IN A WIDE COUNTRY

IN A WIDE COUNTRY

ROBERT EVERETT-GREEN

A NOVEL

Cormorant Books

Canada Council for the Arts   Conseil des Arts du Canada   ONTARIO ARTS COUNCIL CONSEIL DES ARTS DE L'ONTARIO an Ontario government agency un organisme du gouvernement de l'Ontario

Canadian Heritage   Patrimoine canadien    Canadä

The publisher gratefully acknowledges the support of the Canada Council for the Arts and the Ontario Arts Council for its publishing program. We acknowledge the financial support of the Government of Canada through the Canada Book Fund (CBF) for our publishing activities, and the Government of Ontario through the Ontario Media Development Corporation, an agency of the Ontario Ministry of Culture, and the Ontario Book Publishing Tax Credit Program.

LIBRARY AND ARCHIVES CANADA CATALOGUING IN PUBLICATION

Everett-Green, Robert, author
In a wide country / Robert Everett-Green.

Issued in print and electronic formats.
ISBN 978-1-77086-500-6 (softcover). — ISBN 978-1-77086-501-3 (HTML)

I. Title.

PS8609.V4815 2017   C813'.6   C2016-907298-3
                                     C2016-907299-1

Cover photo and design: angeljohnguerra.com
Interior text design: Tannice Goddard, bookstopress.com
Printer: Friesens

Printed and bound in Canada.

CORMORANT BOOKS INC.
10 ST. MARY STREET, SUITE 615, TORONTO, ONTARIO, M4Y 1P9
www.cormorantbooks.com

for Josephine, with thanks for lending me her car

CHAPTER
1

LAST NIGHT I DREAMT I was with Corinne in her white Corvair. My mother owned several cars, but the Corvair is the only one I think or dream about, and the dreams don't change. We're driving on a bright highway or gravel road. Corinne has her hands at ten and two, and she's wearing her cat's-eye sunglasses. I'm sunk low on the red upholstery, feeling the vibration through my spine but also watching from a different angle, as if my own ghost were floating by the car window. I like the feeling of motion, and I can hear the distinctive sound of the Corvair's engine, but I don't know our destination, and that stokes a feeling of dread that increases for as long as the dream lasts. I wake before we arrive.

This recurrent dream began as vague shapes, saturated with apprehension. With repetition, it became as clear and vivid as a Technicolor movie. Instead of eroding the details, the increasing distance in time has sharpened them.

That's the way it is with all my stories, the ones I found and the ones Corinne gave me. I wonder if I could ever strip them back to what I experienced when they were first told. I would have to let them expand to the limit, to the complete set of amplifying details. Only then could I squash them down to the essential point, the way the universe is supposed to expand a million times beyond the reach of light before it shrinks back to an infinitesimal speck.

When someone you love dies, they don't disappear, they retreat into a speck smaller than you can see. All their stories are compressed there too, in that speck, waiting to burst out of it, like a Hollywood chorus line dancing out of a phone booth.

"OH CRAP. JASPER, LOOK AT this thing." Corinne held out the two pieces of the makeup compact that had come apart in her hands. She was sitting at her mirrored vanity in the semi-furnished flat we rented in Winnipeg, in the spring of 1960.

I peered at the coral-coloured plastic, and the wire spring. "The hinge is busted."

"It's almost brand new!" She shook the pieces at the vanity glass in both fists, with a fierce look on her face, as if she were angry with herself and not the manufacturer. Then she threw the mirrored part on the carpet. "I can still use the makeup," she said. "Put that in the Drawer of Shame."

I picked up the mirror and cupped it in my palm. I liked the way my mother's compacts felt in the hand, the way they sprang open, the muffled click they made when they closed. It had taken many slaps from her to convince me not to flip one open and shut like a castanet, not to fondle the soft pad or poke the cake of skin-coloured makeup with my dirty fingernail.

I carried the mirror to the kitchen, where we reserved a drawer for things that were ugly or disappointing: an unflattering photo, a broken toy, or a dress pattern that hadn't worked out. The Drawer of Shame also held things Corinne disliked on sight, which she sometimes swiped to include in the collection. I had mixed feelings about putting the mirror portion of the compact in there, but at least I would see it again when we sorted the drawer, as we sometimes did, discarding items that no longer meant anything.

I returned to Corinne's room, where she was fastening her hair back with a big tortoise-shell clip. She inspected her reflection with a cool, appraising eye, as if the face there belonged to someone else, then began brushing things onto her skin.

I often lurked around when Corinne got ready for work, watching her in the mirror or drawing pictures, usually of warriors bristling with armour and ready for battle. The deliberate rhythm of her makeup ritual had a calming effect on both of us. It was a good time for talking, and especially for telling her anything bad.

"I spilled Coke on the carpet," I said. Corinne stroked a soft brush against the closed lid of one eye, as if trying to smooth away an invisible mark.

"It's not our carpet," she said absently to the mirror. "Throw a rag on it." She dabbed the brush on the narrow cake of eyeshadow, and leaned in to do the other eye.

"They're your shoes," I said. "On the carpet. Where the Coke spilled."

Something between a sigh and a grunt issued from her throat. The brush continued its overlapping strokes, from the eye's inner corner to the edge of the brow bone. "So wet a rag," she said slowly, "and wipe them off." Her lips moved like those of a person dropping off to sleep. "Little mucker."

The mineral-lipped bathtub spout coughed cold water onto the rag. I wiped the patent leather pumps that lay on the carpet outside the bathroom, and pushed the rag down the slope of the inner sole, where the Coke was already drying into a sticky lacquer. The steep arch of those gleaming high heels was permanently fascinating to me, as was the creamy, popcorn-scented sole, from which her heel had ground away the silver script of the maker's name.

I left the rag on the carpet and returned to the drawing I had started on the floor next to her chair.

"There's nothing to do," I said.

"You're doing something."

"I'm sick of drawing. Tell me something."

With a finer brush, Corinne applied a lighter tone to the crease above the eyelid. "Tell you something," she murmured at the glass. "Like a story, you mean." She licked her finger and smoothed the eyeshadow tones together, then drew in the eyebrow, thicker, longer and more arched than it really was.

"Once there was a boy who was very small," she said. "He was no bigger than his father's nose. He never grew, no matter what he ate. The farmer took him to the fields on the brim of his cap. But a giant came and snatched the boy away, and carried him off to his castle."

She leaned in and drew the other eyebrow, slowly and silently. She took so long about it that I almost thought she had played a trick on me and ended the story with the kidnapping.

"The giant's wife fed the boy from her own breast," she said. "He grew and grew until he was a giant himself. He ran away back to his parents, who were frightened to see a giant coming through the forest. He did all his father's work, and brought his mother cartloads of flowers in his arms. But he was so big, he emptied the larder in two bites. When he slept, his body filled the house. His parents went hungry and had to sleep outside. My shoes had better not be sticky."

"They're not," I said, but scampered back and again pushed the damp rag down to the point of the toe.

"When the boy woke up, his parents were gone," Corinne said. "He caught up with them as they ran across a bridge. He stepped in the water to stop them, and shrank back to his tiny size. He floated away, and was swallowed by a fish."

She spat on the black cake of her mascara, made a few quick circles on it with the brush, then dragged the bristles the length of her eyelashes, several times. I started another warrior.

"The king's fisherman caught the fish and brought it to the palace," she said. "When they cut it open, the boy popped out. The king was so amazed, he adopted him and made him a prince. The boy was happy, but told the king he would be happier still if he could see his aunt and uncle. The king sent a golden coach with six white horses to find them, without knowing they were the parents. I thought you were sick of drawing."

"I'm doing the prince," I lied.

Corinne took a red makeup pencil and drew the outline of her lips. The mouth she drew was better than her own, bigger and more shapely. Not for the first time, I thought of how wonderful life would be if I could draw a better me.

"The coach brought the parents to the castle," she said, her drawing completed, the lips still pale between the lines. "When they saw the tiny prince on his throne, they bowed down low. He touched them on the shoulder, and said 'Arise! I am your son.' 'Our son is drowned,' said the father, and began to cry. Each tear became a diamond as it fell."

Corinne wound her lipstick up from its cylinder, and daubed on the colour.

"The prince gathered up the diamonds and gave them to his mother," she said. "When they touched her skin, they became tears again. She knew he was her son after all."

She took a paper tissue and pressed it between her lips, and pulled the comb from her hair. Something about the tone of her last words told me the story was finished.

"Was the king angry?" I said. "Did the parents get to stay in the castle?"

"How should I know? They were happy, that's all. When people are happy, the story's over. Now scoot so I can do my hair."

She brushed her hair, briskly as she usually did, tearing at it from the roots. I went out and closed the door against the coming clouds of hairspray, which made me sneeze. I picked up the Coke bottle that still lay on the rug where I had knocked it over near the shoes, tapped the mouth of the empty bottle against one glossy toe, and said "Arise!" A few last drops rolled onto the patent leather, and shone there like black pearls.

When Corinne came out, I zipped her into her dress. She gave me a long, close hug, as she often did after making herself up. Fresh makeup almost always put her in a good mood, or at least a better one. Her heart beat through the cloth, and the sharp, sweet scents of hairspray and perfume settled around me.

"We need to go somewhere and see about a modelling job," she said.

"Sounds boring."

"Tough luck. We won't be long, and we'll go for supper with Dean right after."

I trudged out to the car and sat so low in the passenger seat, my eyes were level with the bottom of the window. We had an old Sunbeam then, an ugly car that coughed blue smoke.

"Are you going to sulk the whole way?" Corinne said.

"Not if you tell me the rest of what happened."

"There's never enough for you, is there?"

We drove several blocks in silence. The green metal under the window vibrated against my cheekbone.

Corinne took a cigarette from her clasp purse, and pushed the car lighter in. "Okay," she said. "The parents are at the castle and everyone's happy. But the giant comes, and lays siege to get the boy back. The king goes to the castle wall and shouts, 'We've got food for a month. You'll starve first.'"

She let this scenario sink in till the lighter popped out, then lit her cigarette with the glowing coil.

"The giant starts throwing big stones over the castle wall," she said. "The first one crushes a dog. The second kills an ox. The third knocks a big hole in the throne room. The prince jumps on a mouse, and rides out to stop the giant."

"How could he stop him?"

"Give himself up. But he doesn't get to the giant. The mouse runs for a crack in the castle wall, and a cat pounces. You can guess what happens next."

I had seen barn cats with the mice they caught dashing through the straw. They left only the tail, and maybe the hind legs. "What about the prince?" I said.

"That's up to the cat, don't you think?"

We stopped at a light. A little girl was crossing with her mother, skipping on her skinny legs, her hand hidden in her mother's white cotton glove.

"I don't like this part of the story," I said.

The light changed, and we moved on. Corinne took another drag on her cigarette. "What if the cat's actually a witch?"

"That's not better," I said, with a tight feeling in my chest.

"Say she's a good witch. She could carry the prince over the wall, and make him a giant again. He could fight it out with the big lug."

"Just tell me the story the way it's supposed to be."

"Whatever that is," she said. "I told you that already and you didn't like it." She was getting annoyed. "Look, forget this bit. Go back to what it was. They're all at the castle. There's no giant, everyone's happy. The end."

But I couldn't go back. The boy was off his throne. The cat was after him. The ending had unravelled into something bloody left in the straw, or a fight with a giant that might be just as bad.

I would know better next time. I wouldn't ask for more, after an ending that was good enough.

DEAN KEPT HIS CIGARETTES IN a slim silver case with a monogram on the lid, though at home he often pulled them from a shallow tin with the words Sweet Caporal printed on the lid. He needed space to smoke them, because tobacco for him was something that incited large gestures. He would pull the cigarette away from his mouth in a lazy arc, or shoot it forward to emphasize whatever he was saying. There were always flakes of ash clinging to his work clothes or tailored slacks.

Dean had skated into our lives at the Kinsmen Rink, where Corinne used to take me when she was sad or hungover. She wore sunglasses and a snug Mary Maxim sweater, and clung to my arm while we went around the rink at a pace a little faster than walking. We ignored the wise-cracking men who tried to get her attention as they careered past. Dean took the unusual approach of talking to me.

"This rink used to be part of a sanitarium," he said, almost before I was aware of his stocky form gliding next to me.

"What's that?"

"Like a hospital." The spicy smell of his Bay Rum aftershave pricked at my nostrils. "They gave the patients water treatments, and fresh-air exercise. But it was too cold in winter to walk around, so they built a rink."

"A sanitarium's for crazy people," Corinne said, more to me than to him.

"This one was for people with bad lungs," Dean said. We reached a corner, and with an efficient scrape of his skates he went through the curve backwards. Unlike every other man there, he wore dress slacks, and an expensive-looking cardigan. As he turned frontwards again, a massive gold ring with a black stone flashed under my eyes.

"Maybe," Corinne said. "But the rink's still full of crazy people."

Dean laughed, a huffing, stuttery sound. "Crazy people make the world go round. People said Galileo was crazy."

We made another half circuit in silence, and then Corinne said: "I think the world was going around just fine before Galileo showed up."

"But nobody knew that. He had to tell them."

"We always need a man to tell us something," Corinne said.

"He didn't say the world went around," I said, waking up to an occasion to use a dead fact I had heard in school. "He said it went around the *sun*."

Dean bumped my arm with his fist. "You've got a good head on your shoulders. Do you play hockey?"

"I didn't know those things went together," said Corinne. "Jasper, let's go eat."

I thought that was it for Dean, but he followed us off the ice and across the oiled wooden floor. As we stood in line at the rink's snack counter, Corinne removed her sunglasses and surveyed him with sleepy-eyed interest. He was a handsome man with a heavy jaw and dark, glossy hair, and a crease in his brow that deepened whenever he was explaining something, which was often.

"They tore down the sanitarium a few years ago," he said. "The rink's the only thing left."

"How do you know all this? Were you a patient?" Corinne said.

"No, my lungs are great," he said, brushing a few ash flakes from his sleeve. "I just like to know about places."

"Places that don't exist anymore," she said.

"They've all got stories."

"Is that why you came skating? To tell stories to strangers?" Her brows moved together, mocking to his face his serious explanatory look.

"Hell no. I came skating to find a pretty girl like you!"

"You see, Jasper," Corinne said. "They're always on the prowl. Every one of them."

She let Dean pay for our Ukrainian sausages, and he skated with us some more, and then he suggested we all go for a drive. We walked out together through the grey winter light to the parking lot. Our skates clattered into the vast trunk of Dean's blue Lincoln Continental, alongside a builder's hard hat, three bottles of rye and a jumble of broad papers covered with floor-plan drawings.

"Did you draw those?" I couldn't help asking.

"No, all I do with a pen is write cheques, and plenty of them."

"Big spender," said Corinne.

"I got guys working projects all over town," he said proudly. "The money goes out like water."

"Don't be crude," Corinne said. Dean gave her a surprised look, and the stuttery laugh burst out of him, and I felt a dull twinge of pity for him, stuck with that laugh his whole life.

The Lincoln's frigid interior was wide and soft, and smelled of new leather. The car started up with a genteel cough, then rolled over the snow that had drifted in around the wheels. It seemed a long way from the back seat to the place up front where the greenish dashboard light glowed on Corinne's cheek.

We turned onto the Provencher Bridge, and Dean said, "The first time they built this thing, ice from the spring breakup tore out two spans. It was only open a few days and boom, it came crashing down."

"That's nice," Corinne said. "I feel better knowing that, with us way up here and the river rushing down there."

"Don't worry, this thing's solid, even if it's old."

It was dark and bitterly cold by the time Dean dropped us off at our apartment. As the enormous car churned off through the snow, the melodious horn let out a brief chord of farewell.

"Why did we go with him?" I said.

"Because he's nice. Don't you like him?"

"Yeah, but you talk to him so mean."

"Don't be silly. I was only teasing."

We saw him again the next day, and the evening after that he arrived at our furnished apartment in a blue suit and striped silk tie. His cheeks were smooth, he smelled of Bay Rum, and he had a load of fresh-cut flowers on his arm. Corinne was still getting ready, so she told me, who was being stuck with a babysitter, to put the flowers in a vase. I slashed an inch off each stem with a kitchen knife, like a warrior hacking off hands at the wrist.

"You're pretty fierce with that thing," Dean said, and winked, which was a grown-up gesture I found hard to understand. He looked more grand than he had at the rink. His scent and clothing filled the room with proof of his big, expensive life. His appraising gaze somehow made our furnished apartment seem shabbier.

"You can sit on our sofa," I said, with a stiff, embarrassed movement of my arm.

"No, that's okay." He drew a coin from a pocket of his sharply creased trousers. "Here's a quarter for you."

It was a new quarter, so new that his thumb left a faint shadowy mark on the silver. We were messing it up just by touching it. I rubbed it between my fingers, to erase that mark.

"Rubbing it for luck?"

"I don't believe in luck," I said, parroting an axiom of Corinne's I didn't actually believe.

"Haven't you ever been lucky?" he said.

"Maybe I would be, if you gave me another quarter."

He let out a bark of surprised amusement. "Cheeky, ain't you? You didn't thank me for the first one."

"Thanks," I said, but I didn't feel grateful. A quarter wasn't much for being stuck all evening with a babysitter.

"I'll tell you what." He pulled out another quarter, flipped it in the air and slapped it on the back of his hand. "Tails, it's yours; heads, it's not." He stooped a little and put his two big hands under my face, as if I were a little child, then revealed the coin.

"Better luck next time." He slid it back in his pocket, and jiggled the rest of his change. He must have had a few dollars' worth in there, while my entire fortune was the quarter I still rubbed between my fingers.

"How does that prove I'm lucky?" I said.

"You had a chance either way. That's all luck is."

"But I didn't win."

"So you weren't lucky this time." A hint of exasperation crept into his smile. "Jasper, luck's nothing if you don't make up your mind to succeed. If you're really determined, you can do anything. If you made up your mind, you could probably beat me at arm wrestling."

He held up his forearm and clenched his fist. The sleeve of his jacket strained to contain all that muscle.

"That's crazy," I said.

"I bet you could. If you win, you get another quarter." He brushed his hand over the seat of a chair at our dining table, sat down, and planted his elbow on the wooden surface.

"I'm not betting my quarter," I said.

"I don't want it. Look, I'll take a handicap." He made a fist, and stuck out the pinky finger. "You wrestle this."

I sat down, got into position, and gripped the stout little finger. When Dean said "Go," I pulled it down and towards me like a lever. A flash of pain crossed his face. I figured he was going to let me win, but by twisting his finger I got his knuckles to the table a bit quicker than he wanted.

Dean's smile had faded, and a few strands of his glossy hair had fallen out of place. He flexed his fingers, and rubbed the pinky. I had obviously hurt him, but I didn't care: I just wanted his quarter.

Corinne appeared in the doorway in a strapless red cocktail dress and fluttered one hand over her shoulder — my cue to zip her up. I was hooking the eyelet at the top as Dean leaned forward to kiss her, with his eyes nearly shut.

"You'll get lipstick," she murmured, and wiped the red from his mouth with her finger.

The babysitter arrived and pretended to listen to her instructions. Dean made no move to give me my quarter. He had apparently cancelled our bet, and if he had said as much, I would have gotten angry. But what came to me through his uncomplaining silence was disappointment, that I had prevented him from giving me the coin as he had planned.

The handsome couple were going out the door when he dug in his pocket. "Here, Jasper, this one's for luck," he said, flicking the coin fast at me. It flashed in the air, bounced off my fingers and fell on the carpet.

"What do you say, Jasper?" Corinne said.

"Sorry. I mean, thanks." But I did mean sorry, that I had won a coin by hurting him. The door closed.

The quarter on the rug wasn't brand new like the other one, in fact it was almost black with tarnish. Although I knew I would probably spend it the next day, I took it into the bathroom and rubbed it with a little toothpaste, as Corinne did with her silver jewellery when it turned grey. The coin came up so shiny, I could hardly see the difference from the new one. But I could feel it.

DEAN BECAME CORINNE'S LAST AND most determined Winnipeg boyfriend, though neither of them liked the word "boyfriend." He wanted things to be more settled, while she preferred everything to be fluid, including her relationship to material things.

Corinne liked to swipe stuff. For her, an attachment to possessions or money couldn't ever amount to a serious relationship. It was a comedy produced by the rest of the world for her entertainment. If she swiped something, she wasn't really connected to it, didn't have to worry about keeping it, or fret much if she lost it.

Dean didn't understand this attitude in someone who could afford to buy what she wanted. He thought if he bought her enough things, her habit would wither away. But she took stuff even while he was buying her something, like the time she slipped an Eaton's desk bell into her purse while the salesman was boxing a coat for her. It was a few days before Christmas.

"What the hell are you going to do with that?" Dean said, when she pulled the bell from her purse in the front seat of his car.

"Ring it." She put it on the dash and tapped the button a few times.

"Jesus. I don't get you."

"Don't brag about it."

Corinne smiled at me in the back seat, as if to acknowledge that I, at least, got her. Which I did, in that I didn't see anything wrong or unusual about her taking things. She had done it for as long as I could remember. She called it "sneaking," and the rules of sneaking didn't require you to explain why you took something, or even to want it very much.

For a while, Corinne used the clerk's bell to call me to dinner. She rang it with the bravado of a drum major, in the apartment where Dean seldom did anything but wait, restlessly, while she got ready to be taken somewhere. He spent his days putting up new houses for people to fill with new things, and was offended by our crooked plaster walls and worn furniture.

Dean bought me things too, including a plaid tweed jacket, which had brass buttons embossed with lions rampant. He explained that lions rampant were the symbol of ancient kings who lay buried in the abbeys of Scotland. I was awed by this royal garment. Even Corinne said it was handsome.

"But as for these," she said, pointing at the rearing lions on the buttons, "they're not only about kings, or Scotland. Birks uses the same lion. It's their trademark."

"Birks was a Scot," Dean said with dignity.

"Was he?"

Alone in my room, I stood before the mirror in my jacket, stroking the prickly tweed and fingering the buttons. I couldn't wait to wear it somewhere, preferably with Dean in one of his checkered sport coats. At the same time, I felt uneasy about the Scottish kings, rotting in their abbeys, in jackets like mine with lions rampant.

Dean sometimes took me along to his building sites, in a company truck with the words Dumont Do-All Builders painted on the door. He drove fast in the truck as he rarely did in his car, and sometimes left the door hanging open when he jumped out to look down a foundation hole or climb a ladder.

"If you want to be in charge, you have to look like it," he said. "You just have to make up your mind. I'm telling you, Jasper, determination's the key to everything."

He was always building something in or around his house. While he was with Corinne, he put in a Western-themed master bedroom, a backyard stone patio and a basement tiki bar, where he had smoky poker parties I wasn't allowed to interrupt. There were coconuts strung from the bamboo false roof, and grass skirts I helped staple along the front of the bar.

Dean's project for Corinne and me exerted itself on us like a steady headwind. I was to become a practical boy who could fix things and play all games well, or at least keep up. Corinne was to remain an apparently free creature, allowed to say and do unexpected and even crazy things, but prepared to stay "within bounds."

His big front room had a walnut console TV and a long Danish sofa where, after dinner, he would fall asleep watching the hockey game, or *77 Sunset Strip*. I sat on the broadloom in front of the sofa, with my head resting against the tidal breathing warmth of his belly. The air was thick with the tangled aromas of aftershave, cigarette smoke, rye whisky and sweat.

Corinne occasionally came in to watch with us, drawn more by the picture of us together than by what we were watching. Dean would sit up, and we would all be cozy together on the couch. But TV couldn't interest Corinne for long, and Dean couldn't watch without commenting on what he saw. After a little while she got impatient and left, and he slid back into a prone position, and when he stopped talking about what was on the screen, I knew he was asleep. He lay there like a powerful animal unaware of any small creature that might peer or sniff at it. His face looked fleshier than when he was awake, and sometimes twitched into a frown, as if he were troubling over some problem in his dreams. His meaty hand dangled off the couch's edge, with the large gold and black signet ring on one nicotine-stained finger, with the initial "D" pricked out in tiny diamonds.

Dean had a shelf of history books, which came in the mail once a month and filled him with stories that needed to be retold. He was always presenting us with bits of news from the past. When he took us on drives around Winnipeg, we heard about the construction of old city hall, the ruined abbey at St. Norbert, and the Métis settlement where Louis Riel was born. None of these tales held much appeal for Corinne. Dean thought that if he told her enough, or in the right words, she would see how interesting it was, but she never did, so he shifted all his telling to me, and spoke to the back seat the whole time. Eventually she refused to come at all, and then it was just me and Dean, driving around on a story tour of Winnipeg.

"How come you don't have kids?" I asked him during one of these drives.

"I do, but I don't see them. Their mother got the kids. I get the bills."

We floated along in his luxury car in silence, while this information unfurled in the air between us.

"Where do they live?" I said.

"Not far. Just down this street." He spun the wheel suddenly left, almost too late to make the turn. We dived down a tree-lined residential street, with the blare of another car's horn trailing away behind us.

We drove a couple of blocks, then slowed for a ball-hockey game to clear out of our path. One kid raised his stick as we passed; Dean held up a hand in a frozen wave, then stepped on the gas. A block later, the Lincoln slowed again, then rolled to a halt opposite a grey stone house with a huge oak in front, and a wide, empty driveway.

"That's it," he said. "That was our home. The guy who built it hauled in Tyndall stone, the same as for the parliament buildings in Ottawa." The car crept forward a little. "If you look down the side, you can see the pavilion I put up in the backyard."

"What's a pavilion?"

"Somewhere to go, something to build," he murmured, still craning to see the thing he had built and could no longer visit.

"Are you going to marry Corinne?" I said, though Corinne seemed no more likely to marry Dean than any previous boyfriend. He broke out of his pavilion reverie and examined me as if I had only then appeared beside him. I composed my face into a suitably solemn expression.

"You're a funny kid sometimes." He tapped out a Sweet Cap and pushed in the car lighter. He made one of his large smoking gestures with the unlit cigarette, as though to introduce something he wanted to say, but no words came to him on the subject of marrying Corinne.

"You don't ever call her 'Mom,' do you?" he said at last.

"Sometimes," I said, though in fact I never did. For some reason we both smiled at this untruth.

The lighter popped out, and Dean lit up. He took a few puffs, and the car moved off.

"The thing about this part of town, Jasper," he said, recovering his usual explanatory tone, "is that you've got to watch out for flooding. If you're not careful, you wake up one morning and the whole thing's underwater."

THE MORNING SUN SHONE FLAT across the tables as we waited for Sunday breakfast in a café near our apartment. A window washer wiped down the glass outside with a squeegee, chasing the glittering drops to the ledge.

"Can I buy gum?" I said.

A slight frown settled on Corinne's face as she tested the edge of a chipped nail. She put a dime on the Formica. I took it and walked past the cashier's counter, where they had plenty of gum, and ran across the street to the variety store. They too had lots of gum and candy in the front, and spindled racks of comic books, but I hurried past all that towards the gift counter at the back, where watches and pocket radios and a million other things lay scattered together under glass. A small man with black hair raked across his skull crept along behind the side counter and met me at the rear.

"I can show you anything you like," he said with a nervous glare. "Is it a gift?"

"Yes," I said, but the variety of things under my eyes immediately stalled the gift-buying purpose of my visit. I pointed at the first desirable item I saw.

"Can I see the hunting knife? The big one?"

He unlocked the sliding cabinet door, reached crabwise across the chaos of things, and clawed softly at the edge of the knife's leather sheath till he got a grip on a trailing piece of rawhide.

"That's a good blade," he said, putting it on the counter. "You want to be careful with that."

I slid the weapon from its covering. Its solemn, hard weight lay in my hand like a dangerous sleeping reptile.

"Is it for your dad?" he said.

"No, Mother's Day."

"Who's your mom, Annie Oakley?" A bark of laughter burst from his dwarfish body. "Gimme that here," he said, wagging his fingers irritably. He took the knife and set a small jingling carousel of earrings and ornaments in front of me. "This'll do you better for Mother's Day."

I examined the dangling doodads, and tried to weld some imaginary link between one of them and Corinne. It was hard to do with someone watching. My previous gifts of this kind were usually chosen almost at random, when the pressure of the salesperson's attention tripped some internal alarm that forced me to pick something, anything. Before that could happen this time, a mottled stone pendant caught my eye. It had a brown earthy section across the bottom, a narrow darker streak forking up one side like a tree, and black specks floating in a yellow area at the top. I turned it over, and on a tiny sticker read my own name: *Jasper*. I had never seen my mineral self before, and here it was, waiting to be found by me on Mother's Day.

"This one," I said. The dwarf took it from me, spent forever finding a little white box, and another eternity ringing up the sale. I squeezed the box into my pocket and ran back to the café and my cold eggs.

"Why did you go over there?" Corinne said.

"Better gum."

I ate with one hand on the secret in my pocket, and waited a full hour after we got home to let the trail from the variety store go cold. Then I gave her the stone, taking care to show her the little sticker.

"Lovely," she said. "A chip off the block."

"Do you see what it is?"

"I think so. It's a pendant. What do you think it is?"

"A place."

"Yes, you're right. Here's a field, and that's a tree."

"And a flock of crows flying overhead."

"It's a very bare field. And no leaves on the tree."

"It's summer. There hasn't been any rain."

"A drought, by the looks of it. Did Dean give you money?"

"Yes," I lied. In fact I had taken coins over a period of days from Corinne's purse.

She wore my pendant more than any of the other trinkets I gave her over the years. She often fondled its smooth surface as she scanned a menu or talked on the phone, and when anyone noticed it, she told them it was a gift from me. She showed them the tree and the crows, and more or less compelled them to admire me for finding such a thing and giving it to her. It became embarrassing, especially after I decided the stone's landscape shouldn't be flat like the prairies, but mountainous, like the place where it came from, and after which I was named.

Much later, I discovered that jasper isn't found much around Jasper, and that the town was probably named for something or someone else.

*

JASPER WAS ONE OF THE few constants in what Corinne told me about my father. She said he was a geologist who worked for oil companies. He hunted oil in Texas and Venezuela, and was searching for new sites after the first discoveries in Alberta when he died in a plane crash. Somewhere in the northern wilderness, his bush plane sliced through the trees and broke like a toy against the earth. His body was never found. When people heard about it they treated me more softly, and a feeling of lonely distant heroism shivered through me. I was a boy whose father flew in bush planes and was killed. There were worse things to be.

When Corinne told his story, the details sometimes changed. They had already found the oil, or they were still looking for it; the plane went down in a storm, or on a clear day that shouldn't have posed any risk. I assumed she made her changes to suit the audience, the way I gave different people different answers to the same questions, bending the truths of my little life to match what I thought might be normal.

Corinne had only one photo of my father, which I still have. He's sitting on a blanket at a drinking party in the woods outside Jasper, with his eye on the camera and a flask of Canadian Club at his lips. His lean face has a playful look. I spent hours poring over this photo, memorizing his flaring nose and long fingers. I puzzled over the distance between this amiable image and the one in my head, of his plane sheering into the forest. I wanted to warn him, but his laughing eyes wouldn't allow it. No matter what I did, he was going to finish his drink and get on the plane as if nothing would happen.

Over time, I worked out a different version of events. When he gets up from his blanket, he isn't like other men. He stands taller than the trees, and wears clothes made of animal skins and pliable bark. He strides through the jagged landscape with his big knife unsheathed, near the place where my mother lies half-hidden under a blanket of pine needles. He has drunk too much Canadian Club, and as he drags his feet through the boreal forest he stumbles on her big toe and falls flat. They wrestle briefly, then root together, while the stars overhead sing like cartoon chipmunks. After the coupling, he dies, like a spider, and his giant body vanishes into the forest bed. Everything is lost, except the essential fact that he is my father.

Corinne kept his photo in a hinged double frame, facing a shot of my grandfather Ben. He met the same fate as my father, from a different altitude. Ben hurtled to ground from the back of his mare, when she toppled forward near a ditch one spring afternoon. He went down headfirst into the mud and snapped his neck, and lay with his arms folded under him like immature wings. Ben was a great horseman, and probably rolled one eye up at the mare before the world went black, worried even then that she might have lamed herself.

Corinne was about my age then. She was at home when they carried her father in and laid him on the dining-room table. My grandmother Lily got a bowl of water and washed the mud from his hair and face and mouth, wailing the whole time. Only when Ben's face was clean and his eyes safely shut did anyone think to get Corinne out of the room. I heard this part of the story from Lily, who never could tell it without dipping her hands in the imaginary bowl and washing the vanished head, and crying her embarrassed old tears.

CHAPTER
6

WE SAT ON THE FLOATING dock as it rocked in time with the deep rhythm of the lake. Emmett slapped the upper portion of the big rubber hip wader against the grey damp wood.

"I bet I can swim with these on," he said. "A dollar says I can make it to your dock."

"You can't," I said.

"A buck says I can."

A dollar was a lot of money to bet against Emmett doing anything he made up his mind to do. His sunburnt cheeks still bulged with baby fat, his lips were girlishly pink, and his blond eyebrows gave him the expressionless look of a newborn. But his body was lean and strong, and he lived by the iron rule of dares and bets.

"Do you bet?" he said.

I could probably take a dollar from Dean's wallet, which lay unguarded in slacks he had slung over a bedroom chair the day we arrived at his cabin. "Okay," I said. "I bet a dollar you can't."

Emmett responded by pounding the wader's heel like a hammer on the dock with his whole strength, his face twisted into a grimace. That was what he thought of my willingness to doubt him.

"You have to do it too," he said, "and a punch for whoever doesn't make it."

"I don't want to swim with those on." They were his grandfather's, enormous and heavy.

"Are you chickening out?" His face conveyed his contempt for any kind of chickening out, if not the exact consequences this time. Those would not be pleasant, nor short-lived. Emmett kept a strict tally of who around the lake had chickened out, and when and why. He maintained a ledger of shame in his head, and nothing was ever discarded.

"It's too hot."

"That's why we're doing it, to cool off."

I touched the swamp-green rubber. It was blood-warm, and unpleasantly slick. The deep knobby treads on the sole of the boot looked like the molars of a crocodile.

"They're too heavy," I said.

He snorted. "I knew you'd chicken out."

I had had a lot of fun with Emmett at the lake, fishing and swimming and boating. But it was usually better when adults were around. With adults present, Emmett was polite and helpful and perfectly nice. Corinne said he was the nicest boy she had ever met. But when it was just the two of us, Emmett eventually turned everything into a grim contest.

He was already gloating about his impending victory as he dragged the waders up over his legs. He stood up with difficulty. The tops bunched up under his groin.

He took a few awkward steps and hopped into the water with a huge splash. He bobbed up and immediately went under again, then surged back up and grabbed with both hands for the edge of the dock.

"Are you okay?" I said.

"Of course." But already he looked a little less sure. He pushed away from the dock and clawed fast at the water, but couldn't get the boots up to kick. He made it a few yards forward, then slipped under again, and, as he twisted back up to the surface, his wide, frightened eye met mine.

I jumped in and swam to the spot, but before I could touch him, his arm swung around and struck me hard across the nose. I grabbed him under the other arm to pull him up as the pain exploded through my face. He writhed violently and rolled onto his back, and floated there, like the expert swimmer he was. He had kicked free of the waders.

"What the hell are you doing?" he yelled, still gasping for breath.

"Trying to help you, dummy."

"I don't need your *help*. Why are you bleeding?"

I put my hand to my nose, and drew it away all bloody.

"Because you hit me in the face, you dumb cluck."

"Your fault, not mine," he said, and grinned. Now that he was out of danger, he was full of scornful confidence again. I could feel the blood running down my throat. The metallic smell of it mingled with the sharp green odour of the lake.

"You owe me a dollar," I said.

"Tough luck, you said the bet was off." He plunged under the surface, probably to fetch the waders from the mucky bottom.

I swam to our dock and pulled myself out. My face throbbed with pain. Emmett was side-stroking towards his dock, trailing one wader by the heel.

"Cheater!" I shouted, suddenly much angrier as the word echoed across the water.

"Takes one to know one!"

I thumped along the warm grey boards and up the weedy, sandy slope to Dean's cabin. It was bigger, newer and better than the sun-scorched shack built by Emmett's grandfather. The next time I saw Emmett I would make the comparison as harshly as possible, with a punch on the arm.

The screen door hissed behind me as I stepped on the kitchen linoleum. The cabin was so still I thought I must be alone, but when I went into the front room I found Dean and Corinne tangled together on the new sofa, asleep. Their legs were scissored together, their arms lay across each other's bodies, their open mouths were turned in close together, as if they were passing secrets even in sleep. The loud Hawaiian pattern of Dean's shorts bunched around his hairy thighs, overwhelming the light pink of Corinne's shirt, and the white of her panties.

"Jasper?" Corinne murmured, turning her head slightly, but not enough to see me.

"Yes."

She lay there a few moments with her head still turned up a little, as if listening for more.

"Are you having a lovely day?" she said in a lazy voice.

"Not very lovely."

She must have heard the muffling of my voice as I tried to pinch down my bleeding nose. The tangle of limbs shifted, her shoulder fell towards me, and she looked me in the face. I took my hand away to let her see the gore. It was satisfyingly effective in terms of her change of expression, but she didn't spring up from the sofa as I thought she would. She looked troubled but uninvolved, her arm still folded over Dean's dark, broad back.

"What happened to you?"

"Emmett hit me in the face," I said, adding "by accident," as a gift to him and to her, who thought him so perfect.

"Can you clean yourself up?" she said. Something in her voice and manner was asking me to pretend that it was normal for us to have this conversation while I stood bleeding and she lay under Dean's half-naked body.

"I guess," I said, trying to sound sufficiently injured to raise her from the couch. But she turned her face again towards Dean's, ran her hand over his hair, and slid into a closer embrace.

My face in the bathroom mirror showed a bluish-red thickening around the nose, which still oozed blood. It was surely bad enough to deserve someone's attention. I mopped at it with a new white facecloth till it was polka dots all over, and didn't rinse out the blood.

The cabin was too full of Dean and Corinne and their intimate daytime sleep for me to stay inside, so I went out on the deck and sat in a new wicker armchair. A powerboat droned somewhere on the lake, then it too fell asleep. One of Dean's history books lay on an end table, so I opened it and drew lions rampant on the back end paper. The powerboat's engine roared back to life, and a skinny form rose up on the water and bounded along on skis. It was Emmett, gone off to find thrills and adventure without me. I covered the rest of the page with fierce armed warriors, who hacked without mercy at the lions' gaping jaws.

CHAPTER
7

CORINNE WAS ON HER KNEES on the kitchen counter, wiping the cabinets with a sponge, when Dean arrived unexpectedly and said he wanted to take us for a drive.

"I'm not dressed," she said.

"Take a break. This will all be here later."

"Yes, still here, still dirty."

"These old cabinets will never come clean." A grimace twitched across Dean's face. "Look, it's nice out, and I've got the whole afternoon free."

Corinne climbed down and gave him the sponge. "Okay, but only if you finish this while I get ready."

Dean turned the sponge in his hands like a football he was getting ready to throw. "What about Jasper? He can do this. I bet he'd like a drive." He winked at me, as a seal on this treachery.

"No deal," Corinne said. She crossed her wrists behind his neck, and put her face right up under his. "I go only if you clean." Dean scooped her waist in towards him.

"You're crazy," he murmured.

Half an hour later, Dean had finished the cabinets and the Lincoln was sailing through parts of town that usually triggered some story he knew. But this time he drove without a word, as if he had finally gotten the message about what Corinne thought of those tales. The sharp spring air gusted into my face through the rear window, carrying the smells of muddy earth and defrosted dog shit.

We passed along a wide road with a lot of car dealerships next to each other. Dean turned into one of them, under a line of flapping coloured pennants. His face had gone pink and was covered in sweat, though I was shivering from the chill.

"Are you all right?" Corinne said. "Do you want me to drive?"

"No. I've got a little business here. Come with me."

"You're kidding."

"It won't take long."

"I came for a drive, not to watch you work." She took out a new pack of cigarettes and crumpled the silver paper out the window, but didn't light up. The two of them sat there waiting for the other to give in.

"Christ, will you just do this?" Dean said.

We all got out. Dean strode a few steps as if he really didn't care if we followed, then stopped near a row of new cars. He grabbed Corinne's hand and folded something into it.

"This is for you, Baby," he said.

She opened her hand and screamed, her knees almost buckling as she held up the shiny new key. She threw herself on him and hugged him hard around the neck, till he pulled at her arms to stop. "Which one?"

Dean laid his hand on a white Corvair. Corinne turned his bulky frame and climbed on piggy-back, and he trotted her around the car, huffing his quick stuttery laugh. Then we all piled in, with Corinne at the wheel, and squealed out of the lot before Dean could remind her to check her mirrors.

"What about your car?" I said, as the Lincoln vanished behind us.

"They'll bring it over," he said.

"You should have told me," Corinne said, bursting with happiness. "I feel like such a fool."

We drove all over town, past old warehouses and rows of squinty bungalows where no one inside suspected that a brand-new Corvair was driving by. I begged Corinne to beep the horn. I wanted the whole city of Winnipeg to notice us.

After we reached Dean's place, I stood out on the driveway and listened to the ping of the Corvair's engine as it cooled, and ran my hand over the red upholstery. Dean said this model was a Monza, which was the name of a town in Italy famous for car races.

"It's also the place where an Italian king was shot to death," he said. "The guy was an anarchist or something. He came all the way from the States to kill the king." I trailed my fingers over the warm metal. Perhaps the king had travelled to his death in a vehicle like this, adorned with lions rampant.

At dinner, Corinne made a victory wreath from cocktail napkins, and did a little dance for Dean, and put the wreath on his head. When the meal was over, she sat in his lap and stroked his cheek.

"Clear the table, will you, Jasper?" she said. Dean gazed up into her eyes, his face glowing with happiness, and especially with relief.

For a few weeks after we got the Corvair, it was all I could think about. I would go outside at odd moments to look at it, to inhale the smell of the new tires and the faint oily aroma coming from the engine. The pleasure of knowing it was ours was limited by the ache of seeing it sit there idle. It was like an illness I felt in my body even when I was nowhere near the car.

One stagnant Saturday as I lay on the carpet watching TV, Corinne said we were going somewhere. I bounded off to the car without asking where. But the thrill of the engine's raspy awakening and the Corvair's surge away from the curb faded when I realized we were headed for Dean's house, only a few minutes away. He was hosing down his Lincoln on the driveway, with the stern expression he wore while doing any kind of chore.

"Get in," Corinne called out my window. Dean shot a blast of water at the door, and turned off the hose. Then he folded himself smoothly into the back seat, disrupting with one unbelievable movement the natural rule that Dean always rode in the front.

"Where to?" he said.

"I want to look at a boxer dog I might buy," Corinne said, as she stepped on the gas.

"You're joking. What do you want a dog for?"

"Not *for* anything, I just do. Jasper too, probably."

"What do you say, Jasper?" said Dean. He leaned his heavy forearms on the front seatback, and brought his unshaven face near mine. "Do you want a dog you'll have to feed and walk every day, when it's raining or snowing or thirty below?"

"I don't know." Corinne hadn't mentioned it to me, and the prospect seemed unreal. I was absorbed in the present situation of riding to another place that might be many blissful miles away.

"They're not toys, you know," Dean said. "A dog's a responsibility."

"You don't need to tell me," said Corinne. "I grew up with dogs."

"I'd hate to see it end up in the pound, and Jasper disappointed."

"Christ almighty, I haven't got one yet!"

"Okay, take it easy." He stroked her shoulder. "Where are these mutts?"

We drove till the traffic thinned out and the city disappeared behind us. In the field beyond the weedy ditch on my side, the wide skeletal arms of a cultivating machine dragged their harrows through the dirt. In the distance, I could see the shape of a grain elevator, which for me indicated where measured city time ended and endless country time began.

Corinne slowed, and the car swung off the road and along a dirt track near a hand-painted sign: PUPPYS. Three adult boxers raced straight towards the car, then veered around us. We pulled into a dusty yard where a fleshy old man stood wiping his neck with a rag.

"You're the one who called," he said gravely.

"I am," Corinne said, as the dogs leapt around her. One of them had two rows of flabby teats shaking underneath.

"Down!" the man yelled, and the dogs shrank into the dirt. "They're over here." He turned and trudged towards a large shed. The dogs trotted ahead of him and we followed, through the dark, rank shed lined with pens, and out the other side through a chicken-wire gate into a small puppy corral. The little dogs yapped and rolled over each other and stood up to us with the same blackened jowls and rigid posture as the adults. Dean scooped one up.

"Well, you're a charmer," he said, as the puppy wriggled and tried to lick his wrist.

"I thought you were opposed to dogs," Corinne said.

"No, I like them. I just don't want the bother of keeping one."

The old man droned out the breeding history of his kennel, and said all the pups were eight weeks and had their shots. We could have our pick, any one for the same price.

Corinne looked over each dog. She checked its joints and teeth, smoothed down its wiry, short coat and cooed in its worried eyes. Outside the pen, the mother was getting frantic, and became more so as Corinne went through all the puppies a second time.

"Which one do you favour?" said the old man.

"They're very nice, but I don't know. I don't think I want one after all."

"Suit yourself," said the old man. "Come back if you change your mind, but I can't promise there'll be any left."

Corinne opened the chicken-wire gate herself and strode back through the shed. Dean caught up with her at the other doorway.

"I thought we came out here to get a dog," he said.

"I don't feel like it anymore."

"Why not?"

"What's it to you? You said it was a dumb idea."

"Never mind what I said. Tell me which one you like, and I'll buy it for you."

"No."

They faced each other down for a moment, then Dean's shoulders sagged. "Just let me buy you one of those damn dogs," he said quietly.

Corinne got in the car. I slid into a corner of the back seat, as far as I could get from whatever was happening between them. It seemed too risky to say that I had liked those little dogs, that I wouldn't mind walking one in the snow, and that leaving empty-handed felt like losing something. We drove back to the highway in silence.

The city was reforming around us when Corinne swerved into a tiny shopping plaza with a revolving sign. She pulled up in front of an ice-cream place whose pale-blue counter and steel-rimmed stools were visible through the big window.

"Who wants a cone?" she said.

"Count me out," Dean said.

"Don't be a spoilsport." Corinne slid along the seat, pressed her shoulder into him and turned her face towards his.

"I'd rather have a cigarette," he said, looking at her with his head as far away as possible. They stayed that way for a few seconds, then she put her mouth close to his ear, and murmured, "Ice cream first, then cigarettes." Dean wrapped his big arm around her and took a deep breath, as if he hadn't breathed at all since the puppy farm.

*

THE CORVAIR WAS DEAN'S ULTIMATE statement in his long argument with my mother about her relationship to material. He couldn't fathom why she would live with shabby furniture, and steal silly things, but refuse to let him buy her a dog or a new bedroom suite. She had been thrilled and flattered to get the car, but it didn't bring her any closer to his view of the world.

One day as Dean stood in our living room, waiting for Corinne to finish sewing a button on his sports coat, a heavy thump on the floor of the flat upstairs released a light fall of plaster dust from a crack in our ceiling. It landed on his hair and shirt sleeve. He and

Corinne laughed, but as he brushed the dust from his sleeve, his
nostrils twitched, as if at the stench of the old house and its previous
occupants.

"You can't say this is any way to live," he said. "Tell me what
it would take to be quits with it all, and I'll write the cheque."
Without a word, Corinne reached over to the end table, and tapped
the Eaton's bell.

Dean never found out what it took. The bell went into the Drawer
of Shame.

CHAPTER 8

"I LIKE HIM ALL RIGHT," Irene said, looking up at me from the edge of Dean's sofa. "I just have no use for children." Her laughter burst out violently and high before tumbling to a low gurgle. Dean used to say that Irene had a dirty laugh, and I listened carefully to try and discover what made it dirty.

"Jasper's in the prime of life," Corinne said. "Still an innocent animal, not yet a beast." She hugged me close and kissed me below the ear, inhaling as if there were nothing sweeter than the smell of a twelve-year-old boy who didn't like to wash. She too had had a few drinks.

"That must mean it's all downhill from here," Irene said. "*Garçon!* More rum and Coke!" She waggled her empty glass, which still had a cube rattling in the bottom. Her other hand held her cigarette in its short holder, well away from the emerald dress shimmering on her slim torso. Like Corinne's other model friends, Irene carried herself well, even when drunk. She ignored the paw stroking her waist; the man attached to it, a guy named Louie, was sprawled back on the sofa, his lazy eye fixed on her.

Dean had said it would be a party, but it was small for his use of the term. Instead of a crush of people shouting in each other's faces, there were only a couple of Dean's builder friends and their wives, and Irene and Louie and another model named Tina, and me, who would be sent off to bed as soon as Corinne remembered the time. Some kind of brassy jazz was jumping out of Dean's hi-fi cabinet.

I retreated behind the bar, where Dean's builder friends were arguing about the previous night's hockey game. I put a fresh cube in Irene's glass, and some Coke, and plenty of rum. Dean intercepted me, poured some of the drink down the drain, and added more Coke. "She's already high as a weather vane," he said.

I carried the drink to Irene, who took it without thanks or a glance. "Hey, when does this party get started?" she said to the room. The builders' wives smiled awkwardly; they weren't models and had not strayed from each other's side since they arrived.

"Let's play charades," said Corinne. She got Louie to move the teak coffee table out of the way, and divided the room into teams, and gave out pads of paper for people to write things we would act out. Dean and I were a team with Tina, and the builder who hated the Canadiens, and the other builder's wife, who kept her purse on her arm the whole time.

"We'll act out in pairs," Corinne said, smoothing down her dress. "Jasper, you go first with Dean, you're extra and you have to get to bed." She held out the bowl filled with people's folded squares of paper, and I picked one. Dean and I read it together.

"Dean, you've lost already," Louie said, surveying me with a sneer.

"We'll beat *you*," I said. Everyone laughed.

We needed a horse for our charade, so Dean got on all fours and I climbed on his back. I jerked my upper body to get him moving, but he merely pawed the ground.

"Your horse won't go," Tina said. "It must be *Mule Train*!" But it wasn't. Corinne rolled up a magazine and handed it to me, and I whacked Dean's hip with it. He reared up with a deep whinnying sound, and I tumbled off backwards, thumping my head on the carpet. The room reeled above me.

"Why did you throw him off?" Corinne said, springing from the sofa to pick me off the floor.

"I didn't mean to."

"What the hell did you think would happen?"

"*The Lone Ranger!*" Tina shouted.

"Yes!" Dean smacked his hands together. "Hi-yo, Silver, and the horse rears up."

"The Lone Ranger has reins," Corinne said. "He can damn well hold on." She folded her arms around me, welding us into a united front against Dean, whatever I felt about it. Her bare arms were trembling, not from cold but from rage. She had been annoyed with Dean about one thing after another all day, and now it was all coming together.

"Anyway, that round doesn't count," Dean said, tucking in his shirt. "The magazine's a prop."

"A bonk on the head says it does count," Corinne said.

"You can't use props. Everyone knows that."

"Don't be an ass."

Dean's face flushed red. "You're missing a swell chance to shut up."

"This is why I don't play this game," said one of the builders' wives.

"All right, we'll go again," Dean said, and snatched a paper slip from the bowl. "I can do this one myself." He pulled out a comb and styled his hair elaborately, rolling his shoulders from side to side.

"*77 Sunset Strip!*" shouted the builder who hated the Canadiens.

"I love that show," Irene said. "But Kookie, you can't use a comb, that's a prop!"

"I'm just playing by the new rules," Dean said, smiling sarcastically at Corinne. "Props are now allowed."

Corinne smiled back. "You don't have to be a flaming shit-heel about it."

"I don't think we should play anymore," Tina said. "We give up."

"Yay, we win!" Irene threw her arms in the air, and inadvertently kicked over the drink she had put on the floor when Louie removed the table. A dark archipelago formed on the beige carpet. She dropped cocktail napkins on the wet spot, tamping them down with her shoe. Whatever song was playing ended with a brassy flourish.

"Corinne, can you wipe that up?" Dean said.

"You wipe it up. It's your carpet," she said. One of the builders' wives clucked her tongue. Her husband led her away to the bar. The room had fallen silent, the game had broken up, and it looked like the party might go the same way.

"Corinne, this reminds me of that time with Bill, in the north end," Irene drawled. "Hey, everybody, you've got to hear this story!" The music resumed: a cha-cha number.

"We were in this cinder block after-hours place," Irene said, "and a cop showed up, undercover. We heard his police boots on the wooden steps outside, so we all bolted our drinks, except this one guy at the table next to ours. He had a double Scotch or something, so he put it on the floor, not under his own chair, but Corinne's. Lordy, aren't you the perfect homemaker?" she said to Dean, who was on his knees next to her, scrubbing the damp spot.

"It's harder to get out when it's dry and sticky," he said sullenly.

"I'll say!" Irene's dirty laugh peeled down from a high shriek. She was well past the weather vane. "Corinne, you tell the rest."

"The cop prowls around," Corinne said, "and everyone's drinking water, so he leaves. As soon as he's gone, this so-and-so at the next table reaches under my chair for the drink I could have been pinched for. So I move my foot back and tip over his glass. And you know what? The guy mouths a dirty word at me!"

"What a chump!" Louie said.

"So I get up, very ladylike, and dump a pitcher of water on him," she said, miming the action. "Right away my friend Bill hops up and smacks the guy in the face. He goes down like a load of bricks."

"But the funny part," Irene said, "is that Bill hadn't seen any of it! Not the guy hiding his glass, or Corinne tipping it over, or the nasty word. And when we ask him later why he hit the guy so fast, he says to Corinne, 'Honey, I knew if you was throwing water on him, he must have done *something*.'"

Everyone laughed, except Dean, who was still rubbing at the carpet.

"Bill was fun," Irene said. "He was a good sport." She nudged Dean with her knee. "Hey, Mr. Clean, how about another drink?"

Dean stood up. "You're cut off," he said.

"I'll get you one," said Corinne. "Jasper, it's time you went to bed."

I left the room as Dean, with a shocked look on his face, wrenched a chair aside, on his way to change the record. The sounds of Louis Prima's band burst from the hi-fi and followed me up the stairs.

*

I AWOKE IN THE DARK room, which seethed with clamouring shapes. I slid out of bed, so quietly that nothing waiting in the darkness could hear me skimming over the sheet. I went down the hall as smoothly as an Apache scout, towards the light rising from the stairway like a column of smoke. A strange rhythmic rumbling came from the bottom of it. My hand met the spiral railing, and I followed it down the stairs into the bright party room.

Dean lay on his back on the Danish sofa, with his hand flung out near the floor. A deep, grunting snore was coming out of him, unlike any sound I had heard from him before. Corinne and Irene were crouched near his head. I blinked in the bright light till I saw that they were snipping chunks from his hair with a pair of nail scissors. Irene was singing something in a quiet, tired voice:

Every party needs a pooper
That's why we invited you
Party pooper
Party pooper

She grinned when she saw me, and sank onto her bum. "What?" she said, more as a challenge than a question. Corinne looked around in the same unconcerned way she would if I'd walked into the bathroom while she was making herself up. They both laughed. Louie was sitting in the armchair opposite, with his feet splayed out and a glass in his hand.

"You shouldn't be doing that," I said.

"Don't you start." Irene held the scissors near her cheek and wagged them at me.

"Why are you just sitting there watching?" I said to Louie.

"I tried to tell them," he said. He took a sip. A rush of anger at him came up so quickly, I could almost feel it in my mouth.

"Big deal. That's his Scotch you're drinking."

He put the glass down. "Smart-mouth kid. You should show some respect."

"Go to hell, Louie," Corinne said amiably. His head lolled back a bit, as if some tiny spit-soaked missile had arced past without hitting him. He got up slowly and buttoned his sport coat.

"C'mon, Irene, let's say our goodnights."

"Goodnight, Dean," Irene said, and cut out a last snip near the scalp. She stood up and wobbled past the coffee table into Louie's arms. They clung together in their stocking feet, and danced a little.

"Goodnight," I said emphatically, and jabbed Louie in the back.

"Corinne, your kid's a brat."

"Go to hell, Louie," she said, "and goodnight."

"Get out!" I shoved him, and he swung his hand at me, with Irene's arms around his neck, but he was so drunk he toppled back into the chair, taking her down with him. "The boy's a brawler," she said, not disapprovingly.

"Come back to bed, Jasper," Corinne said. She took my hand, led me back up through the column of light, and guided me unsteadily down the hallway. The darkness there was deeper now, and filled with black rage against Louie. She fluffed my pillow and tucked me in, and lay down next to me as she sometimes did when I couldn't sleep.

"Don't be mad," she said.

"Why are you so mean to him?"

"I don't know. It's all silly."

"You're drunk."

"There you go, that's it." She kissed my cheek, gave me a long whisky hug and fell asleep. But I was more alert than I had been all day. I listened through the seething darkness for any sound from downstairs. After a few minutes, I slid out from Corinne's heavy embrace and darted along the hall back down the spiral stair. The party room was quiet; Dean had turned on his side, exposing his butchered hair to the full light. Louie and Irene were still in their armchair, dozing or passed out. Their upper bodies were turned towards each other, her thighs across his lap, her feet dangling above the floor.

I went behind the bar and found a dirty glass, and filled it with ice water. I flitted silently to the armchair, all nerves and energy, and held the cold glass above Louie's head. He could have saved himself by opening his eyes before I counted to ten, but he didn't, so after ten seconds, I tipped the whole glass over his face. Irene's hips quaked as the shock of the water flashed through his body and into hers, though she was hardly wet. She raised herself on one elbow and looked at him with wide-open eyes.

"What happened to you?" she said.

Louie's dazed expression cleared as he saw me. "You little fucker," he said, vehemently but not loudly, which somehow made the fury in his eyes more frightening. I raced up the stairs on a thousand volts, reached my room without touching the floor, and locked the door behind me. It was only when I lay next to Corinne with my heart pounding through the silence that I realized I still had the glass gripped tight in my icy hand.

The next day, Sunday, Dean took us to a party at a country club where his company had built a new golf shop and swimming pool. He wore a sharp blue suit and tie, and smelled of Bay Rum. None of us mentioned the gashes in his hair, which I had plenty of time to inspect from the back seat. They were pretty bad, but to my eye they were less conspicuous than the lions rampant on the jacket I was wearing out in public for the first time.

"Your friend Irene isn't as clever as she thinks," Dean said, as we waited at a red light. "I don't want her in my house again."

"Don't worry, she wouldn't come anyway," Corinne said.

The light changed, and the Lincoln floated through the intersection. Corinne looked over the seat at me, formed her lips into a "shhh" shape, and winked.

At the country club, Dean gave a short speech, chipped a few golf balls into the pool, and showed me how to swing a club. He was always teaching me to do something.

"Dean, what's with the hair?" somebody said. "Lawn mower get away from you?"

"My barber drinks too much."

It rained heavily as we drove back to his house. We went through Market Square and past the old city hall, and Dean mentioned, not for the first time, that a man had been shot in the head there during the Winnipeg General Strike.

"Mike somebody. An immigrant working guy, with a wife and three kids. The police killed him right on the steps of city hall. Jasper should know this kind of stuff. They don't teach him much at that school."

"You have an opinion about that," Corinne said.

"Yes, why not?"

"So write to the principal. Tell him why you keep going on about this stuff. Tell the mayor, and the goddamn prime minister!"

"You want the boy to grow up ignorant?"

"What, you mean like me?"

"No! Jeez! Why do you twist everything around?" Dean gripped the wheel and stepped on the gas, as if more horsepower might suffice to get him out of another quarrel with Corinne.

There was a lot of party food left over, which Corinne served out for dinner on Dean's good china, at his polished dining room table. But the meal had a quiet, ruined feeling, and as soon it was over, Dean went to his history books, to look for a story with a clear outcome.

CHAPTER
9

THE SLANTING LIGHT OF THE last minutes before sunset glowed through the fly-specked screen door. Corinne and Dean, sitting out on the deck, faced each other like bookends, their knees almost touching as they leaned forward in lounge chairs designed to make it hard to do anything but sprawl back. My hand was on the door to push the screen open, but something about the quiet, serious sound of Dean's voice stopped me.

"Why won't you take it?" he said.

"You know why."

"If you don't like it, we can exchange it."

"It's gorgeous. I just can't believe you're offering it. You haven't heard a thing I've said."

Dean said something I didn't catch.

"Oh God!" Corinne said. The legs of her lounger scraped the decking as she flung herself back and draped her forearm across her eyes. Dean remained with his head down and his hands cupped together, almost as if he were praying.

I pushed the door open and stepped out on the warm wood. For a second I thought my presence might change something, but neither

of them looked up. It was a big, wide deck, but with them : that,
I found there was no place on it where I could stand. I walked past
like I had something to do on the beach, with my eyes down as if
I were the guilty one.

From the lake side, the warm light shone over their bronzed
bodies. Corinne lay back on the lounger in her orange ruffled bikini.
Dean leaned forward in his blue terry shirt and Hawaiian trunks,
explaining something with his hands. It all looked exactly the way it
had the previous summer, when they were happy.

I should have stayed in the house, where I could hear or at least
feel what was going on, but I couldn't go back now. I flung a few
strips of festively scalloped seaweed at the lake, and stabbed at the
greying sand with a stick. I began to draw something, a man's face,
and dragged the stick down around the powerful shoulders and
torso, but there was no room where the hips should have been, only
rocks. He was a giant with no legs.

The cabin door banged shut. Corinne had gone in. Dean came off
the deck and strode past me across the sand towards the rowboat,
and began hauling it into the lake.

"Can I come?" I said, running up.

"Get in."

I climbed over the side. He pushed and dragged some more, till
the boat scraped free and bobbed on the water. He got in and swung
the oars out, and began to pull with hard strokes.

"Where are we going?"

"Nowhere."

The oars groaned in the locks and swung out again, trailing
flecks of water across my bare legs. The heavy wooden boat surged
easily through the water. Dean rowed hard out to what felt like the
middle of the lake, then shipped the oars.

"You like it up here, Jasper?"

"Sure."

"You're a good kid." He reached under his seat and pulled out a bottle with a few inches of rye left in it, and took a swig. The lake cradled the boat, taking it in hand now that Dean was no longer forcing it through the water.

"This whole lake was scooped out of the rock by a glacier ten thousand years ago," he said. "It's just a puddle in a pothole. That nice deck I built, it'll rot out eventually." He waggled the rye by the neck. "Nothing lasts, Jasper, no matter what you do."

He put his lips to the bottle, drained the last of it and flung it away. It skipped once on the surface, then floated there like a sea bird. Dean pulled something blue and nearly round from the pocket of his terry shirt, and rolled it between his palms.

"Listen, Jasper, I'll make you a little bet. If you can hit that bottle with this, I'll give you a quarter." He grabbed my hand and closed it on something: a domed, plush-covered jewellery box, with the Birks insignia and lion rampant marked out in black.

"It's only a bet if I put something in too," I said.

"Okay, you're in for a quarter."

"I don't have a quarter, and I won't borrow one."

"All right, something else."

"Can I open the box?"

"Better not. Something bad might come out."

I shook it behind my knee, and felt the soft rattling inside. "What I bet is, if I miss, you can have this finger." I held up my pinky.

He snorted. "I don't get it."

"I mean you can cut it off."

Dean made a choking sound, and for the first time, I thought he might slap me. But he answered in the same quiet voice as before. "That sounds like a good deal, Jasper. Too bad I don't have my knife with me."

A wisp of dizziness stirred behind my eyes. "There's one in the tackle box," I said. The grey metal box lay on the floor of boat, between our feet. Dean flipped the latch and opened it.

"So there is. We're all set then. If you hit the bottle, you get a quarter. If you miss, I chop your finger off with this knife, right here on the edge of the boat." He poked the pointed blade into the wood a few times. "Only thing is, I'm not sure I really want that finger of yours. I don't know where it's been." He huffed out a tired laugh.

"I can't see the bottle anymore anyway," I said. Which was almost true.

He reached out to take back the blue box. My hand trembled as I stuffed it into my shorts pocket.

"I'm keeping this." At that point, with no warning, and invisibly as far as Dean was concerned, my eyes filled with tears.

"You've got a nerve," he said mildly. "What would you do with that box?"

"Just hold on to it for a while."

The whole shore had gone black. Something broke the surface of the dark water not far from the boat, with a sound like a gulp.

"Fair enough," Dean said. "Let's go in."

He pulled at the oars. I gripped the lump on my thigh the whole way back, as if the pocket and gravity were not enough to keep it from flying away over the water. We hauled the boat onto the beach and trudged up the dark sand, with Dean's big arm draped over my shoulder and my legs as heavy as if I had swum the whole lake.

CHAPTER
10

I WAITED IN THE CAR, my cheek pressed against the frame of the open window, my hand moving the handle against the play it had before it actually engaged the window. Dean taught me that phrase, "engaged the window," when one of the windows in his truck jammed. He had removed the door panel and shown me how the spindly metal arm moved on its elbow to raise or lower the glass.

He stood immobile by the cabin, his shirt misbuttoned and his hair uncombed. Corinne gave him a hug at the shoulders with her face turned aside, as she did with her women friends, including the ones she didn't like very much. She walked to the car with a little flap of the hand over her shoulder, not unlike her signal to zip up the back of her dress.

Dean moved a few heavy paces to my window, put a warm hand on my shoulder and gazed at me through the interior fog of whatever was happening to him.

"See ya," he said.

"Sure." I couldn't stop waggling the handle between its two points of resistance.

"Quit that, Jasper," said Corinne, from the driver's seat. Dean squeezed my shoulder and then seemed to remember something. He fumbled in his cottage trousers, brought out a scrap of paper and a carpenter's pencil, and wrote down the number 1961. "I've been meaning to show you this," he said, leaning in my window. "The year we're in is the only one in the century you can turn upside and nothing changes. See?" He swiveled it around a few times, and gave me a tired wink. "Be sure you make the most of it."

He stepped back, and the Corvair roared into life. As we drove away, I watched him in the trembling side mirror. He lifted a hand to wave a second before the trees blotted him out.

When we got to the Trans-Canada, Corinne told me we were starting a summer of adventure. We would go where we liked and do whatever we wanted. We were fancy-free.

"What about Dean?" I said.

"We won't be seeing him anymore."

"Why not?"

"It wasn't working out."

"Why not?"

"Stop saying that. Look, when you're not getting along, every-thing's a reason. You know how he got sometimes. He was a drunk."

A catalogue of all things associated with Dean rushed through my mind. Being a drunk was not one of them.

"No he wasn't," I said, but I already mistrusted my own words. She couldn't be wrong about a thing like that.

"Why do you think he was always falling asleep on the sofa?"

I was too stunned to answer. Dean's little naps, as he called them, were the bedrock of our relationship. Those evenings, as I watched TV with my head resting against his slumbering belly, were periods of complete harmony between us. They were the only times I could be with him and relax into his sheltering male presence without him telling me how to do something, or what I should know.

"Are we keeping the car?"

"He wouldn't take it back," she said. "Believe me, I tried. I wouldn't care if we went back to some rust-bucket thing."

This statement was almost more shocking. Corinne had refused the ring, which I had peeked at before leaving it in its blue box on Dean's bureau, but I couldn't believe she would refuse the Corvair as well. I ran my hand over the upholstered seat, which could so easily have been pulled out from under me.

But Dean's house and patio, and the tiki bar where we had tacked up the grass skirts, were all being swept away by one baffling sentence: *He was a drunk.* How had I not noticed? I would have to revise the whole story of Dean, from our first encounter at the Kinsmen Rink, through all the newly meaningful times when he pulled out a bottle in his truck or dropped something in the kitchen. The year had turned upside down, and he was falling to the bottom of it.

The flat, sunny fields raced past my window, interrupted by narrow stands of trees planted as windbreaks. From the wires limping into the distance between blackened poles along the edge of the fields, a pair of crows took flight, dipping down and rising again with heavy strokes, as if their charcoal wings were soaked with water. Their slow-moving forms were out of sight in a second, receding behind us at a mile a minute, like our whole life with Dean.

"What do you mean, 'fancy-free'?" I said.

"Not tied down. We can do what we want."

"What's fancy about that?"

"Fancy is different. I can wear fancy clothes, but not be fancy-free."

"Why's it the same word?"

"Don't ask me."

"Are we still going to Lily's?"

"Of course, that's why we brought extra stuff." Corinne moved into the empty oncoming lane to pass a pickup truck, which had a couple of sun-browned men riding in the back in grimy work clothes.

"There's nothing fancy along here," I said.

"We don't have to stay on this road forever."

"Okay, let's turn here," I said, as we approached the turnoff to a secondary road.

"I don't think there's much up that way."

I scanned for more escape routes, but they all looked alike. When a car turned from one of those branching roads onto the highway, I needed only a glance to know that the people inside hadn't come from adventurous places, and weren't fancy-free.

Corinne turned off the road at the next town, but only to fill the gas tank. The town consisted of a few buildings with lots of space between them, as if to make way for buildings and people which had failed to arrive. We pulled up in front of a garage with a single pump in front. A man ran over from a nearby house with his mouth full of food and got the pump going.

A truck drove up, and a man in greasy blue work clothes got out. He looked us over in silence, then wrestled a bulky engine part out of the truck bed and into the garage. Once that was done, he approached us.

"Nice little car!" he shouted. "What do you call it — Dinky Toy!"

He ran his filthy hand along the white hood. The creases in his brown face and neck were lined with black. I hated baths, but country people, especially country men, had a relationship with grime I couldn't fathom.

"And this one! Good-looking boy!" He clamped his forearm around my neck, and waggled me hard like a doll. I clung to his arm, and it flashed through my mind that he could break my neck like a chicken bone. I thumped against the steely muscle, and the arm released.

"Yes, he's my good-looking boy," Corinne said as I scooted under her arm. Her voice sounded normal, but she held me tight, and I knew that she too had been frightened by the man's sudden hard grip. His greasy, sweaty smell clung to my skin.

"Where are you headed?" he said.

"Mexico," said Corinne.

"Mexico? You're going the wrong way, little lady!"

"Really? Maybe we won't go there. Jasper, where do you want to go?"

"Alaska."

"To see the cute little Eskimos?"

"Yes, the cute little Eskimos." I began to hear Ricky Nelson's voice in my head, singing "Travelin' Man," and Corinne could hear it too, because she shifted her weight from side to side as if dancing, with her arm still firm around my chest. The greasy man looked confused.

"I don't know if you can get to Alaska now. It's pretty boggy this time of year."

"Maybe we'll hire a plane."

"I've got a cousin, flies up north," said the gas man. "They make good money, them bush pilots. Especially on emergency. He told me one time he flew a fellow down to hospital in Edmonton, they paid him double wages!"

"My dad died in a bush plane," I said.

"Jeez, I'm sorry to hear that," said the greasy man. I lowered my head like one who had suffered, and my father's lonely heroism settled on me, and a sneaky wind stirred along the ground, rustling the tall grass and whipping the dust into a gritty swirl that made us blink.

Corinne paid, and the gas man ran to his shop for a free candy bar for me and an air-freshener card for her. The greasy man shook my hand with his blackened paw and waved as we drove off, growing smaller and smaller in the side mirror till he dissolved in the heat shimmering over the road. He disappeared so much more slowly than Dean, who had been blotted from the mirror in a second with his hand going up and no time to wave. It was such a long time ago, that morning, though the sun was still hours from setting. My stomach contracted, and a salty taste reached the corner of my mouth. I palmed away the tear and bit into my candy bar; it smelled of motor oil.

*

THAT NIGHT I DREAMT OF a giant who marched up from the earth on legs as thick as pillars. He pushed the clouds aside with his hands as the earth spread like a carpet under his mighty feet. He was striding hard to get somewhere, his voice crashing off the mountains with a sound like garbage-can lids hitting the pavement. But those big legs couldn't keep up with him, and he began to stumble. His hands lost their grip on the clouds, his face slipped under their shadow, and the earth shook as his gigantic body crashed to the ground.

CHAPTER 11

WHATEVER HAPPENED THE DAY BEFORE, whatever words were thrown about before bedtime, Corinne always woke me gently, speaking close to my ear: "Jasper … Jasper." I sometimes listened for that voice in my dreams, the way you wait for the wind to moan again at a barely open window. She never shook me, and didn't say any of the half-mocking things people say to sleepers, as if being awake earlier made you the better person. She preferred to rouse me as late as possible, even if it meant we had to rush to get somewhere. I was perfect while I slept, she said, merely myself when awake.

"Jasper." I could feel Corinne's breath on my ear as she stroked my back. I sat up on the creaky motel bed. She was already in her bra and panties. The clips of her garter belt trembled as she went into the tiny bathroom.

With the thin pillow bunched under my head, I surveyed our square, panelled room in the Malibu Motel. It looked drearier than it had the night before, and much shabbier than our apartment in Winnipeg. Someone had hammered nails into the corners of the uneven ceiling tiles, which were scalloped with brown stains. The concave centre of the overhead light fixture was dark with a heap of dead bugs. Corinne had freshened the air on our arrival by swinging the door on its hinge like a giant fan, but the atmosphere had reverted to a heavy odour of old smoke and mould.

I got up and yanked open the window. A thin stream of cool air ran across the cigarette burns lined up on the sill. I could imagine what Dean would say, and how he would look, if he found us in a room such as this.

I walked over the gritty carpet to the bathroom. Corinne leaned over the cracked sink, trying to make up her eyes in a hazy mirror suspended by a nail in the wall.

"Where are we?" I said.

"Near some town. A lot of little towns out here." The mascara brush lifted from the end of her lash.

"Was there really a horseman who rode between them all?"

"What do you mean?"

"Dean said all these prairie towns are as far apart as a man rode each day."

"As a man *could* ride," she said. "So he'd have a place to sleep at the end of the day."

"I think he meant one rider," I said. "At the beginning."

"At the beginning? What do you think, one guy rode across the country, starting towns everywhere?" She laughed. "Dear old Dean, what junk he's filled your head with!"

I slid away from the bathroom, embarrassed for Dean, and for myself. I'd drawn pictures of the first rider. He was lean and tall and wore a long cape. He rode hard with his back bent and his whip raised, galloping towards the next town on his big horse.

"I'm hungry," I said.

"Me too. Get some clothes on."

I dressed while Corinne finished her face. She came out and rolled her nylons on, then stood up and began to fasten the garter clips.

"Why are you wearing nylons?" I said.

"I don't know. I just feel like it."

We ate a hurried breakfast at the motel café, then slammed the door on our dismal room and got in the Corvair. Corinne drove slowly over the gravel to the highway's edge, then shot quickly onto the asphalt and away. That was the best feeling in the world, to zoom through a fast acceleration to the road's right tempo, tires holding the sunny ground but letting it all go.

A midday haze lay over the fields. Horses grazing near a distant stand of trees looked shimmery and unreal. We passed a scattering of buildings and a grain elevator with a name painted in black on its brick-red side: another fly-speck town, a day's ride from the last. Another town not visited by Dean's first horseman, whom I had imagined shadowing each step of our summer journey.

"You know, I think I was wrong back there," Corinne said. "There was a horseman, like Dean said. He rode all across these plains before there were any towns."

"You're lying."

"I'm not. He rode a big stallion that the Indians couldn't tame. He lived on strips of dried buffalo he kept in a rawhide bag. At the end of each day, he rubbed his hand on a lump of coal and left his mark."

"What kind of mark?"

"A handprint. He put it on a stone, or a tree. Then he bedded down under a quilt made of beaver pelts."

"Why did he leave a mark?"

"People coming after would see it," Corinne said. "They'd know they had found a good place to settle down. But in warm weather, the buffalo came, and they all had fleas in their coats. When the fleas bit, the buffalo wanted to scratch. They scraped their hides against trees and rocks, and rubbed off the horseman's handprints."

"Is this a real story, or are you making it up?"

"A story's a story. Do you want to hear the rest or not?"

"Sure." But she didn't tell the rest right away. She reached for a cigarette, and pushed in the car lighter. I pressed my open hand against the red-upholstered door and imagined it was a stone or tree trunk.

"When the rider's marks were gone," Corinne said after a few more miles, "people couldn't find the right place to settle. A lot of them kept going, all the way to the ocean, because they couldn't find what they were looking for. That's why all these towns are so small. Because of the fleas on those buffalo." The lighter popped out, and she lit her cigarette.

"What happened to the buffalo?" I said.

"Hunters got most of them. The fleas took the rest."

The sweet smoke from her cigarette drifted over me in lazy whorls. I was getting an idea for another drawing of the first rider, with the rawhide bag slung over his back and the beaver quilt lashed behind his saddle. The horse would gallop as before, but there'd be a buffalo in the distance, waiting.

I thought there might be something to draw with in the glove compartment, so I released the latch. The Eaton's bell tumbled into my lap, along with a small china shepherdess who had lost her head long ago. There were a lot of other things in there too, all from the Drawer of Shame. They should have been in a kitchen drawer in our apartment.

"Why's this stuff in here?" I said.

Corinne took a long drag and exhaled before answering. "I thought we needed a real break from Winnipeg."

"What do you mean?"

"We're not going back to the apartment."

"Are you kidding? What about our other stuff?"

"We don't need it."

I felt dizzy. Dean and his house were gone, and now our place was too, along with most of our things. Our whole life was collapsing into this car. The Corvair, which had seemed to me so roomy and luxurious, suddenly felt like a prison.

"You should have said we were leaving for good!"

"I wasn't sure, and don't shout," she said, her own voice rising. "You can't plan everything. We've got what we need. We'll pick up things as we go."

I recalled with fierce clarity the day we left, when everything had to be done in a mysterious hurry. She had said it was because Dean was expecting us. I remembered all the dresses she packed.

"You knew," I said, "you just didn't tell me. You brought outfits you were never going to wear at Lily's!"

She gave me a sharp look. "Sounds like you already had an idea yourself."

My mind raced through an inventory of stuff in my closet and chest of drawers. There were things in the bottom drawer I was keeping special, but I was so mad I couldn't focus on whether I had packed any of them.

I pulled a folded sheet of pink paper from the open Drawer of Shame. It was a bill from a furrier, stamped PAST DUE. I found a pen and drew a horse, not galloping but standing riderless, with the beaver quilt behind the saddle. The rider stood with his head hidden inside a gigantic bell, of which he was the clapper.

I stuffed the drawing back in the Drawer, and tapped the button on the Eaton's bell, again and again.

"Quit it, Jasper."

I hit the bell faster. Corinne went on smoking for a minute as if she didn't care, then lashed across and slapped me hard. The bell rolled onto the floor.

"You're a rotten liar!" I shouted. The Corvair trembled as she slapped at me several more times, though after the first few, I pressed myself into the door till only her fingertips could reach.

"You watch I don't stop this car right here!" she yelled. "We're a long way from anywhere, Buster."

That was the last thing said that afternoon. We kept on driving for quite a while, as far apart as we could be, till our shouting lay many miles behind us. I no longer knew what I had brought or what I wanted from what we had left behind. I couldn't tell whether I cared. I couldn't tell about any of it.

CHAPTER 12

I PULLED THE WAXY PAPER away from my cupcake. A pool of corn syrup lay in my plate. Corinne was on her second cigarette, idly tapping a nail against the thick china of her coffee cup. We were in a roadside restaurant, at lunch, and the place was getting busy.

I squeezed the fluted paper into a cone shape and propped it upright on my plate. It toppled over against the fork balanced on the plate's rim, and the fork clattered to the floor. The waitress happened to be bustling by and scooped it up.

"Need another, dear?" she said, her bony, worn-out face nearly level with mine.

"He's all right," Corinne said.

"Such a fine-looking boy. You want more coffee?"

"That would be lovely." Corinne held out her cup. She looked relaxed and content, as if her bacon and eggs had been the best meal of her life. But I knew she was tense inside because the moment was coming soon.

The waitress dug in her apron pocket and put a wrapped pinwheel candy next to my plate. "On the house."

"What do you say, Jasper?" Corinne said.

I swallowed a half-chewed lump of cupcake. "Thanks." I had to fight not to grimace as the lump forced its way down. The waitress mussed my hair, and hurried along.

"Don't gobble," Corinne said. I knew she meant I shouldn't make it look like we'd be finished soon. It was better to make a move before anyone thought of bringing the bill. That was the only bad part of this restaurant game: I always had to leave part of my dessert.

Corinne plopped a lump of sugar into her coffee and gave me a long, serious look, as if to make sure I understood where we were in the game. I tried to show that I did, though at the moment I felt she got my meaning, I realized she was not really seeing me at all. Her whole attention was trained on the position and activity of the waitress, the amount of clamour in the restaurant, and the passage of people in and out of the door. The moment was very close. The seconds crawled by.

The waitress carried a stack of plates towards the kitchen. As she pushed through the swinging door, Corinne reached for her purse.

"Come on," she said in a calm voice. We slid out of the booth in unison. I tried to match her nonchalance, though my heart was pounding as it always did. The whole art of sneaking a meal came down to seizing the moment when things were just chaotic enough that no one would notice a woman slipping out the door hand in hand with her young son.

We strolled to the front of the restaurant and pressed past the people waiting for a table or lined up by the cashier. Each step brought us nearer to the glass front door. Corinne had her hand on it when she stopped and turned, so unexpectedly that the fabric of her dress swiped against my nose.

"Go, go!" I whispered.

But she didn't move. She stood there for what seemed an eternity, as if she had forgotten what we were doing, and then her face broke into the kind of open-mouthed smile she used in her model photos. She waved to someone behind me, beyond the throng of people waiting: the waitress, hurrying from the kitchen.

"I almost forgot to pay," Corinne said, as she pushed back through the crowd.

"It's so busy, I might have forgotten myself," the waitress said.

Corinne smiled a little harder when she heard that. She paid and sent me back to the table with a tip. When I returned to the café's front door, she had already gone out to the Corvair.

"What happened?" I said, as we wheeled out of the parking lot.

"Nothing," she said irritably. "They could have seen us."

"No, they couldn't. There was a bunch of people in between."

"You can't always be sure. It was a cheap place anyhow. Just eat your candy."

"What candy?"

"The one she gave you, dummy."

It took me a moment to remember the pinwheel sweet coming out of the apron pocket.

"I left it on the table."

"Oh, you!" She thumped her palm on the steering wheel, nudging the horn. Then she laughed, the kind of sharp laugh that sometimes meant a slap was coming. "The only damn thing we got out of this, and you left it behind!"

"I don't like that kind of candy," I lied.

"Shut up about it then," she said. "It was all a big mistake." But she looked as if she didn't know exactly what the mistake was, or who had caused it to happen.

Corinne and I had snuck meals when I was sure we weren't going to make it, when I walked through the door with my hands on her back, nearly stepping on her heels for fear that someone would grab me from behind. But the few times someone came out after us, Corinne's impersonation of a forgetful mother was so perfect that in the end they apologized for embarrassing her.

It was exciting to get away with it, to drive off shouting details that were unusual or frightening or funny. But this time there was nothing to say that didn't bring us back to those seconds in the doorway, when the moment had been ours and then slipped away.

"What happens in the restaurant, when you don't pay?" I said, thinking I was changing the subject.

"They get mad, I guess."

"Does the waitress get in trouble?"

Corinne didn't reply for a mile or two. Then she said, "Jasper, why are you trying to spoil this?"

"I'm not."

She handed me a folded paper packet of two sugar cubes, with Epp's Luncheonette printed on it. "Put that in the Drawer." I opened the glove compartment, and again the headless china shepherdess tumbled into my lap.

"There's too much in there, let's sort it out," Corinne said. "The little china miss can go."

"Where did she come from?"

"Lily. I kept it only because she liked it. I was just getting used to it, then that oaf knocked it over."

I never saw the oaf she was referring to, but I remembered the loud drunken whispering in the hall, and the man cursing as he lost his balance, and the china head lying at the shepherdess's feet the next morning. For me, that was when she first became interesting.

I put the shepherdess on the seat beside me, and from the glovebox pulled out a flat steel money clip.

"Oh God, I don't want to think about that guy," Corinne said.

The next thing was the furry arm of a teddy bear, which had torn away from the body a week after I got it. It embarrassed me a little to see it, but some obscure feeling still answered the call of that limb, so I pushed it back in the Drawer of Shame, and took out a small, green glass hand. The thumb and fingers curved up around the palm's hollow, which still held traces of cigarette ash.

"What's this from again?" I said reverently, and also with a trace of fear, in case Corinne wanted to get rid of it.

"Some party. I don't care either way."

It glowed in the sunlight like Kryptonite, or better, since Kryptonite didn't have that kind of emerald translucence. I tucked it back
in the Drawer. We considered several more things, till there was a
small pile of rejected items on the seat between us. The Eaton's bell
was not discussed.

"What do I do with these?"

"Throw them out the window."

"Really?"

I rolled my window down and leaned way out with the shepherdess in my hand. The rushing air beat against my face and arm.
Beyond the thick weeds separating the highway from the fields, a
barbed-wire fence marked the property of someone who came
there only a few times a year, on a roaring farm machine. I flung
the shepherdess towards the wire, but it whipped around and
smashed on the asphalt behind us. The money clip, a broken stiletto
heel and everything else flew out and disappeared into a little corner
of nowhere as the wind thudded in my ears. When the last item was
gone, Corinne tapped out "Shave and a Haircut" on the Corvair's horn.

"Are you excited?" she said. Sorting the Drawer had lifted her
mood, though I felt that this new cheerfulness could easily twist into
something else.

"About what?"

"About us being fancy-free."

"Sure." I didn't want to talk about our freedom, so I switched on
the radio and wound the tuning dial through waves of static.

More buildings began to appear, and farmland gave way to indus-
trial buildings, then to supermarkets and houses and a city: Regina.
We pulled up to a new motel with a revolving sign that promised a
heated pool and air conditioning. Corinne swung the car up in front
of the office, and through the glass door I could see a man in a suit
coming out from behind the check-in desk. Corinne put her hand
under my chin and turned my face towards hers.

"Jasper, I want this to be our best summer ever. It can be, for both of us. We can do whatever we want." She searched my face for agreement. "Do you understand? Let's forget about how it started, and begin again, from right now."

The man in the suit carried our bags to our room, which smelled of fresh soap and pine. Corinne said we'd look at the town and have a nice dinner, but first she wanted to freshen up. As soon as she closed the bathroom door, I searched the drawers till I found some motel stationery, and wrote down every numbered fact I knew about Dean: his phone number and address, his birthday, his licence plate number. Then I wrote down the Provencher Bridge and the General Strike and anything else I could remember that Dean had told me about during our drives around Winnipeg.

When I couldn't think of any more to write, I put the folded paper safe in my bag, lay on the firm bed and stared at the fresh white ceiling. Everything around me was so clean and new, as Dean preferred. But without him there, there was no point to this perfect environment. I wondered if Corinne had told him we were fancy-free and wouldn't be back, and whether our phone would still ring if he called.

CHAPTER
13

CORINNE SAID WE WERE WANDERING, but she often had a destination in mind, especially after we reached Alberta. She just didn't tell me till we left the highway and drove down a series of narrowing dirt roads to someone's driveway. Sometimes she phoned ahead, though more often we arrived without warning. "This is an adventure," she would say, as a finger and a pair of eyes breached the trembling window sheers to see whose car could be arriving, unannounced, at nine on a Sunday night.

One afternoon we stopped at a new house that might have been set on the land an hour before. We weren't yet out of the Corvair when a woman Corinne's age burst through the screen door and ran at the car with her cotton dress twisting around her plump thighs.

"I can't believe this!" she said, laughing. "Do you know how many years it's been?"

"Sorry we're late," said Corinne. "Barb, this is Jasper."

"Come in, come in!"

We followed Barb through a cluttered mud room and a kitchen that smelled of roasted meat, into a dining room with lace curtains and a big china cabinet. A man in dirty green work clothes and a pudgy boy sat at the table, their plates scraped clean of food.

"Royal, this is Karen, and Jasper," Barb said. "This is our boy Virgil."

Royal made a slight, solemn nod. "Around here, dinner's twelve on the dot," he said.

"Don't you worry, just sit," Barb said, pressing Corinne into a chair and heading back to the kitchen for our plates. Virgil's slow eyes examined me without expression, while he kicked rhythmically at the leg of his chair.

"I believe you and I have some family in common," Royal said.

"Really?" said Corinne.

"Your dad was second cousin to my uncle Sid," Royal said. "You must have known him."

"I don't think so."

"He farmed up your way. His daughter Debbie's about your age."

"I wouldn't know."

A frown settled on Royal's browned face. Corinne grew up on a farm, and we visited Lily every year or so, and I had seen country people quiz her in their routine leisurely way about how she and they might be linked through relations and friends. She seldom satisfied them. I think she claimed not to know the people mentioned even when she did. I did the opposite, and agreed to everything, whether I recognized the names or not.

Barb brought plates from the oven, loaded with dry beef, crusty mashed potatoes and dimpled peas. "What are you folks up to?" she said.

"Just wandering around," Corinne said.

"Any special destination?"

"I hope so."

"My mom says it's not wandering if you know where you're going," I said. No one had anything to say to that, and for a moment the only sound in the room was the scraping of forks against Barb's crazed china.

"Where's your dad?" Virgil said, drawing out the word.

"He died."

"Oh my goodness!" Barb said. "I'm so sorry!"

Corinne told the story of the plane crash, which this time happened on a cloudless afternoon, like the one we were having.

"How awful!" Barb said. "And you didn't ever get him home. Isn't it hard knowing he's still up in those woods?"

"Not really. He loved it up there," Corinne said. This was new information. For me, the north was a remote unknown region where no normal person would go. His loving it made the place, and him, seem even more mysterious.

"And now you're travelling," Barb said, "trying to forget. You can find out a lot about yourself that way. You remember my brother Lyle? He went all over North America on a motorbike."

"I rode with him a few times," Corinne said, "at night with no lights on, just the moon." She paused for a moment, then added: "Lyle with his shirt off was the most beautiful boy I ever saw."

Barb's round cheeks flushed pink. Virgil smirked. Even Royal smiled a little, though not in a friendly way.

"Lyle's married now, with two kids," Barb said. "He has a nice house and his own shop."

"Big man," said Royal.

"He's done all right for himself."

"With other people's money."

"Will you drop that old dirty bone!" Barb said with sudden fierceness, her face still colouring.

Royal stood up. "Nice meeting you, Karen," he said. "We don't generally have such unusual visitors."

"He means people we don't see much," Barb said.

"No, I mean unusual. No offense."

"None taken," Corinne said, but she looked a little unsettled as Royal went out. Virgil reached for a sugar cube and popped it in his mouth.

"Virgil, why don't you stir yourself and show Jasper the Prairie International?" Barb said.

He and I exchanged a look of mutual suspicion. Then he slid off his chair and led me through the living room, past a wagon-wheel coffee table and a wall of picture frames loaded with satin ribbons.

"Junior rodeo and 4-H," he said, pointing at the ribbons.

"What's 4-H?"

His pug nose wrinkled. "How can you not know 4-H?"

"I just don't."

"It's this thing where kids like me beat up kids like you."

"You wouldn't get a ribbon off me."

Virgil grabbed my arm and wrenched it behind my back for a few painful seconds, then pushed me away. "You'd be easy, like a girl."

"It's easy when you catch someone off guard," I said, thumping his back. My twisted shoulder ached to the bone as I followed him down to the basement. In the middle of the barren concrete room was a huge trestle table made from sawhorses and sheets of plywood, with an extensive railway landscape built on top.

"This is it, the Prairie International," Virgil said.

The tracks ran through fields scattered with tiny hay bales of jute, toy farm machines, and grazing plastic livestock. The front of the train peeked out from a tunnel in a papier mâché mountain range studded with pipe-cleaner trees.

"Did you build this?"

"My dad and me." Virgil touched a control on the board, and the train crept forward with a gnashing metallic sound, its front light glowing feebly. It wound through the countryside, changing routes whenever he moved the switches.

"Watch me wreck it," he said. The freight cars trembled as the train raced towards a sharp corner. The caboose came off the rails at the curve and the train tumbled across the foothills.

"Did you ever ride in your dad's plane?" Virgil said.

"I don't think so. It was a long time ago. Why's your dad called Royal?"

"It's his name, stupid. Want a turn?"

I ran the train around the track once, then sent it speeding towards a hard corner as Virgil had done. The cars flipped over the edge of the table and clattered across the concrete floor.

"You're not allowed to do that," Virgil said. "My dad gives me a fine if I flip it off the board."

"What do you mean, a fine?"

"He makes me do something, like twenty push-ups or sweep the floor. How big's your cock?"

"None of your beeswax."

"You have to show your cock, that's your fine," he said, moving towards me. "It's not bad, I'll show you mine." He unzipped his pants, and pulled out his dink. It hung from his fly like a sleeping piglet. "Your turn."

"I don't want to."

"You can't shirk your fine, or you get a worse one," Virgil said, grabbing my arm at the elbow and squeezing the joint hard. He knew all the painful grips.

"Okay, okay," I said. He let me shake him off, while somehow moving closer. My bum was pressed against the plywood edge of the Prairie International. The huge room suddenly felt cramped and airless; my head was starting to spin. I fumbled my jeans open, and awkwardly pulled the tip of my cock out.

"What happened to it?" Virgil said, bending for a closer look.

"What do you mean?"

I flinched as he poked me there with his finger. "You don't got a foreskin."

I had never heard that word. Virgil grinned.

"You got a girl's cock," he said.

"There's no such thing."

"Yes there is. My friend said they've got a little tiny one, like yours."

"He's wrong. They're blank down there, and hairy."

"How would you know?"

"My mom, in the shower," I blurted.

"She let you see?" He rubbed a plastic cow over his dink. "She showed you?" The piglet stirred. I didn't want to see it stand up, or hear him suggest another fine we could do together.

"You've got a pig's cock," I said.

He struck my chest with his open hand. I grabbed his thick arm to keep from falling backwards onto the Prairie International. He got his arm around my neck and forced my head down so I couldn't breathe or see, but I knew where to reach, and when I found it, I dug my nails into the piglet as hard as I could. Virgil howled and let go, and I rolled under the table and into one of trestle supports. The table swayed and the whole works crashed over onto the floor, with an avalanche of plastic trees, animals, bridges, railway cars and crossing signs.

"Fucking Jesus!" Virgil yelled, in a panic. "You fucking homo! You girl-cock shit!" He tugged at the heavy table, and started to cry, with his dink still hanging out.

I ran up the stairs and out the back door. Far across the field that began almost where I stood, Royal's farm rig trembled through the heat. I tucked myself into my pants, ran around the house to the Corvair, and wondered what kind of fine Virgil would get for crashing the whole Prairie International. I opened the car door, eased onto the burning hot vinyl and waited. It didn't take long. Shouts came from inside the house, then Corinne burst out the door and walked quickly towards the car.

She got in, slapped my arm and turned the ignition. The car spun around and sprayed gravel across the yard. When we reached the edge of the main road, Corinne stopped to wipe a streak of mascara from her cheek.

"Are you okay?" I said.

"Never mind. What the hell did you do back there?"

"It wasn't my fault."

"These damn hicks."

"Do we have to see the brother as well? What's his name, Lyle?"

"God I hope so," Corinne said. Her mouth twisted, and she stepped hard on the gas. I opened the glovebox and slipped one of Virgil's plastic cows into the Drawer of Shame.

CHAPTER 14

BY THE TIME WE TURNED the Corvair towards Lily's place near Chokecherry Bush, the novelty of ambushing old acquaintances had worn off. Corinne sat lower in her seat, smoked more, talked less, and kept watch on time and distance. She said the glare off the hood gave her a headache, even with her sunglasses.

We arrived in mid-afternoon. Corinne stopped the car at the foot of the gravel lane, got out and left the door hanging open. She walked in her flats through the thin windbreak of trees till she found one with a wide fork in its thick trunk. We climbed up onto a ragged wooden platform nailed across the fork, and clung together on worm-eaten boards scarcely wide enough for two. Small birds darted from the branches above, in the even sunlight that speckled the leaves and bleached the sky to a pale blue. A sound like water spilling over rocks came from the immature wheat rippling in the home section that spread out from the edge of the scrubby treed area where we stood.

"My father put this up for me," Corinne said, rocking the boards under her feet. "It used to be bigger, and there were walls. It was my tree house, though it never had a roof. I hid up here all the time.

My own little world." She told me about the tree house whenever we came to Chokecherry Bush, not because I forgot, but because it needed to be retold. I imagined her nestled behind the vanished walls, hiding from the empty spaces that spread to the horizon.

A gust of wind combed through the leaves over our heads, and sent a few dead twigs tumbling through the branches. Corinne squeezed me in her arms and breathed deeply.

"I love this place," she said. "And now for the people."

We climbed down and went back to where Ernie's dogs were circling the car. They ran ahead and barked as we drove up to the house. Lily stood waiting on the porch.

"Here he is, my own young man," she said, as she gripped me in her bony arms. "Isn't he growing up tall?" She pressed Corinne to her fallen bosom, and led us into the dining room. The table was set with plates of sugar cookies and triangle sandwiches whose crusts were already curling at the edges. Lily pressed me down onto the thin cushion of a spindle chair.

"I can't sit anymore," Corinne said. She picked a sandwich and nibbled it by the window. Lily dragged a chair near me and sat with her face close to mine. Her old-lady's perfume yielded to the homey fug of her breath, which smelled like candies mixed with fermenting root vegetables.

"Tell us all your news!" Lily said as her husband Ernie came in, fastening his shirt buttons over his undershirt.

"Nice little car," he said.

"Hello, Ernie," said Corinne.

"What kind of mileage you get?"

"Nobody cares!" Lily said. She stroked the back of my hand with her hard, waxy fingers, as if trying to rub away this question nobody cared about. "I want to hear about their doings."

"Our doings aren't much," said Corinne. "We're mostly visiting."

Lily slumped into me, felled by the difficulty of getting our news. Then she began a recitation of all the doings in their corner of Chokecherry Bush, and her voice slipped into a more habitual register. She talked in slow circles around a few subjects: the bulge in the wall by the fireplace, the neighbour's problems with his septic tank, the new tiles Ernie had nailed on the exterior.

"Asbestos," he said, spurred by a familiar cue. "The house could be struck by lightning, but she'll never burn."

"I think I need to lie down," said Corinne. She left her sandwich on the table and headed for the stairs, with Lily fussing in her wake. Ernie shuffled over and regarded me with a stony squint.

"You're a scrawny one," he said, squeezing my left arm hard under the pit. "You should come outside and help me in the machine shop."

"Maybe later."

"Maybe later. The little prince. Well, your gran's tickled to see you, that's all that counts. Let's see if you can beat me at checkers."

He pushed the plates aside and arranged the board and pieces. He was a fast, impatient player; his leathery fingers hovered over the squares even when it wasn't his turn. I made moves that I knew were lousy as I was making them.

"I knew I'd get you," he growled, as he swept my last man from the board. "Play again?"

"No thanks."

Lily came to collect the plates, and I drifted away into the front room, which was stuffed with furniture and overlapping carpets. The end tables, mantelpiece and piano top were covered with photos and trinkets. The only item of continuing interest to me hung over the fireplace: the enormous head of a moose, shot decades before by my grandfather Ben. The fur had dried out and gone dull, and the big, dark nostrils were cracking.

In a corner by the window, a hardwood stand held the huge dusty Bible Ernie's father had brought over from Holland. Inside, vines and leaves crept up the initial letter, which stood eight lines high: *In den beginne schiep God den hemel en de aarde.* I turned the pages in heavy clumps till I reached the back, where on previous visits I had illustrated the pages in my own way, with stick men and later with heroes and giants like the ones I still drew.

Out the window, beyond the ragged lawn spiked with volunteer rye and alfalfa, the fields waved silver-green into the far distance. Lily's house was a fixed point on the map of our lives, yet to me its position seemed arbitrary. The land had no restraining features, such as hills, streets or other houses.

Lily came into the room and made me sit by her on the hard, old sofa, whose frayed corners bristled with horsehair. Her fingers fumbled for a sweet in the cut-glass candy bowl. A gnarly big toe poked from each of her slippers.

"Tell me about your friends, Jasper, you must have lots."

"Not really."

"A boy like you always does. And girlfriends, too."

"No."

"Don't try and fool me. Do you remember when you did this?" She pointed at the marks on a table leg I had sawn with a breadknife when I was three. She hugged my arm, as if those scars on the wood were something to celebrate. Then she peered into my face, and her whiskery lips moved with some partially formed thought.

"You've got your own little troubles, don't you?" she said, so quietly that there was no need to deny it. The ropy veins on her hand bulged blue as she squeezed my fingers. With nothing else said, we agreed that there were gaps in the grown-up world I couldn't get around, and that it wasn't my fault. She grasped the sorrows of my pipsqueak life, or so I felt at the moment; but the moment passed.

"You're so lucky nowadays!" she sighed, and patted my hand. Then she tutted, and in a different tone said: "You see, look at the bulge in the wall!"

"How did this house get built?" I said, to prevent her from resuming the tale of the bulge.

"My father built it himself, you know that. He walked ten miles from the railway to his own homestead." Her voice followed the contours of a story often told.

"How did he know which way to walk?"

"He knew north from south, not like you." She giggled. She was permanently amused by my inability, at night or high noon, to say where the west home section was, or to point the way to the south concession road.

"Why did he build the house right on this spot?"

"Goodness! Where would you build it?" She grinned at my simplicity. Her father could tell north from south, and knew very well where to build a house on the open prairie.

"I want to ask Corinne something," I said.

"She's got a bad headache."

I climbed the painted wooden stairs to Corinne's room, which was still full of her old books, clothes and pictures from when she was a girl. She lay curled on the bed; her eyes opened as I stepped into the room.

"Can I call Dean?" I said.

She looked as if she hadn't heard, or were thinking of something else. Then she stretched out full length, and said: "No."

"Why not?"

"They have a party line. People listen in. It's long distance. Lily wouldn't understand. She doesn't know about Dean and doesn't need to find out. Why do you want to talk with him?"

"I just do."

"To complain about me?" A faint smile moved on her lips.

"No, nothing about you."

"Jasper, we just got here. Lily wants to fuss over you, not watch you make phone calls."

"Why don't you come down and let her fuss over you?"

"I will. In a while." She rolled over and curled again into her usual sleeping position.

I left the room and crept down the hall to a small room at the back of the house where Ben's things were kept. He hadn't ever slept in there, but it had been Ben's room for as long as I could remember. The bed had a coverlet but no sheets. On his chest of drawers there was a photo of him in his wedding suit, looking newly barbered and uncomfortable.

Mice had nested in Ben's sock drawer and left droppings that rolled around like lead BBS. The adjacent drawer held cufflinks, combs that still felt oily, and aftershave bottles whose vaporized contents were barely perceptible when I sniffed the open tops. There was a scuffed wristwatch with no strap, a partially used matchbook, a worn, empty wallet, and tarnished lapel pins from agricultural fairs.

I had seen all these things before. Their permanence in the drawer through all the years of my life was reassuring, but also fantastical. This wasn't like the Drawer of Shame, which was always changing. Nothing could ever be added to Ben's drawer. No new item could stand up to his old flattened matchbook, though it looked the same as a thousand others. Would anyone notice if it disappeared? I hid it in my fist, but it was too serious a thing to put in my pocket and keep. I pulled a match from the cardboard base and tried to strike it. A sharp whiff of sulphur entered the stagnant air.

Ben's room was the stillest place in the house, but it only intensified something I felt in the rooms reserved for the living. Our apartment in Winnipeg was close enough to other life for me to hear some outside sound at any hour, even when I awoke in the night. It was all connected somehow. But the deep daylight silence at Lily's permeated everything. It was like a spell that the presence of other people couldn't entirely break.

In Ben's closet, moths had riddled his Sunday suit, but his Western shirts looked still wearable. I pressed the lank fabric to my face and inhaled the musty odour. His tan cowboy boots, stained dark at the tops where his fingers pulled them on, emptied little tumbleweeds of dust when I turned them over, and still smelled of sweat and manure. I pulled them on and stumped around the room, my knees bent by the steep, unfamiliar heel.

The hallway floor creaked, and Ernie's face appeared at the door. "Not your size, Sonny Boy," he said as I scrambled out of the boots. "Come away from this shrine, I've got something for you."

He led me downstairs, all the way to the dark and grimy cellar. From a jumble of things on a blackened shelf, he pulled out a foot-long cast-iron locomotive.

"The real McCoy," he said. "Just needs cleaning up."

He spent twenty minutes at the kitchen sink scrubbing it out, then carried the train into the front room and set it on the carpet. Lily put aside her puzzle book and the three of us looked at the locomotive with varying degrees of delight and dread.

"I only ever played with it on winter nights," Ernie said. "But if you're bound and determined to waste this whole sunny day in the house, you can use it."

By the time Corinne came down for supper, Ernie had trounced me in a half-dozen more games of checkers. There was still light in the sky, but the lamps in the front room had been on for an hour, and for once I was desperate for nightfall and bedtime. The day had stretched out and sagged as time inevitably did at Chokecherry Bush, where I always felt like I was avoiding one thing and waiting for another — what, I didn't know.

CHAPTER
15

LILY HARDLY RODE ANYMORE, BUT the morning after we arrived she put on old pants and a car coat and cantered around the corral on her roan Gypsy. She rode with her body hunched forward, as if into a brisk headwind, though the air was still. Dismounting, she clung to the saddle horn with both hands and eased down slowly, feeling for the ground as if she weren't entirely sure it would be there.

"Your turn," she said, and held out the reins for me.

"Go on, Jasper," said Corinne, seeing me hesitate. Like the points of the compass, horses were something I had yet come to terms with.

Gypsy seemed big enough when I stood next to her with one foot cocked in the stirrup. From the saddle, she was huge. The ground shifted below my eyes as she stamped sideways and tossed her head, trying to comprehend the inert bundle on her back.

"Head up," Ernie yelled. "Reins in. Grip 'er with your knees."

I tucked in my knees and elbows, and the horse settled. "G'yap!" Ernie said, and Gypsy began to walk. Every time Ernie made a sound she accelerated, till I was bouncing around the corral, apparently seated on the horse but in fact merely teetering there, waiting for my rigid body to fall to earth.

I willed the horse to slow down, and after a few interminable revolutions she did, coming to a halt where Corinne stood by the rail with carrots in hand. She also had the new folding Polaroid camera Dean had given her. While Ernie carried on bribing the horse, Corinne pressed the bellows release and snapped a picture of the greenhorn astride. I slipped off the horse, we waited a minute, and then Corinne opened the camera and peeled away the print. "You don't look very happy," she said, giggling. She passed it to Lily and Ernie, whose knees buckled with the full heartless uproar of country laughter. I snatched it from them: my face in the smudgy print was a mask of awkward dismay.

Corinne climbed on Gypsy and made a few circuits. The horse's gait smoothed out, its body seemed to lengthen, and the pair of them flowed around the corral in an easy, graceful canter.

"She always had a good seat," Lily said, wiping a last tear from the laugh riot of my photo. Corinne pulled up at the gate and gestured to Ernie to open it. She trotted out and down the drive and disappeared beyond the trees. We waited by the corral for several minutes, then Lily herded us inside to prepare for her guests.

They arrived a half-hour later and made a big hubbub in the doorway, as people in Chokecherry Bush usually did. They were dressed a notch below Sunday best, and brought fruit tarts and refrigerator cookies covered in wax paper. They pinched my cheek or ruffled my hair and said: "Where's Karen?"

"She'll be along soon," Lily said. "She's taking a turn on Gypsy."

The women helped make tea and put out the baked goods on a drop-leaf table in the front room. The men talked about crops and the weather, subjects that still absorbed Ernie's mind years after his fields had all been leased to a young neighbour. Everyone said I was tall, and asked what level hockey I played. That was the extent of their interest in me, till Lily sidled over to her upright piano.

"C'mon, Jasper, let's do our song."

"No."

"You start," she said, and touched the opening chord. I refused to sing. This had all happened before, with the same friends waiting on the horsehair sofa. She played the chord a few times, then could no longer hold back.

There's a long, long trail a-winding
Into the land of my dreams

She sang in her whinnying high soprano, and met the beat with her torso like an ice-skater surging down a frozen river.

Where the nightingales are singing
And the white moon beams

"Sing with me, Jasper," she said in a quieter voice, as if only we two were there. I glanced at her and saw a familiar change that started in her eyes and moved down her face, stiffening her smile and finally overwhelming it. There was no way out of it, but I sang with her anyway, hoping that if I joined in, the change and the sadness might stop.

There's a long, long night of waiting
Until my dreams all come true

Lily's shoulders began to quake, and her voice trailed away, and her head sank over the keys. She played the last chords while I finished the song alone.

Till the day when I'll be going down
That long, long trail with you.

A strangled sound came from near the keys. Ernie got up and whipped away the music. "Like clockwork," he announced, and then to Lily said, in a lower voice everyone could still hear: "The man's dead, for pity's sake. Let it go!"

Someone else arrived, a woman I hadn't seen before, towing an older girl with dark eyes and thick hair that stood out from her shoulders. She had bruises on her forearms and a deep tan that stopped several inches below the shoulder of her sleeveless sundress. Her name was Ginette, and we agreed without speaking that the only right thing to do was to go outside.

"My mom made me wear this," she said, plucking at the waist of her dress.

"It's not bad."

"I hate it. Where's your mom?"

"She went riding."

"Is this your car?"

"Yes."

She opened the driver's door and got in.

"My dad lets me drive if I stay off the main roads," she said as I got in the passenger side. She waggled the steering wheel, checked the ignition for keys, then reached across and pressed the latch on the glove compartment. A creased studio photo slid onto my lap, of Corinne in a wedding dress.

"Is that her?" Ginette said.

"Yes."

"Is she really married?"

"No."

"Then you were born out of wedlock."

"She was married, but my dad died."

"Why isn't he in the wedding photo?"

"They take some just of the woman too." I knew the photo was only a modelling shot, but I would have said anything to deflect those words: *born out of wedlock*. They were a stain that belonged to other people, like the drooling toddler I often saw eating sand at the playground near our apartment, while his mother read a magazine.

"See if there's an extra key. My dad keeps one in there."

I clawed through the tumbling contents of the Drawer, in a fury of hope that there might actually be a spare. Corinne had gone off on a horse, I was stuck again with Lily and Ernie, and a girl with bruises on her arms was ready to drive. But I couldn't find a key. The green hand ashtray slid out of the mass; I thrust it at Ginette.

"See this? It came from a dead Chinaman."

"Liar."

We got out, wandered over to the barn, and threw stones at a rusted empty barrel. Far across the fields, the farmer who leased Lily's land was dragging a weed sprayer behind his tractor, hazing the crop with arcs of silvery mist.

"C'mon," Ginette said, and walked around to the other side of the barn. A flurry of tiny insects flew up as we waded into the high grass. She leaned back against the fence, with one foot on the rail and her bare knee up.

"How old are you?"

"Fourteen and a half," I said, aiming high and adding a half to sound more plausible.

"Do you want to French kiss? My friend Tracy showed me how."

She put her firm arm behind my neck and pulled me towards her. Her tongue lapped wet against my lips and teeth and the tip of my nose as I recoiled.

"Why do you open your mouth?" I wiped my face and spat, and had to wipe again because I never learned to roll my spit into a ball, as other boys did. The strings of my gob caught in the tall grass.

"It's how you're supposed to." Ginette glared at me, and then ducked forward and rammed me with her shoulder. The blow sent me flying over into the grass. She was on me in a second, with her knee in my ribs and her hand pressing my cheek into the ground.

"Bug off!" I said.

She held me for another second, then let go and walked away. The sky whirled as I sat up, in time to see her scornfully flip the back of her skirt to show her white panties.

I was ashamed to follow right away, so I loitered near the fence and pretended to watch the crop sprayer. My heart was starting to pound, as it hadn't done during the kiss, or while the heel of Ginette's palm ground against my cheek.

I waded through the grass to the front of the barn, and went in the human-sized door cut into the giant one made for tractors. The steep interior was dim and cool and nearly empty, except for hay bales stacked into a rough pyramid against the wall. Light streaked in through gaps between the barn boards, all the way up to the rafters, which fluttered with the sounds of birds lighting and re-lighting on their perches.

Leaning back on a bale, I breathed in the barn's heavy odour and went over what had happened. I closed my eyes, and Ginette's arm pulled again against my neck, and her tongue lapped my mouth in that half-nauseating way, and the rough grass stalks scraped my cheek as she held me down.

I opened my eyes and licked my lower lip. It had an unfamiliar taste, nutty and slightly sour. I licked my lips all over, as far around as I could reach. Then I sat up and bent over the hand with which I had wiped my mouth after the kiss, and sniffed the palm till I felt dizzy.

I left the barn and dawdled towards the house, past the grey fence where Ginette had shown her bare knee, and the depression in the grass where she had pitched me over. The places looked so ordinary, I could hardly believe that those things had happened there, only a few minutes before.

As I approached the house, I saw Ginette's mother standing at her car's open door, waving goodbye to Lily on the porch. Ginette was already inside. As the car moved past me, we stared deeply and impassively at each other.

"Don't come in like that!" Lily scolded, striking bits of hay off my back with brisk swipes of her hand. "What on earth have you been doing?"

Her friends stayed another hour. They scanned the horizon as they performed their long farewells in the driveway, still hoping for a sight of the elusive Karen.

"The girl's a will-o'-the-wisp," Ernie said after the last had gone.

"Shush, you," Lily said.

Seven hours after Corinne rode out of the corral, she returned to the house. Ernie, Lily and I were sitting before the console TV, looking through electric snow at a man fiddling while his grandson skipped out some dance steps. Corinne came into the room and flopped into an armchair.

"Sorry I'm late." But she didn't look sorry. She radiated happiness.

Ernie walked out of the house without a word.

"Did you get lost?" Lily said.

"How could I get lost?"

"People get turned around. Sometimes I wake in my own room and wonder where I am. I saved you some dinner." Lily went into the kitchen and pulled the remains of the roast from the oven.

"I'm not hungry," Corinne said. "I should brush down Gypsy."

"Ernie's doing it." Lily said. "I made carrots with that special glaze you like." Mentioning the favourite glaze was as far as she could go towards a reproach.

Corinne came to the sofa and took my hand, and repeated that she was sorry, and searched my face for signs of complaint. They were there, but not to the extent she deserved. I no longer cared that she had disappeared, and wasn't very curious about where she had gone. I was too immersed in the incident of the French kiss. All I wanted to do was to see Ginette again, not some other day, but that same afternoon. I wanted to do it all over, so I could feel it the right way this time, and see what it meant, and know what I should have done.

CHAPTER 16

I CLIMBED INTO THE TRUCK cab and slid to the middle. Ernie cupped his hand near the corner of the windshield and scooped away a horsefly buzzing against the glass. Corinne got in next to me, the truck roared into life, and Ernie banged my knee with a hard jerk of the long gearshift.

The cab smelled of greasy farm dirt and old cigarettes, but that cleared out as we raced along the gravel concession road with the wind buffeting in hard from both open windows. After a few miles, Ernie slowed near a gap in the fencing and plunged the truck down a rutted lane lined with trees.

Loops of rusting wire coiled out of the undergrowth and over chunks of car bodies. The hood of a Volkswagen Beetle leaned against a tree trunk, like a giant's shield. At the end of the lane, in front of a shabby bungalow, a pair of old sedans faced each other with their hoods open, like alligators comparing jaws. A swarthy man in dirty jeans and a T-shirt walked from the doorway of the house towards our slowing truck.

"You're burning oil," he said.

"A little," Ernie said. "Clay, you know Karen, and her boy Jasper?"

"I remember Karen all right," Clay said with a gummy grin. His cigarette pack stuck out from the top of his upturned T-shirt sleeve.

"Hello, Clay," Corinne said.

"You okay riding in the back?" said Ernie.

"Yup." Clay clambered into the open truck bed. Ernie was swinging into his u-turn when the bungalow screen door opened, and Ginette stepped out.

"I want to come," she called, wiping wet hands on her orange top and faded jeans.

"If it's okay with Ernie," said Clay, her father apparently.

Nothing about Ginette's blue dress at Lily's had prepared me to find her living here, at the end of a car graveyard, in a house Dean would have called a tear-down. I craned around Corinne to show that I was there too, afraid that Ginette might change her mind, and that she might not. But she didn't seem to notice me as she climbed over the tailgate.

Birds darted up from the road as we thundered along the gravel towards the homestead cabin Ernie's father had built decades before, from which Ernie wanted to retrieve an old cast-iron stove. I looked back through the cab's small rear window once, but saw only the rim of the tailgate and the cloudless sky. Ginette and Clay were probably squatting in the front corners, out of the dust and wind.

We turned off into a quarter section of wheat, along a barely visible track. Corinne caught at a stem through the window and the whiskered green kernels stripped off into her hand. We were almost at the end of the track before the cabin's low roof appeared.

Ernie's brother, a thick, balding man named Mitch, was already there, with Daniel, a broad-bellied Indian with pitted cheeks. Mitch was tramping a path through the thick weeds that surrounded the house.

Ginette had already hopped down when Corinne and I got out. I made my guilty introductions and wondered how she would be.

"You ride Chester, right?" Corinne said.

"Yes," said Ginette.

"Chester has the same sire as Gypsy," Corinne told me. "Not that you would care."

"Want some gum?" Ginette offered us an open pack of Juicy Fruit.

"No, I want one of your dad's cigarettes," Corinne said, and followed him into the cabin.

"You call your mom by her name," Ginette said. "But you say it funny."

"It was Karen, she changed it." I glanced at Ginette's face, but couldn't hold her gaze. I had spent too much time with her in my head, where she did the same things over and over. Now she was on the loose, looking and acting differently. Her presence, near enough to touch, reverberated through me with a force that made me dizzy. I could smell the musky, faintly sour odour I had tasted on my skin in the barn.

"What are you worried about?" she said. She nudged into me with her shoulder, and we walked together to the cabin door, a few steps that felt as unreal as a stroll on the moon.

Inside the cabin, rags of darkened wallpaper curled off the walls. A few framed pictures, speckled with black mould, still clung to their hooks. The place smelled of rotting wood and whatever animals had lived there during the winter. A grey mattress lay bursting on a rusted steel frame, near a section of floor that had fallen into the cellar.

"People lived in here," I said, as much to myself as to Ginette. It seemed impossible that someone had slept and dreamt on that bed, yet the cabin still felt like a dwelling more real than any motel.

"Yeah, and now it's only mice," Ginette said.

The men were inspecting the vast stove, which took up half the tiny kitchen. Its black iron sides were decorated with festive whorls and curlicues. Leaves and vines twined over the ceramic tiles that ran up the back to the tarnished steel hood. Ernie swept the debris from the stovetop with his arm and pulled at the handle of the white enamelled oven door. The dry springs sang.

"Let's go out," Ginette said.

We entered the jungle of weeds behind the cabin. The air seethed with the pulsing rasp of crickets. We worked the long handle of an old pump hidden in the weeds, till the hollow heaving sound rose up the pipe and spewed water. Ginette caught some in her hands, drank a little, and flicked the rest at me. I grabbed her arm, but had no idea what to do with it. She shook me off and moved towards a tiny shed, which had lost its door and smelled worse than the cabin.

"That skunk could be dead by now, but the stink will never go," she said. She yanked up a stalk of Queen Anne's lace, leaned against the shed's blackened boards, and rolled the white clustered flower head over her chest. I faced her as close as I dared, but still couldn't meet her eyes.

"What does your dad do with all those cars?" I said.

"Fixes them up and sells them."

"Does he get much?"

"What do you care?" She tapped my shoulder with the flower head, twice, and broke whatever spell I was under. I looked her in the face. She flicked away her gum, gripped my shirtfront, and pulled me towards her. I got rid of my gum too, and just before our lips met she said: "No spitting."

I leaned into her and she lapped at me as before, like a snail crossing and recrossing my mouth. I fixed my eyes on a knot in the dark wood, and held firm against the slightly disgusted excitement seething up in me. It was easier to do if I kissed her as much as she kissed me.

"You're supposed to close your eyes," she murmured. We kissed some more like that, blind to each other, and a shivery relief came over me, because even with the smell of skunk around us, our Juicy Fruit kisses were less revolting than the one at Lily's.

A shout and the sound of splintering wood reached us from the cabin. We left off kissing and listened, searching each other's eyes for a reason to stop or go on. From close up, with my burning hands on her waist, her eyes and nose seemed bigger and her chin more pointed.

"My dad knew your mom at school," she said. "He said she slapped his face once, in front of everybody."

"Why?"

"Don't worry. He acted like it was funny."

A loud crack resounded from the cabin. Ginette pushed me away. "Let's go back," she said.

Daniel and Clay were kicking with their heavy boots at the wall around the kitchen window. Chunks of dark wood flew out with each kick.

"What's happening?" I said, my mouth still tingling.

"They're going to pull it out this way," Corinne said. "Where were you?"

"Exploring."

"I'll bet."

Ginette and I wrenched pieces of broken timber from the upright posts. We kept pulling at boards till torn pieces of wood lay all over the long grass, and our bare sweaty arms were black with dirt. Ernie backed the truck around. The men shuffled the stove out in short bursts of effort.

"She's a heavy one," Clay gasped as they set it down by the rear of the truck. He retrieved an unfinished cigarette from behind his ear and lit it. "What do you want with this old thing? Ain't you got a new stove?"

"You can get good money for one like this," Ernie said.

"Not around here."

"I'll haul it to the city. I know a dealer."

"Wheeler-dealer." Clay grinned as he supplied this obligatory rhyme.

"I remember eating off this stove," Mitch said. He laid his thick, filthy hand on the black iron, near the tiles. "Mam would set a pot of porridge here at night, and by morning it was cooked perfect. *Smakelijk eten, smakelijk drinken*," he sang tunelessly.

"What's he saying?" Corinne said.

"Eat your breakfast," said Ernie.

"*Hap hap hap, slok slok slok.*"

"Mitch, nobody cares about that." Ernie seemed annoyed by this outburst of Dutch kitchen chatter.

I stepped through the kitchen's exploded wall. Sunlight shone on the dirty Delft-blue tiles, hidden for decades behind the stove. I pressed my palm on them, and when I withdrew it, enough of the dirt had transferred to leave a faint negative hand print. It was like a reversal of what the first horseman had done, before the settlers arrived.

"Their own father built this place," I said to Ginette, who was jabbing at a loose tile with a stick. "They grew up here. Why would they let it get so wrecked?"

"Ask them. It's an old dirty dump now." The grout crumbled under her prodding and the tile fell to the floor. I picked it up.

"Do you want this?" I said.

"No, what for?" She broke it against a wall stud.

With its side torn open, the kitchen had become part of the out-doors, but the rest of the house remained a house. It looked nothing like our apartment in Winnipeg, but it too had been abandoned, with pictures left on walls and a mattress still in the bedroom. What had become of the things we left behind, including the ones I hadn't known I was giving up? A shiver of resentment passed through me. I couldn't imagine our place emptied out, but was also having trouble seeing it as it had been. I'd had no chance to look it over one last time and remember. It was like Dean, who disappeared before I knew he was out of our lives for good.

More grunts and shuffling noises came from outside, as the men heaved the stove onto the tailgate. They walked it one end at a time towards the cab, and lashed it there with ropes. Bound in Ernie's truck, it looked smaller and less grand than it had in the rotting kitchen. A thin reflected veil of clouds drifted across the steel hood.

I told Ernie I wanted to ride in the back, and climbed up beside the stove with Ginette. Clay piled into the cab next to Corinne. As the truck rolled through the field and sped along the gravel concession, Ginette and I clung to each other on the trembling metal floor, and licked the grime off each other's lips.

LILY WORE MAKEUP ONLY WHEN she went to church, and her hand was no longer steady. She came downstairs in a pink Sunday dress with crooked lipstick and blotches on both cheeks. Corinne took her into the dining room and repaired her makeup in the inert white light that filtered through the window sheers. From the brown Bakelite radio in the kitchen, Ernest Manning droned through his *Back to the Bible Hour* address, which Lily heard, or least turned on, every Sunday morning.

"I've got to go." Lily's short heels shifted impatiently on the wooden floor.

"I'm almost done."

"You'll come later, won't you? People would love to see you."

Ernie wasn't a religious man, and stayed in his work clothes to drop Lily off in town. Then he came back and spent a half-hour fussing with an engine before dressing for the church social. Corinne took away the book I was reading, which had "Karen" scrawled inside the cover, and told me to put on a nice shirt and pants.

"Why do I have to go at all?"

"Because I do."

I took out a black satin Western shirt I got from a brief cameo in one of Corinne's fashion shows. As I fastened the snaps, the cactuses and cowboy boots embroidered on the creamy yoke led me into familiar fantasies about the adventures I could have as a character on *Rawhide* or *Wagon Train*.

Those dreams vanished like cobwebs in a fire when I went outside and faced Ernie, now suited in grey wool. He said nothing when he saw me, but his face lit up with the joyous ridicule I heard in every remark that made people laugh in Chokecherry Bush.

"I have to change," I told Corinne, who already stood by an open door of Ernie's Buick in a green floral dress.

"You look fine," she said.

"No I don't."

"That's a beautiful shirt and it fits you perfectly." The authority in her voice, not maternal but professional, soothed my fears enough to get me into the car.

We drove to Chokecherry Bush and Lily's Baptist church. Faint wisps of hymn singing reached us as we stood waiting in the bright sunlight. Near the unpainted church steps, a pair of crows fought over some morsel in the weeds.

The singing ended, the church door opened, and the sound of the organ swelled out. The preacher stepped on the porch and shook hands with everyone as they came out: the men with their brown faces and boxy suits, the women in their Butterick dresses and small pinned hats.

Lily led us into the meeting hall behind the church. Ladies from the church auxiliary stood behind folding tables loaded with kettles of tea and lemonade, and plates of cookies and Rice Krispie squares. Ginette approached in her hated blue dress, with a cookie in each hand.

"Holy moly, where did you get that shirt?" she said mournfully.

"It's from a fashion show," I said, mistaking what she said for a real question.

"Don't say that! Come outside." She gave me a cookie and I followed her towards the rear door with my head down, though everyone was looking only at Corinne, the one elegant woman in the room.

We went outside. A few other boys, in suits and shirts like their fathers, had draped their jackets on a low bough of an oak.

"Look, a real cowboy," one of them said. Everyone laughed. The black satin of my shirt glowed in the sun like fresh tar.

"Shut up," said Ginette. A sharp-eyed mousy girl appeared at her side, straining not to laugh. "This is Tracy."

"Very fancy," said the instructor of French kissing, hiding her mouth behind her hand.

"Jasper and I took a spin in his sports car the other day," said Ginette. "We got up to eighty."

"Liar," Tracy said.

Someone shoved me from behind and said, "Hey, do you know Buffalo Bill?" I turned and faced a wide-shouldered boy with pimpled skin and blond, short hair that stuck up like straw.

"Drop dead, Randy," Ginette said.

"Can you get me Bill's autograph?"

Ginette jumped at him, and he ran towards the tree with his hands up in mock terror. She chased him down and gave him a hard fist in the back.

"Bill, I'm dying!" Randy yelled, and sank to the ground laughing.

"True love," said Tracy, apparently bored by these shenanigans. Her matter-of-fact tone stung more than the shame of seeing a girl spring to the attack for my sake. I stumbled towards the commotion. Everyone stared as I approached Randy in my gleaming cowboy shirt, all waiting to see what I would do. But my arms wouldn't leave my sides.

"Fuck off," I told him at last.

"Mercy!" said a plump woman standing in the doorway of the church hall. She stepped out, her wide skirt swaying like a big, soft bell. "We don't use such language here. Did you talk that way, Randy?"

"I was just trying to be friendly." His friends laughed.

"In that case, you boys shake hands. Go on!"

Randy and I briefly touched palms, a sign of peace that put a look of real hatred on his speckled face. He rejoined his friends.

"I was sure you were going to hit him," said Tracy. Ginette folded her arms into a discontented square, which confirmed I should have.

"Is it true you live in your car?" Tracy said.

"No, we had a place in Winnipeg."

"Where's your place now?"

"We're travelling."

"Where will you live when you stop?"

"I don't know."

"That's what I'll do someday," Ginette said. "Leave, and not care where I end up."

"Big talker," Tracy said. "You wouldn't get far."

"Shut up," Ginette said. "This whole day's a nightmare." She left us and ran back into the church hall.

Tracy smirked at me. "What are you waiting for?"

I darted towards the door and pushed my way through the crowd. Ginette stood at the drinks table, her head down, the base of her neck showing under her bushy hair.

"I poured you one," she said, handing me a glass of lemonade. I took a sip, and stroked her bare arm.

"Don't," she said, pulling back. "Everyone can see." At the same moment, she moved so that our free hands were hidden under the table edge and took mine in hers. My heart thumped under my throat.

"Do you like Randy?"

"No, I hate him." Her strong, chapped fingers felt my hand all over. I stared stupidly at her solemn eyes and frosted pink lips. We drank our lemonade, poured some more, and the vague clamour of every useless thing around us sheltered us like a blanket.

Someone touched my arm: Corinne, with her mouth drawn into a tense line.

"Leave that, we're going," she said.

"We just got here," I said, feeling like I had arrived only that moment.

"My mom can drive him back," Ginette said.

"Thanks, but we have to go," Corinne said. She yanked me through the crowd towards the exit. From the front door I glanced back for Ginette, but couldn't find her face among the many staring at us.

"I didn't do anything," I said as we got outside.

"I'm not saying you did."

She led me towards Ernie's car, no longer pulling but holding me close. We got into the back and sat together on the hot vinyl, her hand still clinging to my arm. She was trembling.

"God damn these holy rollers!" she said.

A shadow crossed the corner of my eye as someone appeared at my window. It was Randy, his elbows on the frame, his fingers jiggling the door lock, his face inches from mine. He blew a burst of cigarette smoke in my eyes.

"Hey, Bill," he said. "Remember what you told me? You can have it back double."

"Leave him alone," Corinne said. "Get away from the car."

Randy didn't move. "Speaking of you, what's your married name?"

"You little shit!" Corinne said.

I flung my door open, trying to get him in the legs, but he jumped back. I leapt out and lunged at him with both hands, but before I could touch him, he grabbed my wrists. His grip was like iron.

"I don't fight little girls," he said, and flung me back so hard I toppled over, just missing the edge of the open door.

"Jasper!" Corinne said.

"Mommy's calling." Randy and his loitering friends decamped in a quick, rolling saunter. I got my legs under me and sat on the car seat with my back to Corinne and rubbed my wrists.

"Are you all right?" she said. "Where the hell's Lily and Ernie?"

A moment later they came out of the church hall, looking more than usually old and holding hands as I hardly ever saw them do. Lily touched her eyes with a pink handkerchief as they walked towards us. Ernie's trouser cuffs dragged on the tough weeds that flattened themselves on the baked earth.

They got in, the car moved off, and the breeze cleared out the stifling warm air. No one spoke till we were out of town and on the road back to the farm.

"God almighty!" Corinne said at last.

"Please, dear," Lily said from the front seat. From the sound of her voice, I knew she was still crying.

"You heard what she said."

"A lot of people were very happy to see you."

"You heard, and you didn't say a thing. And there was more outside!"

"Let it go, the both of you!" said Ernie. He switched on the radio. Scraps of hymn singing drifted in and out of the buzzing static.

*

THAT NIGHT, WHEN CORINNE CAME to see me to bed, she told me a story about a voice crying from deep inside a village well.

"The villagers thought someone had fallen in," she said. Her eyes, wiped clean of makeup, were fiercely wakeful. "The well was too narrow for any of the men, so they sent the strongest boy down on a rope. When the rope went slack, they called to him, but he didn't answer. For two days and nights they called into the well, but never heard a sound in return. On the third day, the women wailed and tore their clothes. The men said the well was cursed, and dug a new one."

"What happened at the church?" I said. "What did they say to you?"

"Never mind. Why do you always interrupt!" she said, twisting the edge of my coverlet with both hands. "Seven years passed. Again the villagers heard sounds from the old well. They remembered what happened to the boy, and decided to fill the well with stones. When the first stone fell, a voice in the well said, 'This one's bread.' When the second stone went in, the voice said, 'Here's a precious diamond.' When the third stone fell, the voice said, 'This is your last goodnight.' By the next morning, all the villagers were dead."

"What a terrible story!" said Lily from the doorway. "Why are you frightening the boy at his bedtime?"

"Let me finish," Corinne said sharply. "The strong boy grabbed one of the stones pitched into the well, and killed the troll who had kept him prisoner for seven years. The villagers woke up and pulled the boy out. They had a big party. With lemonade."

CHAPTER 18

THE DAY AFTER OUR TRIP to church, Corinne woke me early.

"Are we leaving?" I said, not fully awake. The sun was beginning to touch the bluebells on the wallpaper.

"No, you can sleep. Tell Lily I've gone out. I won't be long."

"Are you taking Gypsy?"

"No." I closed my eyes, somehow assured that if the horse stayed behind, Corinne really might not be long. I opened them again after what seemed only a moment. The room was full of light, and my forehead was damp with sweat. A distant clatter of pans reached me from downstairs, followed by Lily's voice, calling me down for breakfast.

I fumbled into some clothes and a minute later sat at the table with frog-like stillness. Ernie's empty plate was already smeared over with cold grease and egg yolk.

"Corinne said she'd be back soon," I said.

"In time for supper?" Ernie said.

"They're leaving today, no thanks to you!" Lily told him as she loaded my plate.

Ernie waited out my breakfast, then took me to the garage and made me wash some greasy bolts in gasoline. He crawled into the mechanic's pit under a car he was working on and got me to pass tools and unfamiliar parts down to him. But I couldn't distinguish them quickly enough.

"Forget it," he said. "Find something else to do."

But on the farm, outside, it seemed you could only ride a horse, fix things, make them grow, or kill them. On a blackened garage shelf, I found the slingshot Ernie had made me the year before, and took a handful of fence staples. I fired one of these into a flock of birds hunting for bugs on the lawn. A violent rustle of wings flashed up into the trees, but one bird remained on the grass, its feathers splayed at odd angles, its talons clutching the air, its eyelid twitching shut.

I sprang up from this murder scene at the sight of Ginette coming over the lawn on a horse, presumably Chester. I made a guilty gesture and threw down the slingshot.

"It's only a bird," she said. "Want to go riding?"

"We're leaving."

"Right now?"

"This afternoon maybe."

"So come now. Get on with me."

She trotted near the fence and shifted forward on the saddle. I climbed the rails and got on behind her, and put my arms around her waist. The horse lurched as it stepped down from the lawn to the gravel driveway, pitching me softly against Ginette's warm back. She wore a Western shirt with sleeves rolled up to the elbows and light cotton pants.

"Where are we going?" I said as we turned into the shallow ditch that ran along the road.

"Somewhere. You said you liked not knowing."

We moved beyond the trees and the sun's glaring heat seeped into our clothes. I could feel Ginette breathing and smell the dusty odour of her hair, along with the sharper smells of the horse and the plants crushed under its hoofs. A brittle wail rose from crickets hidden in the weeds.

"Randy says he beat you up," Ginette said.

"He's a liar."

We rode the length of two quarter sections and then turned towards a slough at the edge of a field. Ginette spurred her horse across a shallow bit of water and into a stand of trees more dense than the thin woods that divided the quarters. We slid off, and Ginette lashed the reins to a tree trunk. We sat in a brushy area where we couldn't see anything but the trees, the sky, and each other. Then I saw nothing at all, as we closed in without speaking and exchanged our slithery, warm, still-awkward French kisses, with eyes closed as you were supposed to.

A bit of Ginette's hair got between our mouths, and as she pulled it away we broke contact and I caught a glimpse of her. Her swollen lips were parted, her eyelids trembled, her cheeks glistened.

The weight of those kisses gradually brought us to earth till we lay side by side. Ginette held me tight to her chest, but kept her hips drawn away. I got one leg over both of hers, and followed it across till I was on top of her, and for a moment we lay with our bodies full length against each other.

"Don't," she said, and threw me off. She sat up and so did I. We each hugged our own drawn-up knees as if a draft had come through. But the wind hissing in the leaves overhead did not touch us.

"Do you know what happened at the church?" Ginette said.

"No."

"Kitty Shaw called your mom a tramp."

I didn't understand. For me, a tramp was a cartoon man who carried a bulging kerchief on a stick. But the word's new, unfamiliar setting scraped at me the same way as Randy's remark about the married name and Ginette's about being born out of wedlock.

"Why are you all so mean?" I turned my face from her and laid my head on my knees. Through the trees, the stagnant slough water shone like a darkened mirror.

Ginette moved closer and leaned against me, pushing till I lay again on the ground, which fell away a little behind my head. She clambered over me and kissed me more intensely than before.

"How old are you really?" she murmured.

"I told you."

"Tracy says you're younger."

"She's not as smart as she thinks."

She rolled her cheek against mine and put my hand on her cotton-covered breast. She slid her hand down to my crotch, lingered there almost weightlessly for a moment, then squeezed at me through my jeans. I flinched and tried to sit up, but she pushed me back and leaned on me with her forearm. Her wide eyes stared right through me as she squeezed and stroked me through the denim. We kissed again, our mouths gaping wide, my whole body so tense I could barely breathe. A button from her breast pocket came loose in my hand.

Ginette swivelled around till her thigh lay across my chest, and opened my pants. She pulled my cock free and dropped her head. I flinched violently from the shock of that contact, and lifted my head, but her knee pinned me at the breastbone. At first I was too tense to feel anything, but then something stirred and spread through my body like lava while she lapped at me from a long way down, her boot scraping the ground near my ear.

After a few gasping minutes, a tremor exploded through my hips and split me open to the sky. Ginette rolled off and spat something into the grass. She spat again, with her shoulders hunched and trembling. She dragged the back of her hand across her mouth and looked around at me, her face distorted by what she had gone through with.

"If you ever tell, I'll kill you," she said.

"I won't." The words barely sounded from my dry throat. My fingers and mouth tingled as I tucked myself back into my pants, feeling as if nothing could cover all that had been exposed.

A bird shrieked from the treetops. We stood up and moved away from the spot. We got back on Chester, recrossed the shallow part of the slough, and rode out from the trees and along the ditch. Ginette's body and mine both felt uncomfortably moist, and strange to the touch. Chester's tail swished against my ankle, and the thudding fall of the horse's stool joined the scraping, rustling sound of its hoofs finding rocks and soil under the weeds.

After the first quarter section Ginette pulled my hand underneath her. My fingers lay between her light pants and the saddle leather, stunned into inertia at being in contact with the warm delta of her crotch. She ground her hips forward, and with her hand worked my fingers against the fabric.

"C'mon, it's your turn," she said, a little breathlessly. She removed her hand, and I took over her movement, stroking the cloth near the seam. Ginette's hips writhed against my hand, the saddle creaked, and the horse plodded on. Suddenly her head jerked back and crashed into my cheek.

"Keep going!" she said. I rubbed more quickly against the damp seam. My eye watered from the blow to my face and my hand was beginning to ache. Ginette's stiffening body pitched forward, then her head hurtled back, but this time I was ready and caught the impact on my shoulder. She twitched for a minute and then lolled back limp against me. I had to strain forward and grip the saddle horn to keep my seat.

We rode like that for an uncomfortably long time, my arm stretched out, fingers clinging to the horn. A faint hum started up from far behind us, then grew louder and more familiar. Ginette sat up and pulled my other hand out from under her. I knew before the car slowed beside us that it was Corinne.

"Isn't this cozy?" she said through the open window. The dust rolling in behind her drifted into the ditch and settled on our sweaty skin.

"Chester doesn't mind double," Ginette said.

"Are you heading back? We're leaving as soon as we're packed. Or I can take Jasper now."

"No, it's okay."

The car zoomed off. We rode in silence the rest of the way. My arms lay loose around Ginette's hips. When we reached Lily's drive, Corinne was already packing things into the Corvair.

"You both look cooked," she said, examining us and running her palm down Chester's glistening neck. "Come in for a cold drink."

"No thanks," Ginette said. The horse rattled the bit in its teeth, and cast a nervous eye at Ernie's dogs.

"Jasper, go get some water. Hop off a minute, Ginette."

"I really have to go."

"You should at least water Chester at the trough."

"He'll be okay till I get home."

I ran to the kitchen to get two glasses of water. Lily was pulling cookies from the oven.

"Will you eat nut hermits, Jasper?"

"Sure, anything."

Corinne, coming in, passed me on the porch as I went out. "That girl's stuck to her horse," she said.

Ginette, still on Chester, rinsed her mouth and spewed a stream on the ground, then drank the rest without stopping. The horse shifted sideways on the gravel.

"I wouldn't have done that with you if you lived here," Ginette said.

I had to shield my eyes as I looked up at her, towering over me with the sun behind her and the reins wrapped around her fist. She was still close to me; I could have touched her thigh with a small movement of my hand. But she was already far away, and getting more distant every second.

"Tracy was right," I said. "I'm only twelve."

An uneasy smile twitched across her face. "Liar." She dug her heels into the horse's flanks. She had almost rounded the end of the drive when I raised my hand to my face, and inhaled the strange rank smell on my fingers.

When the car was all loaded, with a tin of fresh cookies and some skinny carrots still dirty from the garden, Lily turned a sad face in at the driver's window. She gave Corinne a last hug, and said the words that ended most of our visits:

"Next time you come, I want to hear about *everything*."

A minute later the Corvair raced along the same stretch of road I had travelled with Ginette. The dogs galloped behind us, steadily falling behind into the plume of dust.

"These visits are like booster shots," Corinne said. "The kind that give you a fever."

"Why do we keep doing them?"

"Lord knows."

She lit a cigarette and took a slow, deep drag.

"Why don't we ever see your real friends when we visit?" I said.

She gave me a sharp look. "My real friend is otherwise engaged. Put this in there." She handed me a tattered work glove.

"Is that Lyle's?" I said. "Are you sure you want it in there?"

Corinne's face creased as she took another pull on her cigarette. She made a weary movement with her arm, similar to Dean's explanatory smoking gestures, but said nothing more. She was already retreating, from Chokecherry Bush, from me, from everything.

I opened the glove compartment and stuffed in the glove and a piece of the Delft-blue tile from the ruined homestead, then took out my crumpled drawing of the first rider. I folded it four ways over the button from Ginette's breast pocket and slid it into a deep corner of the Drawer of Shame.

CORINNE LAY BY THE POOL on a woven plastic lounger in her darkest sunglasses and her orange ruffled bikini. The water flashed spangles of sunlight over her tanned skin, her tousled hair and her freshly painted nails as she groped the aqua-painted concrete deck for her drink. I sat next to her on a deck chair, unable to stretch my body out in a place facing the windows of twenty other motel rooms. Even fully dressed I felt that my altered state must be visible in some way.

In the pool, an elderly lady in a flowered rubber cap was swimming slow lengths.

"What's with you?" Corinne said. "Missing your little friend?"

"It's too hot here."

"Get out of those clothes. Go for a swim."

I got up and paced along the pool. My stumpy, deformed shadow quivered on the flashing surface, refusing to hold a consistent shape. Reflections danced around it, and along the blue-painted bottom of the pool.

The elderly lady finished a length of backstroke. She gripped the pool's edge and squinted at me.

"Why are you staring at me, young man?" she said.

"I'm just looking at the pool."

"Stop it please."

I returned to our chairs. Corinne propped herself on her elbows and took off her sunglasses.

"Are you being a pest?"

"I'm not doing anything. She's crazy."

"What's wrong with you today? How did you get that bruise on your cheek?"

"I don't know." The moment when Ginette's head crashed back into my face emerged from the story that had churned through my mind ever since we left Chokecherry Bush. What if that blow had knocked me off the horse? *"How did you break your neck?"* By touching *a girl.*

Corinne put her sunglasses back on and stretched out. "You're not going to mope the whole day, are you?" She didn't look at all as she had in the car the previous day, smarting from one of life's booster shots and blinking away tears. An hour in the sun, and the blank slate of another motel room, seemed to have restored her.

I pulled off my clothes, down to the swim trunks underneath, and lay on the lounger next to hers. My red hands and forearms emphasized the ridiculous pallor of my belly. My bare legs were almost as pale, and skinny. I was scrawny, as Ernie said, and my chest was still hairless.

And yet I had done *that.* I had felt her mouth on me, and that explosion under the trees. I had stroked her down there, till she practically passed out. Before Ginette, it was hardly imaginable to hold hands with a girl, and then only if her hand wasn't sticky and she didn't ask me to explain. I had entered a new part of the adult world.

But as soon as this proud secret inflated my chest, I remembered Ginette's disgust as she spat and wiped at her mouth, and the pungent animal smell she left on my hand, and the hollowness afterwards. She led me to that also. And then she rode off, taking something with her, without even wanting it very much.

"We'll go back eventually. You'll see her again."

"She said she's leaving."

Corinne reached over and took my hand. "In a few years, she'll marry a boy she's known since she was a baby."

I yanked my hand away. "In that case, it doesn't matter if I see her again."

"Don't take it like that."

A couple emerged from one of the doors opposite, with a little girl. The woman put a pocket portable radio on the cement, and Perry Como's voice, coddled by silky strings, rebounded from the hard surfaces around the pool. The couple played in the water with the girl, and the man stole little glances in Corinne's direction, then longer ones. His wife noticed, and glared in our direction.

Corinne sat up as if stirring from a dream and put away her sunglasses. She stepped to the water's edge and dove in as smoothly as an otter. I went to the low diving board and scattered the world with a cannonball.

*

I LAY ON THE MOTEL bed in my clothes, my fingers twisting the smashed-down tufts on the cotton bedcover. From the other side of the wall, the excited muffled voices I had been hearing for several minutes rose into shrieks of laughter. A car's headlights swept across our curtains. The motor drew up near the window, and panted there till lights and engine were extinguished. Car doors slammed, and a moment later the surging voices behind the wall hailed the new arrivals.

The tub in our bathroom began to gurgle. Corinne was taking a bath to wash the chlorine off her skin. She emerged in a warm exhalation of damp air with one towel wrapped around her and another over her arm. As she crouched down and pulled my pyjamas from my bag, I glimpsed the cheeks of her reddened bum under the short towel.

"Get ready for bed," she said. She tossed the cowboy-patterned flannels to me with one hand and towelled her hair with the other.

I took my things into the bathroom and washed before a mirror running with condensation. I wiped the mirror with my hand and watched my solemn, streaky reflection disappear again behind the mist.

Corinne pulled the covers back and I slid in. The sheets were worn and pilled, but pleasantly tight across my torso, and became more so as Corinne sat beside me, still drying and brushing her hair. A new impatient thumping joined the noises next door: they had put on music. Corinne nodded her head in time for a moment, then squeezed my hand and searched my face, apparently without finding anything new there. She kissed my forehead and got up, as if reluctantly, and took out fresh clothes.

"What are you doing?" I said.

"I'm going to go next door and ask them to keep it down."

"Really?"

She gave a little shrug. "Maybe I'll do a bit more than that, but I won't be long."

She vanished again into the bathroom. I opened the bedside table and took out the Gideon Bible, and found a pen. But with a clean endpaper before me, I didn't feel like drawing anything. None of my old warriors seemed appropriate. I moved the pen idly around the page, waiting for some figure to emerge, but what actually came out were the letters of Ginette's name, joined together at first, then in blunt capitals. Then I drew a horse standing on those letters with a saddle but no rider.

An explosion of laughter burst through the wall from the room next door. Corinne emerged from the bathroom, dressed and as made-up as she could be in fifteen minutes, wearing a deep red lipstick I hadn't seen since Winnipeg.

"I could be back in two minutes."

"I doubt it."

She went out, and a minute later the party next door registered the arrival of the pretty stranger. I lay there till I was sure she wouldn't be back soon, then left the bed and the room and headed along the concrete in my pyjamas and bare feet, towards the pay phone at the opposite end of the motel. I picked up the receiver, dialled the operator, and asked to make a collect call to Dean's number.

It rang till I thought she would say there was no answer, but then his voice came on the line, and he said yes, he would accept the charge. The blood thumped so hard in my throat, I wasn't sure I could speak.

"Where are you?" He sounded sleepy, or maybe drunk.

"Near Lethbridge."

"Having a nice time?"

"It's okay. I rode a horse yesterday," I said, and winced at this blunder.

"Good for you."

"Are you building anything?"

"Yeah, a few things. I'm doing a covered pool, with an underground passageway from the house. The guy wants to walk to his pool in his swim trunks, in February!"

A car turned in at the motel parking lot, and its headlights swept the ground near my feet. It pulled in near the room with the party, then swung around to where there were still places to park.

"How's your mom?" Dean said.

"She's okay."

"Does she know you're calling?"

"Not really."

The line hissed with the great volume of air and distance separating him from me. I clung to the receiver and struggled to think of words that would add up to the right thing to say, as time and opportunity leaked away.

"You take care of her, and I'll see you when you get back," he said.

"I miss you, Dean," I said, choking on the words.

"I miss you too, Jasper. Bye."

"Bye."

The hissing continued for a second, then he was gone. I pressed down the lever and held it to delay the dial tone that meant the call was truly over, with nothing said but that Dean still thought we were coming back.

CHAPTER 20

THE HUGE HEAD PAINTED ON the Wonder of the World tent had fierce saucer eyes and a tongue stuck out long enough to cover the chin. A crowd milled around in front, trying to decide whether the man inside was monstrous enough to be worth the money.

There was still light in the sky, but bare bulbs had winked on all over the fairground, strung on wires like Christmas lights. The reedy tunes of the fairground organ fought against the barkers' shouts and the screams coming from the rides. Many more people had arrived on the grounds in the past hour. Boys shoved each other out of the queue for the Wonder of the World.

"Have you been in there yet?" said a male voice near my ear.

I turned and saw a man in a polo shirt and check jacket jingling coins in one hand. He looked like a stockier, homelier version of Ricky Nelson.

"He looked like a big pink rat," I said. "He bent an iron bar, but it looked fake."

"What about the Dog-Faced Girl?"

"She was just ugly."

Corinne and I had already done most of the rides and freak shows.

We had been to the lizard hut and the fat woman's tent. We had seen the Pop-Eyed Man flick his bloodshot eyeballs from their sockets with one jerk of the head and wiggle them there for an excruciating couple of seconds.

"How about Tiger Fish Boy?" the man said.

"I haven't seen that."

"It's at the far end. Want to take a look?" He gestured down the row of tents. He wore a nice watch, had a friendly smile and seemed full of energy — unlike me, who felt dirty and tired out. He saw me hesitate and shrugged like it was all the same to him.

"I'll just show you where it is." He walked slowly, gatheringly, and I went with him because I couldn't think of a reason not to. He said his name was Gary.

We passed the Pop-Eyed Man's tent, which showed the eyes flying out several inches on their stalks, and a saucer ride whose arms rose and fell like the legs of a giant spider. We passed the fairground evangelist, who for the umpteenth time asked: "May I offer you a testimony of what Jesus did?"

"This fair travels all over," Gary said. "They come here in the summer and go south for the winter. How'd you like to be on the road all the time? See new places?"

"Not much," I said.

"Don't like adventure? Here, let me treat you." Gary bought the tickets as I studied the painting on Tiger Fish Boy's tent. He looked like a leaping salmon, but with tiger stripes and a human face. His scales came right up to his big lips and wild, bulging eyes.

We sat on a bench inside the tent while a tough-looking man droned in a nasal voice about beasts of the deep and the Missing Link. He said we were all underwater till our ancestors crawled out and made civilization. Gary handed me a wrapped caramel, and I caught a whiff of his aftershave — Bay Rum, the same Dean wore.

The lecture ended and we filed through a tunnel-like room at one end of the tent. Tiger Fish Boy was lying on his front in a glass-topped tank, bathed in rippling blue light. He wore a tight, striped bodysuit that ended in a fish tail, and his neck was bent near a tilted mirror. Fleshy folds on his throat wavered like gills in the blue light. As we passed, his eye rolled up and met mine, and I realized he was a boy like me, spending his life under glass.

"Creepy," I said as we came out.

"I like unusual people," Gary said. "I'm kind of a rare bird myself. How about you, are you a rare bird? Do you like to do unusual things?" He was rattling coins in his hand again, quicker than before.

I didn't really understand his question, but knew there was something behind it I didn't want to hear. "What do you think they feed him?" I said.

"Hot dogs, probably. You hungry?"

I let him buy me a hot dog with his coins. My feet ached, my eyes were burning. I felt as if I were moving at half speed.

It had seemed incredible good luck, that morning, to be there for the day. But the free passes we got from the man who hired Corinne off the street ran out when she started working at two p.m., and I'd been wandering around ever since.

Gary handed me my hot dog, already loaded with ketchup and sweet relish, and a Coke. "I need to sit," I said, and took a swig.

"We can sit in my car. The lot's right over there."

I saw a cement-stuffed cinder block anchoring a tent rope and sat down. Gary squatted next to me. I bit into the warm, doughy hot dog. Through a gap in the crowd, I noticed a flash of burgundy, slowly moving our way.

"I think you'd like my car," he said. "It's a Tempest, brand new."

"Convertible?"

"That'll be my next one. This one's a real beaut. I had it tuned up nice. Why don't we go for a spin?"

Gary's face gleamed. I could smell him sweating under his Bay Rum. His hot dog sagged in his hand, already forgotten, its ketchup seeping through the paper napkin wrapped around the end.

"We've got a Corvair," I said. "My mom and me. That's her right there."

Corinne came out of the crowd, still ten paces off, in a burgundy suit that resembled a bellhop's outfit, with a skirt and pillbox hat. A tray of cigarettes hung from a braided gold strap around her neck. She held up one finger to show me that her break was almost at hand.

"Sweet Caps? Players?" she said. People strolled past her, only a little more responsive to her pitch than to the fairground evangelist.

"Your mom's a looker," Gary said. "Lucky you. Listen, I'm going to check out the big man. See you later." He got up abruptly and walked away. Gulls rushed at his hot dog as it hit the ground.

"Who's your friend?" Corinne said.

"Just a guy," I said, trying to match her careless tone, which reassured me at least as much as her presence did. And indeed nothing bad had happened. I had seen the Tiger Fish Boy and got a meal on someone else's dime. I took another bite.

"A guy who bought you a hot dog." Corinne's expression didn't change, but suddenly everything about Gary felt wrong. I swallowed the lump of dough and wiener, and threw the rest to the gulls.

"That was a waste," she said, though without the irritation she usually showed when I didn't finish a meal. I drank the rest of my Coke in one long gulp. She pulled my head tight to her midriff and stroked my hair. The stiff fabric of her uniform rasped against my ear.

"Want an ice cream?" she said.

We bought cones from the ice cream truck and crowded together on the bench where cool air trickled down from the open counter. Corinne fanned her neck, and kicked off her heels, and flexed her bare reddened toes.

"God, this coat's hot. Thank heavens this is only for the day. How you been, jellybean?" She brought her face close to mine and wrinkled her nose, as if we were having fun. The smell of sweat and dust and tiredness mingled with her rose perfume.

"Can we go on a ride?"

"No time. Look, I found you something." She reached into a narrow pocket of her jacket and produced a toy derringer with an engraved zinc body and fake ivory handle. I pulled the trigger and the gun let off a bang, and released an acrid puff from the burnt cap.

"Watch out," she said. "Someone will hear, and want his gun back."

"Finders keepers. How much longer?"

"Couple of hours."

"Can I stay with you?"

She wrinkled her nose again, and her weary smile faded. "No, I can't have you trailing after me. Stay where it's light, and watch yourself."

She finished her ice cream, fixed her makeup and wriggled her swollen feet back into her pumps. She moved back into the thickening crowd, and in a phony friendly voice said: "Players? Rothmans?"

Evening was coming on. There was nowhere on the grounds I hadn't been, nothing I wanted to see again. I stayed in the full fairground lights, away from the shadows, on alert for any sign of Gary's check jacket.

Eventually I gave up on the fair and found some deep cover in a weedy strip of ground opposite the giant's tent. The fairground bulbs seemed to glow more brightly than ever on his fierce eyes and enormous tongue. I nested in the rustling grasses and pulled the derringer from my pocket. It was the kind of sneaky weapon that turned up on *Gunsmoke,* in the hands of some slippery character who planned to shoot someone in the back. I stretched out and removed the roll of caps, and clicked away at the stars beginning to appear overhead.

*

WHEN I AWOKE, IT WAS fully dark. I sprang up and stood there in a daze. The Ferris wheel shone against the night sky. The giant's face leered at me from his tent.

I ran from the field and through the crowd on legs still wobbly from sleep, searching for a burgundy uniform. I collided with someone and nearly fell again. A gnarly hand grabbed my arm and righted me.

"May I offer you a testimony of what Jesus did?" The evangelist slid a pamphlet from a bread bag.

"Did you see a woman selling cigarettes?"

His furry eyebrows lifted. "Sure. She's by the office."

I ran to the manager's trailer. Corinne was standing outside, in her own clothes, talking with three or four men, including the stocky manager, who shone his flashlight on me as I walked up.

"Where the hell have you been?" Corinne yelled. "I've been looking for you. *People* have been looking for you."

She grabbed me by the shoulders and shook me twice, then gave me a hard, twisting hug. A single deep sob burst from her. I could feel her belly quaking as she held me close.

"You okay, sonny?" the manager said.

"Yes."

"If you were mine, you'd get a worse thrashing than that. Where were you, anyhow?"

"I fell asleep."

Corinne released me from her hug and slapped me hard across the face. "You lazy coot! When did I get to take a nap?" She grabbed me by the wrist and marched me off towards the parking lot.

We passed the enormous fairground trucks, slumbering together in the deep shadows, and searched the dim rows of cars till we found the Corvair. My cheek still smarted from Corinne's slap as I got inside and slammed the door. Corinne touched my face, gently this time, and pressed her dry, warm lips to my forehead.

"Oh God, Jasper!" she said, and then the tears really came. She sat there wracked with sobs, her head bent over the steering wheel.

"Sorry," I said. I really was, but a sneaky selfish part of me was also a little gratified by her dramatic reaction.

She wiped her eyes with the heel of her hand and started the car. Our headlights swept over the nearly empty lot and we crunched over the short gravel road to the highway. The rush of asphalt under our tires and the air whipping through the car felt like an escape from that endless day.

Corinne lit a cigarette from one of the packs she had snuck from her tray. I raked the mosquito bites on my bare arms and legs, and slid my hand into my pocket for my derringer. But there was nothing there. I ran my hands quickly over all my pockets, but they were empty.

"I lost my gun!" I wailed. It must have slipped from my hand when I fell asleep.

"Losers weepers," Corinne said. She was seldom sympathetic when I lost anything. But this time she reached over and squeezed my hand. "It was a lousy day all round."

"Except for the Pop-Eyed Man. And the roller coaster, and the flying carousel. And the ice cream."

"Except for all that."

There was only one bed in our motel room, so we slept together as we often did on the road. But instead of turning her back to me as she usually did, Corinne held me close, with a fold of my pyjamas clenched in each hand. I fell asleep with her tears on my neck.

CHAPTER 21

WE WERE HOLED UP IN a panelled motel room near the highway. Rain tapped the grey window and plucked at the puddles on the asphalt around the Corvair. I crouched by the glass with a ballpoint pen and scored a convoy of trucks into the soft wooden sill, a new truck for each one that passed. Corinne was lying on the bed in a slim pink dress, flipping the curled pages of a magazine she had found in the bedside table. She had made herself up and done her hair, but was making no move to go anywhere.

"How long are we going to stay here?" I said.

"Maybe another night."

Another transport rig steamed past, sending a greasy mist into the air and a shiver through the window glass.

"Aren't we supposed to be wandering?" I said.

"Don't be smart."

She flipped a page of her magazine, and another, with quick movements that sounded like slapping. The morning was passing into one of those drifting empty days that started with a grey feeling and ended with her yelling at me over any little thing.

Corinne tossed the magazine on the floor. "Let's get out of this dump," she said.

I jumped into some clothes and we stuffed our things into our open cases. We had been lounging around all morning, and suddenly we couldn't leave fast enough.

On the road, Corinne handed me the room key with its oblong wooden toggle, and I put it in the Drawer of Shame. Puddles burst under our wheels as we drove past sodden fields, a machine yard, and a fenced lot of trucks packed in like eggs in a carton. The road got busier, more buildings appeared, and a sign flashed by: Welcome to Edmonton, City of Champions. We were well into town when Corinne did a big blaring u-turn across three lanes of traffic into the parking lot of a movie house with Picnic on the marquee.

"I can't believe they're showing this," she said, jumping out of the car. I caught up with her at the ticket window, where the agent was telling her the film had already started.

"Two please," Corinne said.

"Lady, you've missed half an hour."

"Two please."

We entered the dark auditorium and found seats in a row near the back. The people in the film were at some kind of outdoor party, at night, with paper lanterns overhead. A man was trying to show a girl how to do a slow dance, till a woman in a pink dress came and took her place. She danced with him while hardly moving, holding his fingers at arm's length. I had trouble understanding the film because of what we had missed, but the dancing part stayed with me, because Corinne moved in her seat in time with the music all through the scene. At the end, the dancers ran away together from their normal lives. We stayed in our seats through all the credits.

"I love that movie," Corinne said, sinking a little deeper into the red plush.

"I like movies I can see from the beginning."

She stroked my hand idly, still apparently lost in the waking dream brought on by the film. "There's another feature. Do you want to stay?"

We got popcorn and drinks and found better seats for the second film. It was in black and white, and filled with cowboys who argued about cattle and formed themselves into a posse. They rode hard across the plains and shot Indians off their horses, or were cut down by braves hiding in the rocks.

When we went outside after the second feature, the clouds had cleared away. Everything gleamed in the afternoon sun. Cars and people passed with a new, purposeful heaviness.

"I can't believe it's still light out," I said, my body vibrating from all the hard riding and shooting we had seen.

"Stop shouting." Corinne put on her cat's-eye sunglasses.

"I liked it when the guy jumped from the train onto the wagon," I said, stepping onto a parking curb and leaping away from it. "Did he really do that?"

"Somebody did."

I wanted to say more, about Indians flying from their ponies as they were shot at top speed, but I could feel her mood sinking. All the pleasure she had found in the first film seemed to have drained away, leaving her as morose as she had been at the motel. We got into the car, and Corinne put the key in the ignition, but she didn't turn it.

"What now?" I said.

"I don't know. You think of something."

"Another movie?"

"God, no."

She took off her sunglasses and touched her lashes with the corner of a tissue. A few blackened tears soaked into the paper. She opened her compact to check the damage and put on fresh lipstick, not just to look better but to think better. I touched her arm, but she pulled away. "You're all greasy from popcorn."

She reached behind her seat, as if looking for something to wipe my greasy fingers, but instead she handed me a framed advertisement for a Cadillac convertible. I had seen it before, that morning, in our motel room, hanging by the door.

"Can you believe what people put on their walls?" she said, as if that were the problem with this day.

"I guess they like the car."

"Do you like it? More than ours?"

I shrugged. Corinne didn't care much about cars as long as she had one, but it seemed risky at that moment to say the Cadillac was better. She spat on the dusty glass, wiped it with the same tissue she had used on her eyes, and laid the picture on the seat between us.

We drove back the way we came, until we reached a car lot, with a string of pennants flapping like at the place in Winnipeg where we got the Corvair. Corinne turned in and parked near a gleaming red Thunderbird convertible. A copper-haired salesman was lowering the top after the rain.

"What are you doing?" I said.

"You'll see." She pulled on a pair of short white gloves and got out.

"Hi, folks," said the salesman. "What can I do for you?"

"We want a convertible, like this," Corinne said. The Thunderbird's white upholstery spread out under her gloved hand like the petals of a flower.

"Will your husband be joining us, ma'am?"

Corinne said her husband had owned a mining company, and had been up north to look at drilling sites when his bush plane went down. The salesman looked sombre for as long as he felt necessary, then told us he had a nice little convertible that would be just right for a lady.

"I like this one," Corinne said.

"It's a beaut, but I'm afraid it's already sold."

"It doesn't say sold."

"It came off the truck last night, special-ordered. The customer hasn't seen it yet, but I'm ninety-five per cent sure he'll take it."

"I want a test drive, in case of the other five per cent."

The salesman said he'd check with his manager and strode away to the office. Corinne opened the wide convertible door and got in.

Five minutes later we were flying along the road, with the wind in our hair and the salesman, Darryl, in the back, explaining the features. "You better slow down, ma'am," he shouted into the rushing air. "This is a thirty-mile zone."

Corinne spun the big wheel, and the armrest dug into my body as the car swung into a hard u-turn. We shot past the dealership and back out towards the city limits.

"We'd best go back," Darryl said. "I want to show you some other models."

"But Darryl, I want this one."

"We can get another just like it in a few weeks."

"I can't wait."

"Turn around at the pancake house and we'll talk it over in my office."

We passed the pancake house, and another car lot, and several other places offering new auto glass or a better muffler, and then the buildings thinned out and the road became a highway.

"Ma'am, please turn around."

An ice cream place came into view, shaped like a dish, with a white roof that swirled up like whipped cream. Corinne pulled in, switched off the ignition, and turned to face Darryl over the top of her sunglasses. "Since you've been so patient, I want to buy you a soft ice cream."

"Thanks, but I don't normally take ice cream. I've got to get this car back."

"I promised Jasper a chocolate dip. You'll try one too, won't you, Darryl?"

He smiled and nodded like everything was okay, but his eyes were sullen. We went in and bought dips for me and Darryl, and a strawberry cone for Corinne.

"I don't know about the boy and that cone on this upholstery," he said.

"Jasper's an old hand at ice cream."

We started back. Very soon, a distressed grunt came from the back seat, where Darryl's melting ice cream was flooding down under the dip's sweating chocolate crust, all over his freckled hands.

"Oh, Darryl," Corinne said. "What a mess you're in." We reached his dealership and drove right past.

"What the heck are you doing?" Darryl said, with no "ma'am" in his voice anymore. Corinne pulled in at the gas station next door, and stopped near the air pump.

"We've got to clean you up, Darryl. You can't go back like that."

Darryl flung his collapsing cone on the asphalt and held his sticky hands over the side of the car, with the wrists together as if he were handcuffed. Corinne got a rag and a pail of water from the station, and wiped his hands, and dabbed at a spot on his sleeve, and took a few streaks from the door. He got out and they both examined the white upholstery, but there was nothing. The car was still perfect. Corinne took her purse from the convertible.

"Come on, Jasper, let's get our car," she said.

"Ma'am, I'd be happy to show you other models," Darryl said, recovering himself.

"Some other time."

"I'm sorry, ma'am, but a test drive isn't supposed to go on that way."

"Depends what you're testing."

"I don't get you."

"I know, Darryl." She took my hand and we walked along the lane that separated the gas station from the dealership. The Thunderbird's engine rumbled, and the gravel crunched as the car crept up beside us.

"I don't think you're looking for a car," Darryl said. "I think you're just a joyrider." The "ma'am" had gone out of his voice again, but not in a sullen way like before.

"Think what you like, Darryl. Joy's an important part of life."

We kept walking. The Thunderbird stayed level, crawling along with Darryl's big arm resting on the door. I tugged at Corinne's hand to go faster, but she ignored me.

"Can I call you?" Darryl said as we passed under the pennants. "In case any special opportunities come up?"

"Just give me your card."

We got into the Corvair and drove away. Corinne switched on the radio and sang along, though it was a song I knew she didn't like.

"That was fun," she said.

"I'm tired of driving around."

"Seems to me you're having quite the day. Two movies. Popcorn and ice cream. A ride in a convertible."

We checked into a motel with a revolving cowboy sign and bowled at the alley across the road, and I began to feel that, yes, I was having quite the day. But when we walked back to the motel, there was a car next to the Corvair with a man waiting inside, his head and shoulders dark against the motel's floodlit front.

"Hi, folks."

I flung away Corinne's hand, walked past the smile and the copper hair, and rattled the doorknob of our room. She opened the door and yanked me inside.

"Look, I need to go out by myself for a while," she said.

"That's not by yourself."

"So? You've had nothing but fun all day." Her voice rose. "You're spoiled, that's what. And how about me? Who's spoiling me?"

"Dean did," I said.

She grabbed my arm again and I braced for a slap, but she only gave me a shake, and said in a quiet, furious voice: "Maybe. But he was a drunk, he was always right about everything, and you know what else? He bored me."

I switched on the TV. A monkey was drinking from a teacup, taking quick little sips with its long lips. The people in the grey

TV world laughed, and a man in a bow tie made a show of looking cross. The motel door swept over the carpet and clicked shut.

*

THE NEXT DAY, CORINNE SLEPT till noon. We were emerging from the motel room to find something to eat when Darryl drove up in a pink convertible, probably the lady car he had had in mind for her from the start.

"It's my lunch hour," he said, as he jumped out. "Let's eat."

He grabbed Corinne around the waist and tried to kiss her on the mouth, but she only let him graze her cheek and pulled away.

"Baby, what's wrong?"

"Jasper, wait inside."

I went in and peered between the dusty sheer curtains as Corinne gave Darryl some hard daylight words about how things really stood. He climbed back into the car with a stormy face and sped away, tires squealing.

Corinne was sullen over lunch in the motel café, while I struggled to contain the wicked glee stirred in my chest by the end of Darryl. But when we came out, he and the pink convertible were back, waiting across the street in front of the bowling alley. He was leaning against the car and staring in our direction.

Corinne hurried me into our room and locked the door with the chain.

"We'd better stay inside for a while, Jasper."

"Why is he there?"

"I don't know. He's a mixed-up boy."

We found cards and played gin rummy, checking between the curtains after each game to see if Darryl was still there. He didn't knock on our door, as I thought he might, and when he was gone, Corinne told me to grab my stuff quick because we were getting the hell out of there.

The Cadillac picture still lay on the front seat of the Corvair. As we drove away, I opened the glove compartment to put it in the Drawer of Shame.

"No, throw it out the window," Corinne said.

"There's people on the sidewalk." We were passing a bus stop.

She snatched it and flung it past me through the window. The car trembled, and someone on the sidewalk yelled, and the picture landed on the pavement with a faint, receding smash.

CHAPTER 22

CORINNE HAD A LITTLE RED leather book with abraded corners that she used to keep track of work contacts. When we got to Edmonton, she started making calls, and landed a last-minute job shooting underwear for a catalogue. It wasn't the kind of work she liked, because there was so much barbering to do, but after a half-hour's work in the motel bathroom, she was ready for the camera. She got dressed and told me to pack my things.

We drove across the deep river valley to an old office building with creaky floors and transom windows over every door. We stopped at one on the second floor, and Corinne tapped at the frosted glass. After a long moment the door opened, and a grey-haired woman in a silver-blue dress appeared.

"I'm Corinne. We spoke on the phone."

"Audrey." Silver bracelets rang softly on her arm as she offered her hand to Corinne, and gave me a puzzled squint.

"This is my son, Jasper."

"We're not shooting boyswear today."

"He's only here to keep me company. He'll be quiet as a mouse."

"I had mice in my house once," Audrey said. "They gnawed on things in the walls. Come in."

A brass-studded leather sofa and coffee table stood at an odd angle in the middle of the long, nearly empty room. Metal shelves loaded with photo equipment lined the walls, and at the far end, a wide sheet of white paper hung down to the floor from a roll near the ceiling. A round, bald man with sagging eyes was tightening the screws on a wooden camera tripod, near a table heaped with clouds of lingerie.

"Marty, this is Corinne," Audrey called out. "Jasper here is going to help me with my list. Right?"

Corinne nudged me out of my startled silence. "Sure," I said.

Marty stroked Corinne's hand with his hairy paw, and squeezed my fingers hard. "Don't touch anything, kid," he said. "This stuff costs a lot and breaks easy."

From a corner of the studio came the sound of a toilet flushing, and a moment later a stocky man in a suit and black-rimmed glasses emerged. He came rapidly across the creaking floor, smoothing his steel-grey hair.

"Jack!" Corinne said.

A big smile creased his bulldog face. "Baby! Nobody told me I'd see you here!" He clutched at her, kissing her loudly on the cheek.

"I didn't know you were pals," Audrey said.

"You found a good one here, I'm telling you," Jack said. "I've sold lots with this gal."

Jack Summers was a clothing salesman from Montreal. Corinne had worked for him before, during his regular trips by train across the prairies. In each city on his route, Jack checked into a suite of rooms and called all the women who had bought from him before. Then he hired a local model, or two if he was flush, to show off the new collections packed in huge steamer trunks, which swung open with all the clothes on rails, like portable closets.

"What are you doing here, Jack?" Corinne said. "Did you lose your trunks?"

"Don't you wish," he growled. "No, I've got some stuff in this shoot. I'm trying out a line of lingerie. You can't sell that in a hotel room."

"Jack, you remember Jasper."

"No, I don't. I remember a little boy. This is a young man. You must have done a trade-in. Isn't that right, young man?" He gripped my hand and gave me a glaring smile. "I'd love to stay and play with you kids, but I've got a train to catch. Corinne, I'll be back in a couple weeks. Don't make me come searching for you." He clutched her waist and kissed her again, almost on the mouth this time, and headed for the door.

He had just gone out when another model came in, a blonde in a blue leather car coat, with only a slip underneath.

"What happened to your clothes, Jackie?" Audrey said.

"If I'm going to spend the day in underwear, I don't see the point of getting dressed."

"That makes so much sense," Corinne said, taking Jackie's hand in both of hers. "What are you, a genius? Jasper, unzip."

"Corinne's helping out today," Audrey said. "Stand facing me, you two."

Corinne stepped out of her dress and linked arms with Jackie. They put on their model faces, and turned their shoulders this way and that, and grinned at each other like old friends.

"You gals are exactly the same build," Audrey said. "Same height, everything. From the neck down, you could be twins."

Audrey gave them the first combinations, and they went behind a screen to put on body makeup and dress for the shoot. She handed me a pencil and a typed list of bras, panties, slips and girdles.

"Sit there," she said. "Each time I give them a set, I'll name the pieces and you mark them off. First item is a Sweet Society full-rise panty and modesty bra, plain lilac."

Marty switched on his big photo lamps. Corinne and Jackie came out and stood before the glowing paper. They posed together with linked arms or bodies half-turned towards each other, not bothering about smiles because the heads would be cut off.

"Lilac, not violet," Audrey said, stabbing at my list. "Pay attention, Jasper."

"You won't see those colours," Marty said tersely.

"As you always say, but you know very well it helps me keep track."

After a dozen sets, they took a break. Corinne and Jackie sat in girdles on the leather sofa, and shared cigarettes, and tried on each other's shoes. I perched on one of the broad arms and pried with my nails at the edges of its domed brass studs.

"Marty, you need some heat in here," Jackie called, pulling her coat around her shoulders. He had settled his bulk on the edge of the lingerie table while Audrey smoked near the window.

"Are you kidding me?" said Marty. "I'm sweating."

"We take our clothes off, and he starts to sweat," Corinne said.

"Jasper, how much is Audrey paying you?" Jackie said.

"I don't know."

"You should have talked money first. You'll probably get the shaft." They both laughed. I felt a pang of grief at the thought that I could have asked Audrey to pay me. I was still clawing at the brass studs, which seemed as solid as the bolts on the Provencher Bridge, till one of the heads popped loose in my hand.

"I always give him something," Corinne said, though sometimes she didn't. I would have said so if I hadn't been distracted by the ugly nub of steel left where I pried off the brass head.

"What are you giving him this time?" said Jackie.

"Not a thing." They laughed again and rocked against each other's shoulders. They were going into a silly shared state of mind that I found doubly hard to appreciate as I thought about what Marty might do when he saw his sofa.

"Poor boy," Jackie said. She dug in her bag and handed me a half-finished roll of mints. Audrey clapped her hands, and we went back to work. I put a mint on my tongue and held the roll near my nose, inhaling its scent of sugar and face powder, as Jackie and Corinne posed first with one leg forward, then the other.

By the end of the afternoon, they were giddy from laughing at each other's jokes. They tossed lingerie at each other and did a couple of poses that Audrey said were too racy for any catalogue. But Marty kept snapping.

"I think that's it," Audrey said, scanning the list. "Very good, everyone." She gave me a dollar and Jackie, who had come in a cab, said we should come to her boyfriend's for a drink.

"Audrey liked you," she said to Corinne as we drove through town. "You should stick around."

"That Marty's a piece of work."

"All these camera guys are lechers. And with Audrey sitting right there! They used to be married, can you believe it?"

They laughed over this fact, which seemed to sully both elegant Audrey and fat Marty, whose mischief I hadn't noticed, as he hadn't seen mine. They had been a couple like Corinne and Dean, and married too, but still worked together, while Marty made subtle mash attempts on the models. A little dew of hope settled on my dream of returning to our Winnipeg life.

We pulled up by a long zigzag cluster of identical three-storey brick buildings set back from a busy four-lane road. A sign on the yellowing grass read: *Bel Air Apartments VACANCY*. A huge grey oak leaned over traffic from the other side of the street, in front of an old wooden house stuck in an even row of new stuccoed bungalows.

We got out and walked with Jackie across the park-like lawn in front of the apartment blocks. "My dad was a soldier, and these buildings sometimes make me think of barracks," she said, "but they're all right inside. You'd think it would be easy to go in the wrong building, but Nick never does, and he's blind."

"Really?" Corinne said.

We entered one of the buildings, and walked down the carpeted stairs to the basement. The hallway smelled of frying and new paint.

Jackie tapped on the door at the end of the hall, and eased it open. The room was dark, except for a fringe of light around the heavy curtains.

"Nick," Jackie said. She bent to kiss someone sprawled on the sofa.

"Doll," said a thick voice. Jackie swept open the curtains. Nick sat up with eyes still closed and groped on the table for a pair of sunglasses. He put them on his slim face and smoothed his black hair with a pocket comb. Jackie introduced us and disappeared into the bedroom.

"Corinne," Nick repeated. "That's a name I haven't heard before. Were you shooting too?"

"Yes, and I've changed underwear so many times today, I may have to go without for a while."

"I thought those catalogues are supposed to have the opposite effect."

Jackie returned in a white dress shirt like the one Nick was wearing and a pair of men's trousers with a necktie looped through as a belt.

"I borrowed some of your things, Nick. I wasn't fully dressed."

"That's okay," he said, stretching his arms behind his head. "They'll just smell better." Jackie caught his hand as she passed, and kissed the palm. He felt over that kissed spot with the fingers of his other hand, as if some rare and delicate thing had settled there.

"Corinne and Jasper have been staying in motels half the summer," she said.

"That's the way to live," said Nick. "You come, you go, nobody asks why. Never any bills in the mailbox. Why don't we live in motels, Doll?"

Jackie put on some music, and took a bottle from a low cabinet near the wall. "You've got rye, but no ginger." She poured rye and water for the adults and orange juice with grenadine for me.

"This place is almost a motel," Nick said. "People move in and out. There's four lanes of traffic right outside the window. You can smell the exhaust from here, that's why it's the Bel Air. Get it? This whole neighbourhood's great for phony names. The Sahara's down the street. In Edmonton, in January, I can walk to the Sahara, in the shoppers park. What do you guess is in that park, trees?"

"What's your phony name?" Corinne said.

"Rodney Medwood," he said, turning in her direction. Nick didn't hold his head in the vague way of other blind people I had seen, but followed the conversation with his face. He seemed confident. I had to admire that, while feeling that he shouldn't get off so easily with such a defect.

"What are you, an actor?" Corinne said.

"He should be," Jackie said. "He's crazy about movies. He's such a regular at the Sahara, he talked them into giving him a discount because he only gets the sound."

"Not true," Nick said. "I pay the same as everyone else. It was the boy who got in for nothing. I had a kid come in with me to describe what I couldn't get from the dialogue. I convinced the management he was like a seeing-eye dog. He was getting good at it, but his family moved back to the farm. Do me a favour, Jasper, I dropped some coins in my bedroom this morning. Bring them here, and I'll give you a few."

On the wall of Nick's small bedroom, a carved African mask shot out its wide lips and big painted eyeballs. On the bed, a square of early evening sunlight glowed on Jackie's open car coat. Otherwise the place was as plain as a motel room. A coin shone on the carpet near the bed. I knelt down to look under for more and saw a dark Persian cat nestling near the wall, staring back. I gathered up the coins and, without rising from my knees, laid my cheek on the warm satin lining of Jackie's coat. It smelled of her perfume, and old leather. I slipped my arm inside the sleeve; the satin shivered over my skin like water.

"Why don't you put it on properly?" Jackie said from the doorway.

I jumped up. She draped the coat over my shoulders and pulled the peaked lapels together.

"You look like a little general," she said. I flinched as she dug into one of the pockets and pulled out her Players. "You're cute, kiddo. But I guess you know that." The coat slid back on the bed. I followed her out of the bedroom, expecting she would blab to Nick and Corinne about the coat, but she didn't say a word.

Nick sent me out with his coins to buy mix from a machine in the laundry room, which smelled of dryer-blown air and concrete. From a narrow window under the low ceiling, I could see cars rushing by on the four-lane road, probably heading home. I wanted to leave, to find something to eat, and another motel. I was sick of our wandering routine, but just then I was impatient for it to repeat itself as it should.

When I returned with the mix, the music was louder, the laughter a little wilder. The room was taking on the hazy, insistent feeling of a grown-up party. Jackie took the mix from my arms and poured more drinks.

"How long are we staying here?" I said to Corinne.

"I don't know, and don't whine." She nudged me away and took another sip. "I like it here. You guys know how to live." She had kicked off her shoes and drawn her feet up where she sat at the end of the sofa. We had eaten nothing since breakfast, and the drinks had put her over the weather vane, as Dean would say. Nick said he would call for Chinese, and groped over the phone's rotary dial.

"What's with the old shack across the street?" Corinne said.

"This all used to be a farm," Jackie said. "The house is what's left."

Someone rapped at the door. Jackie opened it, and a short, solid man peered in the room and jingled a big ring of keys.

"Jasper, you want to peek at another apartment?" Corinne said.

"No. Why would I?"

The women left with the keeper of the keys. The music had stopped. I wasn't prepared to be alone with Nick and his blindness, with no other sound in the room, so I went to the hi-fi and turned the record over. Above the cabinet was a framed studio portrait of Jackie in Hawaiian dress, with flowers in her hair and a lei around her neck. Nick remained on the sofa with his head down, like someone waiting alone, as if the whole reason for talking or being interested in things had gone out the door with Jackie and Corinne.

"Why do you have a picture of Jackie on your wall?" I said.

He turned his head towards me. "You mean a picture I can't see? Because she told me she had a good set taken, and I asked her for one. I like to have her around all the time, not only when she comes over."

"Why don't you just marry her?"

"None of your business. Now you tell me something: What does your mom look like?"

"I don't know. She's pretty."

"Of course she's pretty, she's a model. What kind of build?"

"The same as Jackie's," I said, with an authority transmitted to me by Audrey. "From the neck down, they could be twins."

"That's pretty conclusive. Is she blond too?"

"Brunette."

"Dark, auburn, chestnut?"

"Auburn, I guess."

"Eyes, nose?"

"Her eyes are brown, and kind of almond-shaped. Her nose turns up a little, and her lips are nice, but not as full as she'd like."

"This is great, Jasper, very descriptive. What about her ears?"

"They're okay." His questions were starting to annoy me.

"Small, medium, large?"

"As big as a donkey's. And furry."

Nick rocked a little on the sofa as he digested this information. "Every woman must have her imperfection."

"How do you know about different browns?"

"I wasn't always blind. I remember colours. But I must admit, auburn's more a feeling for me than a colour."

"What kind of feeling?"

"I don't know, an auburn feeling," he said. "Like a big old tenor sax."

I heard feet running up to the apartment door, and Corinne burst in. "You've got to come look," she said, dragging me out of the apartment.

"What are you doing?" I said, and shook off her grip.

"Just come. Don't be so boring."

I followed her up the stairs to the second floor, where Jackie and the man with the keys stood at an open doorway. Corinne pushed me inside.

An orange light glowed through the windows of the stuffy living room. Marks on the cream walls and small depressions in the green carpeting showed the positions of departed furniture. Corinne led me through the two small bedrooms, the tiny bathroom, and the kitchen, where some of the floor tiles were curling at the edges.

"What do you think?" she said, her face all lit up with booze and new company.

"About what?"

"Taking this place. Moving in."

I was almost too stunned to speak. "There's no furniture."

"Jackie says Nick can get us lots, right away, and we wouldn't have to pay."

"You said we were wandering."

She pulled me from the kitchen into the bathroom, where my own confused face glanced at me from the chrome-edged mirror. I felt like something was closing in on me, as I had in the car when Corinne said we were fancy-free and had left Winnipeg for good.

"We *are* wandering," she said, kneading my hand in hers. "We'll just do it in one place for a while. We need money. Jackie's got connections. Aren't you tired of motels?"

"Yes. I want to go home."

She held my face between her warm palms and studied me with

a slightly sozzled frown on her face. Then she went into the other room and told the super we'd take it.

It was nearly midnight when two guys showed up with a pair of beds, a Formica kitchen table with vinyl-covered chairs, a scarred wooden chest of drawers and a couple of bedside tables. Jackie brought linens and a percolator from Nick's place, and dishes and cutlery to use till we got our own.

Corinne made my bed where the furniture guys left it, in the middle of the room. I slid in with the fresh sheets tucked in tight, and scissored my legs inside their cool envelope. I usually enjoyed this feeling, but the empty room and distant pale walls made me feel like I was in hospital. I got up, snapped on the light and searched for something to draw with. All I could find were coins, so with the ridged edge of one of Nick's dimes, I put a faint grey line on the wall. The line became a curve, and then a shaggy body with a head, as I drew a large lion rampant with its claws raised towards the door.

CHAPTER 23

THE NEXT DAY, I WOKE up late and prowled through our new home, noting every imperfection as I imagined Dean would. I found Corinne lying in her bed, staring at the curtain-less window.

"Here we are," she said, with a faint smile. Waking up in a nearly empty apartment after a night of drinking seemed to have given her a different perspective on our new home.

"There's nothing to eat," I said.

"I was thinking about that. We could go over to Woodward's later."

"What about now?"

"Maybe Nick has something. Let me put on my face."

"Just come down as you are."

"Let's not have that discussion again. Look, while I get ready, you get busy with the carpet." She pointed at an old pole vacuum standing in the corner.

Twenty minutes later, we went downstairs to Nick's. Everything along the way — the brown stairway carpet, the pale green hallways, the frosted ceiling fixtures — looked different now that I knew I would be seeing them every day. Corinne knocked on the door.

"What if he's out?" I said.

"Where would he go? Though I suppose he could." We looked at each other, as if trying to measure in our minds the distance a blind man could escape from his basement apartment.

Jackie opened the door, still wearing Nick's pants and shirt, with the sleeves rolled to the elbow. "We wondered when you'd turn up."

"We're starved," Corinne said, and walked right in.

"Help yourselves to whatever's in the fridge," said Nick. He was sitting on a kitchen chair under a barber's oilcloth cape, with snippets of hair all around him on the floor.

Corinne pulled cheese slices and bread from the fridge and made sandwiches. She put them on a platter with cocktail wieners and pickled onions. We sat down to this meal as Jackie tipped Nick's head back and lathered his face with a soft bristle brush.

"Did Walter give you a break on the rent?" he said.

"Yes. It seems your name's as good as money in the bank."

"His brother owns the building," said Jackie, "and the furniture store too."

"He's way overstocked," Nick said. "He should pay you for storing that stuff."

Jackie opened a bone-handled straight razor and honed it on a leather strop.

"You do that like a pro," Corinne said.

"I am a pro. The modelling's on the side, for now."

"This is the ritual of kings," Nick said. "Just hearing that sound makes me feel like a million bucks." Jackie put the blade to his cheek, shaved an inch of lather smoothly away, and wiped it on the towel.

"So, no more motels for you," Nick said. "Is this the end of the vacation?"

"More than that," Corinne said. "We were fed up where we were. We needed a change."

"*You* did," I said, choking on her half-truth.

Jackie moved on to the other cheek, stroking away the lather in even, regular sections. "What about the rest of your stuff? You must have left things behind."

"She left it all," I said. The bitterness of that loss surged over me again.

"It's good to purge," Nick said. "Take what you need and leave the rest."

"That's it," Corinne said.

Jackie tipped Nick's head back a little further, and dragged the blade through the lather above his Adam's apple. She leaned over and kissed him on the lips, then giggled as she wiped the foam from her mouth.

"Are you spoiling this man for a reason?" Corinne said.

"We're going to a party. There'll be other models and people in the business. You should come." She made a few more passes with the blade under Nick's jaw and wiped his face with the towel. "We already have a job for Jasper."

"Yeah, you want to tell me about a movie, kiddo?" Nick said, sitting up. With no glasses, his lean face looked older, with pouches beginning to form under the closed, unused eyes. "I'll pay you a quarter, plus a dime for candy."

"Sure!" At the thought of getting candy and cash for seeing a movie, my resentment faded.

Jackie patted Nick's cheeks with aftershave and slid his sunglasses on his face. With those shades, his hair freshly groomed and his face gleaming, he did look like a movie actor, as Jackie said, though not the star. He was more like the friend who doesn't get the girl, or gets shot.

"I'm going outside," I said.

"Who's going to help me clean?" said Corinne.

"Who are you kidding?" Nick said. "Jackie, pour this woman a drink."

Corinne wrinkled her nose. "A bit early," she said, but took the glass.

I left the building and wandered over the scrubby, broad lawn of the Bel Air apartments. On the other side of the road, the uniform stuccoed bungalows marched along the block in an even line, interrupted by the old wooden house with its open porch and immense tree, whose boughs reached over four lanes of traffic. The house looked as arbitrarily placed as Lily's, not because there was nothing around it, but because there was so much, built to such a different pattern.

I crossed the street and circled around the tree, and found a boy, smaller than me, lying on the ground on the other side. He squinted up at me.

"What are you doing?" I said.

"Listening." He lay there as if he were in his own bed. His red T-shirt rode up around his ribs. Bits of dead grass stuck to his blond hair.

"What for?"

"Energy." He shaded the eye with his small brown hand. "There's lots of energy trapped inside the Earth. There's magma flowing down there like gravy. Do you want to see something?" He jumped up and moved towards the alley that ran along the side of the house, half-turning to make sure I followed.

"My grandpa built this house," he said. He seemed proud of this outmoded achievement. "It's the best one around here."

"It's so old," I said.

"My dad says a lot of the new ones are junk."

"My grandpa built a house too," I said, though it was Lily's father who had done that. The boy broke his dragging stride and skipped for a few steps, as if to celebrate the fact that our grandpas had both been clever enough to build houses. I glanced around to make sure no one saw this girlish manoeuvre.

We continued down the alley till we reached a squat electrical transformer. It buzzed like a box of wasps, behind a chain-link fence topped with barbed wire.

"A guy got electrocuted here," he said. "They had to scrub his scorched handprint off the wall." He held out his hand with the fingers spread widet and waggled it as if the current were surging through. I told him about the first horseman and his handprints, and the fleas of the buffalo.

"That's why those prairie towns are all so small," I said, watching his face for signs of belief.

"Then why is there a city?" he said. This obvious question hadn't occurred to me when Corinne told me the story, but the answer came to me with reassuring speed.

"He must have put his mark where the buffalo couldn't reach. What's your name?"

"Dwayne."

"I'm Jasper."

Dwayne put out his hand and we shook on this introduction like grown-ups, as no boys my age would do. Somehow this adult gesture only confirmed that he was younger than me.

"Somebody got buried alive when they built the shoppers park," he said. "He fell in the wet concrete and nobody noticed."

"That's a lie."

He shrugged, and kicked at a stone. "Do you watch Stampede Wrestling?"

I grabbed his wrist and applied the Two-Armed Deathlock, a favourite move of the LaSalle brothers. He flailed at my hip with his fist till I let him go.

"Crumbs, not so hard!" he said. That was the way we started, and the pattern we followed. I often played a little too rough with Dwayne. Something about him gave a sneaky part of myself permission to hurt him.

"Want to see my knife?" I said, and offered him a jackknife I had found at Ernie's machine shop. Dwayne examined it with reverence, though the iridescent plastic covering had come off one side. I flicked it a few times at a grassy strip near the chain link. Each time the point stuck in he got more desperate to try it himself, so after several more throws I let him. He threw timidly at first, then harder and wilder, as the transformer snarled inside its cage. I finally had to pull the knife away from him and put it in my pocket.

"Do you want to get something to drink at my house?" he said.

We walked back and through the gate of his picket fence, whose fresh paint made the house look more shabby. Ruffled curtains stirred at a kitchen window that was propped open with a coffee can. I flicked the jackknife at the neatly cut lawn, sticking the point near a Dinky Toy truck.

"Don't let my mom see," Dwayne said, snatching the knife up and hiding it in my hand. He ran to get drinks. I sat on his rusting swing set and pushed myself off with my feet. Across the yards of the neighbouring bungalows, beyond the far end, a windowless brick wall rose up three storeys, with the word *Sahara* painted across it in enormous slanting letters.

When I returned to the apartment, a bucket of dirty water stood on the freshly mopped kitchen floor. The pipes in the wall groaned: Corinne was having a shower. I stretched out on the thinly padded sofa, which had been the only furniture in our front room that morning, but which now faced a Danish armchair and coffee table. I opened my jackknife and stabbed the point a few times into the wood below the seat cushion. If Dean were at home, he might be getting ready to fall asleep in front of the hockey game.

Corinne emerged from the bathroom with a worn, unfamiliar towel around her torso.

"I should go to this party," she said. "Jackie says I can meet a lot of people. Can you fend for yourself?"

"What am I going to eat?"

"I bought you a TV dinner."

She disappeared into her bedroom. I lay on the sofa and considered the hours of boredom waiting for me in our new home, which felt stranger than any motel we had stayed in. I got up and went into Corinne's room where a mirrored vanity now stood against the wall. She had black panties on and was tipping her breasts into the cups of a matching brassiere.

"Let me go to a movie," I said. "I know where the Sahara is. It's close. I can practise for when I go with Nick."

*

THE GLOWING SIGN AT THE front of the Sahara spelled out the name in the same sloping script I had seen on the rear brick wall. There was no one in the ticket booth, or in the pink and gold lobby, which was lit by moon-like discs floating on the walls. An usher appeared and told me that the film had started and the ticket man was gone for the night, but that he could let me in for nothing if I didn't tell anyone.

I sat in the empty back row and whispered the scenes as I figured I would for Nick. "He's got a gun. He's chasing the other guy through the fairground." I had missed too much to know who was being chased and why, but describing it kept me interested. I thought more about what might happen as I got ready to say what actually did. I felt almost like I was helping to make the story, that I was one of the authors, and that if I told it just right, it would turn out the way I wanted.

CHAPTER 24

I KNOCKED ON NICK'S DOOR in plenty of time before our first matinee. His muffled voice called me in. He was sitting at the table, sunk low over his elbows, with a phone and a few sheets of paper. The air was hazy with cigarette smoke. Confetti dotted the floor around him.

"What are you doing?" I said.

"Working. You're early. Sit somewhere and let me finish." He felt over some Braille bumps on a page of names and addresses, then groped out a number on the rotary phone.

"Am I speaking with Mrs. Podoruk?" he said, in a smooth voice, stroking a small, flat stone in his free hand. There was a saucer of them on the table. "This is Rodney Medwood, and I want to tell you how smart homeowners are beating Old Man Winter with storm windows from Quik-n-Snug." Then he put the phone down.

"Wrong number?"

"No, they hung up."

"Why is there writing on those pages?"

"That's for the real salesman. I'm only the guy who beats the bushes."

He fumbled for a hole punch, made a hole next to Mrs. Podoruk, and replaced the stone in his hand with another. He made a couple more calls, with the same outcome as the first, and punched his paper.

"What's with the stones?" I said.

"Some idiot was washing his car, and I tripped over his hose, and broke my wrist. This one was under my hand when I tried to get up. I got a couple more in similar situations. Then Jackie saw I had a few special stones and gave me some she thought were pretty. Sweet, huh? I guess I'm done with this."

He combed his hair, went into the bedroom, and returned wearing a camel-coloured sports jacket and a spritz of cologne. We went upstairs and out into the afternoon light.

"Jasper, the movies are a solemn subject with me," he said as we walked towards the road. "Like going to church. But the Sahara's got something no church has: comfortable seating. No need to squirm while you wait for the truth. And the truth is what I'm paying you for. I can picture a lot from the dialogue, but I can't tell if there's a gun on the table, or a blob from outer space sliding under the door. That's up to you, Jasper. You've got to say what you see, clear and simple. If you screw up, I won't know what's going on. And then I'll feel bad about paying you twenty-five cents plus candy."

"Okay."

"We're going to the temple of the one-eyed god. He's cruel to those who waste his gifts."

At the sidewalk, he stepped to the curb as if he could see where he was going. Cars rushed by in both directions.

"Don't you want to go to the light?" I said. It was only a half block away.

"What for?" He waited till there was no traffic to be heard, then marched across the road, touching my shoulder only when he sensed that the other curb must be near. We walked to the Sahara where he bought one ticket from the woman in the booth, who greeted him by name and didn't ask about me.

The lobby was crowded, mostly with kids. We pushed past them and down the theatre's sloping aisle, and found seats near the front.

"Here's your dime," Nick said. "Whatever you buy, you've got to eat during the cartoons, or not till the film's over. And don't tell me the cartoons, they're not funny that way."

I went back and stood in line at the candy counter behind three older girls, including a Chinese. They all wore wide summer skirts and short-sleeved blouses and similar shades of frosted lipstick.

"Did he call you?" said one of them, a tall girl with sandy hair.

"Not yet."

"Then he won't."

The Chinese girl saw me watching, and the others looked around too. I stood as if I didn't notice and hadn't heard.

"Isn't that the guy from 77 *Sunset Strip*?" The Chinese girl pointed at a movie poster on the wall. Her perfume drifted over me, rose-like and a bit earthy, through the odour of butter and charred corn. Her glossy black ponytail bobbed a few inches from my face.

"Yeah, he's a dreamboat."

A few stray hairs from her ponytail trailed along her brown neck, near a small birthmark. The outline of her bra strap showed through the thin cotton of her blouse.

The girls got their popcorn, and the foyer that had been crowded a moment before was suddenly almost empty. I bought a Sweet Marie and hurried down the ramp and into my seat as the lights went down. The cartoons exploded from the steep wall of light, and a tremor of glee ran through me at the thought that I was being paid to do this. Nick's face was turned up to the screen like he was sunbathing. The cartoon images flashed over his dark glasses.

The film was about two men with oily hair who were writing songs at a piano. A girl came and quarrelled with the more handsome one, and a fat man rushed in and shouted for more music.

"Pages are flying off a calendar," I whispered. "Newspapers are spinning. People are dancing in a theatre." Those parts were easy, but sometimes the shots changed quickly and I didn't know what to say.

"What's happening?" Nick hissed with a jab of his elbow.

"She's running out the back door. She's in the alley. The song-writer's walking away, she's catching him. They're kissing." The music swelled and the film was over.

"I love that old crap," Nick said as the lights came on. "But you need to sharpen up. I saw more of that movie than you did." He slapped a quarter on my palm and we moved into the aisle. Through the crowd moving slowly up the slope, I saw a glossy black ponytail and breathed in as if to catch her perfume again.

"I want to stop at the Belmont," Nick said on the pavement. "There should be someone there you know." We walked across the parking lot to the Belmont, a restaurant with a big picture window and a neon sign in the shape of a jockey on a galloping horse. Inside, Corinne sat on a red banquette near the door in a floral summer dress.

"How did he do?" she said, as we slid into the booth.

"I see potential," said Nick.

"Nice sport coat."

"Thanks. Jackie got it for me at a sample sale." He stroked the lapel as if it were his cat.

"What was the film?"

"Some old thing I'd seen before."

"Why did you go again?"

"I didn't know it was on," Nick said. "They show something dif-ferent every Saturday afternoon. I don't bother to check, it spoils the fun."

Corinne raised an eyebrow at me. "What if it's a kind of movie you don't like?"

"There isn't really a kind of movie I don't like," Nick said, turning his face up as he had in front of the Sahara's screen. "Besides, I thought you liked not knowing where you're going."

"I like not deciding in advance. You're choosing something with no idea what it is."

"Yeah, well, sometimes you get where you're going, and still don't know where you are," Nick said. Corinne didn't reply, but a faint blush showed on her cheeks. Her fingers strayed to her pendant necklace, the jasper one I had given her.

The waiter came and Nick ordered coffees, and a Coke for me. I looked around at the restaurant's blue walls, where framed photographs showed jockeys flying along muddy tracks or holding huge wreaths next to their horses.

"Why do they have horses everywhere?" I said.

"Belmont Park is a famous racetrack," Nick said. "The Belmont Stakes are part of the Triple Crown. Do you follow the ponies, Corinne?"

"No, but I ride one sometimes. Got a cigarette?"

He offered the pack and snapped open his steel lighter. Corinne drew his hand closer until her cigarette end glowed in the flame.

"I have an old pair of riding boots Jackie got me for a Halloween party," Nick said. "I was Zorro."

"You should try them on a horse sometime."

"Good joke."

"I mean it. With the right animal, it could be fun."

Nick lit his own cigarette, and let the smoke drift from his mouth. I wondered if he was offended by Corinne's crazy suggestion. It was probably the wrong moment to ask something I had thought of a few times already, but I asked anyway.

"Can I try your glasses?"

Corinne flicked at my arm. "Jasper!"

"Why?" Nick said.

"To see what it feels like."

"What it feels like has nothing to do with the glasses." But he held them out, and buried his face in the other hand, though we had already seen his inert eyelids during his shave. The frames wobbled on my nose, and the inky lenses dimmed the restaurant's dark interior to a deep grey. It looked almost the same as when I awoke in my room on a dark winter morning; except that wearing these glasses for real meant you would never see mornings again.

The waiter approached with our Coke and coffee. "Little beatnik," he said.

"Benny, this kid wants to steal my style," said Nick.

"Impossible."

I handed back the glasses and Nick put them on. He pulled out a comb and smoothed his hair, and Corinne sang the line about Kookie from 77 *Sunset Strip*. Nick made a more extravagant pass over his hair, as Dean had done during our botched game of charades.

A couple came into the restaurant with a girl about my age, and exchanged glances with us. There was a kind of friendly recognition from their side, not of our individual selves but of the three of us together, as a unit like them. An awkward smile flitted over Corinne's face. I felt a little uneasy too, while half-wanting to play along.

Nick was unaware that some shift in sentiment had occurred at our table. He chatted happily with Corinne about films they both knew, and when the bill came, held out a handful of change for the waiter.

"Take something for yourself, Benny, and don't be a cheapskate," he said.

*

WHEN I GOT BACK IN my room, I flattened the wrapper of my Sweet Marie on the bed. I had bungled parts of the film, but still got paid and hadn't been fired. I had heard those girls and seen their frosted lips and smelled their perfume — her perfume, rising from that brown neck. I folded the wrapper twice and tucked it under my mattress, and wondered why Corinne and I didn't keep a container that was the opposite of the Drawer of Shame.

CHAPTER 25

THE GIANT SPRAWLED IN THE barber's chair, his skin as grey as Plasticine. The barber had to reach up high to do his work with the razor, not shaving but carving new features into the giant's face. Only the fierce bright eyes remained the same, watching me, waiting for the moment when the giant could spring after me with his terrible new face. I ran away and fell into a fresh sidewalk, tried to run again but couldn't, because my legs were heavy with wet concrete. I crawled under a parked car and my tears hardened into a mask. The car's engine roared, and I knew that the giant was at the wheel.

I awoke on my feet, swaying next to the bed, with a corner of the sheet gripped tight in my fist. It took me a long moment in the darkness to realize that I was in my own room, alone. I sank onto the mattress and watched the shadows with burning eyes, till morning had crept into every corner of the room. But even when it was fully light and Corinne called me to get ready, the feeling of my dream clung to me like a cobweb on my face.

She was already sitting at her mirrored vanity in a bra and slip, with her hair in a beehive, brushing on her eyeshadow. "Hurry up," she said into the mirror. "Jack's a stickler for time."

"Jack who?"

"Summers. We saw him at that thing with Audrey and Jackie. You look beat."

I told her about my dream, which to me was almost as horrifying in the retelling as the first time. Corinne's face in the glass did not agree.

"I don't think it's funny," I said fiercely.

"A giant with a Plasticine face. I'm sorry, I couldn't lose sleep over that." She stroked on her eyeliner. "Maybe you need another story to wash that one down." She drew an even line around the other eye, then hunted in her bag for mascara.

"There was a farmer whose cattle were disappearing," she said. "Every night something broke down his barn door, and every morning he found bones scattered on the ground. He decided to set a trap. He painted one cow all over with rat poison, tied her outside, and shut the other cows in the barn as usual."

She spat on the little cake of mascara and worked at the spot with a brush.

"The next morning, there were more bones on the ground. Loud groans came from the forest. The farmer ran into the woods with his pitchfork. He found an ogre in a clearing, rolling around and clutching its stomach. He drove the pitchfork into its eye with all his strength." Corinne stabbed the air with the inky mascara brush, and then slowly blackened her lashes.

"The ogre roared and jumped up. Just when the farmer thought he might be eaten too, the ogre changed into a boy. It was the farmer's own son, missing for a year. Everyone thought he had run away, but he had been caged by a witch. She cast a spell after him when he tried to escape, and turned him into an ogre."

"What happened to the witch?"

Corinne did the whole other eye before answering. "They tied stones to her clothes and drowned her in the river."

I stood leaning in the doorway with one bare foot propped on the other, and plucked at the piping on my pyjama sleeve. Death by clothing was an impressive new demise. The pitchfork in the eye was also good. Corinne was right: my Plasticine giant was fading before the violent ruin of the witch and the cow-eating ogre. But as usual, there was something unresolved about Corinne's ending.

"How could they tie stones to the witch if she was so powerful?"

"Maybe they tricked her. Maybe she became a cat at night and lost her powers. All I know is that you're still in pyjamas."

"Why do I have to go?"

"I could use some help. Jack will probably give you a nice tip."

Corinne made me put on a clean shirt, in case I met the customers, and my tweed jacket with lions rampant, which I hadn't worn since we were with Dean. I thought it was too much, and too soon; but when we went outside, the sun glinted off my brass buttons and made Corinne's blue satin dress shine. We walked to the Corvair like a royal mother and son.

We drove to a big stone hotel that stood on the edge of the river valley like a castle. I stepped on the red carpet at the brass front doors. Corinne gave her car keys to a man in a purple uniform with gold braid on his cap. It must have been like this for the kings of Scotland, or the Italian king in Monza.

We walked into the hotel and across a lobby carpet patterned with what looked like snakes chasing oranges. The desk clerk rang a bell like ours from Eaton's, and a bellboy slunk towards a fat couple waiting at the desk with their luggage. Corinne called Jack on the house phone.

"If you're going to start off that way," she said into the receiver, "I'm not sure I should come up."

We waited for the elevator with the bellboy, the fat people and a trolley cart heaped with their luggage. We got into the elevator, the operator pulled the scissored interior doors shut, and the elevator heaved upwards. The fat people got off with their things, and two floors later we got out and walked down the silent hallway. Corinne was carrying an umbrella.

"Where did you get that?" I said.

"It just came to hand." She held it out for me to see. It was heavy black cloth with a gnarled wooden handle carved like a snake's head. She opened it with a soft thump, and I realized with a thrill of admiration that she had taken it from the fat people's luggage cart. We walked under its shade to a room at the end of the hall.

The umbrella was still up when the door swung open. Jack stood there with a pipe in his teeth, looking at us quizzically. "The rain in Spain," he said. "It's dry here. Come in."

Corinne collapsed the umbrella and Jack kissed her, not grossly like at Audrey's, but with a peck on her cheek.

"What's with the kid?" he said.

"Jasper's going to be my dresser. He won't get in the way."

Jack examined me sullenly, and then rubbed his knuckles hard against the side of my head.

"Little nipper!" he said. "I've got a present for you. I thought I'd send it with Corinne, but since you're here, you might as well have it in person." He took a pink windowed box from a marble-topped hall table and thrust it at me. Inside was an enormous chocolate Easter egg.

"That's very thoughtful, Jack, but Easter was months ago," Corinne said.

"It's a movable feast," Jack said. "Chocolate's always in season with boys like Jasper. Am I right?"

"It's pink. Boys like Jasper don't like pink. It's a girl colour."

"What do you mean? The pink is for the Easter Bunny. You know, fluff and pink and everything pastel. The Easter Bunny, that's not a girl or boy thing as far I've been told. It's just fluffy and nice. The kids love it."

"Admit it, Jack. You got him a girl's egg."

Jack clamped down hard on his pipestem, then yanked it from his mouth. "Look, it's good milk chocolate. Forget about the box, just take out the chocolate and throw the damn thing away!"

Corinne calmly flumped the umbrella out a few times as if shaking off drops, and tossed it to him. He caught it awkwardly in his left hand.

"It's the Easter bunny, for Chrissake, not the Marlboro Man," he growled, his mouth curling into a grin. "Now do you want a drink or don't you?"

We went into the main room of the suite, which Jack called the display room. There was a sofa and armchairs for the clients, and a coffee table with a book of fabric samples on it. There was also a higher table by the wall where Jack's chrome cocktail set stood amidst bottles of liquor and mix.

But the main things in the display room were the steamer trunks, dark and huge, with stickers and scuffs on their sides and steel on their corners. They stood wide open, with their contents spread across steel rods. I buried my arms and face in the warm, soft fabrics and breathed in the new-clothes smell, which mingled with the cedar odour of the trunks and the smoke from Jack's pipe.

"Are his hands clean?" Jack said as he rattled the drinks in his shaker. "Sit over there, Jasper, and eat your egg."

I sat on an upholstered chair and tore open the box. The egg was lodged in a cardboard nest lined with tinsel strips. I pulled at some of the tinsel, and suddenly the egg was on the floor, with half of it shattered in pieces and the rest wobbling around on the carpet.

"Jesus," Jack said. "Hardly out of the box. Look at this mess. Corinne, will you talk to this boy? Listen, we're going to have a nice day today, right?" His tanned bulldog face was bent sideways right in front of mine. "A nice day. Corinne, please. I've got to change this goddamn shirt." He poured out his drink and went into the tiled bathroom, and a few seconds later we heard the cascade of his pee splashing into the bowl.

"Jack's always a bit tense before a showing," Corinne said. She put the unbroken half of my egg back in the box, gathered up the rest, and dropped the pieces into a deep Oriental vase by the window.

Jack emerged with his new shirt. The first clients arrived. I was sent into the changing room, which was also Jack's bedroom. The routine was that Corinne would model something for the clients, and then return to the bedroom to change. I helped with the zippers and laid the discarded outfits on the bed.

In between changes, I organized battles between Corinne's shoes, opened all the drawers and examined Jack's stuff. I held debates with the pipes in his pipe stand about whether Jack's farts smelled of tobacco smoke and how big a tip I would get.

After a long while, during a lull between clients, Corinne brought me into the display room to eat from a room-service tray of sandwiches and sweet pickles. The sun had heated the room; Jack was wrestling open the window.

"I thought this tour might wind up a bust!" he said, rubbing his hands. "But that crude oil makes a difference in this town. Those beautiful pumps out there! And I always do good business with you, sweetheart." Corinne eluded a pat on her bum.

Jack took a two-dollar bill from his wallet and gave it to me. "Hold on to this, Sonny Boy, and you'll always have two bucks in reserve. Break it, and it'll be gone before you know it!"

"I don't think Jasper cares about cash in reserve," Corinne said.

"Better he should take after you only in looks."

Two more ladies arrived with a little dog, but Corinne didn't chase me back to the changing room. Jack roughed up my hair and called me his right-hand man. He gave me the chrome ice bucket and brass-headed hammer from his cocktail set and sent me out to get more ice from the machine at the end of the hall.

I went out and along the silent, carpeted hallway. There was no one in sight, and many hiding places around the recessed doors. I had almost forgotten about my dream, but the silence and concealed corners of the long hall brought back the grey terror of the Plasticine giant. I clutched the bamboo handle of the hammer in my fist, ready to smash anything that leapt out at me.

I crept the whole way down to the big rattling ice bin and crouched by its sliding glass doors. The chunks I put in the bucket were too big for a glass, so when the bucket was nearly full, I broke up the ice with the hammer. From somewhere down the hall a door boomed shut. I jumped to my feet and flitted back to Jack's room, eyes turned every way at once.

I entered as Jack was explaining the cut of the slim red dress Corinne was modelling. I put the bucket on the cocktail table, and aimed a blow of the hammer at the last large chunk of ice. It broke in a strange spectacular fashion, and the whole silver insides of the bucket collapsed. I had thought the lining was made of metal, and was surprised to see dark-edged shards of glass poking up around the ice.

"That's not the way!" Jack said. He rushed towards me with his empty glass in his hand. "That's not the way, now is it, little man?" A musical twitter of laughter came from the ladies on the sofa. The little dog yapped. Corinne told me later that I had the cutest look on my face, so shocked and innocent, with the brass hammer in my fist.

"Cripes, Corinne," Jack moaned, peering into the bucket.

"Jack, it was an accident," she said. "I'll buy you a new one."

"Seven years I've had this set. It's been across Canada I don't know how many times."

"I saw one just like it in Birks," Corinne said. "I'll get it for you as soon as this guy I'm working for pays me."

The ladies laughed again. I looked into Jack's bifocal eyes and saw that he would have liked to hit me. I hoped Corinne was telling the truth about the new ice set, because if we really were going to buy him a new one, I could probably keep his little hammer.

CHAPTER 26

A DAY BEFORE I WAS to go with Nick to a movie, he told me to come early this time, with Corinne, for a light supper.

"He's going to cook?" she said.

"I guess."

When we arrived at his apartment, Nick came to the door freshly shaved and dressed in a green linen jacket. The table was set with the same ready-to-eat things he usually had in his fridge, only more of them. There were a lot of jars, plates and wind-up cans surrounding a pair of lit candles, along with a squat open bottle of Mateus.

"I hope you don't mind serving the soup course," Nick said. Corinne went to the stove, retrieved a saucepan, and poured out tomato soup for three. We put our cloth napkins in our laps and ate the best that Campbell's could make.

"How's business?" Corinne said.

"Slow," Nick said. "In summer, no one believes in winter."

"I couldn't work at home. I'd never get out of my bathrobe."

"That's easy. You buy more bathrobes."

We finished the soup, and Corinne passed the other offerings around, except for one flat can that Nick held in both hands, the way a squirrel holds a nut.

"This is a special treat," he said. He snapped the key off the bottom and cranked open a snug bed of what looked like slimy mushrooms.

"Christ, where did you get those?" Corinne said.

"Jackie found them." He groped over the middle of the table for the toothpick holder, and stabbed one of the slimy things.

"You know you've got to cook them."

"You do?" His face fell. "I thought they were ready to go."

"If you want to be sick." Corinne took the can to the stove, and put a scoop of margarine into a frying pan.

"What are they?" I said.

"Puppy-dogs' tails," Nick growled with a wolfish grin. The contents of the can spattered and sizzled. I went to the stove to get a better look.

"I'm not eating those," I said.

"I don't know if I am either," said Corinne. She tipped the steaming snails onto a plate and shook out a snowy cloud of garlic salt. "You have to be in the mood."

"You can't crap out on me," Nick said. "Those came all the way from France." Corinne set the snails in front of him. He made a show of enjoying their aroma.

"They stink," I said.

"They don't smell any worse than your gum," Nick said, "and I'm sure they taste better." He reached for a toothpick, stabbed at the snails, and got one on a Ritz cracker. He held this treat before his mouth for several seconds, and a deep silence fell over the room.

"You know, I've never actually done this."

"Now that's a surprise," said Corinne.

"Are you sure you cooked them right?"

"You were ready to eat them raw."

"I remember. And then you put me on my guard." Nick held the cracker in Corinne's direction. "You first. Another nice glass of wine if you do."

"You're already overdue with that, Buster." She nibbled the edge of the cracker, then took the whole nasty mess into her mouth and chewed with a clownish, melancholy look.

"How was it?" he said.

"Wonderful."

I smeared some Cheez Whiz on a stick of celery, and Corinne poured herself more Mateus. Nick put another snail on a cracker, and with childlike assurance popped it into his mouth.

"A bit rubbery, but good." He speared another and waved it in my direction. "This one's yours." A drop of yellowish oil fell on the tablecloth.

"No thanks."

"Come on, Jasper, be a sport," Corinne said. I kept my head down and nursed my celery stick. Nick waggled the snail for a long moment, then put it on a Ritz and ate it.

"Your loss," he said. "By the way, what did you do with your gum?"

"Put it in the ashtray."

"Jesus!" A morsel of Ritz fell from his lips. "Corinne, haven't you taught this boy about *receptacles*?"

"Jasper, don't go gumming up Nick's receptacles."

When our supper was over, Nick asked Corinne to come with us to the Sahara. She declined the invitation.

"The theatre is air-conditioned," he said, a familiar smoothness creeping into his voice. "Not like this place."

"No thanks."

"You can split if you get bored."

"Not tonight."

"Okay, come later for drinks at the Belmont, on me."

"Give it up, Mr. Medwood. What's the story? Not a real sale unless you have to push it?"

"Something like that." Nick seemed cheerful about being turned down, as Rodney always did, but when Corinne collected her things and went out the door, his mood changed. We left the apartment and walked to the Sahara in silence. In the lobby, Nick rattled through his change for a dime, his standard candy offering.

"After all that food, how can you still stuff yourself with junk?" he said crossly.

"It's like dessert."

"Get something that won't stink the place out." I led him through the reek of popcorn to a seat in the theatre, then turned back up the ramp. A few rows from the back, the Chinese girl I had seen before was sitting on the aisle, talking with her friends. I bought some red licorice and sauntered slowly back down the aisle, my eyes fixed on the black ponytail that shivered when she moved, and the brown fingers groping at her popcorn. For a second I was right beside her, but with one more lingering step passed into the dull zone where she could no longer be seen. The lights dimmed.

The film was about an air-force pilot who had a daughter my age and a wife who was divorcing him. She was getting rid of their daughter, too, by sending her to a boarding school. The sad pilot and a younger soldier climbed into a fighter jet they had to fly to a new base across the country. After that, the film was mostly talking, in the jet and on a passenger plane, where the pilots argued about how high they should fly. There wasn't much to describe, and my thoughts strayed back to the Chinese girl sitting in the resonant darkness behind me.

The sad pilot flew on through the night. Suddenly the lights of the passenger plane came into his view.

"The other plane's coming straight at him," I said, my own words yanking me up in my seat. "He's steering under. His plane scraped the bottom of the other. There's an explosion. It's his plane, his plane exploded!"

"Okay, relax!" Nick said. "Like we weren't expecting it."

The passenger plane lost an engine and had to crash land at the nearest airport. Fire engines raced across the dark tarmac and saved the passengers. The music swelled up and the credits rolled over the screen as the Sahara lights began to glow.

"That can't be the end," I said.

"Why not?" said Nick, stretching into a feline yawn.

"They don't show what happened to the girl."

"What girl?"

"The pilot's daughter."

"Her dad died. That's what happened to her. Case closed, Sonny Boy."

The screen still flickered, but there was nothing more about the girl, waiting alone at her new boarding school, the one she had chosen because it was near her father's new base. The principal would call her to his office, a stranger in uniform would be there, and the worst part of her life would begin.

The towering curtains shuddered towards each other and the screen lapsed into the dead blankness that came over it at the end of every movie, so unlike the inviting glow it had before the film began. Nick was already halfway up the aisle when I wriggled through the crowd to catch up with him. I reached him near the front door a moment before he might actually have noticed that I wasn't right behind him.

We came out of the theatre and returned to the everyday world, where everything seemed tinged with the pilot's uncomplaining sadness. My movements became his. I crossed the street with the serene melancholy he had shown as he walked towards his fighter jet. At the curb, I looked back, as the pilot did to wave goodbye to his daughter. I was startled to catch a glimpse of a girl and a ponytail I had almost forgotten, vanishing around the corner of the Sahara.

CHAPTER 27

CORINNE SNAPPED THE LATCH CLOSED on her hard-shelled modelling case and told me I didn't have to come. But it had been a dull, wet day, and I liked the festive nature of a fashion-show fitting, where beautiful women played dress-up in someone else's clothes.

We collected Jackie from her low-rise building and drove to a store under a sprawling sign that spelled out *Kesterman's Modern Miss* in a flowing feminine hand. The store was closed, but a frog-eyed man in a blue suit stood inside the door and, after goggling at Jackie and Corinne through the glass, he turned the latch and let us in.

He led us through the dim interior, under hanging placards for Lingerie and Sportswear, to a lit area at the back where a man was hammering a narrow roll of carpet onto a plywood runway. Audrey and a stock girl stood bent over a card table strewn with index cards while a couple of models waited around in their bras and slips. Audrey looked up as we approached.

"Jasper here thinks if he comes to enough of these things, he'll get my job," she said. "Now, ladies, please, I know it's warm, but try not to sweat on the clothes."

Jackie and Corinne kicked off their shoes and hung up their

clothes, and the stock girl began dispensing outfits from two racks near the runway.

"No hats for Dolly," Audrey said to the stock girl. "We'll save them for these other gals. And find her some shoes with pizzazz, something young."

"I guess we're the old mares here," Corinne said to Jackie as they zipped each other into their first outfits. Another model, dark-haired and tall, rooted through a snakes' nest of leather belts. Dolly, a slim blonde, stepped up on the runway, swirled the skirt of her dress and struck a few pinup poses.

"Don't be cute, just act like you've done this before," Audrey said. She told Jackie she couldn't focus with a run nylon staring her in the face, and sent Corinne to find shoes, because we'd be stuck there all night if she had to pick out every little thing.

"What's she grumpy about?" I said.

"Maybe nervous about the stock," Corinne said. "This ain't Holt's."

Paul, the man in the blue suit, said that for insurance reasons, nobody could roam the store alone after hours. He trailed after us to the shoe section and waited while Corinne chose a pair of pumps covered in pink satin. When the stock girl ran off to find her size, Paul picked up a gold stiletto, and held it near his groin with the heel sticking up.

"Here's a good one."

"Buzz off," Corinne said.

He stepped closer. "Guaranteed to fit."

"Drop it, Buster, I'm not buying." He retreated with a sneer, which rested briefly on me.

When we got back to the others, Jackie was stepping off the runway in a black dress. Corinne headed towards the fitting table to show Audrey her shoes, and Jackie turned her back to me to unzip. I undid the little hook and ran the zipper down to the middle of her spine. In one rippling movement she dropped the front from her chest and pulled the whole thing off her hips. She took a cocktail dress from Audrey's girl and pulled it on. The fabric curled away from her back like the petals of a flower, exposing her in a way that made her seem almost more naked than when she had stood there with no dress.

"Zip, zip," she said.

I tugged at the zipper and the teeth bit into the fabric. As I bent to free them, I felt the warmth of Jackie's back and caught the spicy fragrance of her skin. The zipper swam before my eyes, then the tab came free and slid up easily between her shoulder blades. I felt some moisture on the back of her neck as I fastened the little hook with fingers that seemed separate from the rest of me. A few strands of hair trailed over my hand; I pulled a bobby pin from her coif and pinned them back in place.

"You're really something, kiddo," she said, touching her hair. "There's mints in my purse."

I found her bag, opened it on a counter strewn with silk scarves, and pawed through a jumble of makeup containers, keys and tampons till I found a roll of mints. I put one on my tongue and scanned the room. Everyone was occupied, including Paul, so I slid one of the scarves from the pile into my pocket, almost without looking at it.

The hidden scarf made the fitting drag on more slowly. Audrey fussed over accessories and kept changing her running order. Corinne got me a sheet of blank foolscap from the card table, and I drew warriors with fancy breastplates and helmets that drooped to the shoulders like iron wigs.

The room went quiet as Jackie climbed onto the runway in a white satin wedding gown, with a bouquet of silk flowers. She wheeled around and flung the bouquet over her head, past all the models waiting to catch it.

"It's not baseball, Jackie," Audrey said. "More like salt over your shoulder." Jackie tried again, and this time the bouquet arced down over Dolly, who grabbed at it on tiptoes.

"Okay, that's it," Audrey said. "The long march is over." The models began putting on their own clothes.

Someone stubbed a finger in my back. "What's this?" said Paul. He caught a tiny ear of fabric from the corner of my pocket, and whipped out the scarf. "He's got a scarf," he announced, flourishing it as if he were a magician. He ran the silk through his fingers, looking for a price tag, but I had clawed it off in my pocket.

"That's mine," Corinne said. "I gave it to him to hold on to."

"Why not put it in your purse?"

"If you saw my purse, you'd know." The other girls laughed.

"Paul, stop persecuting people," said Audrey, gathering up her cards. "These gals are pros. Let's wrap up and get out of here."

Corinne snatched the scarf from Paul and tied it around her neck. She and Jackie finished dressing, and I followed them with a nervous step towards the exit. We were nearly at the door when a firm hand gripped my elbow.

"Don't ever come back here," Paul said in my ear, and released me with a contemptuous flick.

Outside, the sky had cleared, and stars were beginning to show in the deep blue above the buildings opposite. I clambered into the safety of the Corvair's back seat. Jackie said she'd come back with us to the Bel Air.

"Did Paul try to mash you?" she said.

"When I was looking at shoes," said Corinne.

"I was in the wedding gown." They both laughed.

"Why do they always put the wedding gown last?" I said.

"The princess gets married at the end of the story, not the beginning," said Corinne. She lit a cigarette for Jackie, and one for herself, and their smoky exhalations seemed to dispel the tension that had crept into their bodies over the previous hours.

"That dress looked good on you," Corinne said. "Ever think of wearing one for real?"

"Sometimes," Jackie said. "But Nick's too dependent on his family.

They even own the window business. I wish they'd butt out, or give him enough to start on his own."

"Ever tell them that?"

"No."

"I would. If he was the one I wanted."

"Yeah, he's the one," Jackie said, almost sadly, it seemed to me. "I've known him since I was fourteen, when he could still see. He probably thinks I still look like that. How about you?"

Corinne told her about the oil up north and the little plane, which this time went down a day before their wedding anniversary.

"That's so sad," Jackie said, touching Corinne's arm and casting a pitying glance at me. "You found the one, and then he was taken away."

We drove on without further comment, and separated in the doorway of our building. When Corinne and I were back in our apartment, she gave me a quick, hard slap on the arm.

"That was pretty sloppy with the scarf, mister. Trying to get me fired? What do you want with a scarf anyway?"

"I was going to give it to you," I said, though I hadn't thought that far when I took it. There were just so many scarves lying there unattended, and such a beautiful chance to sneak one.

She gave me a half-hearted shake, then a more genuine hug, and I could tell she wasn't entirely unhappy about this stolen gift. But our evening at Kesterman's Modern Miss was the last time she took me to a fitting or photo shoot. From then on, her work was entirely her own, neither seen by me nor much discussed in my presence. It was another step in my gradual exile from what Corinne only half-jokingly called the prime of my life.

CHAPTER 28

CORINNE DROVE OFF ALONE ONE afternoon and came back smelling of horses and saddle leather. She had found a stable outside the city where she could ride. As she put on her riding clothes for her second trip out there, she told me Nick was going with her.

"But he's blind."

"So?"

"What if he falls off?"

"They've got a very sweet nag waiting for him. He'll be okay."

I trailed after her to Nick's apartment. He was strutting around in a tweed coat and his Zorro cowboy boots. Jackie was there too, in a short linen jacket, tan stirrup pants and ankle boots.

"This is going to be terrific," Nick announced, gripping his lapels.

"You coming too?" Corinne said to Jackie.

"Thought I'd give it a try. What about you, Jasper?"

"He doesn't believe in horses."

I followed them outside, then crossed the street behind the accelerating Corvair and went down the alley next to Dwayne's house. He was in the backyard, crouching near the picket fence, burning ants with a magnifying glass. He jumped up when he saw me.

"Did you see Venus and Mars last night?" he said.

"No, but I can see your underwear." He fell for it and looked down; I gave his chin the obligatory upward bump.

"Let's go play on the mountain," he said.

He led me down the alley and along another that intersected it, and we came to a grassy vacant lot behind the Woodward's store. The ground had a small rise in the middle, about as high as I was tall.

"You call this a mountain?"

"It used to be bigger."

"You mean you used to be smaller."

"My dad says this whole world's a grain of sand. The sun's a million times bigger. He tells me lots about astronomy. He says we have to be ready for the Space Age."

I said nothing, irritated by Dwayne's habit of flaunting bits of lore from his father. We strolled over the grass, kicking at stones and bits of trash, two boys with nothing to do. Something caught my eye, and I picked it up: a white tubular toy rocket, as big as a large novelty pencil, with a red plastic nose cone. Blue letters spelled USA along the fuselage, and a pilot's face smiled at the window.

"Somebody must have launched it from their yard," Dwayne said, making a grab for it.

"No you don't," I said, pulling it out of his grasp. But I let him examine the hollow tube, too small for any rocket engine, and fondle the red tail fin. "It's only cardboard," I said.

"Can I have it?"

I stepped away from him and threw the rocket, which flew no better than a pencil would, turning over once before it hit the mountain. Dwayne ran to get it, and wiped away the dirt caked on its fin. I took it from him.

"Please?" he said, skipping around me like a little dog.

I threw the rocket again, and again it flipped in the air before skidding down the mountain's opposite slope. Dwayne retrieved it and held it out to me with a pleading look.

"Which is bigger, Venus or Mars?" I said.

"That's easy, Venus." He grinned at the simplicity of my question.

"Which is bigger, a carrot or your dad's cock?" I threw the rocket, hard this time, and it went into the mountain cone first, with enough force to make it bounce back a foot. Dwayne picked it up.

"It broke," he said, handing it to me. The split plastic nose cone came apart in my hand. It was a cheap toy, probably made in Japan. It would have been a good item for the Drawer of Shame; but instead, I thrust it at Dwayne.

"Here. A bit of tape will fix it up."

He cradled the pieces in his hands, then raced around the mountain with the noseless rocket high over his head, making explosive engine noises with his mouth. He did two circuits like that, with a childish glee that I found annoying. I stepped into his orbit, caught his arm, and pretty well forced him to stop running.

"Let's get something to drink," I said.

We went back to his house and his mother gave us lemonade. Dwayne taped the nose cone back in place. He was deeply happy. The rocket looked hardly any worse than before: the pilot still smiled, in spite of his three crashes.

When I got back to the apartment, Corinne was already there, changed and cleaned up from the stables. She usually rode for much longer.

"We left early," she said. "Jackie's horse tested her a little at the start, and it put her off. She stayed in the car the whole time."

"What about Nick?"

"He was great. He wasn't afraid, he wanted to go and go, but Jackie was waiting, so I made him turn back." She made a face, but didn't really seem unhappy about any of it. She was in as good a mood as if she had had a whole afternoon of riding. "Now they're expecting us for drinks and dinner."

We went to Nick's, where he was mashing potatoes for Jackie's spareribs. Over dinner, he narrated every detail of his ride.

"Doll, you don't know what you missed," he said.

"Okay, I get it," Jackie said.

"I wasn't sure I'd do it till I was in the saddle, but then I knew. Boy, did I know."

"Bully for you."

"I want to try jumping. That would be out of sight. Just ride like crazy at some pile of logs, and do whatever it is you do to make the thing jump. Wouldn't that be a blast?"

He went on with his happy boasting, till Corinne told him he was a bore and Jackie got a migraine. The meal ended quickly and Nick shooed us out, muttering apologies, because he could tell this was going to be a bad one for Jackie.

*

FOR A WHILE, NICK AND Corinne went riding a couple of times a week. He tapped on our door and waited in the living room in his Zorro boots while she did her makeup. She told him he could wait in his place till she was ready, but he still came and hung around as Dean used to do; except that Dean hated waiting, because for him time waiting was time wasted. But Nick didn't let on that any minute of his waiting time was lost. He lounged on our sofa, or sat up with arms forward and shoulders rolling as if already on the horse, ready to do whatever it took to make the thing jump.

Once, Jackie arrived an hour before the riders usually left, to cut Corinne's hair. They talked and joked at first, but as the cutting went on they spoke less, and focused more on the regular strokes of comb and scissors that Jackie could see and Corinne couldn't. When the barber's cape came off, Corinne's hair was shorter than I had ever seen it.

"What do you think?" Jackie said, as Corinne examined it in the bathroom mirror.

"It's different."

"A bit more sleek."

"Yes, that's nice."

"A little less Sandra Dee."

Corinne had nothing to say to that remark. She didn't like Sandra Dee, or at least hadn't in the movie we'd seen together.

Jackie was sweeping the floor when Nick arrived. "Doll. What a nice surprise."

"I thought I'd come too," she said, dropping the last of Corinne's cut ends into the bin.

"What for?"

"Maybe I'll try riding again. Or just walk around."

"You, go for a walk?" Nick's face twisted in disbelief. "Don't make me laugh. You'd end up in the car again."

She moved close to him, and draped her arms around his neck. "Look, I just want to get out of the city. With you."

"What, to make me feel bad when you crap out?" He pushed her away. "Forget it. We're not going." He flung himself on the sofa. Jackie swayed a little, then swept the floor over again and tapped out the nearly empty dustpan.

"Doll," Nick moaned.

"Oh, come off it," Jackie said, and somehow those words meant she had given in. Nick sprang off the sofa. Corinne emerged from the bathroom. They went out the door together, chatting happily about the paddock and the horses.

Jackie said we should have an outing, too. She took me to the Dairy Queen and bought me a strawberry sundae. She got nothing for herself and watched me eat the whole thing in silence, smoking, with the cigarette never more than an inch from her lips.

CHAPTER 29

I WATCHED CORINNE IN THE mirror of her vanity as she did her makeup, and tried to see what had changed about her hair. She had had it recut that morning at a salon. To me it didn't look much different from what Jackie had done, but Corinne said it was a big improvement.

"What did you see with Nick last night?" she said.

"A war film, about commandos who bust up some big German guns, on a cliff by the sea."

"Is it hard, telling him everything?"

"When things happen fast. Or when I describe something, and then it doesn't matter."

"Like what?"

"Like at the beginning, there was a crash landing, and we never found out what happened to them." I could still see the plane dipping through the dusky sky, trailing fire and smoke, scraping hard along the runway, spinning once and ending with its nose in the ground. But the main character walked past like it hadn't happened, and the camera went with him.

"Where are you going?" I said.

"Some company thing at the new petroleum club. They want me to stand there while the president gives out awards."

She put on a lemon-coloured dress and white shoes, and then I walked with her to the Corvair. A couple of passing drivers, both men, nudged their horns when they saw her.

The Corvair sped off. I crossed beneath the huge oak to Dwayne's house, where no one answered the bell. I idled towards the shoppers park, and at some distance saw the Chinese girl from the Sahara approaching the public library, a low brick building I hadn't yet visited. She had gone inside by the time I reached the heavy oak door.

I entered as a stout woman came out from behind the desk and crossed the floor to an armchair where an elderly man was sleeping. His open mouth guttered like an idling outboard, then stalled into silence as the librarian shook him awake. A couple of kids pawed over storybooks on the carpet while their mothers flipped through the card catalogue. The Chinese girl was rolling a book cart towards a far aisle, her plaited skirt swaying around her knees. Her white socks had fallen to the tops of her saddle shoes.

I went to the adjacent aisle and prowled along, as if looking for a title, till I was directly opposite her. Her fingers flashed past the gap near my eyes as she returned a book to its place. I crouched down and through the shelves caught a glimpse of her bare tummy as she reached for a high shelf, and a crusty scab below her knee. I moved as casually as I could to her side of the shelf, still pretending to search for a title as she continued her rhythmic movement from cart to shelf and back. Then she was right beside me, almost brushing against me as she shelved one book, actually touching my arm as she held another in front of me, as if offering it.

"Do you mind?" she said. I stepped back and she slid a slim orange-covered volume into its place.

"Are you finding what you want?" she said, without interest, not bothering to look at me. Her perfume barely registered over the stuffy odour of books.

"Sort of."

"These are the women's shelves."

My eyes raked across the suddenly legible titles about knitting and baking. "Oh, no, I'm looking for — I'm not sure you've got it."

"What?"

There had to be a right answer, as there was to every riddle. I settled almost at random on one of Dwayne's favourite words.

"Astronomy."

Her eyes flicked up at me under her flat lids. "Over here." I followed her short-legged stride to a low shelf crowded with textbooks.

"It's all here," she said, squatting down. "Not much. Downtown is better. What do you want to know about?"

"Stars."

"Try this one, and this. If those aren't enough, come and find me."

She returned to her cart. I lugged the heavy books to a table, and bent my head over a random page without absorbing anything written there. We had spoken, I had found the right word, and she had practically asked me to need her again. I listened for the soft thump of books on shelves, and the creaking of her cart.

After several minutes, my eye caught at single words on the page, then phrases and sentences about exploding stars, and the 400 million tons of matter the sun burns every second. It was like a million H-bombs going off at once. A million! In the time I had been sitting there, a vast distant inferno had sent masses of radiation careering through space till some of it entered the atmosphere, fell through the library window, and settled onto the carpet at my feet.

"This one's famous," said the Chinese girl, at my shoulder again, pointing a tawny finger at a speck near a swirl of other specks. "It's in Coma Berenices. Do you have a telescope?"

"No."

"You should. You've got to look for yourself. I'm getting a new one for my birthday." She rolled the empty cart to the desk, and exchanged it for a full one.

In the other book, I found star maps and a constellation drawing of a warrior holding a sword, with stars stuck like badges to his ankle, belt and shoulder. He was a shaggy version of the armed men I drew while Corinne made herself up. Encouraged by the similarity, I sauntered across the floor to where the Chinese girl rustled among the shelves.

"Will you be able to see this with your telescope?" I said, pointing to the picture.

Her smudgy brows moved up in surprise. "You don't need one for Orion. Are those books too hard?"

"No, they're good," I said, and retreated to my table. I would have to read more to avoid mistakes, so I did, slowly and stubbornly, the way I ate when Corinne served things I didn't care for. I chewed over the same sentences again and again, as dust motes drifted in the H-bomb sunlight that had crept over the floor and onto my pants. That warming light gave me a better reason to approach her. I went to the desk, where she was stamping in books returned.

"If the sun's exploding so much all the time, why doesn't it burn out?" I said.

"Because it's a million times bigger than the Earth," she said, repeating something Dwayne had told me only days before. "You should know that. Do you want to take those out?"

"No, I'll read them here."

"Suit yourself."

It sounded like a dismissal. I left my heavy books on the table and returned to the women's section where I found the slim orange book she had shelved in front of me. With a casual look around I pulled it from the shelf and slipped it under my shirt. Her scent might be on it; perhaps it clung to every book she put on those shelves, preserved between neighbouring covers like a pressed flower. I hugged the book to my side as I left, feeling a queasy mixture of excitement that we had spoken, and shame at my mistakes.

When I got back to the apartment, I found Corinne rocking

IN A WIDE COUNTRY | 181

herself on the sofa with her arms wrapped tight around her knees, her face streaked with mascara.

"What happened?" I said.

"He died."

"Dean?" My heart kicked inside my chest.

"No, the president of this thing, this afternoon. We were in a beautiful big garden, and he got up to speak, and pitched over on his face in a rose bed, right at my feet."

Her voice shook. I stood there blankly. This was not about Dean, or Nick, or anyone we knew. The president of something had fallen down dead in front of her, face first into the mud.

"His wife was there," she said. "A very elegant lady, nicely dressed. And when he went over, she kneeled down, with him lying there dead, and she howled." She looked up, and her face broke apart. "Jasper, she just *howled* like an animal!" A shudder went through her body, and I embraced her awkwardly as she sat there wracked with sobbing, once more a girl in Lily's dining room, with her own father stretched out on the table.

CHAPTER 30

I LAY IN BED IN my pyjamas and sniffed again at the cover of the orange book I had taken from the library. *Crochet Tips for Teens* didn't smell at all like the Chinese girl, just old cardboard and glue. I drew a picture in the back, of Orion with a cock that trailed to his knees.

From the silence in the apartment, I knew that Corinne was still asleep. I got dressed, combed my hair with some Brylcreem I got from Dean, and frowned in the mirror like a pop star I had seen in one of Corinne's magazines. I looked good, but couldn't imagine frowning like that all day. It was so hard to find a face that worked.

I went outside and over to the library, trying to suppress my anxious eagerness as I hauled open the oak door. There was no one at the tables, or among the shelves I could see from the entrance. The plump librarian sat alone at her desk, reading. I crossed over to the more remote aisles, my hopes sinking with every step. Perhaps the Chinese girl didn't come every day, or worked a complicated part-time schedule. But she was there, in the last aisle, reading a book off her cart.

"I found you something," she said when she noticed me, as if continuing a conversation from a few minutes earlier. She pushed past me and went to the end of the checkout desk, where she opened a large book to a night-sky photo with a white blotch in the middle.

"This is what it looks like when stars blow up," she said. "This whole cluster, Crab Nebula, is what was left after a star exploded, a thousand years ago."

I bent over the blotch, close enough to feel her blouse against my bare arm, happy beyond words that she had been thinking of me. I caught the scent of her rose perfume, and something sweeter: her chewing gum.

"Chinese astronomers saw it, and marked it on their star charts," she said. "It was so bright, they could see it during the day. They called it a guest star."

"Like on TV," I said.

"I don't watch much TV."

"Me neither."

She offered me a stick of cherry gum, and as I took it, my fingers grazed her palm, just enough to feel a slight moisture there. She held out the book. "You can take this too if you want."

I lugged it to my table, and she returned to the shelves. My fingertips crawled under my nostrils as I sniffed for some further scent from her moist hand. The picture of the Crab Nebula swam under my eyes.

After a while, it settled into a fixed image again, and I decided it looked less like a crab than a duck falling on its bum. It was a cartoon character, missing a few details. I pulled a pen from my pocket and leaned over the page, without any of the alert tension I felt when I drew in the big Bible in Lily's empty front room. At the last moment, some preserving instinct made me glance up, just as the librarian sprang from her chair and sped in my direction.

"Finding what you want?" she said, glaring at the pen that I was already hiding under the table. "Is Marsha helping you?"

"Yes." I smiled, grateful for the name: Marsha.

"Would you like some paper?" She gave me a sheet of foolscap, and a pencil, and I drew a Duck Nebula, with a bill as wide as Daffy's, and a starry warrior jabbing the duck's bum with his spear.

"What are you doing?" Marsha stood at my elbow, looking shocked. There was another girl with her, the sandy-haired one from the Sahara.

"Just thinking about what I read," I said, covering the page with my hand. "Sometimes it helps when I sketch things out."

"Especially if you're bored," said the other girl. She whipped the page from under my fingers. "Look, he's done a self-portrait."

"Quit it, Noreen. You're embarrassing him," said Marsha.

"I'm not. You're the one who's blushing."

"Let's go."

"We're going to the shoppers park for lunch," Noreen said to me. "You can come if you want. You might as well, you're just fooling around here. What's your name?"

"Jasper."

"Haven't I seen you before?"

"Maybe. I live close by."

They moved towards the door. I stuffed the paper in my pocket and followed them outside. The girls' wide skirts swished against my legs from both sides as we walked across the blazing parking lot. Noreen put on a pair of pink plastic sunglasses and Marsha shaded her eyes with a clutch purse.

"The end of summer is the most boring time ever," Noreen said.

"You should have got a job," said Marsha.

"That would be really boring. Jasper, what do you do, to not be bored?"

"Go to movies. Drive around. Lots of things." I told them about Corinne and our summer of wandering, and Dean's cottage, and our day at the fair, and horseback riding at Chokecherry Bush. It all sounded very different from what actually happened, and the way I felt about most of it.

"I'd die to have a summer like that," Noreen said. "Can you really ride? Are you good at it?"

"Pretty good. I like jumping."

"Where was your dad during all this?"

I gave them the story of the bush plane, which this time went down at night, with a bright canopy of stars and a full moon. As the little plane sliced through the northern forest and shattered on the ground, I saw the doomed pilot in the film about the colliding planes, who they had said was a dreamboat. His sad dignity crept over me again, and over my father as he vanished into the trees.

"That's terrible," Noreen said.

"Why would they fly a small plane at night?" said Marsha. "Bush pilots mostly fly by eye."

"Lordy," Noreen moaned. "I can't believe you're asking that."

We went into Woodward's food entrance, and Noreen marched up to the high lunch counter, where they kept iced cakes and crullers and doughnuts under glass. She ordered three egg salad sandwiches.

"That's our favourite thing here," she said.

A flicker of panic ran through me, and I clapped my hands to my pockets. "I don't have any money!"

"Oh. Then you're our guest." Noreen rummaged in her change purse with her freckled hand. "Marsha, you have a job."

We carried our sandwiches through Woodward's and into the shoppers park, and ate on a bench opposite a shoe store. The cherry sweetness vanished from Marsha's scent, which now took on a sulphuric edge from the egg salad.

"This is the only kind of picnic I've had all summer," Noreen said.

"Why don't you ever go to the park? It's right near your house," Marsha said.

"You only like it because of that dome thing."

"You should go there too."

"Why? You've told me everything already a hundred million times."

"What are you talking about?" I said.

"The planetarium," Noreen said, her shoulders drooping as if under a heavy burden. "It's new, the first in Canada, blah blah. Her dad runs it."

"No, he's a presenter."

"And a professor. A real king-sized brain. You should go, Jasper. All the stars are in there." She scooped up a morsel of egg that had fallen in her lap, and licked it from her fingers. "Are you really interested in this star stuff, or are you just trying to impress Marsha?"

"You're impossible today," Marsha said. She stood up and brushed the crumbs from her skirt.

"I'm going to look at shoes." Noreen walked over and examined the offerings in the shoe-store window. Marsha took a compact from her purse and reapplied her frosty lipstick in daubs that barely disturbed her full small lips. A crescent-shaped light from the mirror's surface danced on her cheek. When she was done, she looked directly at me for almost the first time that day. The fabric of her skirt was bunched up against my leg; her knee bumped a slow rhythm against the bench.

"You should go to the planetarium," she said. "If you're interested for real."

"Of course I am."

"There's a show tomorrow afternoon."

"Are you going?"

"Maybe." She lowered her eyes. With her standing so close, that gesture felt more intimate than if she had kept looking at me. I stared up at her moon-like face, feeling deeply happy, though a new worry was beginning to gnaw, about whether and how her *maybe* would turn into *yes*.

"What shoes should I get, Jasper?" Noreen called out. "You must know, your mom's a model."

"You're too broke to buy shoes," Marsha said.

I went to the window. Noreen stood with her forehead against the glass, flexing her toes inside her thin canvas runners. Pairs of shoes fanned out around a semi-circular display that went up in steps like the layers of a wedding cake.

"Those white ones with the bows," I said. "You could wear them right now, or with almost anything."

"You hear that, Marsha? I'm taking him shopping with me next time."

"I've got to go back to work."

"No! What am I going to do?"

A wind was coming up. It blew grit in our faces as we walked back to the library.

"Don't go in with her, Jasper," Noreen said. "Stay out here with me."

Marsha's brows twitched. "Do what you like," she said. "I'll see you tomorrow. It starts at two o'clock." She pulled open the heavy door and disappeared inside. Again, I felt like I had been dismissed; but she had said yes, she would come.

Noreen and I remained on the fiery sidewalk. She took off her sunglasses and squinted at me. "Was it true, what you said?"

"About what?" My mind raced through all my dubious claims about my horseback jumping, the night flight, my interest in astronomy.

"Those shoes. Did they really suit me?"

"We could go back and try them."

She giggled, apparently at the idea that any boy would offer to go with her to try on shoes. But without Marsha, there were suddenly too few of us to do anything, no matter how bored we were.

"I think I have to help my mom with something," Noreen said. She walked off with long, bouncing strides towards the real park, glowing yellow-green in the distance.

I went back to the apartment, counting up the blank hours I had to fill before I would see Marsha again. Corinne was on the sofa, still in her housecoat, painting her nails.

"Where were you?" she said.

"At lunch. What's a planetarium?"

CHAPTER
31

THE FLORAL DRESS LAY WITH its back open under the needle of Jackie's borrowed sewing machine. The little bulb glowed over the spot where Corinne's fingers straightened the fabric close to the new zipper she had pinned in place. She dropped the metal foot; the needle chattered over two straight inches of fabric, then veered off course.

"Damn!" Corinne flipped the lever and yanked the cloth out, dragging threads with it. "Christ, I hate zippers!"

She tore at the errant stitches with a seam ripper. She was wearing an old pair of capri pants and a short-sleeved top flecked with paint from our place in Winnipeg. She hadn't put on makeup and had pinned her hair up just to keep it out of the way.

"Can I have money to go to the planetarium?" I said.

"Who with?"

"Nobody."

She slid the dress back under the metal foot. The machine slowly shunted into action, gained speed, then jammed with a tense whine.

"To hell with this," she said, switching off the machine. "When's your show?"

"Two o'clock."

"I'll come with you. We haven't done anything together lately."

"You'll never be ready."

"You watch. And change your shirt." She went into the bathroom and emerged fifteen minutes later fully made-up, in a wig she kept for fashion jobs when only a blonde would do. She threw off her work clothes and stepped into a full-skirted pink dress with a sash that made me think of gift wrap, and set a narrow-brimmed straw hat with a blue band on the back of her head.

A mournful admiration swept over me at the sight of this instant glamour, which made my clean white shirt feel shabby. She pulled on her short white gloves and was almost out the door when I ran to my room and yanked my tweed jacket from the hanger.

"A bit warm for that," she said.

We walked along the bright sidewalk. It was Saturday, and there were a lot of people out. Corinne's casual splendour affected them like an electrical storm. Men stared as we walked by, sometimes whistling if they weren't with their wives. One driver pulled near the curb and slowed to walking pace.

"Hey, sweetheart, need a ride?"

"Tell him no thanks, Jasper."

"No!" I yelled at the driver, as much to show him I was there too as to refuse the ride. Corinne took my arm, and we headed past the shoppers park to the real park beyond.

I put my hand in my jacket pocket and found a photo postcard Dean had given me of a Métis posing with his ox and Red River cart. On the back, Dean had written "My first truck!" in pencil, so I could use the card again.

"Dean gave me this," I said, showing it to Corinne. Saying his name to her after so long felt strange and sad.

"I might have guessed."

"Why didn't you tell him we weren't coming back?"

"What makes you think I didn't?"

"I phoned him. From one of the motels."

I braced for a slap, but her gloved hand just gave my arm a little squeeze.

"It doesn't always help to tell everything," she said. "He would only have been more upset."

Somehow this remark told me, as nothing else had, how unhappy Dean must have been when we left his cabin for the last time. I hadn't been able to see it all on his face when he walked towards the car and put his warm hand on my shoulder. Hearing about it now from Corinne was somehow worse than the times she had said he was a drunk and a bore. When she was being mean, he still mattered to her, but now that she was feeling sorry for him, I could see that he no longer did.

"How was he?" she said.

"Okay, I guess," I said, recalling the distant, sleepy sound of his voice.

"I still care about him, you know. Even though it didn't work out."

She gave my arm another conciliatory squeeze. But to me the combination of caring and not working out made no sense. I almost said so, the words were right at my lips, but they crumbled into a hopeless feeling that blurred the bright pavement.

We had turned away from the street, along a path that curved into the park. A silvery dome emerged among the tops of the thin new trees, floating there like a flying saucer.

The path met others that turned on each other like gears. The building at the centre of this clockwork, which had looked large from a distance, seemed to shrink as we drew closer. People milled around the dome, filing inside or peering at the zodiac mosaics set into the pavement.

We walked through the wood-panelled lobby, bought tickets, and found seats under the softly glowing rim of the plaster dome. In the centre of the room, something that resembled a many-eyed insect stood on splayed metal legs. I scanned the faces in the curved rows opposite us, and to either side, then leaned forward to see those in front.

"Looking for someone?" Corinne said.

"No," I said, and sat back. The house lights faded, the insect tilted upwards with a whir, and many small points of light burst from its head. The plaster dome filled with stars.

"We hear a lot about the space age," said a man's voice resonating over the dome. "But what do you really know about space? How big is it? What shape is it?"

I could just make out, on the dark floor, the shape of a man — Marsha's father, probably. As my eyes adjusted, the glow from his lectern played faintly over his fleshy cheeks, his full lips, his dark-rimmed glasses. He moved something in his hand, and a green bead of light danced around a group of stars near the rim of the dome.

"These stars looked like a scorpion to the Greeks," he said. "In China, people saw a dragon. In Indonesia, they saw a swan. Just about everywhere, people saw a picture on a surface, almost like this ceiling. But in space, things that look like parts of one picture can be far apart. The brightest star in this dragon looks close to its neighbour, but our whole solar system could fit in the space between them two thousand times over."

Two thousand solar systems. The domed theatre was so much smaller, yet I couldn't spot the one person I had come to see. Was she even here? I craned to make out the shadowy heads partially hidden by the insect's body.

The pointer lit on other constellations, and more vast measurements were given. The domed ceiling was growing to enormous proportions, while we, looking up, shrank to almost nothing. All the wandering Corinne and I had done that summer was only a minute streak on a surface Marsha's father was now comparing to a ping-pong ball. But nothing he said could help me measure the space that had opened, in the park, between me and the last evening in Dean's boat.

Something whirred in the insect's head. The stars shifted across the dome, carrying the scorpion out of view.

"These stars don't appear at the same time as the first ones we saw," the speaker said, outlining a shape I recognized as Orion. "The Greeks decided this was a hunter. He's running from a scorpion that will never catch him. In fact the scorpion falls a little farther behind all the time because everything in space is moving apart."

The insect's head whirred again, and a bigger, more diffuse array of stars flashed into view.

"Some people think the universe expands because it began with a big bang," said Marsha's father. "A better reason is that new matter is being created all the time. It may be only one extra atom per year in a space the size of a skyscraper, but in a universe measured in skyscrapers, that's millions of tons per second. All this new matter condenses into planets and solar systems that push each other apart. The pattern overall doesn't change, it just gets bigger. We say it's in a steady state."

I shifted in my seat again and saw what I thought was a pale reflection of Marsha's cheek. Something passed over it, her hand perhaps, as she swept a trailing hair behind her ear.

"In another way, space is very close to us," her father said. "The Earth is littered with debris from the heavens. Some may have given rise to life on this planet. We ourselves may have formed from the dust of stars. Think about that when you look at the sky tonight. Space isn't just something far away, it's also part of us."

The stars faded, the lights came up, and people began to clap. The sound rolled up over the dome and returned to us from above, like applause from heaven. Marsha's father bowed in all directions and said he would take questions. In the full room light, his smooth, fleshy face and silky black hair seemed too boyish to be connected to his resonant baritone.

An elderly woman below us raised a finger. "Are you saying life on Earth came from a rock, and not the hand of God?"

The astronomer rubbed his hands. "The Bible says God created man from dust. It doesn't say where the dust came from." A ripple of laughter ran around the room.

"The Lord did His work in six days," the woman said. "But you say creation's still going on, with new planets and suchlike."

"Yes, six days, and He rested on the seventh. But the Bible doesn't say He created nothing more."

More hands went up and people asked about the moon and the tides, whether comets were hot or cold, and if flying saucers were real. He hadn't quite finished with UFOs when the old woman stood up.

"You think you're clever," she said, "but you shouldn't be pushing your personal religion here, and with children present." She plucked up her bag and climbed the steps. We all watched her go. There were no more questions.

People moved into the narrow aisles. A giddy apprehension trembled through me as I saw Noreen come up the steps with Marsha, who was wearing a blue gingham dress. I introduced them to Corinne.

"I love your outfit," Noreen said. "Where did you get it?"

"They let me keep it, after a fashion show I was in."

Noreen cooed with pleasure.

"These buttons could be from the zodiac," I said, releasing a well-prepared remark about my lions rampant.

"No, this isn't Leo," Marsha said, peering at the brass figure. "More like a heraldry lion." She turned to face her father, trotting up behind her on the steps.

"Corinne, Jasper, this is my father, Dr. Suan," she said. He held one hand out to Corinne, and with the other fastened the middle button of his suit jacket.

"You made me feel very small today," Corinne said, taking his hand in her white glove.

"I'm sorry. You look just the right size to me." He flashed a dimpled smile. He was a different shape than Dean, and less athletic, but he looked as if he had gone to the same tailor. His sky-blue suit fit him perfectly, his shirt had a fine, creamy texture, and his mustard silk tie suited his colouring.

"Someone else thought you talked way too big," Corinne said.

"People often think about God when they come here."

"I thought about aliens," Noreen said. "You didn't say enough about them."

"I try not to say anything about aliens."

"But you did," Marsha said. "You said life came to Earth on a meteorite. That means we're aliens."

"Bravo, Marsha." Dr. Suan patted his palms together. She gave him a full, round smile that made me want to say something, anything, to make her smile that way at me.

"I liked the part about the new galaxies," I said, "and going steady."

"You mean the steady state," said Dr. Suan. His dimples deepened. Noreen laughed. Marsha winced as if in pain.

"I grew up in the country," Corinne said, "so I'm spoiled for starry skies."

"That's the best kind of spoiled," said Dr. Suan. "Or one of them."

The room had emptied. We moved in unison towards the exit, with Corinne and Dr. Suan in front.

"I only came to keep Jasper company," I heard Corinne telling him. "Not that he needs it, apparently."

"Your mom's beautiful," Noreen whispered, as we went through the lobby.

"She's not usually blond."

"I want every single thing she's wearing."

"Is that all you ever think about?" Marsha said.

"What are you thinking about, going steady?"

We stepped into the broiling sunlight, with my latest blunder still dragging after me. Corinne suggested we get something cold from one of the pedal carts, so we lined up and bought soft ice cream. There were no benches nearby, so Corinne moved under the trees, gathered her full skirts, and settled on the grass. After a moment we all did. My tweed jacket was uncomfortably hot, though I decided I was already too sweaty to take it off.

"When we started these shows at the university," said Dr. Suan, "we didn't have a dome. Just an old parachute, hanging from the ceiling."

"Had anybody ever used it?" I said.

"I used one like it, in Korea."

"Did your plane crash?"

"No, I was a paratrooper."

"Were you scared?"

"Yes," he said. "But once I was out of the plane, it was wonderful. I almost forgot to worry about what was happening on the ground."

"What was happening?"

"The war." His eyes retained their playful look, but he said nothing more.

"He doesn't talk about that," Marsha said. "He's never told me a thing, except about the parachute. And dancing at the canteen."

"You like to dance, Doctor?" Corinne said.

"I used to."

"Nobody stops liking to dance. They just run out of chances."

"That may be true."

Corinne's strange blond curls made her skin glow. Her spotless white gloves lay on her pink skirt, which spread out like a flower in the tree's shade. She looked like a movie star, or a princess on vacation. Her gestures acknowledged in a casual way that everyone was looking at her, those seated and passing by. I might have enjoyed this display some other time, but right now it annoyed me. I felt like I was tagging along to an occasion I had imagined quite differently, with myself in a starring role next to Marsha, and her father a supporting player in the background.

A man strolled nearby with a pocket transistor radio. A sultry slow tune poured from its tinny speaker.

"*Picnic!* I love that movie," Corinne said. "Excuse me!" she called to the man with the radio. "Can you wait a minute?" He stopped. Corinne got up and kicked off her shoes, and began dancing on the spot, moving her hips one way and her arms the other.

"C'mon, Jasper." She held out her hand, but I clutched my knees and stayed on the grass. She glanced at Dr. Suan and hitched her shoulder as if to say, "Who cares?" He got up smoothly and moved towards her. Their fingers touched at arm's length, and they danced from that distance while hardly moving; and I realized I had watched this scene before. It was from the film we had seen together, the day of Darryl's Cadillac.

"Daddy!" Marsha said.

"Shush, it's almost done." The tune trailed away. The man with the transistor radio gave a flicked salute and walked on.

"I wouldn't have missed that for anything," Noreen said.

Marsha dropped the remains of her cone in the grass. "I think it's time to go."

"You're right," said Dr. Suan. "I've spoiled your supper, and now I'm dancing in the park. Let's leave before I do something sensible."

Marsha and Noreen walked ahead of the rest of us towards the silver Rambler. They got in the car, and Dr. Suan made his farewells. I hadn't considered the worst thing Corinne's presence could do to this occasion, but the look on Marsha's face as they drove away told me that something like it had occurred.

"Well, haven't you landed in the honey pot?" Corinne said, as we headed across the park towards the Bel Air. "Where did you pick them up?"

"I met them at the library, and no one got picked up," I said, irked by her lazy good humour. I walked with my eyes fixed on the hot pavement, practically counting the steps until I could get into my room and out of my sweltering jacket.

"There's nothing wrong with that. But can you stand all that astronomy stuff?"

"Yes," I said defiantly. "I liked it when he said we're all made of stars."

"Oh yeah? Which star do you think you're made of, Richard Burton?" She laughed.

"Why do you have to ruin everything?" I shouted, and bolted away from her across the grass, stripping off my jacket as I ran.

CHAPTER 32

NICK DIDN'T WANT TO WAIT inside, so the three of us went out and stood by the Corvair. He drummed his fingers on the roof and faced the traffic rushing past. A silver horseshoe cufflink peeped out from under the cuff of his blue linen jacket.

"C'mon, Doll," he muttered.

A taxi pulled up and Jackie got out, in a pale yellow dress and pillbox hat. Corinne was wearing a white dress of almost the same style, which emphasized their similar build. They approached each other like the twins Audrey said they could be.

"Nice topper," Corinne said.

"Your hair looks good," Jackie said, but her smile faded when she saw what they had done at the salon.

"Of course it does, Doll," said Nick. "You're the best. Now let's go see those fillies run."

We got into the Corvair and drove with little conversation to the track. We walked through the concrete clubhouse, past the betting windows and the enormous board where they posted the odds. The place rang with the hard, loud voices of boys selling racing programs.

The stands above were quiet by comparison, though they were already full of people. We found seats a few rows inside the shady section. On the track, a couple of horses walked past with their grooms. A jockey stood at the edge of the grass oval, surveying the crowd.

Jackie opened her program and read out the horses in the first race. Nick analyzed the prospects for us: one horse finished strong, but had been weak lately; another was better on a muddy field. One jockey was a bum, and another had hands like you wouldn't believe.

"You can't know how the luck will play till the opening races are done," he said, "but my money's on Maid of La Mancha for the first."

"I'm not betting," Corinne said. "But I'll put two dollars up for the first, if Jasper picks."

"You're bankrolling?" Nick said. "Okay, kiddo, shall we double up on the Maid?"

It seemed silly to use up my one race on Nick's horse, so I reached for the program. Everyone waited as I scanned the list of unrevealing names. It was as bad as trying to buy jewellery with a clerk watching. I gave up and picked one at random.

"Pepper Mill!" Nick said. "You're throwing it away. Jackie, what's in the second?"

They reviewed the options for the next two races. Corinne offered to go down and place the bets. Nick said he was feeling jumpy, so he went too. Jackie bought me popcorn and a Coke from a vendor in the aisle, while I considered what to do with the fortune that would be mine if my horse won.

"You see a lot of Nick, don't you?" Jackie said.

"I guess so." I would buy a house in Winnipeg, with a garage for the Corvair, and a gazebo, and a swimming pool with an underground passageway.

"Always with your mom?"

"Except when we go to the Sahara." I would get a big telescope, and Marsha and I would lie by the pool and look at the stars.

"Does she ever go to his apartment without you? Or send you back to your place alone?"

"I don't think so."

A few more jockeys and mounts came onto the track, and I remembered there were seven other horses that could defeat Pepper Mill, including Maid of La Mancha. A flutter crossed my stomach, and my dreams of wealth began to falter, but it was too late to go and find Corinne. She had probably already wasted my two dollars.

"Are you sure?" Jackie said.

Something in her voice caught more of my attention than I wanted to give. I tried to push away whatever it was that was turning this into a secret conversation. She was nudging a puzzle into my view, and I wasn't prepared to offer anything to help solve it, even with her Coke and popcorn in my hands. I definitely made up my mind not to give her a thing.

"Jasper, this is kind of important. Try to remember."

"I don't know," I said roughly. I didn't actually make any effort to remember. A wall had risen up between Jackie and me, and I wasn't going to pay any attention to what was on the other side. I knew it was cruel, but it was an easy cruelty to accept — in fact I kind of enjoyed it.

Corinne and Nick came back, and gave me a slip of paper with my careless choice printed on it. All the jockeys were out now, walking their horses or talking with their trainers. Their silks rippled in the breeze.

"Jasper, do you see number two, Maid of La Mancha?" Nick said. "What's her jockey wearing?"

"Silks and boots. And a helmet."

"No, what *colours* is he wearing?"

"Green and yellow."

"Okay. Keep your eye on those colours. You may not be able to see the number when they're running."

I watched green and yellow for a while, until it occurred to me that my jockey had colours too. Pepper Mill's jockey was dressed in white and red — the same colours as the Corvair. My feeling of doom lifted immediately. I could win this, I would defeat green and yellow and all the others and cash in. I gripped my betting ticket and prayed — not to God, but to my grandpa Ben, the only real horseman I knew.

We waited an eternity for the race to begin. I squirmed with anxiety, but had lost all interest in seeing the horses run. All that counted was the outcome. The racing was merely something that had to happen first.

Suddenly the gates snapped open and the horses sprang out. The announcer's metallic voice called out names I recognized but couldn't connect with anything in the animal mass heaving along the track.

"What's happening?" Nick said, jabbing me with his elbow.

"Can't you hear the announcer?"

"Of course I can. But I want to know what it *looks* like."

"They're all packed together. Green and yellow's in the middle near the fence. He's next to white and red. They're reaching the curve. There's a big bulge of horses. One's out in front, blue and pink. They're going up the side."

"Okay, stop for a second." Nick listened to the announcer's steely patter, his face turned up as it was when we went to the movies.

The horses reached the far stretch. They floated softly along the white line of the fence, distant and silent, as if they were part of some other event, not the thudding, straining contest that had charged past us a minute earlier.

Nick jabbed me again. "What's happening?"

"They've separated out. There's gaps between them, a big gap between blue and pink and the rest."

"I know, I know! What about green and yellow?"

"He's moving up. He's passing white and red." I felt a pang.

"Oh baby, this is it!" Nick said.

"They're reaching the curve. They're all crowding together again."

"That's only the angle," Corinne said.

"They're crowding together," I insisted, "except for two way behind, and blue and pink in front. Green and yellow's moving up."

"Go, baby, go!" Nick shouted. The crowd was getting noisier. The announcer shouted things I couldn't make out. Nick clutched my arm.

"They're around the curve. They're stretching out. They're coming this way. Green and yellow's running hard. She's closing on blue and pink. She's passed him!" Maid of La Mancha had done it. Red and white followed at an increasing distance, but still ahead of the rest.

"It's too late, Jasper, they'd already crossed the line," Corinne said. The horses slowed up, except for the last ones galloping to end a race they had already lost.

"Damn!" Nick shouted. I had to get Corinne to explain why. Maid of La Mancha was second at the wire, so Nick lost. Corinne had bet on Pepper Mill only to show, so I won. By the time I understood this topsy-turvy outcome, Nick had torn up his betting receipt. Corinne shushed my yelling and pushed me out of the row to collect my winnings.

I flew down the stairs and joined the line of other winners. None of them looked as thrilled as I felt. The house, pool and telescope were waiting for me at the wicket. But when I reached the cashier, she took my receipt and gave me $2.26. I stared at her in disbelief.

"The odds change till the race starts, sir."

I went back to our seats. Nick had lost the second race while I was waiting for my winnings, and lost the next one too. Jackie read out the lineup for the next races. He made her repeat things and snapped at her. They were shouting in each other's faces as they went together down the concrete steps to place more bets.

The sun had crawled around to our seats, and the breeze had dropped. Corinne put her arms around me and gave me a sticky squeeze.

204 | ROBERT EVERETT-GREEN

"So, mister, how does it feel to beat the odds?"

"How long do we have to do this?"

"I don't know. Till Nick wins a few races."

"He won't want to stop then."

"No, probably not."

She borrowed binoculars from the only man nearby who had come with his wife, and we took turns scanning the field. The horses were better close up, just as the gamblers were turning out to be better from far off. To my eye, the races all looked the same. I had had my winning experience, and had found it was like having supper; however good it was, you didn't need to do it again right away.

We stayed until the last race. Nick finished in the money only twice all afternoon, and his victories didn't improve his mood. He spoke to Jackie even more harshly after a win, as if a moment of success only confirmed how wrong the rest of the day had turned out.

"Nick's not the type for gambling," Corinne said. "He takes it too seriously."

She told him the same thing in the car. "And why horse races?" she said. "You don't give a damn about horses."

"What do you mean? I've been out riding every other goddamn week," he said savagely.

"For all you bother about that animal, you might as well be on a merry-go-round."

"What's that have to do with anything? You got me into it."

"Don't I know it."

That put an end to the conversation. A heavy silence settled on us all the way to the Bel Air.

Corinne pulled up to the curb and killed the engine, but no one moved to get out. We seemed to be waiting for something.

"I'm sorry, everybody," Nick said at last. "This was not my day."

We got out, as wearily as at the end of a long journey. Nick waited for Jackie to take his arm, but she strode off without him. He put his hand on my shoulder as he walked up the path, too worn out to make it on his own.

After I shut out Jackie at the races, I expected her to change, but she didn't. She hugged me as usual when we parted, and still gave me candies from her purse, and called me "kiddo." But I wasn't convinced. She was hiding something, and I waited for her to show the change I was sure had happened between us. It was my watchful uneasiness that finally did change it, not suddenly with a few words at the track, but over days of holding back and making strange by degrees that were all the more irreversible by being so gradual.

CHAPTER 33

WHEN WE MOVED INTO OUR apartment, I needed to see its sparse-
ness as proof we had only paused in our wandering. But now my
universe was expanding, and I wanted more things in it. I started
lobbying for furniture.

After a few days of nagging, Corinne found me a fuzzy blue-
green wing chair that turned on its pedestal base. I spun myself in
it like a planet until I was dizzy to the point of nausea. I was recovering from this game when Corinne came in and said I had a visitor,
waiting in the hallway outside our apartment.

I staggered past sliding walls and the cascading faces of the kitchen
clock, and found Dwayne standing a long step back from the open
door. He was poised as if to run away, and relaxed only slightly
when I invited him in. Our living room felt more bleak with
another pair of eyes looking at it, so I prodded him through to my
room.

"Where's all your stuff?" he said. Besides the bed and the chair, there
was nothing. My clothes spilled from an open suitcase on the floor.

"In storage. We haven't had time to send for it."

He walked around the room, measuring its emptiness with his

feet, pausing at the window, from which his house and the sprawling oak were visible.

"Have you met any deadbeats?" he said. "My dad says there are deadbeats living over here."

"He's wrong," I said. "I know a guy downstairs whose brother is a millionaire."

"Why's he live here then?"

"He likes it. He doesn't want to be tied down to a house."

"We're not tied down. We just know where we belong," Dwayne said, as if reciting. He sat on the unmade bed and flipped through one of the comic books I had bought with Jack Summers's two-dollar bill. "Where's your dad?"

"He died up north, while he was looking for gold and diamonds." I told him about the little plane, and the snow squall that blew up so thick, the pilot couldn't tell the land from the sky. I said my father had tried to seize the controls to save them all, but the plane crashed into a mountain and exploded.

"Crumbs," Dwayne said in a hushed voice. The comic book slipped from his hands. "Why would they go up there in winter?"

"It was spring. Sometimes it snows late."

"What kind of plane were they flying?"

"I don't know."

"How could you not know what plane it was?" For him, this was the only incredible part of my story.

"I don't remember," I said, annoyed to hear another obvious question from Dwayne that I hadn't thought to ask.

"There's not too many that fly up there," he said. "I'll ask my dad, he works at the airport. When you hear the names, you'll remember."

"Look at this." I pulled him off the bed and sat him in the chair, and spun it around as fast as I could. At first he let out a long, thin squeal of pleasure, but after a minute he was begging me to stop.

"Let's go outside," I said. Dwayne got up and collapsed on the carpet. He found this hugely funny and lay giggling on the floor of our deadbeat apartment, till I said I was leaving right now and he could come or not.

We went down the back stairway to the expanse of parched grass and dandelions between my building and the ones behind it. I taught him the knife game where you face each other and make the other person do the splits by flicking the blade where his foot can't reach. I stretched him out three times till he fell on his bum, but these defeats only made him more cheerful.

"Let's go to my house," he said. "There's more to do there." He was probably right, but it irked me to hear it. I pocketed my knife and stalked around the building, with him skipping alongside. At the sidewalk, I showed him the Corvair.

"This is our car," I said. "It's a Monza. That's a place in Italy where the king was shot to death."

"Why would they name a car for that?"

I couldn't think of an answer. "The engine's in the back, for better handling."

Dwayne laid his small hand on the passenger window and peered inside. "Our engine's up front. My dad doesn't let anyone touch it but him."

We stepped into the road to cross under the massive oak. From the middle of the street it seemed to teeter over us at a crazy angle, its leaves flashing in the breeze like warning flags.

"This tree's going to fall someday," I said.

"It won't."

"Imagine if it fell on your car. That branch would smash your windshield and spear you like a fish."

Dwayne shuddered. "I always sit in the back."

He led me down the alley to his back gate because his mother didn't like boys charging through the front with their dirty feet. I stopped at the fence and flipped the gate latch several times. The sneaky dark part of myself that often roused in Dwayne's presence was fully awake.

"I had a dream about your house," I said. "I was walking by at twilight and heard a voice and saw a face crying up there." I pointed at random at one of the windows.

"That's my window!"

"The voice said, 'I've lost my son, no bigger than my thumb. He was carried away, on his own birthday!' A crow flapped overhead, with something in its beak. I fired at it with my slingshot."

"You sure it was my house?" Dwayne said.

"Of course I'm sure, dummy. The bird screeched, and a tiny boy fell from its beak. I held out my hand to catch him, but as he fell he grew bigger and bigger. When he reached the ground he was so huge, his giant arm nearly crushed me. He tossed me over this fence, and roared, 'This is your last goodnight!'"

"Jeez! What did you do?"

"I woke up."

"Who was at the window?"

"I don't know."

Dwayne studied my face with his hand shading his eyes, clutching his skinny torso with the other arm. The laundry reel creaked in the yard next door, as the old lady there yanked her clothes off the line.

"The part about the voice was a rhyme," he said, "like from a book."

I shrugged, as if to say it wasn't my business to know how things got into my dreams. "Don't make me sorry I told you."

We went in the back door and were intercepted by Dwayne's mother, who was thin and straw-haired like him. She said she was too busy cleaning and cooking to have us running around upstairs, and sent us down to the rumpus room.

The low, panelled room was crowded with furniture, like Lily's house. At one end was a homemade bar, rougher and simpler than Dean's tiki bar. It faced a wall of timber shelves loaded with bric-a-brac.

We played ping pong on his dad's homemade table till the ball shot under the heavy sofa, and then I went to the shelved wall to look at the loot. Dwayne fell in behind as I made my inspection of curling trophies, green glass insulators and souvenirs from trips to the Rockies. I stopped at a stuffed fox, its teeth bared to the gums, its glass eyes rimmed with dust.

"My grandpa shot that," Dwayne said.

"My grandpa shot a moose," I said. "My grandma's got the head stuck on her wall."

"Crumbs!" Dwayne said. "Where do they live?"

"She lives in Chokecherry Bush. He's dead. He was racing some other cowboys, and his horse threw him. He broke his neck."

Dwayne's mouth gaped. "Was it a wild horse?"

"Pretty wild, but he tamed it. I think a snake must have scared it."

Dwayne scanned the wall for something to hold up to a snake spooking the wild horse of a moose-hunting cowboy. Nothing in that clutter could top the dusty fox. Finally he took me over to the bar and showed me a plastic figurine of a black girl with huge pink lips and a grass bikini. He squeezed a rubber bulb near her feet, and both halves of the bikini shot straight out in front. He giggled and poked his finger at the crescent where her bare plastic thighs came together.

"Did you ever touch a real girl that way?" I said. He screamed with laughter, and bumped into me with his shoulder, and as his hair grazed my nose I caught a faint smell, like sour milk. He really was much younger than me, in ways our actual ages didn't register. He had swallowed my fibs about my racing cowboy grandfather, and the dream of the giant boy, but he would never believe the truth about Ginette. His laughter irritated me.

"Who made this?" I said, pointing at the first thing I saw, a criss-crossed Ukrainian Easter egg standing alone on a shelf over the bar.

"My grandma, before she went to Heaven," he said, his laughter faltering at this solemn recollection.

I grabbed a teak-handled bar accessory that had a ring of coiled wire at the end. "What's this, a toilet brush?" But that only made him laugh more.

"I dare you to lick it," I said, so fiercely that he stopped laughing, and refused. I tossed the implement on the bar. "If someone gives you a dare, and you don't accept it, you have to pay a fine."

"I never heard of that," he said.

"It's true. Here's your fine. It's nothing bad. Stand on this chair." He climbed up on an armchair covered in brown, knobbly fabric.

"Close your eyes," I said, and he did so, as obediently as if I were preparing a nice surprise. I took the painted Easter egg from its varnished wooden cup.

"Open your mouth." Dwayne's lashes trembled, and then he stared wide-eyed at the egg.

"Jasper, if you break it, I'm grounded for life," he moaned.

"Nothing's going to happen," I said mildly, and then grabbed him between the jaws in the painful way Corinne did when she was giving me medicine, and poked the egg between his lips, little end first.

Dwayne froze on the chair, as if he were perched on the edge of a tall building. His face shone with fear. I felt a twinge of pity; but the sneaky, vengeful self in charge of this game had one more move to make.

"Now jump off the chair," I said.

Dwayne's eyes creased shut. His hands curled in front of his face. The ceiling creaked right overhead; his mother was moving around in the kitchen.

"Okay, dummy, I was just kidding." I held his arm, and gently took the egg from his mouth. "Nothing happened. I'll wash the slobber off your precious egg, and put it back. Anyway, that wasn't your fine."

"It wasn't?" Dwayne said in a shocked little voice.

I took out my jackknife. "This is the fine. It's for you to keep."

Dwayne turned the knife over in one sticky hand, and with the back of the other wiped the tears from his face. Just then his mother called down the stairs: "Dwayne, come up for lunch."

Dwayne got down from the chair and slid the knife in his pocket. He looked at me with a mixture of fear, disbelief, and gratitude.

"Mom," he called. "Can Jasper eat with us?"

CHAPTER 34

IT WAS ONE OF MY days for the Sahara, and Nick had again invited
us for a little picnic. Corinne was finishing her makeup when Jackie
arrived at our door in a black sleeveless top and grey slacks. She
looked leaner, and her eyes seemed larger, which I put down to some
trick with her eyeshadow.

"I thought I'd see what you two have made of this place,"
she said.

"Not much," I said.

She came into the living room and surveyed our thrift-store
drapes and cottage sofa, and the battered walnut TV console that
stood near the wall on its three good legs and an upended brick. I
switched on our one channel and sat on the sofa, as if playing a part
in a TV commercial about how cozy this desolate room could be.
A man was reading a report about wildfires burning in the forests
near High Level. The name of the town and the northern loca-
tion made me think of the little plane, flying on a day like this one
perhaps, losing its bearings in a blanket of smoke, crashing through
the flaming trees. Perhaps the body lay near High Level, waiting for
a firefighter to tramp through the underbrush.

I glanced up to see if Jackie was taking an interest in these familial flames, but she wasn't watching, or looking around much. She felt my gaze and turned towards me.

"Still a bit sparse," she said with a faint smile. "Show me your room."

I darted ahead of her, pulled the crumpled sheet over the bed, and kicked my clothes a bit closer to the suitcase. Jackie came in and examined the squalor of my little life.

"Did you draw this?" she said, pointing at my large lion on the wall by the door. I had gone over it again in pencil and though it was still only a faint outline, the sun creeping over it made the graphite shine.

"It's a lion rampant," I said.

"I see."

I sensed she didn't, really, and wanted to tell her about the kings of Scotland, but that wouldn't begin to explain it. Besides, I was worried she might start talking to me in a secret way, as she had at the track. I moved towards the door as Corinne emerged from the bathroom, waggling her heel into a plain white flat. Her makeup was more subdued than usual, and she had not changed out of the pale green wrap dress she mostly wore only at home.

"You need some pictures in this place," Jackie said to her. "And house plants."

"I'd only kill them. Are you picnicking with us?"

"I made potato salad."

"Oh. Damn. In that case, I'll leave mine." The white glass bowl was on the kitchen table, where she had left it to cool an hour before.

"Which do you make, German or Canadian?" Jackie said.

"I don't know. I put in boiled eggs and onion."

"Mine has bacon and dill pickle. It's different enough. Bring it."

"Okay," Corinne said. She picked up the white bowl as if everything was sorted out, but I could tell that if there were ever a time for potato salad to go into the Drawer of Shame, this was it. "You're looking very chic," she said to Jackie, in the bright, stiff tone that sometimes came into her voice at awkward moments.

We went downstairs in a silence that was somehow not displaced by the reedy jazz spilling out of Nick's apartment. He was putting out his usual array of cocktail wieners and other treats from jars and cans. Jackie went straight to the hi-fi. "This stuff gives me headaches," she said, and put on something quieter.

Jackie explained the potato salads to Nick, and served out equal portions for the two of them. Corinne did the same for us.

"Like a tasting party for spuds," Nick said, getting some of Corinne's salad on his fork. "Boiled egg. That's a nice change. I think I'll mix the two together. Okay, Doll? You know I still love yours." Neither Jackie nor Corinne looked completely at ease with this outcome.

"I should have brought a bottle," Corinne said. For once, there was none on the table.

"No need!" Nick jumped up, pulled something from the rattling fridge, and returned with a bottle and three glasses.

"Champagne!" Corinne said.

"My brother Angelo imported a case."

Jackie stared at him in disbelief. "I thought we were saving it for a special occasion."

"So, special is now. It's summer, we're all together, and I've got you gorgeous creatures looking after me."

"I'm not looking after you," Corinne said.

"Okay, no need for a fine-tooth comb. The point is we can all be happy." Nick loosened the wire cage, and wrestled out the cork. "Doll, will you pour?"

"I don't feel like it."

"I'll do it," Corinne said, and tipped a little into each glass. The foam coursed up to the rims with a faint crackling sound.

"A toast to all of us," Nick said. "You too, Jasper."

"Wait," Corinne said. She got me a glass, and tumbled two inches of champagne into it. I held up its strangely heavy mass by the slender stem, and we chimed the rims together, like bells brushing against each other. I grimaced as the bubbles pricked at my nose.

"You don't like it?" Corinne said. I was about to answer, but she was talking to Jackie.

"No, I love champagne," Jackie said. She looked absent, and definitely unhappy, and I realized she had been carrying the same unhappiness with her when she came to see our apartment.

"All right, I've got a toast," Corinne said. "To Jackie. For taking us in, being a true friend, and putting up with Nick."

"That's more like it," said Nick. We chimed glasses again. Jackie's lashes glistened with tears.

"This would make a great stirrup cup," Nick said. "I mean for real, before riding."

"Since you mention it, I can't go this week," Corinne said. "Too busy."

Nick's grin faded. "That's too bad. But I guess I can wait a week."

"I might want to look for another stable. Someplace cheaper."

"You get what you pay for."

"That's it too. The grooms there aren't the best."

"They seem plenty good enough." Nick's voice rose. "How the hell would they be better at a cheaper place?"

"Look, things would be simpler if we didn't go for a while."

"For a while? That's crazy! Are you backing out on me?" He gripped the edge of the table and leaned towards her.

"I think I've said what needs to be said."

Nick rolled his shoulders as he sometimes did while rehearsing his ride on our sofa. Then he raised his glass again.

"In that case, I have another toast. To Buttercup, that blessed old nag of mine. Happy trails."

We drank, all except for Jackie. She seemed no more pleased about the apparent end of Nick and Corinne riding than she did when Corinne had toasted her as a true friend.

We ate some more, and more champagne was poured, because Nick insisted there was no point saving any, till drinking or not drinking enough became his whole focus. He ended up finishing the bottle himself, with both women watching him in silence from behind their half-full glasses.

"That's it," he said bitterly, after his last gulp. "I'm happy anyway. You can't force people to have a good time. Jasper, are you ready?"

He put his hand on my shoulder as we left the Bel Air and crossed the street to the Sahara. His legs swayed a little as he climbed the curb, still wearing his slippers, as I only then noticed. I steered him through the theatre's empty foyer and down the aisle as the film was starting.

It was called *Voyage to the Bottom of the Sea*, but it was really about a raging fire in the upper atmosphere. Red flames streamed across the sky as a nuclear submarine emerged from the grey Arctic waters.

"They're pulling a man off the ice," I whispered. "He's got burn marks on him. The ice is steaming."

The sub captain said the flames were in the Van Allen belts of radiation, three hundred miles above the Earth. He wanted to use an atomic missile to blow the burning radiation into outer space, but couldn't convince the world's top brains. He went back to his sub and ordered a crash dive.

"The military cops are running on deck," I whispered. "The sub's diving, the cops are in the water ..." But Nick had fallen asleep. There was no need to describe anything more, and besides, the film bored me. The only good thing about it was the sky burning out of control, like wildfires near High Level. Maybe there was a bomb for them too.

Nick woke up during the final scene.

"They're fighting in the sub," I whispered. "The captain's firing the missile. The sub's coming up, they're all climbing on deck. The sky's clear again."

"What crap," Nick said as the credits rolled. "I should have stayed home." He hauled himself from his seat, his shirttail half out.

"Can I have a dime for later? There wasn't time to get a treat."

"A treat?" he scoffed. "You had champagne. That's plenty enough treat for you, Buddy Boy."

When we reached his apartment, he opened the door and said, "Doll, you still here?", and went several steps into the darkness, and called again, with no response. Then he came back and without another word, shut the door in my face, as if he had forgotten I was ever there. I went home and put the fat, flared champagne cork in the Drawer of Shame.

CHAPTER 35

CORINNE SQUEEZED A TINY BEAD of glue onto the rim of the false eyelashes, then spread the bead into a glistening line.

"Seen your little friends lately? Marsha and Doreen?"

"Noreen. No." Saying a name associated with Marsha intensified the ache of not having seen her since the planetarium, a whole week before.

Corinne pressed the lashes into place along her eyelid. She clamped them lightly with an eyelash curler, and gave the mirror a lopsided blink.

"You should go out and do something. You mope around here too much."

"I mope around just as much as I want." It was nearly noon, and I was still in my pyjamas.

She took the second row of lashes from the tiny cardboard box, then met my eye in the glass. "If you're going to pay court, you've got to keep your pecker up."

"I don't need your advice!" I stalked off to my room and threw myself on the bed. I lay there till the queasy feeling in my gut clarified into anger, then I put on the previous day's clothes and stole a dollar from Corinne's purse, which she had left on the sofa as usual. I went out determined to blow her dollar on the first thing I liked.

But when I got outside, the angry energy went out of my stride. For days I had been unable to go out without being drawn straight to the library, where Marsha never was. I resolved not to go this time, but did anyway, fitfully, hurrying when I felt she must be there, slowing down when I was sure she was not. I was glad to hold the library door for two old ladies, whose creeping progress over the threshold delayed the moment of truth.

Marsha was at the desk, stamping returned books. I skipped past the old ladies and stood in front of her, my body vibrating like a tuning fork.

"Where have you been?" I said.

She pressed the date stamp into the ink pad. Her hair, loose as I hadn't seen before, hung around her face like silken black curtains, pinned above each temple with a barrette.

"We went to the lake," she said, her eyes flicking up. She stamped the card, closed the cover, reached for another book. Nothing in her voice or on her face showed that she had measured the endless week as I had. Our reunion, which felt almost like a miracle to me, had broken her rhythm for only a second.

"You must have seen lots of stars," I mumbled, recalling what Corinne had said about dark skies in the country. At this remark, Marsha's bored demeanour changed into a look of cartoonish glee.

"I got my new telescope!" she said. Her hands fluttered together like birds.

"Was it your birthday?"

"No. I wore them down." She gave me the smile I had seen at the planetarium, and a weight lifted from my heart.

"Do you want to get a sandwich? I have money today."

"Not yet." She reached for another book. "Do something for a few minutes while I finish."

I pulled a book from the astronomy shelf and went to my usual table. Whatever happened now, my days of emptiness were over. I stared at a page about the solar wind, and thought of galleons whipping past the moon, and listened to the soft, regular thump of Marsha's stamp. Gradually other words leaked through from the page, and I read that solar wind was a stream of charged particles, some of which got trapped in the Van Allen belts. I was startled to find this reference to the radiation that had inflamed the sky on the screen of the Sahara only a few days before.

"I can go now." Marsha stood by my elbow.

I jumped up and walked with her to the entrance, and the miracle of our reunion bloomed all over again. We stepped outside into the glaring heat.

"I was reading about solar wind," I said.

Marsha tapped my arm as if I had made a mistake. "You know, the man who discovered that could hardly get it published."

"Why not?"

"Everyone else wanted to be right."

"Couldn't they just agree with him?"

"They did, but only when they couldn't help it. That's how science works. My dad wrote a paper they rejected. But someday they'll admit he's right."

"What about?"

"A star no one else studies. He thinks it's a non-trivial exception to some model of stellar motion."

These strange adult words passed between us like whisky from her father's liquor cabinet. We walked through the parking lot towards the Woodward's end of the shoppers park. The breeze pressed Marsha's light skirt into her thighs.

"That lady at the planetarium tried to get him in trouble," she said. "He has to go see the board."

"She was so stupid."

"She's been there before. She likes to stir things up. There's Noreen."

Noreen and two boys lounged in the shade by the windowless wall of the shoppers park. The boys slumped against the brick as if their lean torsos were too heavy to hold upright.

"Here come the smart people," Noreen said.

"Jasper's buying me a sandwich."

"Good. Maybe he'll get me one too."

"Hey, Marsha, you babysitting?" one of the boys called out.

"Some people are ignorant," she announced.

Noreen abandoned the boys and followed us into the shoppers park.

The glass case at the lunch counter was filled with tall cakes iced solidly in pink, green and white. A tough-looking woman in a hairnet and pale green uniform waited for instructions. I ordered our sandwiches, awkwardly, saying the words like a foreign phrase I had memorized in advance.

"Have you noticed," Noreen said, "how you can say almost anything in front of Jasper and he doesn't look embarrassed, but when he buys a sandwich, he blushes all over?"

"You're not helping," Marsha said.

"Have you ever modelled with your mom, Jasper?"

"A few times."

"Do you ever help her get dressed?"

I shrugged. "I zip up the back and things."

"The back *and things*." Noreen shivered with delight. "Does she have lots of dresses?"

"Stop pestering him," Marsha said. "Let's go eat."

We went to the bench by the shoe store and unwrapped our perfectly square egg salad sandwiches. Marsha's loose hair spilled onto my shoulder, her arm brushed against mine. I bit into my soft sandwich in a state of anxious bliss.

The boys from outside came down the shoppers park, and arranged themselves in front of the girls like emissaries from a foreign power. "Who's this, your new boyfriend?" one of them said to Noreen.

"Yes, Jerry, Jasper's my new beau." I flinched as she draped her arm over my shoulder.

"Jasper, the friendly ghost," said Jerry, stepping closer. "Maybe he'll disappear."

"Bug out, and quit crowding," said Marsha.

He moved aside with an air of mocking deference, and restored our view of the shoe store's window poster for half-price sandals.

"So, will you come?" Jerry said to Noreen. "It'll be fun."

"Like the fun we have talking about how bored we are."

A frown flashed across his face. "That's your big subject, not mine. What about you, Marsha? My house on Friday?"

"Her dad will never let her," Noreen said. "Maybe I'll bring Jasper."

"It's past his bedtime." Jerry sneered in my face. He had moved in front of me, so I swung my foot out and kicked his shin, with as little thought as if a doctor had thumped my knee with a rubber hammer. It wasn't a hard kick, but it went through him like an electric shock.

"You little twerp," he said, with a disbelieving glare. "This twerp *kicked* me." His adolescent baritone jumped up comically high. Everyone laughed. He made as if to hit me, but swatted instead at the mark my dusty shoe had left on his light pants.

"Who's going to be there?" Marsha said.

"Everybody."

The girls went on not knowing for several more minutes, and Jerry kept coaxing while his second stood by in silence. Finally Marsha balled up the wax paper from her sandwich and said she had to go back to work. Noreen and the boys went off down the shoppers park. Marsha said nothing more about Jerry's party as I walked her back to the library, but the subject lay in my gut like an incubating illness.

"Are you coming in?" she said at the door.

"I have to go somewhere," I said, with what I hoped would be a mutually punishing show of self-denial. She studied my face, as if trying to measure the mood behind this lie.

"The moon's nearly full tonight," she said. "Come to my house and you can see my telescope."

"Sure!"

"I've got to show it to somebody."

That impersonal remark dampened the thrill of being invited. It made me feel almost as bad as I had that morning when I wondered whether I would see her at all. A dull shock reverberated through me as I realized how far I had climbed since our first meeting, how much further there was now to fall, and how calmly she remained at sea level.

"I have to check with my mom," I said.

She shrugged at this formality and told me the address. I repeated it to myself all the way back to the Bel Air. By the time I reached my room it had become an incantation that made my whole body resonate. I lay on the carpet and wrote it over and over, entwined with her name, till the overlapping scrawl was too thick to read.

*

I TOLD CORINNE I COULD walk to the Suans' house, but she insisted on driving me.

"It's late," she said, as she ran a soft makeup brush over her cheek. "I want to see where you'll be."

It was nearly ten when we left. The pavement was still warm under my runners as we walked to the car. Across the street, shadows crept over the bungalow lawns as interior lights glowed orange beneath the greying sky.

We drove to the Suans' street, which was lined with bigger bungalows and wider driveways, then crept along the curb, trying to read the house numbers. A man watering dusky flowerbeds with a garden hose flicked the stream at the Corvair, sending a few drops through my open window. Corinne stepped on the brake. Dr. Suan came towards us across the wet grass, still showering his flowers.

"Don't you dare spray me," Corinne said as she got out. The street was still except for the pattering of water dripping on leaves.

"I wanted to get your attention," he said, releasing the trigger on his hose. "You looked like you were going right past. Marsha's waiting for you, Jasper." He gestured up the driveway.

I walked past the dripping shrubbery and the silver Rambler. A square of yellow light from a rear window of the house shone down on a white barrel telescope standing on its tripod on the patio. It looked like a toy cannon about to fire tennis balls over the back fence. Dr. Suan's laughter came to me from the street. His and Corinne's murky shapes were barely visible against the fading white of the Corvair.

The back screen door swung open. Marsha walked out with a quick, elastic step, then veered around me and peered into the dusk at the bottom of the driveway.

"Why is your mom waiting?" she said.

"We nearly drove past," I said, but she shushed me with her hand, so abruptly that I half-swallowed the last word. She stood still and alert, her perfume mingling with something green and bitter from the flowerbeds. Dr. Suan laughed again and a car door slammed. The engine roared up and the Corvair slid away from behind the doctor's dark trousers.

Marsha broke off her surveillance and told me to come inside for a minute. She led me up a short flight into the kitchen, where her trailing scent disappeared into a heavy aroma of boiled rice, fried meat and earthier smells I couldn't identify. A pudgy short woman stood by the sink.

"You eat cake?" she said.

"Jasper, this is my mother."

Mrs. Suan advanced towards the kitchen table, and with a purposeful frown cut two slices from a large white layer cake studded with tiny silver beads. She seemed much more Chinese than Dr. Suan.

"We're going downstairs for a minute," Marsha said.

Mrs. Suan put the slices on two plastic plates. "You go, let him stay."

"Never mind!" Marsha grabbed the plates and rushed outside. I followed and stood with her in the shadows.

"I was only going to show you my room," she said in an irritated whisper. "She'll probably watch us from the window. She didn't want you to come."

I glanced up at the kitchen. The light went out. The whole back of the house was now dark. I scanned the dead grey windows, wondering which one Mrs. Suan might choose to spy on us. Marsha pressed the plate into my hand and we sat on patio chairs and ate vanilla cake as she explained the features of her telescope. Her annoyance with her mother melted into something like love for her fabulous new toy.

"Let's look at the moon first," she said. "It's still too light for other things."

She peered through the eyepiece until she had centred the nearly full moon and found the focus. Then she stepped aside for me to look, her fingers still gripping the eyepiece, as if the moon might float away in the time it took me to bend over. My cheek grazed her skin as I looked at an image much smaller than the extreme close-up I had expected. Its grey blotches and pocked craters were less distinct than in photos I had seen in the library.

"Isn't it wonderful?" she said.

"Yes." Her belly was right at my elbow; I could feel her breathing. The moon swam before my eye.

"Don't jiggle it," she said. I turned my head slightly and settled my cheek against her hand, which still held the eyepiece. The shivering moon stood still.

"What would happen if you tried to talk on the moon?" I said, fighting down the giddiness of feeling her skin on my face.

"Nobody'd hear you. There's no atmosphere."

"They could read your lips."

"You'd be too busy suffocating."

We looked at Scorpius and Hercules and the Northern Cross. They seemed scattered and puny, and remote from the names and stories attached to them. Marsha stood close to me the whole time, as if huddling together were the only way to make the sky fit into that small circle of glass. She showed me more distant things, tiny flecks of light I could barely distinguish, like grains of dust that might scatter if we breathed. Her bodice brushed my bare arm, her warmth radiated through the scant air between us. Mosquitoes sang softly around my ears.

"My father's going to Mount Palomar, in California," she said, in a reverent voice. "It's the biggest observatory in the world. He might take me." Through some spontaneous emotional calculus, I reckoned the distance to this marvellous lookout: infinitely far if I couldn't go, right next door if I could.

We returned to the moon, which had sunk lower in the sky. After the granular mysteries of the deep void, it seemed huge and impossibly bright.

"They're going to fly there soon," she said. "The president said so."

"What president?"

"*The* president. They'll have to invent new rockets. By then, women may be astronauts."

"Won't they all suffocate?"

Before she could answer, something grated on the patio stones. I looked up from the eyepiece, and the backyard world returned, full of sleeping inanimate shapes. The end of a cigarette glowed and curved down from the smoker's face.

"You must be getting bitten," said Dr. Suan.

"I'm going to the moon," Marsha said. "We just decided."

"Can you sit still that long?" He put his heavy, warm hand on my shoulder, and a rich whisky aroma reached me. "In any case, Jasper's got to go home first."

"Not yet," she said.

"It's past eleven. Say goodnight, Jasper. I'll drive you."

"Goodnight." The prompted word sounded awkwardly formal. I groped at Marsha's dark shape and caught her wrist. Our palms slid over each other, our fingers clasped lightly for a moment, then she darted forward and gave my cheek a kiss, half a kiss. It was over before I knew it was coming. Her hand left mine and she bumped the table in her retreat. The outdoor light flashed on, and I caught a half-blinded glimpse of her head showered in light, and of Mrs. Suan catching her arm to pull her inside.

We got into the silver Rambler and Dr. Suan backed it down the drive, his cheeks glowing green in the light from the dashboard. He steamed along the road much quicker than Corinne had done.

"Did you have a nice time?" he said.

"Yes."

"The last time we had a boy in our yard, I think I put out the wading pool."

"I'm older than that."

"That's not what I meant."

The dark zigzag profile of the Bel Air buildings came into view. I thought he would drop me off, but he got out, and we walked a purposeful diagonal across the grass to the door of our block. The usual smells of the place assailed my nose in a new way as I led him up to our floor, hoping at every moment he would decide he had gone far enough. He rapped at our door, and a minute later it opened, just wide enough to reveal Corinne's face, her hair still wet from her bath. She held her robe close at the neck.

"Special delivery," said Dr. Suan.

"I'll say. Did he behave?"

"The house is still standing."

"Get in, you. Say thanks to the doctor."

I spoke the word as ordered and slipped inside. I went straight through the darkened front room to my wing chair and turned slow, blissful circles, my toes tracing orbits on the carpet. I was entirely filled up with this golden evening. Marsha's touch and presence had somehow fused with the distant stars into a cosmic intimacy I could still feel on my skin. I touched my cheek where her hand had rested and buried my nose in my shirt sleeve, in case any of her scent had transferred itself to me.

I heard a muffled laugh. Dr. Suan was still chatting quietly from the hallway with Corinne. She leaned against the half-open door, her bathrobe still clenched around her throat.

It was always good to overhear what adults said in private, and it was more on general principle than out of real curiosity that I crept through the darkened living room and lurked as near as I could without being noticed. But as my body mimicked the alert stillness of Marsha's on her patio, I felt a flicker of the sharper interest she had shown in the chatter at the bottom of her drive, as I hadn't while standing right next to her.

After another minute, Dr. Suan left, without my having made out more than a few isolated words. The apartment door closed, and I retreated through the shadows to my room, still strumming with my thumb the tines of the plastic fork Mrs. Suan had given me with my cake.

CHAPTER 36

"JASPER ... JASPER."

Corinne's voice came from somewhere inside my sleep, as she patted my cheek with her warm palm. My tongue dragged against the dryness inside my open mouth. There was a dream still moving under my eyelids, but it slid away and I couldn't stop it. She shifted my bent arm back and forth a few times, like a bird's dormant wing. That was as close as she ever came to shaking me awake.

"Your friend Dwayne's here," she said.

"What time is it?"

"Seven."

"Why so early?" I had scarcely spoken when Dwayne threw himself on the bed across my legs. I sat up, like an open jackknife springing together.

"Are you out of your skull?" I shouted. Dwayne slid to the floor.

"They're cutting down the tree," he groaned. "They're taking it."

I was in my clothes and down the stairs almost before he could catch up with me. The road had been blocked off with sawhorses, in front of which a policeman mechanically waved cars up the side road. On the grass on our side, opposite Dwayne's house, a sparse crowd of boys and men stood staring into the big oak.

A squat, yellow vehicle twitched its long hydraulic arm among the upper reaches. Something up there snarled and chewed into the wood, shivering one section of the tree's broad canopy. A minute later a large bough dropped to the street with a festive shimmering of leaves. The chainsaw's angry whine dropped to a steady gurgle. A few boughs already lay on the road, though I couldn't see where they had come from. The tree looked almost the same without them.

Dwayne's father stood on his lawn talking to a city worker in dun overalls and a hard hat. They surveyed the spot where the mechanical arm jerked among the boughs, as if watching an unusual spectacle that had nothing to do with them. But as another bough fell, Dwayne's father's head drooped and he swayed from the waist with his arms crossed.

"It's our tree," Dwayne said miserably.

"The part where it's growing belongs to the city," I said, recalling a formerly useless tidbit fed to me by Dean.

"It's our yard."

"The city owns the first few feet," I said, with the narrow pleasure of someone reciting facts that are true but unreal.

"Five feet," said a man standing nearby.

"It's our tree and everybody knows it," Dwayne told him.

"Sure they do, sonny."

A few more boughs came down, and the tree began to show its losses. The onlooking men began to chat and make jokes among themselves. The novelty of what was happening in the tree had settled into the magnetic tedium of watching a man do a repetitive task. Their attention was briefly diverted by the arrival of Corinne, in capri pants and a half-sleeve top, with a kerchief around her head to cover her unbrushed hair.

"What a shame," she said. Dwayne turned to her with his mouth twisted into a soundless moan, his anguish renewed by her show of sympathy. She put her arm around me as if I, and not he, were the one suffering. I could understand that she who worshipped a tree with boards nailed into it at Chokecherry Bush would feel something about this event, but the feeling itself eluded me. The gnarled, colossal trunk of this tree was not climbable, and had no place to hang a swing. Immature acorns already littered the asphalt and would have been followed by a million leaves in the fall. What else could you do with this tree but cut it down?

The steel cage with the man and the chainsaw were now fully visible, jerking between the few remaining clumps of foliage. The men on our side of the street stopped their joking. We could all see and feel the end coming.

"What if they stopped cutting before the last one?" I said to Dwayne. "Wouldn't that be weird?"

"They should have stopped before the first."

"But it's almost all gone. Don't you kind of want the last one to come down?"

"No, are you crazy?" he said. I knew he was lying, and nearly said so, but he was in tears already.

The last bough tumbled softly onto the others, like something falling onto a coil-spring bed. The oak's grey arms stretched naked over the street, no longer a tree but a bare, writhing trunk covered with whitish sawn scars. It was a deformed living version of the blackened wooden poles holding up the phone wires.

"That's her done," someone said, and from the other men came a murmur of approval, of a job properly completed.

A large truck came through an opened gap in the sawhorses and more chainsaws coughed into life, and the men from the city cut the boughs into chunks they could drag and push into the truck's wide box. The air smelled of gas exhaust and fresh sawdust.

"We should get a branch," I said.

"What for?" Dwayne said.

"We could make a slingshot."

We both ran into the road. Dwayne kept going to the other side, but I stopped near a worker who was dragging a bough behind him like a tail. The leaves, still healthy and green, swished behind his heavy boots on the sunlit pavement.

"Are you going to chop down the trunk?" I said. I asked only because I wanted to see it happen, but when I spoke the words, they became Dwayne's, as if I were saying his lines in a film. For a moment, his feeling became mine and his sadness reached me, as it hadn't through what he had actually said or done.

"Nope. Somebody else will."

"When?"

"No idea. Might be a while. You can't play down here."

I snatched up a supple branch and carried it to the curb, upright, like a peacock's fan. I sat on the grass and gave my find little flicks to make the leaves rustle the way they would if the real wind were moving through a real tree. Footsteps slapped the asphalt and Dwayne bounded onto the grass beside me. The events of the morning had filled him with energy.

"My dad says I can't make a slingshot."

"Why not?"

"He says what would I use it for."

"What did you tell him?"

"To shoot birds."

"Dummy, no wonder." I examined the branch, and found a junction that was about right, though the arms curved a little and weren't the same thickness.

"Can you get a saw or something?" I said.

"No, he won't let me."

"What about later? He's got to go to work, doesn't he?"

"I can't."

"Just sneak it out for a minute. This will be the handle."

"Cut it with a knife." A drying tear trace was visible on his cheek. He made a sound with his lips like a chainsaw buzzing and gripped the branch where the handle would be. I yanked it away.

"They're not going to chop it down, you know. The guy told me."

"What will they do?"

"Leave it like that."

"That's stupid," he said. "But if they do, it'll grow back."

"No it won't."

"Yes it will. Even a stump will grow back." He seemed proud of this statement.

"Not if they tear out the roots."

"Why would they do that? They'd have to dig up half the street."

"Maybe they will."

"You're crazy." His face had a wild, mad, exhausted look, and his tears were coming back. "You're a liar," he shouted. I wanted to grab his arm hard, but his dad was probably watching to make sure no slingshots were made from the ruins of his tree.

"You're ugly," I said.

I ended up carrying the branch back to the apartment and into my room, unnoticed by Corinne. I put it in my closet, where it stood till all the leaves drooped, though to my surprise they didn't fall off. They hung on like withered green gloves. I told Dwayne I got a terrific slingshot out of that branch, but never agreed to show it to him, and didn't make it either.

CHAPTER 37

NICK'S DOOR WAS SLIGHTLY AJAR, as it often was on warm days. When I nudged it open, a man I hadn't seen before surveyed me from the sofa. He wore an expensive-looking silver-grey suit.

"What do you want?" he said, as if I were the stranger there.

"Is Nick here?"

"He's busy." Nick came from the bedroom with a sheaf of his punched calling papers, looking the way I felt when Dean demanded to see my homework.

"Jasper, this is my brother Angelo. Can you beat it for a few minutes?"

"Wait," said Angelo. He tossed me a quarter. "Watch my car, will you?"

"What do you mean, watch it?"

"See that nobody touches it."

"Which one is it?"

"It's in front. You'll know."

I went out and found a long, lemon-gold Cadillac, top-of-the-line. I walked the length of it, from the short, crisp tail fins to the wide grille up front, inspecting every flawless inch. It was so new, I could hardly believe someone had slid onto the leather seat and sped around town to our address from wherever it was that Cadillacs belonged.

I held Angelo's quarter as I would have held the key, and for a second it seemed absurd that the coin could not in fact open the door so that I could smell the upholstery, see my face in the rear-view mirror, and feel the worldwide span of the big steering wheel. That was all beyond my reach, though in another sense the car was a little bit mine. Angelo had given me custody.

Our street looked different with this wonder sitting on it, not better but shabbier. I considered what could happen to a car like this, parked in broad daylight on this now-shabby strip. Someone might try to steal it, of course, or scrape the paint with a knife, or a key. Or a coin. I backed up several paces and squatted on the grass. In an ideal world, it would be possible to score the Cadillac's paint with Angelo's quarter from one end to the other, and have this obscenely damaged car coexist in the same space as the pristine vehicle standing before me. The one would not cancel out the other. It was like those times when I imagined killing some animal I was playing with, and felt the killing and the playing going on at the same moment.

Dwayne's father drove up, home from work, and parked his Chevy on his driveway. He saw the Cadillac, and me squatting nearby. We had never spoken, but the few times we had seen each other convinced me that he counted me among the deadbeats of the Bel Air. He probably thought I planned some mischief on the Cadillac. I felt a flicker of anger and thought of standing up to shout that I was only doing my job, but he was already going in his front door.

Some older boys came along and inspected the car as I had, but in the opposite direction. At the tail fins, they noticed me staring hard at them. One of them asked if the car was mine. The others laughed.

"I'm watching it for a guy I know."

"You mean in case somebody steals it?"

"I guess."

They laughed again, and loitered around the car, and actually touched the paint. I jumped up and stood closer, and they laughed some more. Like Paul at Kesterman's Modern Miss, I was having to stick with people and things for insurance reasons. I was relieved when the boys sauntered away.

Five minutes later, Angelo came out and walked quickly to his car. He opened the door as if it were any ordinary car door, and at the last moment before he got in, gave me the faintest hint of a nod. As he sped smoothly away, I felt some vague sense of lost opportunity. I stood with his coin on my palm, wondering whether I should spend it right away or put it in the Drawer of Shame.

When I got back to Nick's apartment, he was slouched on his sofa, tying a narrow ladder-patterned tie. One of his upholstered chairs lay on its back.

"Did you have an accident?" I said.

"No," he said firmly. "Is Corinne coming?"

"She's out working," I said, following her instructions. In fact, she was in our apartment.

"Yeah, she's a busy gal," Nick said absently. He whipped the tail of his tie around and drew it down straight. "There may not be much in the fridge. Make me a sandwich with whatever there is, and pour me a rye on ice."

On the way to the kitchen, I found his saucer of stones smashed face down on the floor. The pieces lay like the petals of an exploded flower, with the stones scattered among them. Nick must have heard the china scraping as I picked them up, for he said: "Throw that away."

"The stones too?"

"No. Get another saucer."

I found an old one in a cupboard with a garland of painted flowers curling around its rim and made us sandwiches with processed cheese slices and margarine that was still a lard-white block in wax paper. That was strange: Jackie usually whipped in the orange colour, though I wondered why, since he couldn't see it.

At the sound of ice rattling into his glass, Nick rose and shuffled to the table.

"I hope you're enjoying life," he said, "because you've got it made right now, Sonny Boy. No money worries. No need for a job. Nobody thinking you should do something, or that you can't."

"Did Rodney Medwood get fired?"

"Ange would never do that. But he's a big one for proving things. You've got to prove something or other to get very far in his books." He bit into the soft sandwich. "No, if I were you, I'd think twice about growing up."

We finished our melancholy picnic. Nick put on one of his nicer jackets and we climbed the stairs. Outside, he tripped on a break in the pavement, and staggered a step. When he had righted himself, he flung his stone into the street, hitting the door of a passing Buick. The car braked hard, then moved off more slowly.

"Bastards," Nick said. He strode into traffic, holding his hand out at the first horn blast. I stayed on the curb until the way was clear, then ran across in time to reach the opposite side with him.

I got him into a seat in the Sahara and then went out for a chocolate bar. I came back down the ramp as the newsreel was running. A tank was rolling along a street, next to a boy riding his bike to school. A soldier was slathering mortar on a brick, like guys who worked for Dean. The announcer was saying something about a wall of hate.

"What's this?" I said to Nick.

"Politics."

The film was called Taste of Fear and it began in a place that looked like my idea of Jasper. There were snowy mountains in the distance, and a calm lake with a small boat floating on it, like Dean's rowboat at his cottage. Two men reached from the boat into the water, as if to pull up a fish they had hooked; but what they hauled into the boat was a drowned girl.

The scene shifted abruptly to an airport. "A man's picking the girl out of her wheelchair," I whispered. "They're driving away in a big car."

"I thought you said she drowned," Nick hissed.

"She did. Maybe this is another girl."

"Can't you tell?"

"No," I said, though they looked similar.

"Jesus!"

The girl rolled around a big house in her wheelchair, looking for her father, who everyone said had flown away on a trip. She kept telling them he was dead. Suddenly we saw a chalk-white body with bulging eyes, submerged in a disused swimming pool.

"What? What is it?" Nick could tell from the music, and from the way I flinched in my seat, that something terrible was on the screen.

"He's dead."

"Christ, we know that! What do you *see*?"

I wanted to tell him, but was too cowed by those frightening eyes. I kept my face covered for the rest of the film, glancing up only when people stopped talking.

"She's in the car. The driver's getting out. The car's rolling forward. It's headed for the cliff." The car and the girl went over the edge and crashed onto the rocks below. After that, there was a lot of talking and explanation I couldn't understand.

"What's wrong with you tonight?" Nick said savagely, as the lights went up. "You're lucky they blabbed so much."

Outside, thin high clouds streaked the deepening blue of the sky. A few cars wheeled through the concrete desert around the shoppers park.

"I'll walk you to your place," Nick said as we reached the Bel Air.

"No, it's okay." But he carried on up the stairs, bumping and groping more than usual, like a real blind man for once. At our door, he cinched up his tie.

Corinne was bent over Jackie's sewing machine, working on the dress she had abandoned for the planetarium.

"You're here," Nick said, with no trace of satisfaction, tł ᵤgh he had come only to see her.

"I'm battling my old foe, the replacement zipper," Corinne said. "How's Jackie?"

"In the pink. She jumped out of a cake the other day." A little animation came into his step as he paced out the distance to our cottage sofa. "Some accountant was retiring, so all the other accountants got stinking drunk. Jackie swiped a nice bottle. She said it was the least she could do for those poor slobs." He flopped onto the sofa.

"What about you? How's the window trade?"

"I'm fed up with windows. In fact, I've got a great idea for getting out of them. I could use a drink, by the way."

"Jasper, pour Nick a drink," Corinne said, while showing me that the drink should be small. I poured out his rye, and he told us his scheme for a new business. Someone would take orders for food over the phone and then send a catering truck to the customer's house.

"They park the truck, cook everything right there, and bring it to your door. Like a restaurant in your driveway. In fact, that's my slogan."

"Sounds good," Corinne said.

"Yeah, doesn't it. But Ange says it's outside our business. We're not in food, we have no expertise, it's too much outlay. But I'm boring you with this."

"Not at all." But he was boring her, and I could see it, and he could probably hear it. Corinne was always bored when Dean talked for more than a minute about one of his building projects.

"Jackie's going to be mad," Nick said.

"Maybe she could make him listen."

"Are you crazy? A guy like Ange? That would be the kiss of death."

"So try him again later," Corinne said, impatience creeping into her voice. "Get someone else in on it. Maybe he'll pay more attention if you have another partner."

"You don't understand." Nick waggled his fingers in his glass and licked them, like a baby. "Hey, did you find another stable?"

"Not yet."

"Let's try the old place again. Maybe those grooms have smartened up." He turned and faced her, as he hadn't yet done during their conversation.

Corinne pressed the pedal on Jackie's sewing machine, and the needle chattered over the fabric. From where I stood I could see she had gotten the whole long zipper to lie down and behave. She flipped the lever, pulled the dress from the machine and gave me a solemn wink, which somehow confirmed we were both waiting for Nick to leave.

He was still turned towards her on the sofa, holding out for an answer to his comment about the grooms. He waited till her silence filled the room, then said his farewells and left.

*

AT BEDTIME, I MADE CORINNE tell me a long story, and then asked her to leave the light on.

"You getting scared of the dark again?" she said with a smirk. I couldn't tell her about the body in the pool, but I convinced her to leave the door open enough for a wedge of light to keep the bulging eyes from reappearing in my room.

When I finally fell asleep, I dreamt I was in the girl's car, speeding along a mountain road. The tires squealed like gulls as the car flew around the corners till it smashed through a rail. The seat melted under me, and I sank through the bottom of the falling car with nothing but rocks and water below. I opened my mouth to scream, but all that came out was a half-chewed piece of chocolate, which tumbled with a trail of brown spittle onto an open library book. I awoke in the darkness and as I tried to remember where I was, figured I could maybe tear out that spoiled page without anyone noticing.

CHAPTER 38

I TOLD CORINNE I WAS going to church with the Suans.

"You must have it bad," she said.

She ironed my one white shirt while I ran to Nick's to get him to lend me a tie. After a quarter-hour of begging, he let me have a clip-on bow tie, red and flecked with tiny emerald dots. The sight of it at my throat drew me up taller, like a flower straining towards the sun. In that exalted state, I waited at the curb for the arrival of Dr. Suan's Rambler.

The car pulled up a few minutes later, and I got in the back next to Marsha. She looked out with dismay at the dandelion fluff drifting over the Bel Air's scrubby lawns.

"I didn't know you lived here," she said.

"Marsha, Mrs. Devon lives here too," said Dr. Suan.

"I thought you would wear other pants," Marsha said.

"Which ones?" I slid my palms over the spots of missing wale on my blue corduroys, which were stealing attention that should have gone to my tie.

"Never mind." Her hands, gloved in white cotton lace, lay crossed in the lap of her pink satin dress. Her Sunday scent tumbled over me like a slow avalanche of flowers. The car moved into traffic, and a gust of air brought a competing manly aroma from Dr. Suan's freshly shaved cheeks. Mrs. Suan appraised me with a jaundiced smile from the front passenger seat. She also wore pink, a few shades darker than Marsha's.

"We have a new young minister," said Dr. Suan. "He's shaking things up." The sun gleamed on the sleeve of his sky-blue suit. The Bel Air was still in sight behind us, and already I was dreading getting out of the car with this flawless family.

The United Church building was almost all roof, with a mile of shingles descending from a high peak. But inside, windows appeared in the sides of this rigid tent, and a wall of stained glass glimmered behind the shining altar. Everything glowed in an even, magical light.

Marsha edged into a pew, her skirt rustling over the oak. I sat next to her with my feet drawn under to avoid comments about the scuffs on my shoes. An organ sounded, and we sang from a book Marsha held up with one gloved hand. As my voice dodged around the unfamiliar tune, I felt a gloomy pleasure at the sight of a pea-sized tear in the lace near her thumb.

The new young minister droned into a microphone for a few minutes then called for children twelve and under to leave for Sunday school. I sat in quiet terror while the children left, in case anyone asked how old I was, and then the minister began a much longer speech about the patience of Sarah. I forced myself to sit as still as Marsha did, the better to hear her skirt slide over her slip at the slightest movement.

Two ushers walked soundlessly down the carpeted aisle, passing silver trays that piled up with white envelopes as they floated from hand to hand. The organ sounded again, we all stood, and Marsha sang near my ear about thrones and dominations, while the minister paraded down the aisle behind a glittering gold cross.

Afterwards we went to a new Dairy Queen and ordered chocolate sundaes. Everything was clean and light and proper, as in the church, with the Suans in their perfect clothes of pink and blue. The sundaes arrived in boat-shaped glass dishes, with a maraschino cherry perched on each one.

"What church you go to?" said Mrs. Suan.

"Baptist, I guess."

"It's all the same God. I think so."

"Same God, different voices," Dr. Suan said as he took a spoonful of his sundae. The notched silver cufflink on his snowy cuff somehow confirmed that the God we had visited that morning was not the same as the one who ruled over Lily's church.

"I was wondering," I said, preparing a question I had rehearsed in the car. "How can there be world without end if the sun burns out someday?"

"There are millions of worlds and solar systems besides ours," Dr. Suan said. "One disappears, others arise in its place. Your cherry's gone, but the sundae's still there."

"But doesn't it mean the cherry shouldn't end?"

"It must end, but that's not it," said Dr. Suan. "God doesn't end and neither do we."

"But why make a sun that burns out?"

"That's why we go to church, isn't it, Daddy?" Marsha said. "Because the sun burns out."

"Wonderful," said Dr. Suan, with an indulgent laugh. I smiled too, as if agreeing that this sideways riddle was a wonderful answer. I took a gulp of ice cream that seared my throat with cold all the way down. Mrs. Suan said a few Chinese words to Marsha, who showed no sign of hearing them, except that she daubed a paper napkin at a streak of chocolate sauce under her lip.

"It's our nature to be overwhelmed," Dr. Suan said. "In past times, people thought the heavens were an array of spheres moving around the Earth. The regular working of this system was proof of God's presence. Now we need a bigger story. And so we've been allowed to discover a universe more vast and wondrous than we ever imagined."

"I prefer the minister sermon," said Mrs. Suan, crinkling her nose.

The glass door flashed open. Jerry came in past us with two other boys, and took a table near the back. He said something, and they laughed and gawked in our direction. Marsha must have noticed too, but she gave no sign of it. Our table slipped into an awkward silence, so I asked Dr. Suan about the Van Allen belts, and whether they could catch fire, and if an H-bomb would blow the flames out.

"We don't know much about those belts yet," he said. "But I'm pretty sure they won't catch fire."

"Why not?"

"Because they haven't already." He smiled at the neatness of this answer. At the other table, the boys laughed at something Jerry was saying and goggled again at our table. I knew I hadn't kicked him nearly hard enough.

"Suppose the world is only one year old," said Dr. Suan. "Suppose mankind has been around for about an hour, and that Van Allen discovered those belts two seconds ago. They weren't burning when he found them. Something about those belts had prevented them from catching fire for the whole hour we've been looking at the sky."

"Daddy, you're confusing him," Marsha said.

"How am I confusing him?"

"Because the Earth isn't only one year old."

"Jasper, do you expect your hair to catch fire any time soon?" said Dr. Suan.

"No."

"Why not?"

Because there was no flame nearby, because I was no closer to the sun than he was, because nobody had a magnifying glass over me to make me smoulder like an ant on the sidewalk. I could have said any of those things, but what I did say was:

"Because the Earth isn't only one year old?"

Dr. Suan laughed. Marsha frowned and put her napkin over the remains of her sundae. "Can we go now?" she said.

The damp back of my shirt peeled away from the vinyl seat as we got up to leave. A metal chair leg scraped the floor near the back of the restaurant, and Jerry appeared before Marsha with a nervous, insolent look on his face.

"I'm not talking to you," she said to him and turned sharply away. Mrs. Suan gave him a withering glare. The Suans walked towards the exit, their faces flushed from the heat. I was near the door when Jerry thumped me in the back.

"Hey, not a ghost after all," he said.

"Watch yourself, young man," Dr. Suan called from beyond the door he was holding for me. "Come on, Jasper."

I walked with him out to the Rambler, feeling shamed but also victorious, because I was the one getting into the back seat with Marsha, and Jerry was seeing me do it. On the sweltering upholstery, Marsha was fanning herself with one limp glove. "I want the sun to burn out right now," she said.

"You asked about H-bombs," Dr. Suan said as if the Jerry unpleasantness hadn't happened. "This isn't my field, but we can definitely use those for peaceful purposes. With quite a small bomb, we can make a new harbour in Alaska. We can get oil from the northern tar sands. I've heard the Premier is actively considering this method."

He started the engine, and pulled out of the lot. A warm breeze moved through the car.

"How do you get oil out of the ground with a bomb?" Marsha said.

"The intense heat turns the sand to glass," he said. "The oil floats free. You just pump it out and refine it."

"Won't it be radiated?" I said.

"We can probably control the radiation. These are technical problems. When we work them out, we'll be able to move mountains in a few seconds."

Marsha sighed, though whether because of the bombs, or Jerry, or my bungled answer about the burning hair, I couldn't tell. Whatever the reason, our church expedition seemed a failure. But when we pulled up in front of the Bel Air, she squeezed my hand tightly in hers, still in the remaining glove, without looking at me. I felt the pattern of the lace pressing into my skin.

I looked for its imprint after they drove away, but there was nothing there.

CHAPTER 39

DWAYNE RAN UP TO ME on the Bel Air lawn.

"There was something in the paper about Monza. My dad told me. They had a race. One of the cars spun out and killed everybody."

"The king too?"

"No. My dad says they don't have kings in Italy anymore." He seemed proud of this discovery.

"Why not?"

"They just don't."

"How could the car kill everybody?"

"The guy spun out. He crashed into the crowd. I saw the photograph."

We ran through the dry, stubbly grass and across the street. Dwayne stumbled as we reached the curb and scraped his knee, and stood there a second pressing down on the whitened spot where the blood oozed out in one glowing blob.

"Come on!" I said.

He winced and hobbled after me, and we went in the front door as we never did. The air in the front room was stuffy and sweet from the heat slanting through the closed windows and the flowery scent of air freshener.

"My mom's at the store."

"Where's the paper?"

"I don't know. My dad threw it out, maybe."

"You didn't save it?"

Dwayne looked stunned, then lit off for the kitchen. The canister under the sink was empty. We dashed out the back, as if a garbage truck might arrive at any moment and snatch the contents of the can before we could get to where it stood beyond the fence. I yanked off the lid, and we pawed through a few stinky days in the life of Dwayne's household, pulling at pieces of newsprint stuck to scraps of food.

We gradually got the whole paper out of there and spread the crumpled pages over the sloping ground between fence and alley. The story of the crash at Monza filled the upper half of a page. A line of oil spots ran across the photo of a crowd of people standing behind a fence at the top of a short incline. The remains of a car lay on the track below, like a trampled bug.

I read out the story in the pungent air beside the garbage can. Two cars had touched wheels and one zoomed up the incline, throwing the driver and spinning through the spectators. The driver and eleven others were killed.

"The race continued with shocked crowds pushed back and cars roaring around the track for two hours, past the bodies of the dead strewn over the grass and covered with newspapers," I read.

"Why didn't they stop?" Dwayne said.

"I don't know."

We sat in silence, the cars racing through our minds, on and on, past bodies covered in newspaper. Two hours: I could tell an entire film to Nick in less time. I read out the sentence again, about the shocked crowds and cars roaring past the bodies of the dead, and it sank into my memory and stayed there, every word.

The blood on Dwayne's knee had dried into a rusty worm. The breeze plucked at the newspapers on the grass and sent one floating and tumbling down the alley.

"You said there were no kings, but the driver was a German count," I said.

"That's not a king, and he's German."

I tore the story from the page. A car drove past us down the alley. Its dusty plume caught the newspapers, and the pages began to shift. We jumped on them, and chased down the few that skimmed away. We spread them out again and ran up and down that bit of alley, taking turns veering up the scraggly incline and trampling the newspapers. We made race-car noises and ran over the pages till they were torn and scattered along the dusty asphalt. Then we gathered them up and clapped them into big noisy balls of newsprint that blackened our hands. We pushed them back into the steel garbage can and slammed the lid on them. On the bodies of the dead.

We were filled up with energy, but our game was done; so we wrestled on the close-clipped lawn of Dwayne's backyard. I fought a little too hard, as usual, and hurt Dwayne more than I meant to, and had to promise to buy him a Coke. We got up with the smell of crushed grass on our filthy hands.

That evening, over Kraft Dinner, I told Corinne about the crash. I said it happened in a Corvair Monza like ours. She paid no attention till I got to the part about the drivers racing on for two hours while the bodies lay on the grass.

"Who told you that?" she said.

"It was in the newspaper." I pulled the torn scrap from my pocket, and proudly spread it out.

"Take that dirty thing off the table," she said. It looked greasier than it had in the alley.

"Why didn't they stop the race?" I said.

"I don't know, doesn't it say in your paper? Don't put it back in your pocket, throw it out."

I folded it up smaller than before and held it under the table. "Give it," she said and took it from me, and went to where the garbage was. But instead of throwing it out, she put it in the Drawer of Shame.

Even though it was in the newspaper, I imagined that the story of the crash belonged to me because of Monza and the driver who was almost a king. I told Nick about it.

"Yeah, I heard on the radio," he said, indifferently.

"Did they say the race continued with shocked crowds pushed back, and cars roaring around the track for two hours, past the bodies of the dead strewn over the grass and covered with newspapers?" I recited.

"That's ugly," he said. "Where did you get that line?"

"It was in the paper."

"What are you, a parrot?"

We went to the Sahara. The first thing was a newsreel about the crash at Monza. They showed the count in his white racing suit, climbing into a low cigar-shaped thing that didn't look at all like our Corvair.

"*Von Trips was all smiles ...*" the announcer said in his brisk newsreel voice.

"He's in the car, it's moving," I whispered to Nick. "All the cars are going past."

"*... the odds-on favourite to take the Formula One crown ...*"

"The cars are far away, coming towards the camera," I said. "People are watching from the top of the slope, behind a fence." My heart started to pound.

"*On the second lap, disaster struck ...*"

"Two of the cars are leaving the track. One's veering up the slope. He's hitting the fence. The car is spinning, through the fence and the dust. Other cars are speeding past."

"*Von Trips died instantly.*"

"People are lying on the ground." I almost said they were sleeping.

They lay in the sun as if taking a nap, beside their straw hats.

"... *a tragic end for West Germany's bright hope* ..."

"They're picking something white off the grass," I whispered. "They're putting it on a stretcher and running it across the track. A hand is dangling down. It's his hand, dangling down!"

"Okay, okay, take it easy!" Nick said. "You don't have to tell me any more. Eat your candy bar."

Tears sprang into my eyes as I bit into my Sweet Marie. I couldn't really believe in the deaths of those on the grass, lying so casually among their straw hats, but I felt pain in my heart for the count, climbing into his little machine, racing off towards the horizon, being flung on the ground like a rag doll.

They showed the winner with his grinning, dirty face. "*When Hill learned what had happened, he burst into tears and was too shocked to speak.*" But on the screen, Hill kept smiling. He didn't yet know what I knew. The newsreel ended. There was nothing about cars roaring around the track for two hours past the bodies of the dead. There were no newspapers.

Before the crash, Dwayne had shown little interest in the murder of the king at Monza. But now Monza was in his personal geography, as near and remote as Athabasca or Slave Lake.

"How did they kill the king?" he said. I was teaching him to play checkers, on the carpet in his rumpus room.

"He was giving out medals to athletes. Somebody shot him."

"One of the athletes?"

"No, dummy, they were getting medals. You can't move that way. You have to go forward."

"You went backwards."

"That's because this one's a king."

"So who killed him?"

Dean hadn't given me many details, but I figured I could guess how it went.

"He rode to the games in a jewelled black carriage, with a lion rampant on each door. The six white horses had silver shoes and bridles trimmed with gold."

"Did they shoot him in the carriage?"

"Shut up and listen. The carriage drew up at the palace of athletes, and the trumpets played, and the king crossed the royal red carpet. He gave the athletes their medals, and touched their shoulders with his sword, and said, 'Arise.'"

"And then he got shot."

"No, he went back out on the red carpet and the crowd cheered. A man stepped up with a bouquet of flowers, and a gun hidden inside. He shot four times, and the king fell dead on the steps of city hall."

"You said it was the palace of athletes."

"Same thing."

"What happened to the guy?"

"They put stones in his pockets and drowned him in the river. You can't move that."

"Why not?"

"You have to move this one, because this one can jump. You've got to jump when you can, it's a rule."

Dwayne jumped, and as he carried off my piece, I saw that he could have jumped once more and taken my king. But he was so happy to jump at all, and new to the game as well, so I kept silent.

"You know, these pieces look like little cookies," he said, after I had beaten him. "Do you want a cookie?"

CHAPTER 40

ONE MORNING, WHEN MY RITUAL library visit came to nothing, I decided to go to Marsha's and call on her there. I walked towards her neighbourhood full of hopeful energy, as if my deciding to go to her house uninvited marked a new stage in our relationship.

I passed a house where an enormous black dog lay panting on the stoop. It came over to me, trailing strands of spittle from its huge, square jaws, and trotted along next to me, tail beating against my leg.

The dog was still with me when I reached Marsha's house, and it loped ahead as I turned up the drive. I heard a sharp cry, and something smashing, and rounded the back of the house to see Mrs. Suan cowering against the screen door, with the dog lapping at a puddle of milk around a broken bottle. The milk crept over the patio stone and soaked into Mrs. Suan's slipper.

"You're getting wet," I said.

She gaped at me, unable at first to say anything. "What is that?" she gasped.

"I think it's a Newfoundland."

She looked as terrified as before, as if she had never seen such an animal.

"It's only a dog," I said.

Her body sagged as if she were about to faint. She wrenched the door open but caught her foot on the threshold and tumbled heavily. The pneumatic screen swung against her trailing leg. The dog was sniffing her slipper when Dr. Suan appeared from inside in a white dress shirt and pyjama bottoms.

"Wait here," he said to me and got her up and inside. During the long time it took him to come back, I pushed the shards of milky glass into a pile with my running shoe. The dog lay on the drive, licking its jowls.

Dr. Suan returned with his trousers on, and heard my story while he put the shards of glass into a small orange crate.

"My wife thought it was a bear," he said so solemnly that my urge to laugh died in my throat. "They don't have this kind of dog in Hong Kong."

"Can I see Marsha?" I asked.

"No. You have to take this animal away. It followed you here, so when you leave, it will probably go with you." He flipped open the little spring-loaded milk delivery door, as if to make sure this ruckus hadn't impaired its functioning, and went back inside.

But the dog wouldn't follow me. It remained on the driveway as I walked partway down the block and back again, twice. The second time I returned, Marsha was standing on the asphalt in shorts and a madras shirt with a hairbrush in her hand.

"Why did you bring your dog to my house?"

"I didn't, and it's not mine. It just followed me."

"My mother said it came ahead of you. She didn't even see you at first. That's why she was so scared."

"She was so scared because she thought it was a bear." I started to laugh. But Marsha had no laughing to do about the dog that was not a bear. She told me her family had never owned a dog. This seemed to compound my crime. No matter what I said to dissociate myself from the dog, she wasn't satisfied.

"My mother's in bed. I may have to stay in all day. Everything's a mess."

"Can I come in for a while? Maybe the dog will go away by itself."

"Are you crazy? You can't come in now."

"When, then?"

She stared at me with a look of wild disbelief. I thought she might shout at me, tell me to go to hell and never come back. But instead she said: "I don't know. Some other time."

The dog was not mentioned again, but Mrs. Suan regarded me with sharp suspicion after that, as if I might produce strange animals at any moment. She held it against me, and Marsha did too.

*

A FEW DAYS LATER, SUNDAY, I took a different route to the Suans'. An extra car stood on the driveway, and another was parked in front. The inside front door stood open. As I pressed the doorbell, voices and the slap of flip-flops echoed down the driveway from the back-yard. Marsha appeared around the corner of the house with a tray of dirty dishes in her hands.

"I can't see you now," she said. "We've got company." Her skin glistened, her ponytail sagged behind her neck.

"What about later?"

"No." A burst of loud male laughter resounded between the houses. Dr. Suan came into view with a highball glass in his hand and a cigar end in his mouth. His face was bright red.

"Jasper!" he said, with a look of pained hilarity. "What are you doing here?"

"I'm just leaving."

"No, no." He sucked on the cigar and blew out a cloud of rank smoke. "You stay. Marsha needs company."

"He already said he's leaving!" Marsha shouted, and ran up the steps through the front door.

Dr. Suan clapped his hand on my shoulder and gently pushed

me towards the backyard. Two couples stood near the patio table where Mrs. Suan was mopping up a spilt pitcher of something. One chair was overturned, ice cubes glistened on the grass, and a large wet patch darkened the trousers of a man in a Hawaiian shirt. His wife dabbed it with a handkerchief as he tugged at the wet cloth.

Dr. Suan tossed his cigar end on the lawn. "This is Marsha's friend, Jasper."

"Look, Winston, we better push off," said the man in the Hawaiian shirt.

"Plenty of time. Take your pants off, I'll lend you a pair." Dr. Suan tugged at the man's belt.

"They wouldn't fit," he said, pulling away. "We really must go. Thank you, Jennie!" Mrs. Suan, still bent over the table, lowered her head a little more.

"Don't be a party pooper," said Dr. Suan, as Marsha emerged from the house.

"Daddy, will you stop!" she said. She gathered up more dishes, looking like she might cry. I felt a pang of sympathy, but also hoped she'd cry a little, because I hadn't seen that yet, and she might need comforting.

"I'm joking," said Dr. Suan. "Everybody sit down and relax." But the Hawaiian couple carried on around the corner of the house and away.

"We should go too," said the other man. "Thanks, it's been swell."

"We haven't talked yet," said Dr. Suan.

"We've been talking for three hours. We have a meeting on Tuesday. We'll talk then." He and his wife left the backyard with a light step.

"Marsha, bring Jasper a Coke," said Dr. Suan.

Marsha glared at me and marched into the house. Dr. Suan led me inside and up to the kitchen, where he yanked the bottle of Coke from Marsha's hand and passed it to me. She rushed down the back stairs to her room and slammed the door. Dr. Suan sat me down at the kitchen table.

"No need to hurry," he said as I swigged the bottle, desperate to get out of there. "We have all the time in the world." His glossy head sagged. He ran his hand over the Formica, slowly, like a child discovering it for the first time.

"Do you ever think about infinity, Jasper?"

"Not really."

"This kitchen is 120 feet square," he said. "Enough room for me and you and everything here. All contained, very limited."

He turned on his chair, pulled off his loafers, and stretched out his bare toes.

"But there's no limit to the minute events occurring in your body, right now. And if there's no limit" — he paused as a belch rumbled up — "that must be infinity."

Mrs. Suan carried in the last of the party things from the yard and ran a protesting blast of water into the kitchen sink.

"This is not comfortable," said Dr. Suan. "Come in the living room."

He shambled across the broadloom and sprawled on an orange armchair at one end of the teak living-room set. I sat on the sofa. On the Chinese lacquer coffee table, a shiny black rock the size of a date sat on top of a solid cube of maple.

"Your father was a pilot, right?" he said.

"No, he was in oil."

"But he..." He made a diving motion with his hand. "In a plane?"

"Yes."

"Too bad." A deep frown settled on his face. "You asked before, did I crash? Not me, but others I knew. Impossible! Your friends die, people you love. You wonder, Why didn't I die? You wonder ... What do I do now, with all this time?"

I drained the last of my Coke. "I think I should go."

"No, no, it's okay, I don't talk about those things!" he said, waving both hands as if to settle me in my seat. "My wife's from Hong Kong. Not like me, I'm from Medicine Hat." He grinned, and pitched forward, and braced his elbows on his knees to light a cigarette with a heavy glass lighter on the coffee table. He sat back again and pulled on the cigarette, and I noticed that a tear had run down his face, all the way to the jaw.

"You're looking at my little rock; you know what it is?" he said. "A meteorite. It's glassy from the friction of the atmosphere. Go ahead." He motioned to touch it, and I ran my fingers over its silky surface, more to please him than myself. "Everyone wants to touch," he said. "They talk about going to the moon, or Mars. All very scientific. I want to go too! Nobody admits that we also want to touch." He leaned forward and stroked the little stone. He was the opposite of Dean, who talked less as he drank more.

"You know the Pleiades?" he said. "The constellation?"

"I think I saw it with Marsha."

"No, you didn't." A look of something like disgust flickered over his face. "They come later, in the fall. The six daughters. The Chinese saw seven, but we see six. They were very advanced, the Chinese, great astronomers, scientists, everything ... But the Pleiades! In Korea, we had pictures of girls, pinups. You know what I mean?"

"Kind of."

"Kind of! But at night, in the field, we had nothing. Just a rifle, in the mud, waiting there all night. So I looked at the horizon, for the Pleiades. The beautiful daughters of Atlas. And behind them, Orion, back from the hunt. They're clean and gorgeous, he's filthy and hot. Of course he chases them. And does he catch them?"

"I don't know."

He shook his head slowly, as if beginning to see at last how stupid I really was. "Do they ever talk about Mother Nature at your school?"

"I guess."

"They think the Earth is a nice green mother, and up there nothing but rocks whirling around. But the cosmos gives birth all the time. Like a big dirty sow." He took a deep drag, and blew the smoke at the ceiling. "New worlds, new galaxies, no beginning, no end. The universe opens her skirt to let them out. We're only the dust from all that. The dust of stars, brought to life, to run around on our little rock."

His chin sank towards his chest, and the ash fell from his cigarette onto the carpet. I had heard the last part before, about the dust and the new worlds, but this time something came clear to me in a new way. He had touched a bell in my chest, and it started to vibrate, and I sat there absorbed in that feeling while his hand scratched his belly.

"Get me some water," he said without opening his eyes.

I went to the kitchen. Mrs. Suan stood by the counter, tense and immobile. She looked at me with contempt, filled a glass and took it into the living room. Dr. Suan was already snoring. She drew the cigarette from his fingers and tucked a silk cushion behind his head.

I made for the back door, and had my hand on the screen, when I heard a sound from the basement. Marsha gestured to me from the bottom of the stairs. I crept down and she pulled me into her room. We sat on the floor with our backs against the bed, opposite a wall covered with star charts and pictures of movie stars. Her short, bare feet were marked with dirty lines from her flip-flops.

"Why did you stay with him?" she said.

"What was I supposed to do?"

"Walk out."

"He was talking to me the whole time."

"He was talking because there was someone in front of him. He won't remember a thing tomorrow."

"So what's so bad?"

She let out a deep sigh, and for a moment her head leaned against mine.

"I hate when he gets like that," she said.

"Who were those people?"

"Junior faculty. They've seen it before." She looked at me uneasily. "Look, don't tell any of my friends. I'll be so mad if you do."

"I promise," I said, unsure whether it was good or bad that her friends were people other than me.

"Look, this came yesterday." She reached over to her bedside table and pulled a letter from a fat manila envelope. It said her letter had been received, and they looked forward to her visit to Mount Palomar, and would be happy to give her a tour.

"Isn't it exciting?" She leaned into me, and gave me a hug from that awkward side-by-side position, and the pall of the afternoon seemed to lift from her. My chest expanded under the press of her arms, with the vibration from the dust of creation still going on inside. After the trouble upstairs, things were turning out better than I could have hoped.

Heavy steps sounded overhead, not walking but staggering. A voice began to shout.

"Get out," Marsha said quickly. She sprang from the floor and shoved me from her room and up the stairs. I darted out of the house to the shrill sound of Mrs. Suan yelling at her husband in Chinese.

CHAPTER
41

CORINNE WALKED ME TO SCHOOL along a sidewalk covered in wet leaves to a long yellow building with a round red bell bolted onto the brick. I went inside and became the strange new boy, ordered to sit at the front of the class, to catch up with things I already knew, and be thoroughly inspected by everyone else. The large calendar on the wall, with a month of school days squared in green, confirmed that our life of wandering was definitely over, and with it any hope of returning to Winnipeg. I spent much of the day dreaming of a new kind of wandering that included Marsha, not as she and I actually were, but in some future state of ideal mutual understanding.

School emphasized the differences between me and everyone I knew. Dwayne was in a lower grade with little girls in pigtails whose skipping games filled the area behind the school with clouds of whirling ropes. Marsha was in another school up the road where all the girls wore lipstick and some boys had cars with engines that rumbled as they crawled along the curb.

Dwayne found me at recess and paraded me, his older friend, before his classmates, blind to the sneers of kids in my grade. He waited for me at the end of the day and tagged after me out the front door. Marsha and Noreen were passing along the sidewalk in their fall sweaters, binders clasped against their breasts.

"Who's your little friend?" Noreen said.

"Dwayne. He's actually my neighbour," I said, straining for a face-saving distinction.

"I remember going here," she said, surveying the children running around in front of the building. "It seems like such a long time ago. Are you really supposed to be here? Couldn't you skip a grade or something?"

"How could he do that?" Marsha said impatiently. I thought she looked at me strangely, but everything she did was so magnified in my eyes, I couldn't be sure.

"I don't know. You did."

"I skipped a grade, too," Dwayne said, unaware that this remark made everything worse.

We lingered together another minute, examining the glass wall that had come up between us, searching for any conversation that could withstand the presence of my damning little friend. The girls turned to leave. They were halfway along the block when I ran after them and caught Marsha by the arm.

"Are you mad at me?"

"Don't be stupid." She pulled her arm away.

I reached into my pocket and gave her a little star-shaped pendant I bought with money I found down the back of Nick's sofa. I figured she might hold Dr. Suan's patio party against me, and had decided to buy my way back into favour.

"What's this for?" she said, but not in a way that needed an answer. She flipped her ponytail up and fastened the chain behind her neck, then fingered the little star. A shy smile spread across her face. She showed it to Noreen, then hugged me at the shoulders, and the strangeness of the previous minutes melted away.

"There might be some meteors this week," she said. "Come and watch them with me." She touched the little star and clasped my hand. Everything was right again, so easily after all. And yet, as she and Noreen walked away without me, the feeling returned, that she had not really forgiven me for seeing her father drunk. I was stained by it, as I was by the episode of the dog.

"Who's the chink?" Dwayne said, as we started for home.

"She's not a chink."

"What is she then?"

"A girl I know."

"Even if you like her, she's still a chink."

"You better stop saying that." I made as if to hit him, and he flinched. The word "chink" had applied itself to Marsha several times in my mind, with a secret harshness I enjoyed, but it was equally pleasant to put it aside, and let her off.

"She's not a chink," I said. "But her mother is."

The school receded behind us, and so did the perspective it imposed. Dwayne was my friend again; we could talk as usual, and I began to look forward to whatever snack his mother might have ready for us.

We got within view of the mountain and saw a shopping cart abandoned on the grass. We both broke into a run.

"Let's do Wild Mouse!" Dwayne shouted.

"What's that?"

"It's a roller coaster at the exhibition. It twists and turns like crazy." He shook the cart and gave me the frenzied grin he used whenever he wanted to do something crazy. Then he sprang over the side, hunched down on his runners, and shook the cart some more. I grabbed the handle and ran the cart over the uneven ground, with hard turns every few steps. Dwayne flung his head from side to side and yelled over the cart's metallic rattling. I wrestled it around the mountain till my wrists ached too much to go on.

"Go, go!" Dwayne shouted, shaking the cart again. "It's not crazy yet!"

That sounded like a dare. We took off again, and the Wild Mouse became a crazed rat. I ran hard and veered harder. On the third turn, one of the forward wheels struck a hole. Dwayne lurched hard against the front of the cart, and the whole thing toppled over sideways with a crash. The handle's edge raked my ribs on the way down.

"Holy crumbs!" Dwayne wailed. He slid from the cart with his hand clamped to his face. Blood ran out between the fingers, and down the inside of his forearm. I had to pry the hand away to see his pulpy nose, and the jagged cut across his cheek. His white shirt was already spattered with blood, so I got it off him and pressed it to his face like a pillow. We jogged like that along the lane to his backyard. His mother saw us coming from the kitchen window and was already out the door by the time Dwayne rushed up, crying, and pressed his bloody, half-naked body into her arms.

She got the shirt away from his face and felt his nose with the tip of her finger. She asked what happened, and Dwayne blubbed out the story in a few muffled statements. It was damningly simple: I had run wild and crashed the cart.

Dwayne's mother had always liked me, or at least given me the benefit of every doubt. But now she showed me a much harder look than the vague smile she wore when I ate her cookies.

"Maybe you shouldn't always do what Jasper tells you," she said.

"It wasn't my idea," I said. I pulled up my shirt to show her the painful scrape across my ribs, but there was only a red mark, and no blood.

"We'll have to take a cab to the hospital," she told Dwayne. He wailed again and flung his treacherous self at her bosom. She held him close and shot me a searing glance that assigned me the full blame, for this and probably other things too. They went inside to phone for a taxi and let the screen door swing shut in my face.

I crossed back to the Bel Air full of fury and vengeance. It was Dwayne's idea, my ribs hurt too, and I wouldn't take the rap. But when I rehearsed the whole incident in my head, and others related to Dwayne, I found that the blame had stuck to me after all. It had seeped through to me somehow, through my clothes and my skin, and I couldn't see how to get rid of it.

CHAPTER 42

I TAPPED AT NICK'S DOOR, then quietly opened it. He was sprawled on the sofa, flipping his lighter open and shut. He had his houndstooth jacket on, and one tasselled loafer.

"Do you still want to go to the Sahara?" I said.

"Sure." But he made no move to get up, and continued flipping the lighter.

"It starts in ten minutes."

"I'm all ready. As you can see."

"You still need a shoe."

"Yes, *Mom*." He lurched up and groped for the other loafer.

We walked to the Sahara in silence. Nick hadn't combed his hair, and his shirt looked like he'd pulled it from the hamper. I thought maybe he had been drinking, but I didn't smell anything on him. We waited behind three other people for tickets, but when we got to the window, Nick just stood there.

"One adult," I said, more as a cue to him than to the ticket girl, who knew us and already had his ticket halfway under the window.

Nick sank down lower in his seat than usual. His jacket lapels crowded up towards his chin, as if he were shrivelling into his clothes.

"Are you okay?" I said.

"A-okay. Now start the damn movie."

The feature began with a man talking behind a desk, about how the movie had no story and no script, but lots of Jerry Lewis. It was all shot in a big hotel surrounded by palm trees.

"The bellboys are lined up," I said. "The manager's inspecting them. They're all walking off in different directions, except Jerry Lewis. He's turning this way and that. He doesn't know which way to go."

"Christ," Nick said.

I tried to describe the pranks that happened one after another. "He's handing the woman a car engine. He's putting a bra on a hanger. He's throwing room keys at little shelves."

"The guy never talks," Nick said. "I'm a blind man at a movie full of sight gags." He stood up and started moving out of the row. We went to the manager's office, where Nick tried to get his money back.

"Look, mister," the manager said. "I'd like to help you. But you were in there over thirty minutes. That's our cut-off. Thirty minutes, you don't get no refund. Plus, the boy's in for free. Like we always do for you."

"Nobody told me it was a silent film!"

"It isn't. There's talking and music and everything."

Nick argued for a few more minutes, then tore up his ticket stub and threw the bits on the floor. The manager stooped and picked them up.

"This place stinks tonight!" Nick said. He stormed through the empty lobby, nearly colliding with a standing ashtray, and banged through the front door. He was ready to plunge into the road without pausing, till an eighteen-wheeler barked its horn at him.

His pace slowed by the time we got to the Bel Air's front door, but then he ran up the stairs, instead of down to his place. He was at our door before I caught up with him, tapping his nails on the wood.

I turned the handle, but the door was locked.

"Corinne's probably in the bath," I said. But when we got inside, the place was empty. The clothes she had been wearing when I left were flung on the bed.

"Did she say she was going out?" Nick said.

"No."

He sat on the sofa and crossed his arms. I thought he would say something more, but he stayed silent.

"Do you want anything?" I said.

"No." He hugged himself and rocked back and forth. "Thanks, but I decline. Tell me something, Jasper. Listen, I've been wondering. What I want to know is ... how's school?"

"Okay. Kind of boring." It was the same answer I gave any adult faking an interest in my education.

"I guess it would be," he said. "How about your teacher? Is she any good?"

He had his lighter out again, and since he was leaning over, he looked as if he were directing his fake question to the shiny thing in his palm. He might as well have been. He had never shown the smallest interest in what I thought or how I was doing — in any part of my life. I only realized how complete his indifference had been at this moment when he pretended to care.

Several seconds passed without an answer from me. I didn't intend to say nothing, but as the nothing went on, it became the right answer. Nick had dragged me from the theatre before the movie was done, and made an embarrassing fuss with the manager, and he wasn't going to get a single word from me to help him stay on our sofa till Corinne got back.

On that point, we understood each other completely. After another minute, he got up and left the apartment without a word.

Corinne returned while I was watching Danger Man pull himself out of a plane wreck. She was wearing a flashy blue dress, her cheeks were flushed, and her hair was mussed.

"How was your movie?"

"We left before the end. Where'd you go?"

"For a walk."

"Who with?"

"Nobody. You should be in bed."

A little later, she came into my room, and sat on the bed, and stroked my hair back from my forehead.

"Why did you change to go for a walk?" I said.

"I usually change when I go out, haven't you noticed? You should change more often. Your shirt was smelly today." She gazed at me with a look of complete happiness, as she did at unexpected times, but this time I felt she was looking right through me. And something else was missing.

"You didn't put on your lipstick."

"I did too," she said, and a look of confusion briefly disturbed her blissful expression. "Oh, I already took it off — before I came in here."

She smiled, and tucked me in, and kissed my forehead with her naked lips. She blew me another kiss from the doorway, and went away as if everything were completely normal, though we both knew she didn't go on walks by herself, and never took off only part of her makeup.

CHAPTER 43

IT WAS SURPRISINGLY EASY TO convince Corinne to let me go to the Suans' house in the middle of the night to see the meteor shower. I lay down in my clothes at my usual bedtime and sprang up as soon as she touched my arm. We left the dark apartment without speaking. The Corvair coughed into life, its exhaust note sounding newly abrasive in the hush, and we drove under the pale, regular sunbursts cast by street lamps that lit the way for us alone.

Dr. Suan was on his front steps when we arrived, and came towards us as I got out. Corinne hadn't put on makeup or brushed her hair; she drove off with a wave before he reached the car door.

"Come," he said, and led me up the drive to the rear of the house. The back-door light shone feebly on Marsha, who was spreading an unzipped sleeping bag on the grass.

"I'm getting bitten," she said.

"Then you didn't put enough on," said Dr. Suan. Marsha squirted some bug repellent onto her hand, and mine, and we wiped it on our faces and arms till all I could smell was its lemony chemical odour. On the patio, Dr. Suan extended the squeaking legs of his tripod.

"Don't touch this once I open the shutter."

"I know, Daddy, I know," Marsha said.

The feet of the tripod scraped the patio stones as he searched for a stable spot. Marsha picked the heavy camera off the table and trained it on me.

"Don't waste a shot, there's not enough light," said Dr. Suan.

"I know, Daddy! I was only looking." She sighed with exasperation.

"Are you going to watch too?" I said.

"No, I'll get it with this," said Dr. Suan, "if no one bumps the camera." He fastened it to the tripod. "Do you understand about long exposures, Jasper?"

"Of course he does!" Marsha stamped her runner on the patio stones.

"Why don't you settle down, young lady, and offer your guest some lemonade."

"Do you want a drink?" Marsha removed a tea towel from a pitcher on the table and poured two glasses.

"Do you know what you're seeing tonight, Jasper?" said Dr. Suan.

"Meteors, I guess."

"Rubbish from a comet. Dust and grit we see only when it burns up in our atmosphere. But this shower isn't very reliable. You might not see much. You should have been here a few weeks ago."

He was still fussing with his camera, whose lens now pointed straight up from the tripod. Marsha sat down on the sleeping bag. I joined her, and we waited for Dr. Suan to finish.

"Don't mind me," he said.

At that, Marsha stretched out full length, and I beside her did the same. The cotton-stuffed flannel smelled faintly of charcoal and pine needles. The star-filled sky above seemed more deep and impressive than any I'd seen before, even at Chokecherry Bush, where Lily often tried to make me admire God's heavenly home. But that display had seemed static, while the sky over Dr. Suan's backyard was filling up with new stars and planets every second. Those specks of light had rained down their life-giving dust, which after a long evolution had become two beings on a sleeping bag, looking up.

The yard light went out. "Shutter's open now," Dr. Suan said. "Have fun." The screen door wheezed on its pneumatic arm, and we were alone, lying together in the dark. Marsha's scent stole up to me from under the bug lotion, seeming to carry the warmth of her body with it, like a blanket spread between me and the cool air. I turned my head towards her, but she kept her eyes up, waiting for something to dart across the sky.

"He forgot to say it was a bit cloudy last time," she said, as if trying to make up for not inviting me to the better meteor shower.

"Did you watch anyway?"

"Of course." Her elbow jerked against me. "There."

"Where?"

"It's gone now. They only last a second. There, again."

I saw nothing, and nothing the next time she jabbed me, though I was really looking by then, letting my eye rove over the whole sky, determined to catch something.

"Don't try to spot them," she said. "They're always somewhere else. Just keep your eyes open and they'll appear."

A hair-thin streak flashed at the edge of my vision, and I called it out to her, more excited by the telling than the seeing. A few more happened in quick succession, so subtly that I was only sure they had happened because of the little grunts of pleasure coming from Marsha.

"Isn't this exciting?" she sighed.

"Yes."

Marsha patted my open hand on the sleeping bag, and I closed my fingers on hers. She drew them out as carefully as if she were extracting a splinter, and curled her hair behind her ear. A few strands moved from under my cheek.

More meteors streaked by, and then they trailed off. For a long time we lay there waiting for more, with the universe spread wide above us. My eyelids burned from so much staring and too little sleep, yet it had all finished so soon. I waited in dread for the moment when Marsha would sit up and declare the evening over and I would have to go home. But then a ghostly green light rippled and flexed over the back fence.

"Look, the aurora," she said.

The light slimmed down to a glowing vertical fold and flared out again, this time arching quickly across the sky. Marsha groaned and gripped my fingers on the sleeping bag. The green became lighter and spread into a hazy band, like a much smaller Milky Way.

I knew a little about the Northern Lights, so with a sense of making a small payment against a lopsided debt, I propped myself on one elbow and explained to Marsha how they were caused by sunlight reflecting off the Arctic snows.

"That's ridiculous," she said, releasing my fingers. "It's nothing to do with snow. It's photons firing out of an excess flow of radiation."

"Sunlight is radiation."

"Yes, and this comes from the sun too, but it's plasma, slopping over at the pole. Didn't you read about the solar wind, and the Van Allen belts? You forget everything so easily."

I wanted to say I forgot nothing that really mattered, nothing about every moment I had spent with her. But instead I waited out the silence that had to pass for her bruising comment to fade. I was still turned half towards her on one elbow, teetering on my hip.

"What are you doing?" she said. "You're going to miss it all."

I leaned over awkwardly and kissed her in the lapping, slobbery style I had learned from Ginette. For a moment, her mouth lay under mine, soft and full and unresisting, and it seemed that she accepted me after all, that my errors and stupidities were all forgiven, and the whole world was happiness. Then she squirmed out from under me and sat bolt upright.

"What are you doing?" she hissed.

I sat up too, more slowly. My pulse thumped in my throat.

"Why did you have to do that?" She no longer sounded merely shocked or angry, but sorrowful, which was worse. "Don't you know you're the only one I can have over like this?"

"I'm sorry," I said, with a buzzing heaviness in my head, like the feeling that sometimes came when I awoke in a motel room I couldn't recognize.

"How could I be so dumb?" Marsha said.

"You're not dumb." I should have said more, but no words came. She seemed to be waiting for some further explanation. Her hand moved to her face, which I could scarcely make out in the dark.

"It's just ..." I said, and stalled again, blocked by the gathering heaviness in my chest. My eyes drifted up towards the colours bunching and rippling in the sky like ribbons slowly dancing around a knot. "I mean, what's wrong if I like you a little?"

"Jasper, you're just a kid." She put her hand to her face again, and I realized she was crying.

It was too late to pretend I was older than I was, but not to prove I had the right to kiss like that. I had recently learned a word for the other thing Ginette had done with me, from Dwayne of all people, who heard it from a cousin who knew the names for everything. It had trickled down from the secret adult world to me, who had already done that thing; and so, under the intimate canopy of stars, I used my new word for the first time. I even felt a sad glimmer of pride, as I told Marsha: "I am not. I got a blow job from a girl once."

She stood up. "Okay, everything's ruined now. Don't say another word. Just go."

The sleeping bag's zipper scraped my hand as I scrambled up. The screen door opened, and Dr. Suan came out.

"Is it finished?" he said.

"Yes, it's over," Marsha said. He approached the camera, and the shutter closed with a faint click. The colour had gone out of the sky, and we were back to the dim reality of the Suans' backyard, from which I was being expelled, probably forever.

"I'll run you home," said Dr. Suan.

"Thanks, I can walk."

"I promised your mother."

"I'd rather go by myself."

I turned on my heel without saying thanks or goodbye, thinking that this would be a punishing gesture. The yard light flashed on, and in spite of myself I looked back. Marsha was stooping for our lemonade glasses, clearing up the same way she had at the end of Dr. Suan's miserable garden party. In her weary movement I caught a reproach sharper than the ones she had spoken.

CHAPTER 44

FOR DAYS AFTER THE METEOR shower, I didn't see Marsha anywhere, not even in the library. She didn't stray past the door of my school, though I looked every day, and sometimes rushed to the door for fear of missing her.

I ran everywhere to tire myself out and went to bed as early as I could. The ceiling of my room still glowed with the last orange rays of the sun when Corinne came to smooth the covers over my shoulders.

"Are you sure you're not ill?"

"Just tired."

"You go to bed so early, and then I hear you rustling around for hours. Why don't you stay up longer?"

"What for?"

Each morning I woke up exhausted from some cloudy struggle that tangled the sheet around me. I lay there grasping for some shred of what it was about, until the hopeless feeling of the previous day returned.

One day Corinne told me we were going to have Nick and Jackie over for dinner.

"Why?"

"I know, it wasn't much fun last time. But they've been good to us. I feel like I should do something."

She counted our motley kitchenware and decided we had enough dishes, with only a little washing before dessert. She made macaroni salad and boiled spareribs and got me to daub them with barbecue sauce using a balled-up paper napkin.

I was folding other napkins into pyramids when our guests arrived. Jackie was as dolled up as if she had stepped off a runway. Nick looked haggard, smelled more strongly of smoke than usual, and had a drink in his hand.

"Nick couldn't wait," Jackie said dryly.

"Better to be safe than sober," he said. They sat on our cottage sofa, and again the room seemed more barren with people in it than without. Corinne got Jackie a drink in the nicest glass we had.

"Wanna hear the news of the day?" said Nick, pressing his shoulders into the thin upholstery. "Angelo's selling his window business."

"I'm sorry," Corinne said. "What does that mean for you?"

"He says he'll find me something else."

"Like what?"

"Like who knows." He fished out his lighter and flipped the cap a few times before lighting up.

"I think this could be good," Jackie said. "This could be the break he needs."

"Yeah, I'm really catching a break here. You'd have to be out of your skull not to see that. Think of all the things I could do for Ange. He could make me a rodeo rider, or a trapeze artist. That could be kind of reassuring, to be snatched from the air by a pair of strong arms every night." He rubbed his elbows. Beads of sweat stood on his forehead.

"What'll become of Rodney Medwood?" Corinne said.

"Oh, this really is Rodney's big chance," said Nick. "He's gonna be a star."

"In movies?"

"Old movies. He'll be what they used to call a romantic juvenile."
Corinne lifted her glass. "To Rodney Medwood, child star."

"No, the romantic juvenile wasn't a kid. He was the nice young
guy who marries the sweet, innocent girl. But off-screen, he gets in
deep with the bookies. He becomes a dope fiend. He loses his swank
house and swimming pool, and ends up selling storm windows."

"At least he gets the girl," Corinne said. "To Rodney and his girl."
They drank, and Corinne went to put the ribs under the broiler
while Nick and Jackie sat on the sofa like strangers waiting for
the same bus. I slid out of there and hung around the kitchen till a
light haze of sweet-smelling smoke issued from the oven. Everyone
crowded around our little table, and Corinne dished out the food
on our mismatched plates.

"I have news too," Corinne said. "I'm leaving town for a few days.
A salesman I know wants to do a little tour with his new collection.
Five places in four days."

"That's great," Jackie said.

For me, it was more than great. We would soon be skimming
along the highway in the Corvair again, with all pains left behind. I
hugged Corinne's arm.

"The thing is," she said, "I need someone to look after Jasper while
I'm gone. I was hoping he could stay with you, Nick."

I flung away her arm. "No!"

"With me?" said Nick, gnawing a rib. "I'm no babysitter."

Corinne took my hand, but I yanked it away. "He practically looks
after himself," she said. "He'll mostly be at school, or running around
with his friends."

"Does he cook for himself too?" Nick said.

"He can serve things out the way you do."

"I don't need someone to do things the way I do. I've got too
much of that already."

"Well, boo hoo," said Jackie. "Who's the salesman?"

"A guy named Jack Summers," Corinne said. "He works out of Montreal."

"He's a jerk!" I said. A fierce, sudden rage boiled up in me, against Jack and his stinky pipes and the rotten deal Corinne was preparing.

"Ah, but he can pay," Nick said. "Here's to jerks who can pay." He raised his glass, but no one joined his toast. He hadn't shaved, he looked a mess, and his life was falling apart. It was ridiculous that Corinne thought he could look after me.

"Is there something for Jackie in this?" he said.

"Not this time."

"She's swung a lot of things your way, you know. You've had it pretty good here."

"You've all been very kind."

"Everyone's bent over backwards for you," Nick said with a sneer. "My brother doesn't know you, for Chrissake, and you're eating off his table."

"Shut up, Nick," Jackie said. But he leaned in for more, and for once I was completely on his side.

"You've had favours from all of us," he growled, "and now you want more, and when we ask back, you say 'Not this time.'" He groped for the bottle, but Jackie snatched it away and got up with Corinne to clear the plates from the table. This dinner party was turning out worse than the last, but I didn't care, because Nick wasn't going to play along.

The women returned, and Corinne served cubes of red Jell-O with whipped cream. Nick took one mouthful, and said, "You know they make this stuff from horses."

"What are you talking about?" Jackie said.

"Gelatin. They boil it out of horses' hoofs."

"What the hell's wrong with you?" Jackie said. "You're acting like a goddamn louse!" She left the room and flung herself on the sofa. Corinne took one more bite of her Jell-O, then went into the kitchen and tossed the rest in the garbage.

"Okay, you know what?" Nick said. "Forget it. I can take Jasper. We can bach it together for a few days. Right, Buddy Boy?"

"I'm not staying!" I yelled. I jumped up and my chair went over, and I was out of the apartment and down the stairs before Corinne could call me back. I ran through the dandelions and over the street, past the scarred trunk of the big oak and onto Dwayne's porch, which I hadn't visited since the Wild Mouse.

I rang the bell, and Dwayne came to the door. He had stitches across his cheek, and a purple bruise on his nose.

"I can't see you anymore," he said through the fly-specked screen.

"Why not?"

"My dad said."

"The Wild Mouse was your idea."

"You did it too wild." In the way he spoke, I recognized something of how I had felt since the night of the meteors. I felt a twinge of pity for him, and for myself, who had done everything too wild and too mean, with no time left to do anything differently.

But then another feeling came, of being dismissed again, this time by a little twerp I had befriended practically as a favour. I stood, choking on words I couldn't sort out, until I found something I could say with real conviction.

"Your dad's a jerk."

"You're the jerk," he said quickly, but with more sorrow than anger, and swung the door shut. I kicked at it hard enough to hurt my toe.

I wandered down the road to the Sahara, where they had a pay phone in the foyer, and dialled Dean's number, shovelling in coins I had taken from Corinne's bag. The phone rang a long time before anyone answered.

"Hello?" It was a man's voice, but not Dean's. I thought with a sudden panic that he might have moved somewhere where he couldn't be found; but when I asked for him, the man said to hang on. There was a pause, during which I could hear him shouting for Dean across a hubbub of other voices. He was having a party. I couldn't believe he had resumed his social life, and was not sitting alone in his house waiting for Corinne and me to return.

Finally he came to the phone. "Yeah?"

"It's Jasper."

"What a nice surprise. Where are you?"

"In Edmonton."

"Is everything okay?"

"Sort of." My chest contracted. I couldn't say any of the things bursting to come out. Someone laughed close to the receiver at the other end, a woman.

"Listen, I've got a lot of people here right now, can we talk another time?"

"Okay. I miss you."

"Me too, Jasper. Bye."

I went outside and stood for a long time at the bus stop and got on the first one that arrived, without any thought of where it was going. When we reached the end of the line, the driver shambled the length of the empty vehicle to ask where I was headed, and whether I was lost.

CHAPTER
45

AN APRICOT SUMMER DRESS LAY on Corinne's bed. I never liked the dress, or the colour.

"Why are you so mad about this little trip?" she said.

She was making herself up to suit the dress, with lipstick one shade darker, blush a little warmer than usual, eyeshadow a cool grey-green to counter the warmth of everything else. It was very well balanced and pretty in its way, but still I hated the colour and the dress.

"Jack's no good with kids. You know that."

Her hair was pinned back while she did her face. In a minute she would brush it out and look very fancy-free with that hair, those lips and that outfit. But still I despised the dress and the colour.

"We'll be rushing around, driving and showing every day. It won't be much fun."

Her shoes lay on the carpet next to the bed, a pair of white lattice-tops with medium heels. She wore those shoes the day Dean gave her the Corvair. In those shoes she danced for him on his patio, with a big present on the drive that from his point of view turned out to be worth exactly nothing.

"You've got school. I don't think other kids skip every time a parent goes out of town."

"School's a waste of time," I said. "I've learned more from Marsha." The name popped out before I could stop it. Hearing it in my own voice made me realize how long it had been since I had any reason to say it aloud.

"I bet you have."

In the mirror she gave me a knowing look. I refused it with a scowl that even to my eyes looked ridiculous.

"Listen, would you rather I ask if you can stay over there? At the Suans'?"

Here was a beautiful offer that would have seemed like a dozen Christmases if she had suggested it a week earlier. I wanted to cry, but my face was numb.

"No."

"I don't mind asking." She brushed out her hair.

"Where are you going?" I said.

"Red Deer, Calgary, Lethbridge, Medicine Hat. Some other place I don't remember."

"No, I mean tonight. Right now."

"To see a friend."

"Who?"

"Just a friend. I won't be late. We'll sit together before you sleep. Jack will be here tomorrow first thing."

*

HER HAND ON MY BACK the next morning conveyed a feeling of hurry and departure that woke me more abruptly than if she had shaken me. She was already dressed and made up. It seemed a long time since she sat in the same spot in the apricot dress, telling me she would be back before I knew it, promising we would do something special together soon. Now she was saying the same things in other words, with a bloom of fresh perfume and her bag by the door, with a fall coat draped over it.

"Jack's waiting, I've got to run," she said, crushing my neck in an uncomfortable hug. She walked out of the room with a rustle of skirts, the apartment door boomed shut, and I nestled into my pillow, almost believing this could all be sorted out with a little more sleep.

When I woke again, half the morning had slid by, lost hours that seemed like a gift or head start. Corinne and Jack were probably in Red Deer already, setting up in a hotel room as usual. It was really happening, and here I was, alone.

I crawled out of bed and dug in my suitcase for Jack's brass hammer, the one I kept after smashing his cocktail shaker. I banged a few dents into the windowsill with it, then tossed it into the Drawer of Shame. My clipping about the Monza crash was still in there, and I read it again, trying not to skip ahead to the line about cars racing on for hours past the bodies of the dead. The scarf from Kesterman's Modern Miss was there too, and though I knew why, it was harsh to find that my calling it a gift had made no difference.

A blouse was sprawled over the foot of Corinne's bed. On the floor of her open closet, a dress lay crumpled around a wooden hanger. I went through all the drawers in her vanity, looking for clues to mysteries I couldn't name, but found nothing aside from the usual tiny bottles and brushes.

I dressed and went outside, and since it was nearly lunchtime, walked over to Woodward's and stood before the cabinet of cakes. I meant to ask for an egg salad sandwich, but some defensive instinct at the last moment made me choose roast beef. The bench opposite the shoe store was empty, but I went back outside and ate sitting on the curb, my knees drawn up under my chin, my eyes blinking against the grit thrown up by cars wheeling past to park. I arrived at school after classes had resumed for the afternoon, and told the teacher my mother was ill.

When I got to Nick's, he was on the phone, making a Medwood

call. He sounded smooth as always, but he was unshaven and his shirt looked slept-in.

"You're early," he said.

"School's been over for an hour."

"I meant for the movie. I've got a few more calls. Keep quiet or make yourself scarce. And stay out of my room."

I sat on his sofa, where I was supposed to spend the night and two more, and listened to Rodney make his pitch against Old Man Winter. Only one call kept him talking long enough to punch the twin holes that marked an interested prospect, but that was enough to rouse him to shave and change his shirt for the film.

The Sahara was nearly full when we arrived. I found seats near the front as usual, then went back up the aisle. Marsha stood at the refreshment counter with Noreen and another girl — the same trio from our first encounter in that very spot. Marsha's glance slid away from mine, and she walked with the other girl towards the ladies' room.

"Here you are, back from the dead," said Noreen. "Look, I bought those shoes." She pointed down at her white summer pumps, the ones with the bows on top, from the store at the shoppers park. "Remember the time we looked in the window?"

"Yes."

"Remember the time you kicked Jerry? Like this?" She gave me a brisk, hard kick with the point of her new shoe. Nick's dime slipped from my fingers onto the carpet. She stooped quickly and picked it up.

"Finders keepers," she said, her scorn drifting over me like snow. "Now get lost so Marsha can come out of the ladies'."

It hadn't occurred to me that she would know, that Marsha would tell, that my kiss would no longer be a secret blunder in the darkness of her yard. The whole lobby seemed to fill up with the news, even as people dwindled away and into the theatre.

The cartoon had a bitter taste. Nick noticed through the noise of Elmer Fudd's shotgun that I wasn't ripping open a chocolate bar.

"You better eat that thing," he growled. "I don't want you messing with it during the movie."

I groped under my feet till I found a thrown-away wrapper, and crinkled the sticky paper in my hands so Nick could hear. A furious sequence of things I should have done or said in the lobby coursed through my mind.

The film was a beach movie about a boy who surfed and swam and had perfect hair and lots of friends. There was just one snooty girl who didn't like him, no matter what he did to prove how swell he was.

"He's surfing another high wave," I whispered. "Everyone's watching but her. Stupid cow."

"Hey, stick to the facts," Nick warned, too loudly, because someone shushed him from the row behind us. Nick swivelled around. "Jasper, what's that sound?" he said. "Is there a train coming in?"

"We're trying to watch the movie," said the man behind.

"Don't worry, it's not going anywhere."

The man leaned forward. "I suggest you shut it, pal."

"It? It?" Nick kept his face turned towards the man, as if he were really staring him down from behind his dark glasses. "I resent your pronoun, *pal*."

Someone in our row shushed, and Nick faced the screen again. The girl in the movie said something mean, and jumped into her convertible.

"She's driving into the mountains," I whispered. "He's following. She's going faster, there's lots of turns. She's hit a tree. The boy's out of his car, pulling her out." The wail of a police siren filled the Sahara.

"Is she dead?" Nick said, not attempting to whisper. "That stupid cow?" Several people shushed this time, and the man behind us cursed.

"They've got her on a stretcher," I whispered. "Her hand's hanging limp. He's holding her hand."

The girl lay unconscious in the hospital bed, looking perfect and normal except for the clean white bandage around her forehead. Her parents stood by like sad statues, and the boy was there too. Her eyes opened, and in the close-up, I could see that someone had put her pink lipstick on fresh. Who would do that on a dying girl? But then the music told us she wasn't dying, and not hating the boy anymore either, and they were hugging on the pillow, and the movie was over.

"Well, boo hoo," said Nick, as the lights came up.

"If you don't like it, why don't you stay home?" said the man behind, now standing. He towered over us like a giant with his big, hairy hand on the back of Nick's seat.

"Why don't I stay home?" said Nick, turning his head slightly. "Because, *pal*, it won't let me."

"What won't let you?"

"My disease."

The giant leaned back as if he smelled something bad.

"What kind of disease?"

"Medwood's Disease, if you must know," said Nick.

"I never heard of an illness that made you go to the movies. Especially in dark glasses."

"He's blind, too," I said.

"Gord, will you quit it. Let's go," said the woman beside the giant, pushing against his stubborn bulk.

"Okay, okay." He shuffled towards the aisle.

Nick remained in his movie posture, with his face still turned up towards the blank screen, as if this ruckus were beneath his notice.

"We paid the same money, pal!" the giant shouted from the aisle. "The exact same money as you."

He trudged up the slope. I scanned the crowd disappearing before him, afraid that I might see Marsha, and that I might not.

"Why do they let idiots in here?" Nick said. He jumped up as if he wanted to confront the giant again. But by the time we had gone up the aisle and through the lobby, his feet were dragging. At his apartment door, he stood a long time fumbling for his key .1ough the door turned out to be unlocked.

"I'm beat, kid, I'm going to bed," he said. "Linens are in here." He tapped on the closet, then went into his room and shut the door.

Bedding down on Nick's sofa gave me a strange new perspective on a familiar room. I closed my eyes and tried to imagine that I was in a hotel room. Instead, my mind returned me to the lobby of the Sahara, my encounter with Noreen, and the news that Marsha was telling everyone about my stupid kiss. The stain was spreading, and there was no way to stop it.

CHAPTER 46

NICK'S DOOR WAS AJAR AS I approached, but now that I had the right and obligation to be in his apartment, I felt more hesitant, not less, about walking in. I nudged the door a few inches. Nick sat at one end of the sofa, cradling Jackie's upper body in his arms, while she lay stretched out with his cat curled near her ankles. I started to back away, but Jackie said, "No, it's okay." Her mascara had gone messy around the eyes, but she must have stopped crying some time before I got there.

Nick, free of glasses for once, stroked her cheek, while she searched his face for something. They stayed like that for another long moment, as if I weren't there, and then whatever was happening between them ended.

"What's new with you, Jasper?" Jackie said. "Done any more drawings?"

Usually I kept my pictures to myself, but Jackie had liked my big lion rampant, so I pulled a new drawing from the binder under my arm. She looked at it from her reclining position, with Nick still bent over her.

"What is he, a jockey?" she said, and I remembered that a picture of a man on horseback might not have been the best image to show her. But it wasn't a jockey, it was the lone horseman, with his beaver quilt and rawhide bag of coal. I told her about the handprints and the buffalo, and about how the fleas kept people moving west.

"What happened to the rider?" Jackie said.

I couldn't imagine a plains horseman riding to the Pacific, so I said: "He went north, I think."

"They don't have horses up north."

"Maybe he got tired of horses."

"That can happen," Jackie said. Nick cradled her a little more in his arms, and kissed her forehead.

"He could have gone north by plane," I said.

"They didn't have planes then," Nick said, "and he couldn't have made a mark unless he dropped things."

"They'd get lost in the trees," Jackie said.

"Maybe that's why there are so few towns up there," I said. "Everything got lost." I didn't mention my father's plane, but its familiar lonely feeling came over me.

Jackie handed me my drawing and sat up. Nick straightened himself as if from a long sleep. "We should go to the Belmont for dinner," he said. "I'm sick of everything here."

Jackie went to fix her face and Nick put on his camel jacket. We walked out of the Bel Air into the cool evening. As we waited at the sidewalk for traffic to clear, Jackie said, "Too bad about that tree."

"What tree?" said Nick.

"The big one in front of the old farmhouse. The one they stripped of all its branches."

"I never heard about that tree."

"It used to shade that whole part of the street."

I told him about the cage moving among the boughs, and the chainsaw ripping the wood, and the foliage shimmering as the boughs dropped. We went over to the trunk, and he gripped the gnarly bark, and felt around its girth.

"How has this been here all this time?" he said.

"Maybe you forgot," Jackie said.

"Are you kidding? Remembering where things are is the only way I can get around."

At the Belmont, we sat in the same booth where Nick and I had found Corinne after our first time at the Sahara. The same waiter came over.

"Eddie, this is a special night," Nick said. "I expect the best."

"For you, the best of the best." Eddie recommended the chef's special pork tenderloin.

"Sounds good, we'll all have that," Nick said. "Two rye and gingers, and a Coke for our young friend."

Jackie took Nick's hand in hers. "You look nice," she said. "I love this jacket." Nick's face still seemed gaunt to me, but his jacket was sharp, his shirt was pressed and his cheeks shone almost as much as when Jackie shaved them with a straight razor.

"The best threads I own all came from you, Doll," he said. "By the way, did you ever get your sewing machine back?"

"Not yet. Why?"

"Just wondered." He leaned over and kissed her cheek. Jackie's face twitched at his touch.

"How do you know about my sewing machine?" she said.

"I walked Jasper home once. No big deal!" That was true, it was no big deal, but the words sounded guilty. Jackie withdrew her hand from his.

Eddie brought our drinks. The restaurant door opened, and Dr. Suan came in with two other men, including one I recognized from his patio party. They looked around for a table, and as they walked towards it, Dr. Suan gave me the faintest of nods. He too had heard the news it seemed, maybe in a version that didn't include a slobbery kiss in his backyard.

"So, Jasper," said Nick. "Why don't you like this guy Jack?"

"He's mean."

"Is he young? Old?"

"Old. He smokes a pipe and sweats a lot."

"Poor guy," Nick said. He seemed pleased with this information, more so than Jackie.

"Let's talk about something else," she said.

"Okay. How come you didn't tell me about the tree?"

"I just did," said Jackie.

"I mean before. And why did they cut it?"

"Because of the cars," I said.

"That's ridiculous," Nick said, and he resumed his complaint from the first time I met him, about the four lanes of traffic outside his window, and the fumes, and the Bel Air's phony name.

"Why don't you drop that old tune?" Jackie said. "I've heard it plenty before, and I'm sure Jasper doesn't care."

"Oh, no? Maybe he does. It might surprise you, what I pick up about people."

"Let's not get into how much you know about other people," Jackie said.

"All right. What do you care about, Jasper?"

"I don't know."

"I'll tell you," Nick said. "Their sporty car, getting candy before the movie, and maybe some little girl we haven't seen yet. Am I right?" The softness I had seen in him on the sofa with Jackie had vanished. I felt a dull hatred for this man, who cared nothing about me, but who had nosy ideas that happened to be correct.

"You see, I'm right," he said. "He's clammed up." He took another sip of his drink.

"Why are you picking on him?" Jackie said.

"I'm only teasing. You can't blame a guy. I mean, he's been *dumped* on me," he said with sudden vehemence.

"You said this was going to be a special night."

"It is, Doll. What do you want? Another drink?" He touched her arm, but she jerked it away.

By the time the tenderloin arrived, the dinner had taken on the same ruined feeling as our last meal with Dean. Nothing Nick said was right, nothing Jackie felt was understood. Finally we all focused on our plates and sawed at our meat.

My eyes drifted over to Dr. Suan's table. He was deep in conversation, about non-trivial exceptions maybe, or the sow of the universe. It was painful to look at him, but I kept doing it, and gradually the hurt inside my body seemed to shift to his end of the restaurant. I hoped he would get drunk, so drunk that everyone would notice and talk about it the next day. Word of it would get around to Marsha, and she would feel bruised also, on account of the same table at the Belmont where my hurt had settled now.

"Like a regular little family," Eddie said to us, as he brought the bill.

*

I AWOKE IN THE DARK on the sofa, with a weight on my chest: Nick's cat, purring and kneading my pyjamas with his claws. I rolled over, and the cat leapt into the dark void of the carpet. A wedge of light shone across the floor from Nick's bedroom door, which had not been so much ajar when I went to sleep. The cat must have pushed it open.

A murmur of voices came from the room, along with another quiet sound, irregular and moist, which I slowly recognized as Jackie crying. I remained stock still, listening as hard as I could, but no clear words emerged.

I peeled off the sheet in one light motion and crept close to the door. No sound came from the room, and I thought perhaps I had missed it all; but then I heard Jackie's voice quite distinctly.

"When my heart breaks, it hurts," she said.

There was no reply, no more talking, just the uneven sounds of her sobbing, and then of a bare foot meeting the floor, and of the doorknob rattling slightly as someone's hand touched the other side. I remained frozen, and waited for the door to be pulled shut. But instead, Jackie appeared in that wedge of light, her arm across her bare breasts, her eyes swollen red, her lips trembling, her skin yellowish. She looked less like herself than a coarse and bleary replica.

I fell back from the door and stumbled to the sofa like someone not fully awake. I sank down and lay with my nose against the pebbled fabric of the sofa back and forced myself to breathe like a sleeper, though my heart pounded against the cushions. Jackie said nothing. There was no sound, until the bedroom door closed with a definite quiet click. From the opposite direction, the refrigerator motor shuddered into action.

Behind my tightly shut eyelids, I could still see the unprepared face Jackie showed me, disfigured by the bruising inside her body; and also the look she gave me in the second before I turned away. It was a sharp, accusing look, as if I was to blame not only for hearing and seeing her like that, but for everything else.

CHAPTER 47

I ARRIVED HOME FROM SCHOOL to find Angelo's Cadillac parked in front of the Bel Air. There was no point going to Nick's while it sat there, so I squatted near the car as I had when I was being paid to watch it. The feeling of it being a little bit mine came back to me, though with no obligation to protect it this time. Someone could smash into it with a truck and it wouldn't be my business at all. Mud had spattered the hubcaps and the lower part of the chassis. The Cadillac no longer looked quite so perfect, though it was still fine enough for me to feel how sad it was that I would never slip behind the wheel of a car like that with Marsha.

I waited there a quarter hour, until Angelo emerged from our building and bustled towards his car. He barely noticed me on the grass and didn't seem to recognize me.

"I saw your car. I've been watching it for you," I said.

His suspicious look relaxed somewhat as he remembered. He pulled a quarter from a pocket of his pinstriped suit and tossed it to me without a word.

In the apartment, Nick sat at the table, stroking his cheek with one of the stones from his saucer. His Medwood papers were spread over the table, next to the phone and a half-empty bottle of rye.

"Open a window, will you?" he said. "It stinks in here." It smelled the same as usual to me, except for a trace of Angelo's expensive, leathery cologne. I pulled open the window behind the sofa.

"You should be happy you're an only child." He poured more rye in his glass, and took a good slug. "If a friend goes bad on you, you can get rid of them. But family, you're stuck with that!" A scowl tightened on his face.

"I'm going to my place for a while," I said.

"Nobody's stopping you."

I went upstairs to our apartment. Everything was as it had been the morning Corinne left, though it looked a bit more abandoned. I found some paper and drew the Cadillac, with a tree bough rammed through the windshield. I opened my closet and pulled out the last remaining branch from Dwayne's tree. I could still make a slingshot, and flaunt it from afar, to show him what he gave up by turning me away. Instead, I pulled off one withered leaf for the Drawer of Shame, and shoved the branch out my bedroom window.

I found canned spaghetti in the cupboard, warmed it a little on the stove, and spread it over a slice of stale bread with the mouldy bits pinched out. I ate this supper in front of the TV, and watched 77 Sunset Strip. The fatherly dreamboat from the plane-crash film was there as usual, no longer in uniform, but still burdened by the pilot's sadness.

Evening came on, and it occurred to me that Nick probably wouldn't care if I didn't go back to his place. I put on my pyjamas and got into bed, and as the last light faded on my ceiling, tried to convince myself that Corinne was in the next room, reading or painting her toenails.

When I awoke, the room was fully dark, and alive in a way it hadn't been before. The apartment's smudgy stillness seethed around me like a malevolent fog. I threw off the covers, pulled my corduroys over my pyjamas and jammed my feet into my runners. I ran out of the apartment and down the stairs to Nick's, where the door was still unlocked and the light was still on. He lay asleep or passed out on the sofa, fully dressed, with the rye bottle empty on the table.

I looked him over with careful impudence, annoyed to find him settled where I was supposed to sleep. His unshaven jaw had slipped open and his sleeper's breath gurgled in his throat. It was an angular, raspy kind of sleep, unlike the rumbling, round slumber I had felt against the back of my head in front of Dean's sofa in Winnipeg.

It would be an ugly job to get Nick shifted to his own bed, so I threw a blanket over him and went into the bedroom. There, another idea came to me — Corinne's idea — and it propelled me out of the apartment and the building. I ran along the sidewalk full of desperate energy, my midget shadow bounding to giant size each time I passed a lamppost.

I ran all the way to Marsha's street, stopping a block from her house to nurse the stitch in my side. Most of the houses had fallen into the dead, grey sleep of things at night, but as I snuck up her drive, I saw a pale light glowing over the backyard. The bulb in the kitchen was on. I crouched by the backyard bushes where the ground was wet from Dr. Suan's evening watering.

He strayed by the kitchen window in his bathrobe, passing out of sight as he tipped his head to drink from a tumbler. The light flicked off, and I counted slowly to a hundred, to give him time to get back to bed. While I counted, I looked up at the clear night sky, where the universe was still opening her skirts to release the work of creation. It was soothing to stare into that sparkling void, even though my troubles had started there, and in this very backyard.

I reached a hundred and stood up. My back touched the bushes and my pyjama shirt soaked through. I writhed against the damp, crept over to Marsha's basement window, and tapped the dark glass with a pebble, gently at first, then more sharply.

The curtain moved, an orange light glowed on, and through the narrow gap in the cloth I saw her bare legs dart away from the bed. A moment later the inside back door scraped against its frame, and Marsha's wide eyes searched me out through the crack in the door.

"Oh, it's you!" she whispered.

"Who did you think it was?"

"Nobody. What are you doing here?"

"Can I come in?"

"No. Are you crazy?"

"You've got to let me in."

"I can't. Go home, Jasper! You'll get me in trouble."

"I can't go home."

"Of course you can, just go!"

"I can't, you have to let me in."

"Oh, God!" she hissed. She pushed the screen door open. I slipped in like a ghost. In a moment we were down the carpeted stairs and behind the closed door of her room, staring at each other in the orange light of her bedside lamp.

"What's happened?" she said, clutching the neck of her baby-doll nightdress, searching my face with fierce eyes, listening for any sound from the rest of the house.

"I'm on my own."

"What do you mean, on your own? Where's your mother?"

"On the road."

"She just left you here?"

I felt the phrase like a slap, and a sob came out of me, as unexpected as a hiccup. Marsha jammed her palm on my mouth. I pulled it away just as quickly.

"Sort of," I said, glaring at her, trying to show I wouldn't cry.

"What do you mean, sort of?" She plucked at my pyjamas. "You've been in bed somewhere. Why didn't you stay there? How did you get wet like that? Jasper, I'm so mad at you!"

There was a bump over our heads, and sounds of movement, and the snap of the light switch in the stairway. Marsha froze, then shoved me down on the floor next to her bed, on the side away from the door. She slid under the covers with barely a rustle and turned off her lamp. I lay flat with my head partly under the bed, facing the streak of pale light under the door.

"Marsha?" Dr. Suan's voice sounded in the stairwell. His weight came down the stairs, and he murmured through the door: "Are you all right?" The pale line under the door widened, and light spilled across the carpet towards the bed. A few long seconds passed; then the door closed, the steps retreated, and the stairway light snapped off.

"Don't you dare move," Marsha whispered. We lay still for several more minutes, and then her orange light came on again.

"You're really messing things up," she said, glaring down at me. "I've got an exam tomorrow."

"I can sleep on the floor."

"Why are you even here?"

I wanted to tell her about Corinne going off with Jack Summers, and Nick being drunk on the sofa, but it was too complicated. So I said my grandfather had been thrown from his horse, and was badly hurt, and Corinne had rushed to see him.

"That's terrible."

"He might die."

"I'm so sorry."

Her face softened, and I felt a tremor through my whole body. She slipped off the bed and sat on the floor beside me, and took my hand. The scent of her hair and skin came over me, as it hadn't for a long time, and something in me uncreased and stretched out at this fragile hint of a return to things as they had been. All the distress of days past melted away and I struggled not to let it show on my face, but tears of relief ran down my cheeks. She brushed them away with her fingers.

"Why didn't your mom take you?"

"I've got school, and my neighbour said I could stay with him," I said, "but he got really drunk."

With the mention of things as they actually were, I turned my face towards hers, now close enough that I could have kissed her again. Her lips pursed and her eyebrows moved together. "Why do men drink like that?" she said, releasing my hand. The true part of my story wasn't helping.

"Why have you been avoiding me?" I said.

"You know!"

"But that was a mistake," I said, not thinking where this statement might lead.

"What do you mean?" She searched my face with her dark eyes, and I saw that there was one thing she wanted to hear from me, a better lie that would put everything right.

"I mean … I like you, but not that way."

"Then why did you kiss me?"

"I was just trying it out."

"Really?"

"Really."

She looked so relieved, I wanted to cry. But my lie had taken hold of my face, and stayed stuck there while she hugged me and kissed my cheek, with her arm around my waist. She was so very happy I didn't like her that way.

"Did I show you what they sent me from Mount Palomar?" She jumped up and searched for the manila envelope, and again showed me the letter, about how they looked forward to giving her a tour of the facility.

"But we need to sleep," she said. "And you should get out of that wet top."

I pulled off my corduroys, and she found me a T-shirt. She gave me a blanket and one of her pillows, and I lay down again on the floor next to her bed. She turned out the light, and moved around on the mattress for a minute.

"Goodnight, Jasper."

"Goodnight."

It didn't take her long to fall asleep. I listened to her breathe and inhaled her scent from the pillowcase under my cheek. A crushed feeling spread deep across my chest, under the soft, worn cotton of her T-shirt. This was a much worse ending for the night than if I had dragged Nick off the sofa, drunk and abusive as he might have been. Everything was ruined now, and forever, just when I had made her believe it was all sorted out.

I rolled on my back and as I gazed at her shadowy form on the bed, my cock stirred, and stood up to its full, useless length. I gripped that untimely stump, and in the darkness and silence, under cover of her peaceful breathing, I took the last lonely pleasure I would ever get from Marsha's presence.

*

SHE WOKE ME, NOT GENTLY as Corinne did, but by shoving the heel of her hand against my shoulder. A feeble light glowed through the curtains of her small, high window.

"You have to go. My parents will be up soon."

I rolled over, and my hand strayed onto something small and sharp on the carpet: one of her earrings. I hid it in my palm and clambered into my cords and shoes. We crept up the stairs. She gave me a brief, impersonal hug, and I slipped into the clear early light. I walked home quickly, my eyes on the sidewalk, my fists in my pockets, her rhinestone earring digging hard into my palm.

CHAPTER 48

THE PAPER GARMENT SLEEVE CRACKLED up and over the hanger, and slid down onto my bed. Corinne held out a silver-blue sharkskin jacket. She had come in with her bag and modelling case, and hadn't yet taken off her unbuttoned coat.

"What do you think?"

The fabric was soft and cool, like water. The buttons were smooth, too, with a dimple in the centres where the thread was.

"Try it on."

I slipped the jacket from the wooden hanger, which had the same breezy script stamped on it as the paper sleeve: Young Men's Style Shoppe. The coat hung on my shoulders with a lank, silken heaviness. The cuffs almost reached my knuckles.

"Looks good," Corinne said.

"It's a bit big."

"Just a little. There's room to grow." She seemed different somehow, and not just because she wore a new pink dress under her coat. She had the feeling of travel about her, of being fancy-free, though she had been working a set itinerary and not wandering.

On the paper sleeve, next to the lettering, a brushy drawing showed a smiling, long-legged guy in sharply creased trousers, with his jacket slung over his shoulder. I went to the bathroom and looked in the mirror, turning my left shoulder forward, then the right. The jacket looked sleek all right, but I didn't much resemble the cheerful customer of the Young Men's Style Shoppe.

"How'd you get on with Nick?" Corinne said, as she took off her coat.

"Okay."

"What have you been up to? How's the junior astronomer?"

"All right." I put the jacket back on its hanger.

"How about Dwayne, did you see him?"

"What do you care?"

I thought she might get mad, but she took my hand and said, "Don't be sulky. We'll go out for a nice meal later. Do you like the jacket?"

On the hanger, with its silver-blue sheen and narrow lapels, it looked sharp. And it was mine. "It's nice. Thanks."

"It's partly a gift from Jack. He sends his love."

I dropped jacket and hanger in a heap on the paper sleeve. Corinne straightened it out again, and buttoned it, and hung it in my closet next to my real jacket, the plaid one with lions rampant.

"Was the dress a gift too?" I said, feeling poisoned by the words.

"You like?" She smoothed the pink fabric over her hips, and struck a model's pose. The cut and the colour suited her, but I suppressed any sign of approval.

"I see there's no pleasing you right now," she said, irritated at last. "Let's go see Nick. I got a gift for him too."

"I'll stay here."

"No you won't. We'll both thank him. Look at this."

She opened a narrow, flat box of thin cardboard, and lifted a fold of tissue paper on a red necktie with three tiny mounted figures on it. They were jockeys, racing their horses around a curved white fence.

"He won't be able to see that."

"He can feel it. It's embroidered."

We went downstairs. It occurred to me that it would be good to hear what Nick had to say about me, rather than be confronted by Corinne with it later. My head swam a little as I realized how unpleasant things could get if he denounced me as a spy, or blabbed about the night I hadn't stayed there.

I was going to walk into his apartment without knocking, but Corinne stopped me and rapped out "Shave and a Haircut." We heard movement inside, and after a long moment Nick appeared in the half-open doorway, in his socks and bathrobe. The curtains on the wall behind him were drawn, as they weren't when Jackie was around.

"What do you want?" he said.

"I came down with Jasper to thank you," said Corinne.

"You're welcome," he said in a dull voice.

"Going to ask us in?"

He stepped back and made an ironic showy bow. We entered the stuffy, shadowy apartment, which felt as oppressive as when I had awakened to the sound of Jackie crying. The heap of my bedding still lay on the end of the sofa. I half-expected Jackie to appear again with her arm across her breasts, this time to accuse Corinne.

Corinne groped for the wall switch and snapped on the overhead light. Nick tucked his bathrobe a little tighter around his body and stood up straight, like a soldier braving out a bad inspection. His hair and unshaven face looked greasy. He smelled of sweat and tobacco smoke.

"So, thanks for taking care of the boy," Corinne said, glancing around the apartment as if she hadn't been there before. "How did he do?"

"Not bad, for a nosy kid. He may have run a bit wild when I wasn't looking, but he survived. How about you?"

"It was okay. We stopped at one place that wasn't worth it."

"Some rain must fall. Want a drink?"

"No, I'm bushed. I brought you something." She gave him the

narrow box. He groped inside, and the tissue fluttered to the floor.

"Feels nice," he said, stroking the tie with both hands. "What colour?"

"Burgundy. It's Italian silk."

"There's something stitched on it. Can't tell what."

"It's three horses at the track," she said. "They're running, and you're winning."

Nick's fingers crept over the stitches. "That's a grey," I said as he felt out the first horse. "The jockey's in white and gold. That one's chestnut, and looks like it's gaining. That's the fence, and right there's the leader, another chestnut with gold and white silks."

"They should mix up those colours more," Nick said, "but I won't complain if you say I'm winning." He reached into his bathrobe pocket and drew out his open palm, empty. "Tough luck. I seem to have lost my betting receipt." He draped the silk tie around his bare neck and held an end in each hand. Somehow that token of his usual dressy style brought back a bit of his old swagger. "We should go riding again, eh?"

"I don't think so," said Corinne.

"Lost your taste for it?"

"No, I just think it's over."

"I was starting to get the hang of it. We should try again. You can't stir a guy's interest and then leave him flat."

"Look, I'm grateful about Jasper, it was a real favour to ask," Corinne said, her voice still nice, but with a hint of hard news in it. "But I'm not riding with you again."

Nick shrugged as if it didn't matter, like he'd expected no better answer. But his head sank a little, and it seemed to me that he had still held out hope, that Corinne might relent and make things again as they were, whatever the consequences.

"Sure thing," he said. He fingered the tie's pointed end. "Thanks for dropping in. I'll think of you whenever I tighten this around my neck."

CHAPTER 49

I PUSHED OPEN THE SCHOOL'S front door and stepped alone into the bright late-afternoon sunlight. The weather had turned clear and warm again. Little kids chased each other around the shrubbery more wildly than usual, filling the air with shrieks.

A group from the high school approached along the sidewalk. Jerry was among them, and Noreen, and a couple of Jerry's friends, and Marsha. She was in the midst of the group, and since they were all taller, I caught only glimpses of her glossy ponytail, her soft woollen sweater and the plaid skirt swaying above her knees.

I took a few steps down the walk, raking my fingers along the zipper of my open jacket till the flesh tingled. Jerry's glance strayed over me and didn't register, as if I had fallen too far from his social orbit to be worth a sneer. Marsha followed his brief turn of the head, and when she saw me, her lips compressed into an almost-smile, not unfriendly, but not welcoming. It only lasted a second, yet I felt it conveyed her complete daylight response to the events of my night at her house. Relieved as she might be that I didn't like her that way, I could see there would be no renewal of things, only a more definite end.

I waited for them to pass, hoping that I was wrong, that Marsha might turn again and ask me to walk with her. When she didn't, I dawdled until a decent gap opened between me and her group, then moved along in their distant wake. I didn't look at them directly, but was morbidly aware of the plaid skirt and ponytail, and the boys' intermittent barks of laughter. No one from their happy, sauntering group looked back the whole two blocks I trailed after them.

At the apartment, Corinne was still in her housecoat, smoking in a chair by the window, looking pale and anxious.

"I talked with Audrey," she said. "She says there's nothing happening. No work."

"That's too bad."

"It's a crock, that's what it is. There's got to be something. It's fall, people are buying new wardrobes. This town's full of money." Her lips tightened as she took a drag. "I think maybe Jackie put me in Dutch with her."

"Why would she do that?" I said, not really needing an answer but curious to hear one.

"If you're new and you start doing well, others get nervous." Corinne flicked her hand, as at some bothersome insect. "You never know about people, till you really know them."

"There must be other people."

"Yeah, great. Start over from scratch. Not so easy."

A dormant wish stirred in me, like a long-buried seed when it feels warmth creeping through the soil. "Maybe we should go back to Winnipeg," I said.

"Look, I've got problems enough. I don't need you whining about Winnipeg, or anything else. Got it?"

The sharpness of her tone knocked me back a step. But I felt a sneaky, dark satisfaction from knowing that things were collapsing for her, too, and hearing her say "Winnipeg" gave me hope. Maybe she would think about it, in spite of what she said.

I went into my room and removed from my pocket the two

sticks of green chalk I had taken from my classroom. I broke them into inch-long pieces, and dragged them edgewise around the pencil outline of my large lion rampant on the wall. The thickened chalk line made the whole image feel larger and more menacing, but it also changed something about the gaping jaws. They seemed now to be not only fierce, but fearful as well. I stood a long time trying to see how that had happened, and to decide whether I should do anything about it.

*

THE NEXT DAY, SATURDAY, AS we ate our late breakfast of bacon and eggs, someone thumped on our door. It was Walter, the super. He thrust a white envelope at Corinne and left without a word. She opened it, and read the short letter inside.

"Angelo wants his furniture back," she said. "And he needs the apartment for his cousin. His cousin!"

"Can he do that?"

"I don't know. Who cares? I don't like this place enough to fight for it." She stuffed the letter into the Drawer of Shame, and left the drawer open. That seemed a special mark of shame, that a new item could not be shut away.

"What now?" I said.

"He'll take the furniture this week. We'll have to sit on the floor while they laugh. Not likely!"

She threw the rest of her breakfast into the garbage, as if the food were tainted by this news, then jammed the plate in too. She opened the fridge door and slammed it hard enough to make the bottles rattle, then grabbed a handful of cutlery from the draining board and flung it across the linoleum. She scanned the room with a wild look, apparently trying to decide what to attack next.

I jumped from my chair and pried at a curling corner of linoleum with one of the knives scattered on the floor. Corinne caught me by the arm.

"Don't," she said. "It'll only make them feel better." She pulled me up and gave me a long, close hug, and some of the hard disappointments of the previous weeks relaxed their grip on both of us.

"Let's get ready," she said. "I could use a drive."

The little time it took to pack made me feel how thinly we had rooted there. I actually spent time rearranging things in my bag, to drag the process out, to make it seem less like yet another escape from temporary lodgings.

I put the bag by the door and draped my two jackets over it, the plaid one from Dean and the new one. Corinne was still cramming the contents of her vanity into her modelling case. I returned to my room and rubbed the remains of the green chalk on my hand, and pressed it to the wall, on my lion rampant, right where the heart would be. It made a fainter impression than I wanted, so with the remaining shards, I scribbled zigzag lines down the fingers and across the palm, till my mark had the jagged energy of an electrified hand.

We carried our bags and boxes downstairs. At the first landing, I said: "Are we going to say goodbye to Nick?"

"Why bother? He's in on this too."

A small wave of grief lapped over me, not so much for Nick as for other farewells I would not be making. We trooped out and carried everything to the Corvair. A paper Woodward's bag filled with the contents of the Drawer of Shame went on the floor of the passenger's side, and the boxes we couldn't fit into the trunk settled on the rear seats. We exchanged glances across the roof of the car and then slammed the rear doors on the evidence of our life in Edmonton.

Time had seemed to rush at us ever since Corinne opened Angelo's letter, but now it slowed to a crawl. I got into the car as I had so many times before, yet it took a portion of forever to do so, aware as I suddenly was of each part of that ordinary movement. I pulled the door, and it swung shut with a peculiar finality. Corinne's compact opened on her palm, she raised the mirror to her face, the lipstick dragged across each lip, the lips rolled together, the compact closed, the sticky tube of colour spiralled into its cylinder. I turned my head, which felt newly heavy and slow. Through the glass, our squat brick building looked solidly itself, though the cough of the Corvair's engine told me that the whole structure was about to vanish like a fairy-tale castle. The car began to move, and my head swivelled to follow my staring eyes, as Dwayne's house and the tree, and the Sahara and the shoppers park, and all the ghostly passages that linked them were whisked away and gone.

We drove through midmorning traffic as if nothing unusual was happening. Eventually the buildings and people thinned out, and the road took on the ribbon-like seriousness of a highway. The prairie opened calmly around us. Swathing machines moved across the land, tumbling the ripe crops under their rolling wooden arms. Driving into the countryside felt like reversing time, travelling back into our wandering life. The Bel Air was turning out to be a motel after all, as easily left and obliterated as any other. But as the city skyline in my side mirror levelled down to nothing, I felt something in me being torn away.

A grain elevator flashed by my window. At this recurrent sign of our wandering days, the anxious hope revived in me by Angelo's letter rose though my chest, and I asked the only question that could fix everything.

"Are we going back?"

"To Winnipeg?" Corinne's face remained inert behind her cat's-eye sunglasses. Her brown hands were steady at ten and two. "You really are terrible with directions. No, we're headed the other way, to Vancouver."

I wasn't ready for this twist in the story. Vancouver was for people who couldn't find what they were looking for, she had said so herself. Stay or go back had been my only options, though I now saw as if for the first time that the Corvair, like a king in checkers, could cross the board in any direction.

"Why Vancouver?"

"I know people there."

"You said you didn't want to start over again! You said that was a lousy idea!" The words burst out, but my voice sounded distant, muffled by the pulse thudding in my ears.

"Don't shout at me! I didn't write that letter." Corinne's voice rose at the mention of the humiliating document. "You think I'm in charge of everything. It was my fault we left, my fault we kept going. Everything my fault! Never mind how much fun you were having, lying out under the stars! I'm the wicked one, ruining everything!"

She dabbed her fingers under the corner of her sunglasses, then slapped my arm, quickly but not very hard. I touched the spot; there was a little moisture there, from her tears.

"We'll go through Jasper," she said in a trembling voice. "It's clean and fresh up in the mountains. We'll stop at the hot springs. I think we both need a break."

My spirits rose a little at the mention of Jasper. I had never seen that mythic place, except in a postcard Dean had found for me, of pale grey mountains with their knees covered in forest. He had put it in a small frame and propped it on his tiki bar.

"You might like Vancouver," Corinne said. "Everyone seems to end up there eventually."

I pressed my open hand against the door. There was just enough green chalk powder left to make a very faint mark on the red upholstery. Corinne took my other hand in hers and gave it a squeeze. I sank low in my seat and rode with my cheek against the trembling door that bounced against the bone with each bump in the road. Apart from that sensation, I was numb.

The paper bag full of things from the Drawer rustled at my feet. I pressed the button on the glove compartment and started pulling things from the bag.

Corinne felt inside her handbag without looking, and after a long moment of rummaging, pulled something out: a ridged, square, silver cufflink. She gave it to me, and I turned it over in my hand, sure that I had seen it before. It took me another moment to recognize it as Dr. Suan's.

"Okay," Corinne said. "Let's sort the Drawer of Shame."

CHAPTER
50

THERE WAS A LOT OF yelling in our lives after we got to Vancouver, and not just between us. Corinne found work, and a decent apartment on Commercial Drive. But some kind of turmoil was going on inside her, and it flashed out unpredictably, at strangers, her friends, or at things too big and intangible to be stuffed into the Drawer of Shame. I understood, because I was becoming the same way. My anger at her was seeping into every part of my life.

Late one afternoon I found her squatting in a corner of the living room near the kitchen, on the beige wall-to-wall carpet. It was the one thing she hated about the apartment, and it was no longer beige: she had covered almost the whole thing with red paint.

"What?" she said as our eyes met, in the brusque tone she took on when she had been drinking. She moved onto the kitchen linoleum and dipped her brush into the paint can.

I squatted down and looked more closely at the rug. The paint had soaked into the upper fibres, but further down the beige showed through, like dyed hair growing out. I touched the surface with one finger; it was already starting to stiffen. I wanted to laugh but stifled the urge.

"Are you crazy?" I said in the sullen way that had become a habit almost whenever I spoke to her.

"I knew you'd say that. You've gotten really boring since we moved in here." She lashed the brush at the last remaining square of beige rug, jamming it into the fibres to push the paint down.

"You know he's going to be furious," I said. The landlord had mentioned the wall-to-wall more than once when we looked at the place, as a contemporary selling point.

"Who's going to tell him? It already looks a hundred per cent better," she said, and then in a softer tone, "I just couldn't stand it anymore."

It took a few days for the rug to dry completely. To my bare feet, the stiff fibres felt like a field of cut straw. It was a little corner of Chokecherry Bush, relocated to our place in Vancouver, but painted red.

My anger came out at school, where one afternoon I was sent to the office for punching another boy during recess. I maintained it was a shove, but since his nose was bloodied, I was the one sitting in front of the principal's grey steel desk.

"You're new here," he said without interest, not looking at me but at the playing field beyond his wire-shielded office window. "I should really call your father in about what you did today."

"He's dead."

His bifocals glinted as he looked around. "I'm sorry. Is this a recent loss?"

"He died in a plane crash, when I was little." I told how he had been a pioneer in oil exploration, whose bush plane had gone down during a lightning storm. That seemed about right for the occasion.

"Tragic. And quite young too, I suppose. How old was he?"

"Thirty," I said, with almost no hesitation, though I didn't actually know his age, and was startled to realize that I hadn't thought to ask.

"He must have been quite a go-getter. Where was he from?"

"Wetaskiwin," I said, after a slightly longer pause. It was the first name that came to mind, plucked from the air to cover another gap in what I knew and had somehow never tried to find out.

"You don't seem too sure."

"He grew up on a farm near Wetaskiwin," I said, more firmly, but with a rising sense of uncertainty that extended beyond the name of a town.

"My wife's from that part of the country. You must still have family there." The principal gave me a chilly smile. "Perhaps there's a connection somewhere."

"Maybe."

"Do you ever go back for the fair?"

"Which one?"

His pale eyebrows twitched. "The big August fair in Wetaskiwin."

"Sure." Here was another country person trying to fit me into the mental map of his relations. As usual, I was ready to agree to whatever link was proposed, though I scarcely took in his chatter about a town I'd never visited and a fair I hadn't heard of. I was focused on the things I didn't know, and the lightning storm I had just invented, and all the other variable ornaments to the story, which for years had seemed normal but suddenly no longer did. Something was being dislodged and damaged inside me, I could feel it. My palms were sweating, I was almost panting for breath. I was sure the principal would notice, but he was busy searching in one of his desk drawers for something.

"You seem like a smart boy, Jasper," he said, in the same dull voice I had heard when he first spoke. "You've had a tough break, but that's no excuse to bash someone whenever you feel like it." He closed the drawer and rose from his seat. "Now stand up and put your palms out."

I stuck my hands out over his desk, and he gave me two sharp blows on each one with a heavy leather strap. The second ones stung like fire; my hands curled up by themselves like paper in flames. Much as they hurt, I felt I was getting what I deserved, though not for the reason he imagined.

"Now go back to your classroom, and try not to show yourself here again."

I left his office and the school. I wanted to plunge my burning hands in snow, but the streets were wet with rain, under the grey Vancouver sky. There was no way to get rid of the pain, nor the shock that was spreading inside me. Something old and well protected had cracked open in the principal's office, before he ever touched me with his leather strap. I couldn't yet find the words to say what had happened, but for the first time the lonely distant heroism that so often shivered through me when I spoke about the little plane was challenged by another feeling: shame.

*

I HADN'T TOLD ANYONE THAT Corinne had painted the carpet, even at school, where people would have screamed with laughter to know. But the landlord must have sensed a change, because as I climbed the stairs, still stunned by the events of the afternoon, his bear-like form appeared on the landing above me.

"Back from school? Is your mom around?" he said quickly. Without waiting for a reply, he went up ahead of me, two steps at a time, and rapped on our door. We stood there together for a long moment, waiting, as if neither of us lived there. Then he seemed to remember, and said to me, "Let me in for a minute, I want to check the plumbing." I could tell he was lying, but it didn't matter because the door opened and Corinne popped out, dressed as if for a modelling job.

"Ed, how nice, I'm on my way out. In you go, Jasper," she said, shoving me into the apartment and pulling the door shut. From the other side I could hear Ed muttering about the pipes, and Corinne assuring him that everything was okay, and that she was in a hurry. But Ed still wasn't happy, and after a bit more discussion he forgot about the plumbing and demanded to be let in. "I just want to look around, that's my right," he said, his big voice rising to a shout.

"Yes, but you can't storm in any old time," Corinne said calmly. "I've got to run, and the place is in a bit of an uproar. Come back tomorrow, if you really want."

Ed said nothing, and after a moment his heavy steps retreated, but then he yelled up from the landing, "Tomorrow morning, first thing!" I heard the sharp peck of Corinne's heels as she followed him down.

I got ice cubes from the freezer and cradled them in my hands. Ten minutes later, Corinne burst through the door. "Get ready, we're leaving," she said, kicking off her shoes and darting into her room.

"Leaving for where? I thought you were working."

"No, I just had to get rid of him. Why are you wet? Grab your stuff, we're getting out of here."

She began tearing clothes from hangers and shoving them into a suitcase. I was jolted for a moment by her frantic movements, but then a strange calm came over me.

"What's the rush?" I said. "He said tomorrow."

"The man's a brute. You didn't see his face. He seemed like a teddy bear when we moved in, but no. I don't want to have it out with him, three flights up." She jammed things into her case as if physically repelling the idea of facing Ed's wrath.

"So we have to take off, again," I said, dropping my ice cubes on the carpet. "Not because of him, but because of you!" My calm turned to fury. I shoved her suitcase onto the floor.

"Shut up!" She grabbed my shirt and slapped my face. In spite of my burning hands I gripped both her arms, and she grabbed my elbows, and we stood there locked together, with all the bad feelings of recent days tangled between us.

"They gave me the strap today," I said through my teeth, as if she were to blame.

"Oh, God!" She released me and ran her fingers over my swollen palms, as though trying to read something there. To my surprise, she didn't ask why, or who, or anything, as if my reddened hands were another inexplicable setback imposed from outside.

"None of this should have happened," she said quietly. "I made a mistake. We'll move on and make a better start."

"I'm not going."

She put her case back on the bed and repacked the things that had fallen out, more methodically this time. "Get your stuff together. We'll have a nice dinner somewhere. We can talk through everything then."

"I don't want to have a nice dinner. I want to go back to Winnipeg."

"We'll stay in a hotel for a few nights, maybe with a pool."

"You're not listening. I don't want to stay with you. I want to go back and live with Dean." I was feeling breathless again. My own words reached my ears as if from somewhere outside myself.

Corinne kept packing in a state of enforced calm. "I know you miss Dean, but he's not set up for that kind of thing. What makes you think he'd agree?"

"I'll call and find out." I marched to the phone and dialled his number, and after a few endless rings he answered.

"It's Jasper," I said. "I'm in Vancouver, and I don't want to stay anymore. I want to come back and live with you." I blurted this out in a low voice with my head down, but once it was said I glanced at Corinne. She had left her packing and was watching me closely.

"He says maybe I can," I told her. She looked stunned. I gave her the phone and left the room. I didn't want to see her yell at Dean that he had a nerve, and that it was impossible. He had not actually said I could come. He said it was a nice idea, and if I wanted we could have a serious talk about it someday, and maybe he should talk with Corinne.

But she didn't shout, or speak even loudly enough for me to hear from the doorway of her room. She talked with Dean for nearly an hour, slumped on a corner of the bed. I roved through the apartment, distractedly snatching up my things, dragging my feet over the stiff carpet.

Corinne called me into her room. Her face was a blank, though she had obviously been crying.

"If you want to stay with Dean for a little while, you can," she said. "We could both use a break. I'll sort things out here, and you can come back in time for Christmas. But do you really want to go?"

I hesitated, more from surprise than doubt, though I couldn't guess how things would be with Dean, without her there. It was a dream I hadn't imagined coming true, and with so little resistance. But everything was changing. Whatever had split open in the principal's office was still coming apart inside me, and there was no way to put it back the way it had been.

"Yes," I said.

*

TWO DAYS LATER, CORINNE PUT me on the train. She held me in a long, close embrace on the platform, drawing me into her like the air itself. She didn't seem to notice I was already miles away in my mind.

I rode alone through the Rockies and onto the open prairie. As we passed the whistle-stop stations, each one the same, I remembered the first horseman, riding as far as a man could ride in a day, leaving his sooty handprint as a sign for others. That was another story I had wanted to believe, one I had made true for myself by wishing. I pressed my open hand against the trembling window; it left no mark. I sank back into my seat and followed the rush of country with my eyes, as I measured with my gut the distance I was moving from my mother, and from all the stories of our life together.

Dean was waiting for me when I got to Winnipeg. I never lived with Corinne again.

CHAPTER
51

WHEN I DREAM ABOUT CORINNE in her Corvair, she's always the same age. Her skin is unlined, her hands steady at ten and two. She has her foot on the gas, and as the car rumbles over the asphalt, I feel a slow dread creeping through my chest. I'm seldom aware that she is dead, though the dreams began only when she was no longer alive.

The last time I went anywhere with Corinne for real, she wasn't able to drive, or even dress herself without help. It took an hour for the two of us to ease her thin arthritic limbs out of her loose house clothes and into a pink suit, and for her to make up her face. Getting her seated at a table in a café was an awkward puzzle of weights and angles that abruptly ended when she wrenched her aluminum cane from between the table legs and plopped into the chair.

We met in mid-afternoon, which at that stage was her best time of day. It was hard for her to move much before noon, when she gradually increased her mobility and speed, like a car in neutral rolling down a low grade. At about five p.m. the grade reversed, and she began to slow down, until she had to be lifted from her armchair and carried to bed.

The café was new, made from resinous pine logs. We sat on the side overlooking the distant mountains and the closer forest and the very near tour buses in the parking lot, moving round each other like silver elephants. We were in Jasper, my namesake town, where Corinne had settled years earlier with her husband Sam.

She didn't wear much makeup in those days, only enough to put a hint of colour in her wrinkled lips and tissue-paper cheeks. Her eyes were bright like a fire running on a fuel that won't last. She was living some new kind of accelerating time, while everything around her went on at the usual pace. I poured her a cup of tea, and the seconds ticked by no faster than they normally did; but, in another way, that brief act seemed to squander time on an incredible scale. Surely we should have been doing something better with all the time it took to fill her cup.

"How can I feel so close to someone who twists everything around so much?" she said with a barely audible laugh. "Half of what you remember never happened, or at least not the way you think it did."

Her fiery eyes made her words sound like an accusation from another world, but she was cheerful. We were out in public, her energy was at its peak, and she looked as good as she could. But though she gripped the thick teacup with both hands, she couldn't help spilling a little on her plate.

"I remember more than you do," I said.

She swatted the air dismissively. "You mean you make up more! Or muddle up the details."

"I take after you."

"All the bad things from me! I don't think it works that way. Your stories always make me wonder, 'Who's that terrible woman he's talking about?'"

"But you still laugh."

She started to smile, but a spasm of pain flashed over her face, and her neck went rigid. "Goddamn," she said through her teeth. The teaspoon shook in her gnarly fist. I moved to touch her hand, but she didn't like that kind of thing when she was hurting. A few seconds passed, and the demon ravaging her bones went back to sleep.

"You *are* terrible," I said, as if nothing had happened. "That's what I like about you."

"Good to know I still have what it takes," she said, with a grin that was halfway to a grimace. She touched her compact, probably wondering how she looked after her brief agony, but she didn't open it.

"If you're my age and a woman, you're invisible to man and beast," she said.

"Who do you want to notice you, besides your husband?"

"Sam hasn't seen me for years, and doesn't expect me to see him either, though unfortunately I can still see the way he dresses. You know, you're getting very thin on top." She wanted to show that she could still see me all right, and that time was galloping up on her son too. But there was no percentage for her in that remark, as Sam would say. She raised one shoulder in a tiny shrug, and made a fluttery movement with her fingers on the pine table, like dance steps that had no other way of coming out.

I could see that her attack had weakened her. Soon she would be getting restless to leave, and it would be too late to ask what I had come to ask.

"I want you to tell me something," I said, reciting a script I had rehearsed in my head a hundred times. "I don't want evasions or fairy tales. Who was my father?"

I expected some kind of startled reaction, but her papery face didn't change. She just looked at me more attentively while my heart thumped in my chest. The commotion of this exchange, it seemed, was all going on inside me, the only one who had prepared for it.

"When did you start thinking about that?" she said.

"A long time ago. In Vancouver."

"In Vancouver." She covered her mouth with her hand. This news seemed more troubling to her, that her accepted story had lost its force so long ago, without her knowing it, and while we were still together. She stayed like that for many moments, not saying any-thing, searching me out with her fiery, frightened eyes. I thought: when she takes her hand away, her mouth will open and I will hear the truth.

"You're not going to like it," she said at last, in a quiet voice. "He wasn't someone you were fond of. I didn't like him much either." She tried to lean in closer, but her brittle spine resisted, and she ended up merely dipping her head lower, while still holding me with her flaming eye. Her fingertips noiselessly clawed the tabletop.

"You remember Jack Summers, the salesman I used to travel with?"

"You're joking."

But she wasn't. The saddest ghost of a smile crossed her lips, without easing the fear in her eyes.

I sank against the banquette. I had expected someone else, Lyle most of all, the beautiful, shirtless prairie boy on his motorbike — her great lost love, as I had come to imagine him. Not sweaty Jack Summers, of the stinky pipes and glaring eyes, and the steamer trunks filled with soft, new clothes he scolded me for touching. I had no good feelings about him, and now he was returning from the past to do me what felt like a fresh injury.

"Why him?"

"It wasn't anything planned, God forbid," she said, recovering herself a little. "We were in Saskatoon, at the Bessborough Hotel. A snowstorm shut down the city. We got tired of playing gin rummy."

A mirthless hilarity shuddered through my body.

"Funny, isn't it?" she said, with a faint quizzical smile.

"What you're saying is that I was a substitute for gin rummy."

Her feeble smile crumbled, and a large tear tipped from her pale eye down her wrinkled cheek. It would have taken no effort to inflict a lot of pain on this frail old lady, crying quietly in a room full of strangers. But instead I leaned across and took her hand, from old habit as much as from sympathy.

The gesture acted on her instantly. She gripped my fingers and her face brightened with a relief beyond what I thought she deserved.

"Who was the man in the plane?" I said.

"There was no plane."

"What about the guy in the photograph?"

"He was just some guy."

No plane. Just some guy. There was no surprise for me in these admissions, but watching her make them was like passing a door that had seemed shut for a long time, and suddenly hearing the latch click.

"Why didn't you tell me?"

"I was afraid of how you'd be, and what you'd say," she said. "I would have had to tell Jack, and nothing good would have come of that. And after a while everyone knew about the man in the plane. I couldn't just kill him off."

We both smiled at this little joke, in spite of ourselves. But he was well and truly killed off now, even as a fiction that, in her mind, had endured as a story I still believed. He had vanished into fairy tale, like Dr. Suan's steady state theory of the universe.

"Is he still alive?"

"Jack? No, he's gone. I think I need some more tea."

I filled her teacup. The act seemed normal again, no longer a bizarre squandering of time as it had before. It was the time past that was running strange now.

"Why did you wait so long to ask?"

I had known that question would come, but it took me a moment to find the answer. "I didn't want any more turmoil."

"You were afraid, too," she said, giving me a hopeful, complicit glance, which for the moment I couldn't accept.

"Let's say I didn't need any more fathers."

"You got the one you wanted. Dear old Dean."

"He sends his love, by the way." I signalled for the bill.

"Was everything all right?" the waitress asked.

"Very nice," said Corinne. In a quavery voice, she sang me a little song she made up years ago in Winnipeg, when we used to look for spangled warriors in the frost on the window.

I pray you don't have icicle spurs
Unless you ride an icicle horse.

*

A MONTH LATER I VISITED Corinne for the last time. She lay between crisp hospital sheets, a ghost in her blue cotton gown, her mouth not quite closed, her eyes turned towards the door. On the blanket, the fingers of one hand kept closing on the palm, as if grasping at something that was slipping away.

I bent over her and warmed her cold, flexing hand in both of mine. Her eyes rolled up to take me in, but her expression didn't change. She had abandoned her face, or the morphine had taken it from her. A fine gold chain had pooled in the hollow at the base of her throat. I straightened it out, and the jasper pendant I had given her came into my hand, with its crows and tree and prairie field.

Corinne's face was ashen, her faded brown eyes the only points of real colour. She would not have wanted to look like that, even in a hospital bed. I found her purse and took from it a round lady's compact, and began padding colour onto her wrinkled cheeks. This movement had so often been the prelude to a story that I began to improvise one, without knowing if she could hear or understand.

"There was once a beautiful princess who had a fine horse that ran as smooth as silk," I said, rounding her chin and padding over her temples and forehead. I searched the handbag until I found eyeliner, an eyebrow pencil and a pink lipstick.

"Her father the king was a horseman too. One day he was thrown from the saddle and broke his neck. The spell that maintained his kingdom was broken, too. His castle collapsed into a small tree house with no roof. His daughter's fine horse turned into a cat. Her velvet riding cloak became a cotton shift."

I brushed the eyeshadow above Corinne's flickering lids. The movement made her slack mouth look more normal; her lips usually parted when she worked on her eyes.

"The princess wept. A tear rolled over her palm and became a child, the size of a bead. She nurtured him as he grew, sometimes pampering him, sometimes shutting him in her pocket."

I drew the eyebrows with even strokes of the brown pencil, thickening them as Corinne used to do.

"One day the boy grew tired of the pocket and escaped through a hole. The princess couldn't find him anywhere. This time she cried enough to fill a basin."

Corinne's eyes began to droop as I started the lower lip. "The sun cast her reflection on the basin of tears. She was still beautiful, but a crease of sorrow had formed on her brow. The same crease marked the face of her son as he rode away on the cat that had been her fine horse."

Corinne's lids settled over her eyes. I wanted a proper ending for my story, but I couldn't improvise a tale as well as she could. The boy and the princess should come together again, but how? Should it be a happy ending or a sad one?

I put away her makeup and surveyed my work. It was an improvement, but it hadn't masked her pallor any better than the colour they had put on my grandmother Lily, when she was in her coffin. A queasy feeling ran through me: I had made Corinne up to look like a corpse.

A soft moan escaped with her shallow breath, and her eyes flickered open. Their gaze seemed to want to hold mine, though her face showed no expression. Perhaps she was fastening on me the way a baby would, with no real sense of what she was seeing. The moment for my story's proper ending might already have slipped away; but that fear only made it more important to say everything I could.

I leaned in closer, kissed her cool forehead, and whispered, "No blame." I cupped her head in my hands, kissed her again, and added something I hadn't told her for a long time. "I love you." I searched for a response in her dull eyes, which now seemed more like a screen than a window. But I could feel that she was seeing me, and wanting to.

After a while the nurses came in, drew back the covers, and fluffed her pillows. They dragged her up the bed a bit, and a spark of feeling came into her eyes, fear perhaps. She sank again into the pillows, and the nurses smoothed the bedding and laid her inert arms on the blanket. The fingers of one hand still made a small gathering movement.

I waited with her for the rest of the long afternoon. Time no longer ran rapidly, as at the log cabin café, but trickled away, one shallow breath at a time. The sound of efficient steps passing in the hall reached us from another world. Every now and then that world came into the room, to check on an old woman wandering motion-less in the failing light, towards a destination everyone could predict but no one knew.

I HAVE NO PHOTOS OF Jack Summers, nothing but myself to prove he ever existed. I last saw him at the castle hotel in Edmonton, when I shattered his ice bucket with the little hammer. He had been ready to hit me then, and I had almost wanted him to, because there were clients in the room and he might have blown a sale. But he sold four outfits to those ladies, whose little dog barked as the paper sleeves rustled down over the garments. At the end of the after-noon, Jack stuffed some cash in a hotel envelope for Corinne, and kissed her cheek, and rubbed his knuckles hard against my scalp. He told Corinne to watch out for this little corker, but she said he had it wrong: I was the one who looked out for her.

She took my hand and we walked with arms swinging down the wide hotel hallway. We rode the elevator to the main floor, and crossed the lobby carpet whose pattern looked like snakes chasing oranges.

Outside, the sky had filled with dark, heavy clouds. Corinne gave her modelling bag to the man in the purple uniform, and led me around the side of the hotel, to the top of a long wooden staircase that zigzagged down the hill to the river. A large drop spattered on my cheek. We looked at each other and laughed as we realized we had left the stolen umbrella in Jack's room.

We climbed down the stairs as more raindrops speckled the bare, grey wood. The heel of one of Corinne's curvy black pumps caught in a gap and snapped off, but she carried on barefoot, right to the bottom. We walked over the damp ground to the riverbank, and skipped stones across the swift water, and threw fist-sized rocks that landed with heavy plops. Finally Corinne tossed in her shoes, which were cracking and had already been resoled twice. One of them bobbed on the surface for a moment before sinking.

The sky rumbled. Corinne's beehive hairdo was collapsing; she pulled out the pins and let it fall. She folded her arms around me, and pressed my head next to her bosom, and inhaled as if there were nothing sweeter than the smell of a boy who didn't like to wash. I felt her heart beating through the damp satin.

We climbed back up the wooden stairway, as the rain lashed down. By the time we reached the front door of the castle hotel, we were soaking wet. Corinne stood in her bare, muddy feet on the red carpet while the man in the purple uniform brought us her modelling bag and the Corvair. He also gave her a small hotel towel for her face, which was streaked with mascara.

"Thanks," she said, and she tossed the towel without using it into the back seat, and we drove away with the windows open.